THE DAGGER'S PATH

Perie needed to turn. He had to see what was behind him, had to know what his father saw. Yet he was frozen, unable even to turn his head. Da's face was pale as milk, his gaze stark with shock. In that moment Perie's world, all he'd ever known, skewed into insanity. He opened his mouth to scream, but his breath was torn from him.

Da reached out, picked him up and hurled him through the air with a strength Peregrine would never have dreamed he possessed. The air filled with harsh sound. And he was falling, falling . . . plummeting down the slope. He crashed through leaves, breaking branches, careened off something else at a breathless pace, hit the ground and skidded and plunged feet-first into the air as if he'd fallen off a cliff. Then, just as he finally drew in enough breath to scream, he slammed into something so hard the air was driven from his lungs. Even then he didn't stop. He cartwheeled, rolling down a slope so steep he couldn't halt his fall, until he thudded into a tree trunk.

Pain. Pain everywhere. He wanted to scream, but to fill his lungs with the air he'd need to cry out – that would hurt too much. His sight sparked with flashes of light. Everything doubled, then blurred. He couldn't focus. His hearing rang with noise coming from inside his head.

He faded in and out.

Time passed.

Briefly, he was aware of voices, of words shouted in the distance. But not his name, not his father's voice. Pain swelled. He moaned. He heard screams, screams that rent his soul. Then, for a long time, he wasn't there at all, but somewhere else, bleak and dark.

By Glenda Larke

The Mirage Makers
Heart of the Mirage
The Shadow of Tyr
Song of the Shiver Barrens

The Stormlord trilogy
The Last Stormlord
Stormlord Rising
Stormlord's Exile

The Forsaken Lands
The Lascar's Dagger
The Dagger's Path

The Dagger's Path

GLENDA LARKE

www.orbitbooks.net

ORBIT

First published in Great Britain in 2015 by Orbit

A CIP catalogue record for this book
is available from the British Library.

ISBN 978-0-356-50270-0

Typeset in Minion by Palimpsest Book Production Limited,
Falkirk, Stirlingshire
Printed and bound in Great Britain by CPI Group (UK) Ltd,
Croydon, CR0 4YY

Papers used by Orbit are from well-managed
forests and other responsible sources.

MIX
Paper from
responsible sources
FSC
www.fsc.org   FSC® C104740

Orbit
An imprint of
Little, Brown Book Group
100 Victoria Embankment
London EC4Y 0DY

An Hachette UK Company
www.hachette.co.uk

www.orbitbooks.net

This one is for you,
Duke McGuigan,
with much love and the hope that
you will always have time for a good book

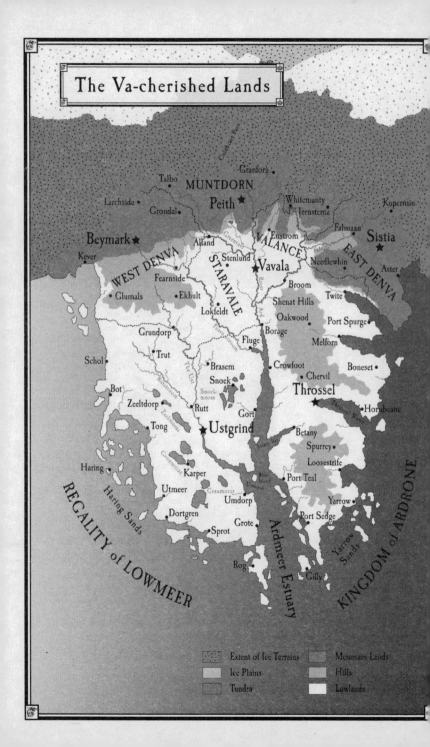

The Va-cherished Lands

Extent of Ice Terrains
Ice Plains
Tundra
Mountain Lands
Hills
Lowlands

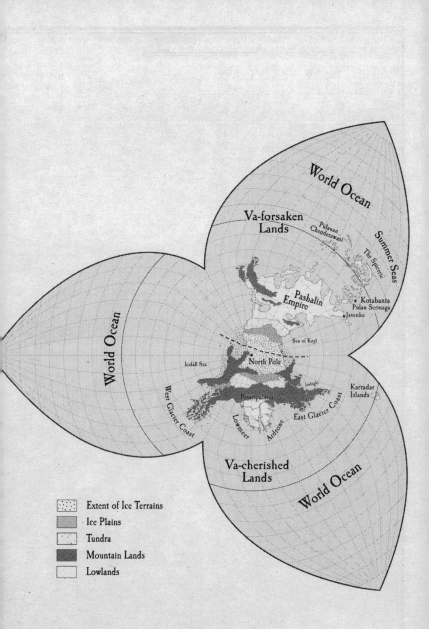

Twenty-three years before

The sorcerer stood in the doorway of the nursery, unobserved, savouring the moment. Emelia, the nurse and the baby: a scene of domestic tranquillity, lit only by the glow of candlelight, for it was already two hours past sunset. The nurse, her back to him, busied herself folding the child's clean linen with her chapped red hands. Emelia was holding the baby, a besotted expression on her exquisite face, singing to the child she held in her arms.

Did she really think such a thin and reedy sound would lull anyone to sleep? Her voice always had been her most unattractive feature. Still, it did seem the babe slept, for he was silent and still, his plump face barely visible within the wrappings of a crocheted shawl.

His son.

Little do they know, any of them.

"A scene of such domestic bliss," he said pleasantly and stepped into the room.

Emelia gave a squeal of delight. "My lord! Is it really you?"

Typical. As if I could be someone else.

He held up his hand to halt her headlong rush at him. "Contain yourself, my dear. You'll wake the boy."

She stopped then, obedient, and sank into a curtsy, wobbling awkwardly because her burden unbalanced her.

She has the right blood lines, remember that.

He waved a dismissive hand at the nurse, who bobbed and waddled from the room in almost indecent haste. He enjoyed seeing how the respect of servants and lackeys was always tinged with something more disquieting. Not *quite* fear; after all, he paid them well, never raised a hand to them and rarely dismissed anyone, but they sensed his power nonetheless. He suppressed the glimmer of an amused smile.

1

"Well, my dear, let me see my son." He held out his arms.

Carefully, she handed over the sleeping boy, her joy dampened. He saw and recognised it in the slight tremor of her fingers, the tense muscles along her jawline. *Good.*

"I expected you long since," she said.

"I don't know why. I told you I'd be gone a year, and it is almost a year to the day. Do not chide me." *Do not dare.*

A flicker of uncertainty in her eyes. "Of course not, my lord."

"I had no qualms about your ability to deliver our son into the world with a minimum of fuss, and then to care for him well." He glanced down at the child still sleeping wrapped in his blankets. "He seems healthy."

"Indeed he is." She was relaxing, and there it was: the faint note of accusation at his long absence that he'd expected to hear. "Five months old and thriving."

She couldn't resist it, could she?

Cradling the baby carefully in the crook of his arm, he began to unwrap the shawl until he'd exposed one plump little hand. Gently, he uncurled the tiny fingers. His smile widened as he gazed down on the palm so exposed.

Perfect. Oh, so perfect.

At last.

He could scarcely believe it; after so many attempts, he had the first of the sons he needed. "You have done well, Emelia."

"Thank you, my lord." She hesitated, her gaze doleful, the flush tingeing her cheeks betraying her.

He smiled encouragement. "You have something you wish to ask me?"

"You said – you said, if it was a son and healthy—"

"Why so hesitant, my dear? There are no secrets between us now."

Her lips parted with delight; her eyes shone. "We can wed soon, then?"

"Indeed. I promised, didn't I? You've proven yourself. I regret I ever had to demand such proof from you in the first place. It was . . . ungallant."

"Oh, never so! I understand the necessity of a man such as you to have an heir, my lord."

2

"So true. Put the child down in his cot and come with me. I have a gift for you, down in the courtyard."

"Oh!" She scurried to the cradle and tucked the child into the bedding, discarding the shawl.

"Bring that," he said. "It's cold outside."

Obediently she snatched it up from where she'd dropped it.

"It's a chill night. Maybe this is not a good time . . ." he began.

"Oh, how can you tease me so! Is it a new carriage? You can show me from the parapet walk!"

"So I can." He held out his hand and she took it shyly, ducking her head like a child. He curbed his exasperation and led her out of the room, picking up a candelabrum from a side table as he went. There was no one about in the passage or on the spiral staircase; he'd already ensured that would be the case.

When he opened the door to the battlements, a blast of salt-laden air raked his face and threatened to tear his coat from his shoulders. The candles blew out. Emelia squealed. *Of course.*

Plunged into the darkness of a cloud-ridden night, he halted briefly to give his eyes time to adjust. The parapet walkway dated back to the days when this had been a remote castle guarding the whimsically named Yarrow Narrows against coastal marauders. On one side, the crenulations of the parapet overlooked the sea; on the other, below – a long way below – was the inner bailey, nowadays simply called "the courtyard", as if renaming it could make a defensive keep in this wild location seem more homely.

"Pickle it," he said and tossed the useless candlestick over the railing. The moan of the wind and the roar of a turbulent ocean was enough to smother any sound of the brass hitting the stone paving. "Someone has already doused the torches in the courtyard. I don't think you will see much."

She groped for the railing. "Let me look! Where is it?"

"Right below us."

Bending over, she peered into the darkness.

"Ah, Emelia, you know what I have always loved about you?" he asked, whispering into her ear. "You are always so delightfully gullible."

She turned her face towards him, but the dark hid her expression. Puzzled, probably. She always was so *unaware*. He gave a low laugh,

3

and bent to grab her legs. In a single, fluid action, he lifted her off her feet and thrust her body forward, propelling her across the balustrade.

So easy.

She didn't fight him. There was no struggle. In her shock, she didn't even scream on the way down, or at least if she did, he didn't hear it.

Leaning against the handrail, he studied the darkness below. He could just see the white patch of the shawl, still clutched in her hand. A nice touch, that. The devastated mother, betrayed because he'd decided not to wed her.

He chuckled.

There'd be whispers. There always were. He didn't mind those; they added to his mystery. Those who worked for him, though, ultimately they kept their silence. They knew who paid for the ale in their goblets or the linen of their coats. He looked after his retainers, and they knew it.

He returned to the nursery where his son still slept. He halted for a moment, gazing down on the boy, but didn't touch him. "Sorry, lad," he murmured, "you may be my firstborn son, but you're not ever going to be my heir."

He moved on to knock at the adjoining door. "Nurse!" he called.

She was there immediately. "My lord?"

"Look after your charge. I fear I have upset the Lady Emelia. I informed her I was leaving again in the morning and will not soon be returning. She has retired for the night to her room and asks not to be disturbed."

The nurse blinked uneasily before bobbing another curtsy. "Of course, my lord. The wee lad will be in my good hands for the night."

He smiled his thanks and left.

On the morrow, after the body was discovered, he would double her annual stipend.

1

Between the Cherished and the Forsaken

Lookout duty aloft lent itself to the pleasant diversion of daydreams. Memories too, but memories were a trap, because you didn't always know where they might lead you . . .

The mast creaked under the strain of wind-filled sails, the tang of salt and wet canvas saturated the air, but in the crow's nest, memory had snared Ardhi in his past. He smelled the smoke of mangrove charcoal burning in the kilns and heard the hammering in the forges of the metalworkers' village. His thoughts lingered in that other world, recalling the greying *attap* roofs of the houses on stilts and the rows of fish drying on the racks in the sun.

His grip on the railing in front of him tightened as he remembered the day he'd gone there to see the blademaster, the *empu* Damardi. He'd been sick with guilt and shame. His pounding heart had matched the sound of the hammers; the whiff of molten metal had tasted bitter to his tongue.

With clammy fingers, he'd straightened his loose jacket, brushed a streak of dirt from the hem of his pantaloons and checked for any untidy strands of hair escaping from under his cloth headband. He'd made sure that his kris, his father's coming-of-age gift, was neatly tucked into the waist of the *sampin* wrapped around his hips. Finding nothing that would hint at disrespect for the man he was about to visit, he'd walked on past the lesser smiths until he came to the house of Damardi, the greatest krismaker of all.

Once there, he did not mount the steps to the *serambi*, the raised porch, as a normal visitor might. Instead, he'd knelt on the bare swept earth in front of the house. He'd taken the plume he carried from its sheath of protective bambu and laid it on the ground. In the mango tree overhead, the bird they called the macaque's slave scolded its noisy warning at his intrusion.

The villagers went about their business, muttering to each other while they ignored him with calculated insult as he knelt there in the heat. Remorse suffused his face and neck with red. They all knew his careless words had brought the unimaginable to the Pulauan Chenderawasi. He'd told the pale sailors of paradise birds, and they'd come a-hunting.

They'd shot Raja Wiramulia with their guns, killed him for the golden plumes of his regalia even though they knew nothing of their true *sakti*, the Chenderawasi magic with which they were imbued.

Kneeling there in the metalmaker's village, mortified, Ardhi wanted to die.

The village boys were less mannerly than their elders. They spat on him and whispered as they passed by, "Betrayer. Traitor. Moray, moray, moray!"

He shuddered and hung his head at the insult. The despised moray eel was the hated assassin of the reef, darting out of its dark crevasse to seize unwary prey.

An hour passed before Damardi stepped on to the *serambi* and placed his hands on the railing. "Who comes to speak to the blade-smith?" he asked, looking down on him. "You, young Ardhi? How dare you bring the Raja's plume here, still stained with his blood!"

"The Rani bade me ask for a kris to be made, *empu*. Who else is skilled enough to craft such a blade?" He picked up the plume and held it in both hands, offering it to the old man. Damardi would need some of its barbules to fold into the metal.

Yet the blademaster swelled with rage. "Such a kris is borne only by a warrior-hero in the service of the Chenderawasi. Are you such a hero? Are you even a warrior?" His scorn was scarifying and his grief seared.

Yet Ardhi couldn't look away. "*Empu*, it is the Rani's wish."

Tears slid down the creases of Damardi's wrinkled cheeks to pool at the corners of his mouth. He made a gesture with his hand without turning around and, in answer, his granddaughter emerged from the door behind him. Lastri.

Lastri, with her long black hair and lithe body, her shoulders bare above the tight wrap of her breast cloth. Lastri, whom he had loved so well. Lastri, who'd swum naked with him in the lagoon by night, and lain in his arms on the sand after they'd made love by moonlight. Lastri, who had pledged herself to him, just as he had sworn his love for her.

Now she carried half a coconut shell cupped in both hands and the curve of her hips shivered him with its reminder of all he'd lost.

"The Rani sent me the blood of the Raja," Damardi said, his voice cracking as he gestured at the contents of the shell. "This will be used to damask the blade." His unflinching gaze fixed on Ardhi's like the eye of a sea-eagle on its prey. "I must obey Rani Marsyanda. I will make this kris, although every song in my soul screams at me that you are unworthy of it. Leave the plume. Return after two moons, and the kris will be ready."

"Two months is too long, *empu*. The kris is needed now."

"Revenge can always wait."

He licked dry lips. "It is not needed for revenge. That, I could achieve with my bare hands."

"Then why?"

"The pale men still have the other plumes. They took them on board their ship and sailed away. I need the kris to follow the regalia, that I might find and return the plumes to their rightful place."

Lastri gasped, her eyes widening. Damardi's knuckles whitened as his grip on the porch railing tightened. "These pale men, these ugly banana skins, do they know the power lurking within the plumes?" he asked.

"No."

"At least you had a rice grain of wisdom left in your empty, traitorous skull."

He hung his head in silence.

"But a kris containing the *sakti*, the magic of the Chenderawasi? Such a kris cannot be made in an hour, or a day, or a single moon. The metal must be folded and refolded, the blade must be waxed and soaked and damasked to its edge. Every step must be perfect, otherwise how can it be endowed with its *sakti*? Two months, Ardhi."

"And there's the hilt," Lastri murmured. "Who is to craft and carve the hilt?"

"The Rani. She will use . . ." But Ardhi couldn't finish the sentence.

"I know what she will use," the old man replied, scowling. His eyes glistened. "And she will have already cut what is needed from the body of her husband."

With those words, Damardi appeared to shrink before Ardhi's eyes. The wrinkles on his cheeks burrowed deeper and his eyes shadowed darker under the heavy overhang of his brows. "Very well," he whispered. "I will craft a Chenderawasi kris, but to do it in seven days, a price will have to be paid."

"I will pay it."

"You do not know what it is."

"*Empu*, if a price has to be paid, then it is mine to pay, and it shall be done."

"Indeed." Damardi nodded. "You will stay with me for those seven days. Your strength will aid me. But when it comes to the power of a Chenderawasi kris, your promise to sacrifice your life will be the spark that awakens the Raja's blood and the plume-gold of his regalia. There is no other way. For without a sacrifice, the *sakti* of this kris will rouse too slowly to give it life."

Grief-stricken, Ardhi bowed his head. "I need to live, *empu*. I need to live to seek, find and return the plumes."

Damardi frowned, considering. "Then the day you return with the plumes will be the day of your sacrifice. That promise and those undertakings I will fold into the blade. Your blood to be spilt, and your life freely given to the blade of this very kris. If you do not return the feathers, then the kris itself will turn on you in punishment and take your life no matter where you are. You have no future beyond your quest, Ardhi."

He nodded, his grief cold with fear and rock-hard in his breast. The time of his death had been decreed. *So be it.* Yet he wept at the thought.

He was only eighteen.

Glancing at Lastri, he winced. Her face was a mask, her eyes dulled with grief, but her stance said something else. She was enraged, furious at him for what he had destroyed: their future together.

"Now go," Damardi said. "Build a fire in my forge, so we may heat the metal. I have the best Pashali iron, and we will mix it with the darksilver sky iron from the heavens, collected long past in the mountains.

8

We shall add the root of the graveyard tree and the leaves of the tree of life. This kris will have a bird's-eye damask at the point and the stem, to ensure that its future is auspicious. Its power will carry the *sakti* of the islands across the seas to aid your task." A tear trickled down his cheek. "You are not worthy of such a blade."

Pulauan Chenderawasi. The nutmeg islands.

Agony to have the memories play again and again before his eyes – yet how to stop them?

Perhaps it is punishment, Ardhi thought. Perhaps it was all just to remind him that even if lives were ruined, he had to believe in the rightness of what the kris was doing. The path of the *sakti* of the Chenderawasi was always true.

He looked up at the sails of the *Spice Winds* and dragged his thoughts back to the present. He had to understand why the dagger had brought the four of them – Saker, Sorrel, Piper and himself – together on board this ship on its way to the Spicerie.

Splinter it, though, now is not the time to think about it. He was on lookout duty. He turned his attention to the ocean.

On the horizon ahead, the Regal's aging galleon, *Sentinel*, wallowed along with its impressive array of cannons. Keeping pace to either side of *Spice Winds* were the two other new fluyts designed for spice cargoes; and far behind, with a topmast splintered, limped the elderly carrack *Spice Dragon*. It was a miracle that on this, the first day of watery sunshine they'd had since leaving Ustgrind, the Lowmian fleet was still together. It had taken a whole moon month to emerge from the storm-scoured waters of the Ardmeer Estuary, followed by fourteen more miserable days of appalling weather as the fleet rounded the Yarrow Islands and lost sight of land.

His mind began to wander again, to a sun-sparkled sea where the waters were brighter, the skies a deeper blue. Even the seabirds there spoke other tongues . . .

The kris at his hip slithered in its sheath, pushing against his thigh. He jerked in surprise. The blade hadn't as much as glinted for weeks, let alone moved of its own volition. He drew it out, and the point swung downwards. He looked through the slats of the floor of the crow's nest to see what had prompted its awakening.

9

Sorrel, who rarely left the hastily converted storage cuddy that was her cabin, was on the weather deck with Piper, glamoured so none of the sailors could see either of them.

Ardhi felt a stab of sympathy at her loneliness. Captain Lustgrader had decreed she stay away from the crew at all times – except for Banstel. Barely thirteen years old, the ship's boy milked the goats, washed Piper's swaddling and brought Sorrel's meals to her.

He might have known that she would sneak up on deck now that the weather was better. She had courage and determination, that woman. He admired the set of her shoulders, the lift of her chin at any hint of adversity, the steel in her gaze when she was threatened. What he didn't understand was why the dagger's *sakti* had manipulated the weather to ensure she couldn't leave the ship, as she'd wanted. As for Piper, the baby – he couldn't fathom who she was at all, or why she was here.

He fingered the hilt of the dagger, taking courage from the feel of the Raja's bone beneath his fingers before slipping it back into its sheath. He should have felt satisfied. Those bulging sails around him were filled with cold northerly winds driving the ship towards the Summer Seas.

He was heading home. The three pillaged plumes of the Raja's regalia were safe in his baggage, and the fourth feather, the one he had been granted by the Rani to aid his task, was close by in Commander Lustgrader's hands. He could retrieve it once Saker no longer needed to use its power to coerce Lustgrader.

Sri Kris had prevailed in the Va-cherished Hemisphere, had done everything that had been required of it.

Except kill him.

Skies above, why did he find that so hard to accept? He'd agreed to it! Yet his spirit rebelled and his thoughts darkened with defiant anger. He wasn't eighteen any longer, but he wanted to lash out at his fate, wanted to do anything just to go on living.

Down on the deck, Sorrel looked up at him. Her gaze locked on his, and her mouth curved up in a smile. Without thinking, he smiled back and felt a sudden surge of desire. For her perhaps – or maybe just a longing to find desire and passion in a woman's arms again, someone, somewhere, before he died.

*   *   *

The ship's bell rang. His watch in the crow's nest over, he scanned the horizon one last time. *Spice Dragon* was falling out of sight behind. Not a good idea to scatter too widely, not when Ardronese privateers might be waiting to pick them off, although that was unlikely while their holds were still empty of spices.

As he headed down the shrouds, a wind-rover approached the ship, skimming the waves. He halted his descent to watch, fascinated by its effortless grace as it banked. Its wingspan was greater than his own outstretched arms. It rose to cross the ship just over the mizzen mast, then swung around behind the stern, only to return at a lower level coasting towards the aft deck. Saker was standing at the stern rail, and Ardhi didn't need to be told he was calling the bird in. It wasn't the first time either; the man had done this at least once before on this journey, perhaps more.

Witan Saker Rampion, masquerading as Lowmian Factor Reed Heron. *There's more to you and your witchery than you guess.*

The wind-rover matched its speed to the ship, cruising, spreading the feathers of its tail and dropping its legs, flying lower and lower until it touched down on the decking. It folded its wings over its back and ruffled them uneasily, then lowered its head to hiss its aggression.

The helmsman, with his back to the raised poop at the stern, didn't see what was happening, but other sailors working further along the deck noticed and gaped. Saker knelt beside the gigantic bird, stroked its head and neck until it relaxed, then bent to do something to one of its legs. From above, Ardhi couldn't see exactly what, but a few moments later the bird rose from the deck, its spread wings easily catching the lift of the wind. It banked away from the ship and vanished between the swell of the waves.

Ardhi climbed on down to tell the officer of the watch about the lagging *Spice Dragon*.

2

Va-forsaken Magic

Gunrad Lustgrader, commander of the fleet of the Lowmian Spicerie Trading Company and captain of *Spice Winds*, sat at the desk in his cabin. Lying in front of him, next to an empty length of bambu, was the paradise-bird feather Reed Heron had gifted him. Billows of gold and orange and red enticed him to stroke the plume, to revel in the sensuous thrill of its touch. The glow of its ambient light was warm and welcoming. Magical.

For a moment he was transported back to the islands of the Summer Seas and inhaled again the perfume of the flowering cinnamon and the musky scent left around the villages at night by roving civets. The warm coral sands scrunched underfoot once more and the glory of birdsong filled his ears, sounds so ethereal that tears pricked his eyelids.

He wrenched himself into the present.

Scupper that. The plume was uncanny and it held him in thrall. He knew that and fought it, so why was it a battle where victory always seemed just out of reach?

On his last voyage, he'd seen men in Kotabanta happily disintegrate into drooling fools after inhaling the smoke of burned tree sap. Such madness! The rational part of his mind told him he was like that, drugged, no longer in command of his own destiny, captured – not by smoke – but by cursed sorcery from the Va-forsaken Hemisphere.

That bastard scut, Heron. He's to blame.

Appalling snatches of the day they'd met, not fully recalled and never quite in focus, floated through his memory. He couldn't dismiss them as inaccurate; they stayed, nagging, an ache eroding his sanity.

Tolbun, first mate, had even bluntly told him that the whole ship's company wondered at the way he fawned before Heron, and puzzled over why he'd ever allowed that flirt-skirt and her squalling baby on board.

He knew his behaviour was deranged, yet couldn't change it.

One day soon, Factor Heron, I'll see you keel-raked, your skin shredded on the barnacles, your back flayed to the bone, and if you survive that, I'll hang you from the yardarm. As for that lewdster female, he'd throw her overboard with the baby in her arms. Lightskirt and babe, they were in this together and they would die together, rot them both.

The dream was pleasant, but if he thought too hard about ways of turning it into reality, his stomach cramped and his head ached as if his skull had been cleaved. The moment he wanted to speak to anyone about Heron, his words dried up in his mouth, or turned to paeans in praise of the man. He'd discovered it was better to say nothing.

Sometimes he wondered about the lascar in his crew too. After all, he was a Va-forsaken nut-skin. Maybe he ought to throw him overboard, just in case. He closed his eyes and considered the idea. Voster and Fels, two of the ship's swabbies: they were a couple of rogues who could make an accident happen. If he paid them enough, they'd even resist the temptation to wag their tongues about it afterwards.

Tempting, but no. Ardhi the lascar was a blistering good sailor. The way he scampered about the rigging in the roughest of weather like a giddy-brained spider! Besides, he and Heron were teaching the crew and the factors how to speak Pashali. If he did rid the ship of Heron, he'd need Ardhi alive to teach or they'd be at a disadvantage in spice negotiations. Better still, the lascar came from the nutmeg islands, and knew all about the paradise birds. He hadn't managed to pry much out of the man yet, but he would. There were ways.

His fingers aching with nebulous desire, he forced himself to thread the plume back into the bambu. He flattened his hands on the desk, waiting for his fingers to cease their trembling.

"Banstel!" he roared.

The cabin door opened immediately and his cabin boy stepped inside. The lad had finally understood it was best not to keep the Commander of the Fleet waiting. Unfortunately, his hair was stuck with what looked to be hay and his shoes were filthy.

"You smell like a goat!" he snapped. "Next time you come in here looking like a street urchin, your backside will be striped and you'll be sleeping on your stomach for a week. Understand?"

"Aye, sir."

"Tell Mynster Yonnar Cultheer to report here immediately. Then bring us a carafe of rum cider, nicely mulled."

Forgetting to acknowledge the order verbally, the lad scurried out. The goosecap; his mind was as unkempt as his appearance!

While he was waiting, Lustgrader reread the sealed orders he'd received just before they sailed from Ustgrind. Not for the first time, he had to resist the urge to crumple them up and toss them into the sea. Yonnar Cultheer wouldn't like them, and Yonnar was the Merchant of the Fleet, the representative of the Company's power aboard.

Banstel, now less tousled but still smelling of goat, delivered the jug of warmed cider at the same time as the black-clad merchant settled into the larger of the cabin's two chairs. Lustgrader waved the boy out and half-filled two pewter mugs himself. Retrieving his shaker of ground nutmeg from its locked cabinet, he sprinkled a generous taste on top of the liquid.

"Clove, cinnamon, dried apple, nutmeg," he said, inhaling the steam from his own drink after handing Cultheer his mug. "Not too many people can afford a luxury like this, eh, Mynster Cultheer? One of the few pleasures of being a sea captain who has sailed to the Spicerie and back."

"Indeed."

His agreement was without any inflection of enthusiasm and Lustgrader gave an inward sigh. Merchants could be tiresome. Unimaginative, sober men, they tended to put the Company's interests ahead of everything, including the well-being of the ship's officers and crew.

He chose his words carefully. "I want to speak to you about some instructions I received, signed and sealed by Regal Vilmar, and written, I believe, by His Grace, personally." He picked up the letter from his desk. "These instructions are of a highly confidential nature. You can pass on the information to your factors with the understanding that if they say a word to anyone else, either on board ship or on land, the punishment will be severe. A matter of treason."

Yonnar's eyebrows rose. "You intrigue me. And I wonder why you inform me of this only now?"

He ignored the implied criticism. "We are instructed to make the procurement of more plumes of the paradise bird our primary concern, taking precedence over the acquisition of spices. They are to be considered the property of the Basalt Throne and the Lowmeer Spicerie Trading Company will be reimbursed accordingly."

In shock, Cultheer dropped his mug on the desk, splashing liquid, and sat bolt upright. "What? Is this a jest? Commander, surely His Grace can't be serious."

"Regal Vilmar is not renowned for his levity, and you should watch your tongue."

"Of course. You caught me by surprise." Flustered, he mopped at the spilled drink with his pocket kerchief. "But this *is* an expedition privately funded by the merchant shipping companies of Lowmeer. They've all invested a great deal of money and will never countenance placing more importance on feathers than on spices! How could the Regal possibly reimburse the fortune we would lose?"

"Allow me to finish," Lustgrader said, tone cold even as he revelled in the man's discomfiture. "We are to buy or seize as many feathers as possible and keep them in good order under lock and key. No other member of this expedition is to be permitted to own or keep such plumes, on pain of summary execution. Plumes are to be delivered directly to the Regal and handled only with gloved hands." He stared at Cultheer. "Mynster, these are orders from our monarch, not suggestions."

Cultheer took a deep, controlling breath before he replied. "I can't tell my factors to spend their time shooting and plucking birds!"

"I don't think that would be a solution, either. The factors need to devote their whole attention to the buying of spices. I just want you to be aware that in order to please the Regal, we have to return with a great many feathers."

Cultheer shook his head in a puzzled fashion. "Why does he want them? They may look pretty on an Ardronese lady's hat, but *our* Va-fearing women are not so foolishly frivolous! No one in Lowmeer is going to pay a price that matches a picul of spices. We are not overdressed peacocks like the Ardronese. Does His Grace not realise one small sack of quality cloves or nutmeg would buy a man a manor house on Godwit Street?"

Lustgrader shrugged. "I do not question my liege lord. Unfortunately for us, the men who killed the bird on my last voyage are dead. They didn't make it back to Lowmeer. No one knows exactly how they got the bird, or whether there were more such creatures out there. Consider this too: the islanders came after us, all the way from Chenderawasi Island to the port of Kotabanta, on Seringa Island, just to demand the return of the plumes! They even said our men had killed the Raja of the islands, but my sailors strongly denied that. They swore it before the ship's cleric, and I've no reason to doubt their truth."

Cultheer snorted. "There might have been a good reason for them to lie. If they'd really murdered the ruler of the island, you would have had to give them up to island justice. I've no doubt the islanders' vengeance would have been savage."

"I'd rather believe God-fearing men than Va-forsaken nut-skins!" he snapped. "However, the fact that they came such a long distance to demand we deliver up these men for whatever they did, together with the plumes they had, indicates that the Chenderawasi people are not likely to cooperate and supply us with more plumes, no matter how much we offer. Probably the birds are sacred, or some such foolish superstition. I have tried to pry more out of that Va-forsaken lascar we have on board, but you'd think he didn't understand a word I said for all I could get out of him."

"So what's your solution?" Cultheer had calmed enough to sip his drink, and his eyes lit up as he savoured the flavour.

"I suggest that we recruit some natives from another island, Seringa perhaps, and bring them with us to Chenderawasi, where they can go bird-hunting with some of our swabbies. The Regal must get what he wants, and we must obtain our spices."

Cultheer frowned unhappily and fiddled with his mug. "Yes, but what if your sailors really did kill the Raja? Or perhaps I should say, what if the islanders believe they did? They won't welcome our return. We are more likely to be met with spears and clubs."

The cold of doubt in the pit of Lustgrader's stomach kept him silent.

"Pity we have to go to Chenderawasi at all," Cultheer said. "We could buy their nutmeg in Kotabanta, albeit for a higher price."

"We have half a dozen factors there on Chenderawasi, don't forget – their warehouses filled with nutmeg and mace! Or so I trust. But we don't have a choice now, anyway. The Regal's instructions are clear."

"I mislike this, captain. It appears we have two masters in Lowmeer, one the Company and the other our monarch, and we have to please both of them. Not to mention Chenderawasi savages enraged by the death of birds."

"We are five armed ships, Cultheer. More fire power than any previous fleet. Our factors there are well armed. These islanders have nothing but a few daggers or spears. I do feel, however, that the more we know about them and their birds, the better our trade will be."

There, he'd planted the suggestion without mentioning Factor Heron. *Now, Cultheer, it's up to you. Use your brains, man . . .*

"I could lever some more information out of the lascar," Cultheer suggested. "Or better still, ask someone else to do it. Factor Heron. He's always chatting to the dusky fellow. Said it's because he's interested in learning the language of the islands."

Lustgrader smiled. "You do that. Find out all you can. About . . . about . . ." He ached to tell Cultheer exactly what to say, but the Va-damned sorcery wouldn't let him. He raised his mug in a toast instead. "Drink to our success. Spice – and feathers!"

He doubted Heron would tell Cultheer or anyone else the truth about the power of the plumes, but sometimes you learned a lot from people trying to hide something. Most of all, he just wanted Heron to know that the traders of Lowmeer would be hunting the birds, that therefore others knew how the plumes could be used. He wanted that Va-cursed factor to feel the fear of the stalked, because he *was* being stalked. And one day, he, Gunrad Lustgrader, would find a way to send Factor Reed Heron to perdition where he belonged.

"Keel-raked," he said aloud, after the merchant had left. To his ears, the words were rich with promise. He took a deep breath and smiled.

"How can Ardhi's dagger be some kind of . . . sorcerous blade with the power to influence the weather? Saker, that's curdled crazy."

Sorrel hugged Piper a little closer to her breast, her disbelief warring with her fear that he was right. Around them, the life of the ship continued, but no one noticed her. She was blurred into the background of sand-filled fire buckets, and Saker was attempting to look as if he was dozing in a patch of sunlight.

Sunlight, at last. She was so fed up with rain and cold and cloud. It had been the weather that had imprisoned her, not Captain Lustgrader's orders that she was to remain below and not converse with the sailors or the factors. Now it seemed the weather had been the least of her problems, for Saker was talking of something she had not wanted to think about at all: Va-forsaken magic.

She had seen it in action. She'd seen the way the Chenderawasi plume had entranced Captain Lustgrader. She'd even once briefly glimpsed another world because of Ardhi's dagger – but, oh, how hard it was to acknowledge that she could be powerless in the face of something so alien and utterly without conscience.

"It was responsible for the storms? Just so I could not be landed anywhere on the Ardronese coast as we'd planned?" She snorted. "I've never heard of anything so absurd! Look at me. I'm a nobody. I started life as a yeoman's daughter, then a landsman's wife, and finally a servant hovering somewhere between the status of a lady-in-waiting and a despised chambermaid."

"You're not a nobody, not to me," he said.

Once her heart would have lurched to hear that; once she would have blushed with pleasure, but not now. He was the one whose actions had brought her to virtual imprisonment on this ship and it rankled still. "Well, that's sweet of you to say so, but it doesn't change anything."

"If it wasn't you the kris wanted on board, then it was Piper."

"That's silly. She's just a baby." But the thought that it could be true tore her fragile equanimity to shreds. Appalled, she started shaking. "Because she's a twin? Or because she's Mathilda's child?"

"How can any of us know why? Maybe Va-forsaken sorcery is doing this to prevent us getting her to the Pontifect." He glanced at her. "You're shivering! Are you cold?"

She shook her head, but her stomach griped with terror and she leant forward, hoping to relieve the pain. A royal child. And a twin. Maybe a devil-kin. "Can feathers and daggers really command the winds?"

"That's the kind of witchery they have in the Va-forsaken Hemisphere, it seems. Ardhi's kris and those golden plumes – they're all steeped in what he calls *sakti*."

She hunkered down lower into the shelter of the longboat hoisted above the deck. "It's evil, then. Sorcery, not witchery."

"Maybe, maybe not."

"But it's from the Va-forsaken Hemisphere!" She stared at him, astonished. "And it's forcing us to do things we don't want to do." When he didn't reply she asked, "Where is Va in all of that?" She thought he paled in the moments before he answered.

"We both have witcheries that tell us Va-faith has power," he said, his eyes troubled. "A power that came in answer to our prayers when we were in dire jeopardy. I saw an unseen guardian with my own eyes. I spoke with her. Va exists, Sorrel." His words were clear enough, but conviction was lacking in his tone.

He doubts, she thought. *And perhaps so do I.* She looked down at the child she held. "Are you sure about Va? Perhaps it's just Shenat belief that is true and real. Shrines and their guardians. Because I wonder at a deity who allows a child to be born a devil-kin."

"We don't exactly know the truth of what devil-kin are." He sighed. "I can't know the mind of Va. All I know at this moment is that you and Piper and Ardhi and I are all heading towards the same place for reasons we don't understand, commanded by forces we can't resist. All we can do, every time we are faced with a choice, is to hold on to what we believe is right. I trust the instincts that tell me Ardhi is not an evil man, although I do believe he will put Chenderawasi interests before ours. I'm sorry, Sorrel. I can't offer you anything more than that."

"Coercion of any kind has to be wrong. If we can't choose freely, then how can any choice we make have any value?"

"I hold tight to the belief that the idea of a child born innately evil, without any say in the kind of person they will grow up to be, must surely be anathema to Va."

"I'll tell you what else must be anathema to Va," she replied bitterly. "That horrible coercion you exerted on Lustgrader using the plume. That was despicable." Her revulsion returned with the memory. "You're a witan! How could you do that?"

He winced. "I did it to save your life. And probably Piper's too. If

I hadn't, at best you'd be languishing in an Ustgrind jail for stealing the plumes. At worst, you'd already be dead."

She blinked back tears of frustration and rage. She hadn't stolen the plumes: he had! "Saker, this is ridiculous. I can't sail all the way to the other side of the world with the Regala's child! I'll leave the ship at Karradar. I'll buy a passage back. I still have most of the money you gave me."

"If Lord Juster Dornbeck's ship is in Karradar when we arrive, we'll ask his advice."

She was puzzled. Why would Dornbeck help her? She was hardly a noblewoman in distress. It was doubtful he'd even remember who she was. Sick with worry, she asked, "What about Lady Mathilda and the other twin? I failed them. I was supposed to get help for them!"

"I did send the Pontifect a message before we sailed. I didn't know then though that you'd be on board too, so I've tried sending messages since. Several, in case some didn't arrive."

"How?" She stared at him blankly.

"My witchery."

"Oh! You were sending a message with that huge bird."

"Trying to. Who knows if I was successful?"

Before she could say anything more, Piper started crying, her awakening sudden, her demands imperious. Sorrel dropped their glamour instantly. The crying of an invisible baby would raise questions better not asked.

"Oh, pox," Saker muttered. "Here comes Cultheer."

She was already on her feet, ready to go, but was too late to avoid Yonnar Cultheer's attention. He strode down the deck, clutching his black cloak with one hand in a vain attempt to keep it from billowing out behind him, while his other hand anchored his tall-crowned hat on his head. *What a fusty bolster he is*, she thought. *So attached to his idea of what's appropriate, he won't even dress to suit the conditions.*

His face was thunderous as he came up, words spewing out of his mouth before he'd even reached them. "Didn't you hear the orders that were given concerning this woman, Heron? She is off limits! And you, you hussy, do not dare to speak to my men."

She raised her chin and glared at him. "Would you have me stay silent throughout this voyage, Mynster Cultheer? All the way to the Spicerie?"

"You aren't going all the way to the Spicerie, mistress! The captain is going to throw you off the ship in Karradar."

"Perhaps, but I go nowhere in silence, not to please you, or anyone."

She nodded to Saker and headed towards the companionway to return to her cabin, hushing Piper as she went. Nausea rippled through her guts in waves. Brave words were all very well, but what if she was marooned in the Karradar Islands without any way of getting back to the Va-cherished Hemisphere?

All she'd heard about the islands told her they were not a safe place for a single woman, let alone one with a baby. She'd heard it said that in Karradar you could hear all the languages of the world, commit all the sins ever invented by mankind, and worship all the gods ever known, if you so desired. Its main function was to act as a revictualling port for trade ships, and a place for sailors on shore leave to gratify their whims and lusts.

Sweet Va, why am I here? When I accepted my witchery, I said I would serve Va-faith, but I still don't know what it's asking of me!

After dinner that night, Cultheer spoke to the factors about the paradise birds. Saker sat and listened, hoping the expression fixed on his face was as bland as he thought it was. Inside, he felt wretched. That foolish old man, Regal Vilmar! He ought to have learned from his own experience how dangerous the plumes were; instead, with rattle-brained idiocy, he thought he could use them to his own advantage.

Well, at least Cultheer's given me an excuse to be seen with Ardhi.

When he went looking for the lascar in the morning, he found him scrubbing the residue of sea salt coating the carriage gun on the weather deck.

"Bad news," he said, speaking Pashali for secrecy. No one else on the ship spoke the language with anything close to fluency. "The Lowmians want more plumes. What did you call them? Your Chenderawasi gold."

"Chenderawasi'mas," Ardhi said quietly. He was as taut as a wind-laden sail.

"They want to hunt the birds," he said, and passed on all Cultheer had said. For a moment he thought the lascar was going to hurl himself in rage at the only officer in sight, Mate Tolbun, who was standing with his back to them as he berated one of the swabbies on deck.

He grabbed hold of Ardhi's arm. "That won't help, you muckle-top," he said. "You'd end up in the brig looking forward to a lashing." Gradually he felt the tautness under his hand relax, and released his grip. "I'm sorry."

"My crime, my guilt," Ardhi said finally, his eyes dark with pain. "Tell Cultheer I've never seen a paradise bird. That when I told those sailors on *Spice Dragon* about them, I was in my cups, as drunk as a rat in a wine barrel. Tell him I just passed on information I'd heard. Tell him that I thought it was all legend anyway."

"Unlikely they'll believe that, given what happened later."

"I know, but say it nonetheless. As for other information about the Chenderawasi Islands, I'm already spreading tales designed to strike fear into the heart of every superstitious sailor. Do you know how impressionable they are?"

"Indeed I do. I wish they'd place as much faith in Va as they do in evil spirits and good-luck charms. But, Ardhi, be warned. Cultheer said this order to find plumes came direct from the Regal, written in his own hand. That means Vilmar worked out how to use the power of the plumes. This whole business isn't going to go away. Even if this fleet sank in its entirety before we reached the islands, there'd be another fleet, and another."

"I'm not a lackwit." The expression on his face was grim. "I brought this on my people, and it's up to me to solve it."

"How?"

He made a sound that was part groan, part laugh. "Come now, Rampion. You've thought it through. You and Sorrel, or maybe Piper and Sorrel and you, are going to fix this. Why else would you be here?"

"I've had a belly full of your Chenderawasi *sakti*, Ardhi. You reckon it's all up to us to solve your problems, so you can go home and live happily ever after?"

"Me? I don't get to live at all!" He gave a bitter laugh.

"What makes you so certain?"

Ardhi changed the subject. "I owe you an apology."

"You can't undo my anger with a piss-weak apology! After what you've done to me with your wretched Va-forsaken witcheries, you should be on your knees begging for my forgiveness. Mine, and Sorrel's!" He took a breath. "So which of the numerous crimes against us do you want to apologise for?"

Ardhi bent to scrub the cannon with extra vigour. "That time I came to steal the kris from your room."

For a moment Saker didn't know what he meant. Then he gasped. "Hang me for a beef-witted dunce. That was *you*?"

"You didn't guess?"

"No, of course not!" He'd been hit on the head and his memory of that night was confused. He'd woken in the morning, suffering from an excruciating headache, to find his window and door still latched on the inside, although one board from the window shutter had been misplaced. He vaguely remembered a fight, but he'd never been quite sure what had happened. He couldn't see how anyone had entered his room several storeys up, so he'd eventually concluded he'd fallen somehow during the night and hit his head.

Flabbergasted, he asked, "You followed me all the way from Lowmeer to Throssel? How did you know where to find me? Fobbing damn, how did you even know who I was?"

"I didn't." Ardhi kept his head down as he brushed the underside of the gun barrel. "I didn't know your name, just that you were a witan. I'd seen your medallion, remember? I found you by following the path left by the dagger. I thought that was what Sri Kris wanted. But when I tried to steal it back, it wouldn't come. It wanted to stay with you. That was when I knew I'd wasted my time on that journey. So I turned round and went back to Lowmeer to look for the stolen plumes."

Saker blinked. "Dear oak, is there *anything* that's happened to me over the last year or more that hasn't had something to do with that blasted dagger?"

Ardhi gave an exasperated shake of his head. "I should have known when that kris abandoned me in the warehouse, it was for a reason. I should have waited. Instead I ended up fighting you, and that's what I want to apologise for." He straightened and looked him in the eye.

"Damn you to beggary, Ardhi! Doesn't all this make you sick in the stomach? No man should be at the beck and call of magic. Where is our free will? And what about Sorrel and Piper? Why are they here?"

He turned away to look over the bulwarks at the sea. "I might be able to answer your question properly if I knew who Piper's parents are."

"Why would that matter? I'm not certain who her father was, and I'm never going to tell you who gave birth to her. It's not my secret to tell! And really, it has no bearing on you or your problems."

"Then I can't even begin to guess why either of them is here. I can tell you this much: I believe in the rightness of Chenderawasi *sakti*. It has kept our island and our people safe. I do not believe it is evil, any more than you believe witcheries are vile."

"But can you assure me that it has the interests of anyone else at heart? What does it care about us on the other side of the world?"

"I don't know."

"No. Exactly. You don't." He banged the palm of his hand down on the bulwark in his frustration. "And yet you still obey!"

Ardhi gave the faintest of smiles. "Just as you obey your Va and his shrine guardians, even though you don't know what any of them wants."

He couldn't think of a reply to that.

3

The Petition Writer's Son

"So I can never have a witchery?"

"Reckon not."

Peregrine Clary looked over the back of their laden donkey, Tucker, and pulled a face in response to his father's answer.

"You heard what the shrine keeper said," his father continued. "Not your choice, lad; the shrine guardians do the choosing, not you. They pick fine, upright folk, not the grubby son of a petition writer."

"Be hardly my fault I'm grubby! Nobody can keep clean on the road, not if they don't stop at a proper hostelry. Reckon it'd be fun to have magic."

"Witcheries aren't magic; they're Va-bestowed gifts. Magic, that's sorcery – and believe me, if the old legends are true, we don't ever want to see sorcerers again. They were dark days when such as them walked the earth. Anyway, you don't need a witchery. You can read and write. Be never wanting for food or ale when you can write a letter or a petition. Or read one."

Peregrine snorted. Their meals were often more beggarly than sumptuous, not to mention too far apart. The idea of using some kind of witchery to make a living was much more appealing. Being able to call up a breeze for the fisher folk's sailboats, for example. Or calm a horse, or cure a case of the meazle, or lure fish. That would be fun. And people *paid* for services like that too.

"Will we get to the bottom of the valley afore nightfall?" he asked, hoping it was so.

They were moving down a track carved into a hillside. On the right, the slope rose so steeply you'd have to claw your way up it on all fours; on their left, the land fell away almost as precipitously, clad in a rough tangle of trees and bushes and rocks as it plunged into the darkness of thick forest below, everything so sunless and soggy that just looking at it made chills creep up his back.

"'Fraid not. We be losing light already. We'll camp as soon as we find a flat spot, and be grateful the weather's fine. Leastwise it be warmer here than up in the pass."

"I wish we'd gone another way. The valley roads have villages and inns. This way there be naught." Worse still, the hotpot meal they'd had with the shrine keeper up at the top of Needlewhin Pass seemed a ponderous long time ago. "'Sides, this forest is eerie. Reckon not too many folk come this way."

"They don't, but this be shorter. Don't whine, Perie."

He sighed, but made sure his father didn't hear. He'd be glad when they arrived in Twite down in the valley. He *liked* towns. Towns were interesting. But oh, travelling between East Denva and Ardrone was as dull as a dish-rag. And why did it look so dank and dire when hill country was supposed to be where Va-faith had started? The track was so narrow and *mean*. The forest canopy met overhead, cutting off the last warmth of an evening sun. It might not be raining, but it was going to be horribly cold.

Now *that* would be a good witchery: the ability to conjure up warmth.

His train of thought broke as his father grabbed his shoulder and halted. He was staring downhill, but Perie saw nothing untoward. He tilted his head, listening. Then he had it; not what there was, but what there wasn't. Sounds.

No birdsong. The forest had fallen abruptly silent, as if the whole world had stopped breathing. Dread tendrilled along his skin like a cold breeze, then blossomed into horror. Yet he saw nothing. He couldn't think. He whirled to look back the way they'd come. Still nothing.

He wanted to flee, but couldn't move. Tucker brayed, eyes rolling, nostrils flaring. A smudge of darkness sucked the light out of the air. Rot overwhelmed his nostrils; a tight grip squeezed his chest. Panic, telling him that his world was about to end. He wanted Da to say nothing was amiss, but his father was staring straight past him, his face contorted in fear.

Perie needed to turn. He had to see what was behind him, had to know what his father saw. Yet he was frozen, unable even to turn his head. Da's face was pale as milk, his gaze stark with shock. In that moment Perie's world, all he'd ever known, skewed into insanity. He opened his mouth to scream, but his breath was torn from him.

Da reached out, picked him up and hurled him through the air with a strength Peregrine would never have dreamed he possessed. The air filled with harsh sound. And he was falling, falling . . . plummeting down the slope. He crashed through leaves, breaking branches, careened off something else at a breathless pace, hit the ground and skidded and plunged feet-first into the air as if he'd fallen off a cliff. Then, just as he finally drew in enough breath to scream, he slammed into something so hard the air was driven from his lungs. Even then he didn't stop. He cartwheeled, rolling down a slope so steep he couldn't halt his fall, until he thudded into a tree trunk.

Pain. Pain everywhere. He wanted to scream, but to fill his lungs with the air he'd need to cry out – that would hurt too much. His sight sparked with flashes of light. Everything doubled, then blurred. He couldn't focus. His hearing rang with noise coming from inside his head.

He faded in and out.

Time passed.

Briefly, he was aware of voices, of words shouted in the distance. But not his name, not his father's voice. Pain swelled. He moaned. He heard screams, screams that rent his soul. Then, for a long time, he wasn't there at all, but somewhere else, bleak and dark.

He emerged from the blackness, clawing his way back inch by inch.

The wind had picked up and now gusted through the trees over his head. Close by, damp leaves and soil; the sap smell of a broken branch. Further away, a whiff of sweat and unwashed skin, smoke of a fire, horse manure.

Sweet pickles, I hurt . . .

A lot.

Da, please come back soon . . .

No. Not Da. Da had thrown him away.

Why . . . ?

His tears fell without sound.

When the black returned, he welcomed it, let it swallow him whole. It was easier that way.

* * *

Gerelda Brantheld cursed herself for taking the shortest route over the hills between Twite and Sistia. The track was rough, and by the look of it, Needlewhin Pass was still a long way further up. She had to walk her horse because the trail was so fobbing steep. Worse, judging from the mud and ruts, she was following close behind a large troop of horsemen and pack animals also travelling upwards. Traders, she assumed. They'd certainly churned up the ground.

Serves you right for listening to that whey-faced woodcutter outside of Twite. Fellow had said the path was good. He'd lied. She'd been so anxious to finish the tasks the Pontifect had sent her to do, so keen to return to Vavala as quickly as possible, that she'd been prepared to make the climb. She ought to have guessed it would be a mistake; what was the expression? "Better the horror you know than the outlandish that lies in wait." She snorted at her own unease.

The forest was so thick that on her first night out she'd ended up having to call it a day even before the sun was fully set. And now that she was on her way again in the morning, the track was wet and slippery, her horse slow and unhappy and she'd barely slept. This reeky forest had spooked her all night, and she was normally as unimaginative as a log.

Pox on't! Fritillary Reedling, the things I do for you . . .

As she plodded on leading her mount, she let her idle thoughts drift to Saker Rampion. Strange how often she'd brought him to mind since that day they'd bumped into one another in the Shenat Hills. She'd heard about his subsequent nullification, and later still, Pontifect Fritillary Reedling had informed her that he'd managed to survive it.

Gerelda had laughed, unsurprised.

Of course he'd survived. He might have been a rattle-brained idiot on occasion, but he would never be an easy man to kill. They hadn't met again since then, and she felt a pang of regret. She enjoyed his company and yes, if she was honest, she'd enjoyed renewing their bedroom intimacy. He'd learned a lot since their student days.

She smiled at the memory. *We really should try to see each other more often. We should plan it, not leave it up to chance.* It would be good to talk to him about all the worrying things she'd been seeing and hearing. *He always listens*, she thought, *that's why. He listens carefully. I wonder what he's up to now? I'll have to ask Fritillary . . .*

Leading her mount, she rounded a bend in the path – and stopped dead. In the middle of the track was a mound of bloodied bones and skin. A fresh kill, by the look of it. Her mount laid his ears back and snorted as it caught the whiff of blood.

What traveller left a mess like that in the middle of the track? Loutish bastards.

She calmed her mare and tied it to the nearest tree, then walked on to take a close look. There was no one in sight, thanks be, but by the look of it, there had been a string of campfires burning along the trail the night before, where men had roasted meat and feasted. If this had been a trader's horse train, it had been a large one.

Crouching on her heels beside what was left of the kill, she examined the animal – or animals – they had butchered. She'd expected to find the remains of a deer, or maybe a goat they'd brought with them; instead she found the head, tail, legs and skin of a donkey.

Beggar me speechless, someone ate a donkey? Besides being as tough as a sun-dried fish, any beast of burden was usually worth more alive than eaten. Maybe it had broken a leg.

She glanced around, still puzzled. There was evidence of too many people. Too many fires: one every twenty paces or so along the track. Each one surrounded by the remains of their meal. She was misliking this more and more. A merchant's pack-train should have a lot of linked pack animals, but not all that many hands to look after them. These mountains were not particularly lawless; traders didn't need more than a couple of armed guards, if that. So what the rattling pox was going on?

Guessing that most of the fires had been built for warmth during the night, she looked closely at the largest, the one where most of the roasting had taken place. And was shocked, shaken to her core. A disembodied foot, hacked off at the ankle and still wearing a leather red-tongued boot, lay off to one side. And there, cast away into the ashes of the fire: that was a human legbone. She picked up a stick and poked it, rolling it over until she was certain she was right, only to reveal something worse. The cooked flesh had been hacked away from the bone with a knife.

Her knees buckled, almost failing to hold her upright.

Va help us all, they slaughtered and ate a man!

Her gaze swept the trees on either side of the trail, her imagination – the one she'd once been so sure she didn't have – supplying her with a stream of possibilities. She was surrounded. They were there, in amongst the trees, laughing at her. Waiting for her to snap with fear, waiting for her to run so they could give chase. The fox after the rabbit, and she was the rabbit. They'd let her think she was escaping, only to catch her just when she thought she was safe.

Come on, this is not you, Gerelda, milk-livered and as scared as a moldwarp in its burrow.

She took a deep breath. There was no one there. The camp had been abandoned much earlier that morning, and the men had proceeded on their journey up towards the pass. But who were they? Not traders, she was sure of that now.

Hunting for clues, she scoured the campsite. She found the dead man's other foot, still clad in its boot, and more sickening evidence that he'd been eaten. Taking a calming breath, she forced herself to search for a clue to his identity. The saddle packs, probably for use with the donkey, had been thoroughly searched and the belongings scattered. Doubtless the murderers had taken the valuables, but a broken pen, a spilt packet of ink powder, some poor-quality parchment and a broken portable desk-board told her the owner had been an itinerant scribe of some sort.

As she rifled through what had been left muddied and torn on the ground, she found clothes for a much younger lad. Someone of perhaps eleven or twelve. She sat back on her heels, feeling ill.

A child. A lad. Eaten as well? Sweet cankers, not that.

Swallowing bile, she hunted again through the bones and ashes and charcoal looking for any sign that more than one person had died there, but there was nothing. No sign of a lad among the debris. Perhaps the scribe had bought clothing to give to his son, waiting safe in a village somewhere. There was no way to know.

She examined footprints, counted the number of different boot-sole patterns, looked for where they'd hitched their mounts. She discovered a number of puzzling round marks on the soft soil near the base of a tree. She counted the remains of ten fires; evidence of approximately ten men per fire. Units of ten: one hundred men altogether. That had the feel of a tight organisation: royal guards, or an army contingent. Those round marks? Made by the butt-ends of staves leant against the tree trunk. No, not staves: lances. These men were a troop of lancers.

But when had the King's army ever turned to eating travellers? The idea was ridiculous.

So who were they?

One hundred men, many of them mounted, about two hours ahead of her, heading up towards the mountainous border country; men who didn't baulk at killing and eating other men. Ahead of them, but still on the Ardronese side, a single shrine, hardly enough to interest them as a destination to pillage. Beyond that, the pass and the vast forests of East Denva, dotted with the occasional mine or quarry.

She shivered, forced herself to walk, not run, back to her horse. A feeling of dread was wrapping itself around her, reshaping her calm into abject terror. Va-damn, was this some kind of perverse witchery?

No, never that. *Sorcery.* The thing that people laughed into non-existence, the same way folk poked fun at myths, or at tales of elves and sprites told to children. She'd never believed in such things.

Now . . . ?

Now, she was not so certain.

Her fright was telling her to turn around, to go back to the safety of Twite, but rattle-brained terrors had no business trying to rule her head! So . . . so she would follow these men without ever letting them see her, and once she could pass them without them knowing, she would ride on to Sistia. There she would attend to some Va-faith legal matters the Pontifect had asked her to look into, after which she would ride like the wind for Vavala to tell Fritillary what she had seen.

She didn't like this, not one bit.

She didn't like the whispers, the rumours she'd heard, either. Wives who spoke of their husbands training as lancers "for when they were needed to defend Va-faith"; mothers who spoke of sons disappearing from the farm or the village; townsfolk who told of journeymen vanishing without trace, leaving the tools of their trade behind. Not many such folk, but a lad from a village here, a man from the farm there, a handful from a neighbouring town. She'd heard a cleric speak about those serving Va – not as clerics, but as soldiers.

Fox, she thought. In Ardrone, anything to do with Va-faith was in the hands of Prime Valerian Fox. That man was as reeky as a barrel of rotting maggots. *But, fiddle-me-witless, even he wouldn't countenance eating human flesh, surely?*

Riding upwards, all her senses alert, Gerelda had never felt so vulnerable. She'd been in many tight spots over the years while working as the Pontifect's legal investigator, proctor and agent. She'd known fear before, but never had she felt that she was drowning in terror as she was now, every nerve screaming at her to turn and flee, even as her more rational self was telling her there was little need to be so fearful. The horsemen were unlikely to be keeping much of a watch to the rear, not on this lonely track. Once she'd passed the fires, her horse was untroubled; she herself could neither hear nor smell anything tangible that was worrisome; she had no intention of challenging those ahead of her – so what was the problem? She concentrated on staying alert and watching the forest on either side for any signs of ambush.

Her vigilance paid off, but not in the way she'd expected. A mile or two past the fires, she spotted a large pool of dark, congealed blood. Nearby, the broken branches of a bush at the edge of the track indicated someone had left the road. Curbing her anxiety, she dismounted to take a better look. A trail of broken twigs, crushed leaves, dislodged stones and scraped bark told her whoever it was had tumbled down the slope, skidding and sliding and flailing as they went.

She squatted, studying the quantity of blood. There was enough to tell her someone had died there. A man had been slaughtered, probably by sentries positioned along the track to guard the camp. His body had been later taken to the fires to be dismembered and cooked. But that wouldn't explain the trail of broken vegetation. No, someone must have escaped the horror on the track.

The clothing that belonged to a lad . . .

Frowning, she stared into the forest. No movement, no sound. The slope was too steep and wooded for a horse. She would have to leave it on the track, along with her packs, if she wanted to investigate. Given all she had seen, that would be foolhardy. Better to mind her own business. She climbed back into the saddle.

They killed a scribe. They ate him. His legless feet were still in their boots . . . What if there really had been a boy and he was out there somewhere, alone?

Sweet Va, she so *hated* not knowing the facts.

Sighing, she dismounted again, tied up her horse and began to slither down the slope, following the trail of broken twigs and scuff marks. The hillside was so steep she had to anchor herself on saplings and bushes, not letting go until she'd singled out another lower down to grab. Further below, she was grateful for her caution: the person she was following had obviously sailed over a steep drop. She peered over the edge, but couldn't see anyone. The trail of broken bushes and crushed leaves continued downwards. She contemplated jumping, but decided that would be to risk a broken leg. Instead, she scrambled sideways looking for a way around the drop.

Blistering pox, it'll take me an hour to get up that slope again, it's so fobbing steep. More like a bleeding cliff.

Once she had circled around the steep section, she worked her way back until she'd picked up the trail again. A few paces deeper into the undergrowth, she found him. Scratched and gouged, he'd started to climb back up to the track. She could see the trail he'd left behind. He was crawling, his face bruised and swollen, his clothing ripped, a shoe missing. He looked broken, exhausted, terrified. He was covered in mud, and there was plenty of blood mixed in with the filth.

Her heart sank. *Oh, what in the name of the Flow am I going to do with him?* Aloud, she said, "Don't be frightened. I'm not going to hurt you."

"My da," he said. "Where's my da?"

Fiddle me witless, what the pickle do I say? "Was he wearing a pair of boots with tongues of red leather?"

He was silent, but his eyes widened.

"Did you have a donkey?"

He stared at her, his lip trembling, then nodded dumbly. One arm clutched the other arm tight to his chest. Broken collarbone, at a guess.

He nodded.

"Then I'm sorry, lad. No easy way to say this. He's dead."

He stared at her, a long bewildered stare. "Tucker's dead? The donkey?"

"Yes. And the man who wore boots with red leather tongues. Him too."

There was a long silence. When he did speak, he sounded more puzzled than believing. "Da threw me down the slope. Why did he do that?"

"To save your life, I would think," she said. "There were armed men, a troop of them. They killed your father and your donkey."

Nothing on his face told her he'd understood. Instead, his legs buckled. She caught him just before he hit the ground.

4

In Another Man's Boots

It took Gerelda three hours to haul the lad back to the track. Concussed, he drifted in and out of consciousness, sometimes able to clamber up with her help, but mostly just a dead weight. At least when he wasn't awake he wasn't in pain.

Once back on the trail, she was glad to see him sink into oblivion as she stripped off what was left of his clothing and washed his scratches and scrapes as best she could with water from her water skin. She applied an unguent to the worst cuts, then dressed him in culottes and a shirt of her own. His collarbone was definitely broken, so she fashioned a sling for that arm, tearing up the only skirt in her pack. She hated skirts anyway.

Having made him as comfortable as possible in her own bedroll on the ground, she squatted beside him. His colouring – a thick shock of dark, unkempt hair, dark eyes and skin a mite more tan than most – told her he had Shenat origins. He was thin and wiry, probably not more than twelve years old. His accent was more that of East Denva than of Ardrone.

Well, she couldn't babysit a child. She had a job to do.

She should just leave him there and ride away. If he was the son of a scribe or petition writer, he ought to be able to read and write. She could leave him a note telling him to walk on down into the farming valley of Twite. He'd be there in a day or two. Well, maybe three, if he was slow, and he would be. She guessed that was where he and his father had been headed anyway; it seemed likely that they had been coming down into the valley when they'd met the men travelling upwards.

His eyes sprang open as though he'd heard her thoughts. "Don't be leaving me," he whispered.

She hedged. "Not yet a while. But I'm not going your way. You were going down towards the Twite road, weren't you?"

He went to nod, winced and said instead, "Yes. We've been in East Denva." He frowned. "Did you . . . did you say my da was . . . dead?"

"Yes. I'm afraid so." She squatted beside him. "I found his body a short way further down the track. And the donkey too. Sorry. They were killed by whomever it was you met on the way."

Fig on't, if he goes back down the road, he'll find the remains. She'd not spared the time to bury what was left of the man, and it wasn't a sight a lad of his age should see.

He struggled to sit up, biting his lip to stop himself crying out. "Who killed him? I didn't see anybody! And why would they do that anyways? My da wouldn't have hurt anybody. Never even carried a weapon, him. Always said folk don't hurt scribes." He eyed her sword and the fear in his eyes deepened. "Why've you got one? Never seen a woman wear a sword afore." He looked around, frantic. "Da? Da!"

She laid a hand on his shoulder. "I'm not lying, lad. At a guess, those men didn't want anyone to know who they were and where they were headed. Your father – and you – were in the way. Simple as that. Wrong place at the wrong time."

He shook his head violently, which made him dry retch. When he ceased his fruitless heaving, he whispered in protest, "Da writes petitions. He drafts contracts and such. Folk don't hurt us none. I never saw anybody!"

She reached out to pat his good shoulder. "Look, lad—"

He pushed her hand away. "Who are you?"

"I'm a proctor. That's a kind of lawyer. I work for the Pontifect. My name's Gerelda Brantheld."

He had suspicion written all over his face. "That's a Lowmian name."

No gullible sluggard, this lad, then. "I was born in Lowmeer, but my home is in the city of Vavala now."

"Show me this dead 'un. It won't be my da." His denial was vehement. "My da wouldn't let anybody kill him, not just like that."

"What's your name?"

"Peregrine Clary. Folk . . . folk call me Perie mostly."

Shenat naming, combining a bird and a herb in this case. "Well, Perie, I think your father was taken by surprise. I'm going to continue up over the pass, where those men were heading. I intend to warn the Denvian authorities about them. They were soldiers of some sort. And you need to continue downwards, to wherever you were going, where you'll be safe. I can give you food and some money, but I can't come with you."

He tried to stand up, gasped in pain and sank down on to the bedroll again.

"You have a broken collarbone. Only time will cure that. I suggest you rest up here for the remainder of today, then set off down this track when you feel able to walk. It'll take you a day or two to reach the valley where someone will give you shelter."

He rose to his knees and then carefully stood up with her help. "I want to see this dead 'un," he said. "Now."

Gerelda stifled a sigh. Fob it, she couldn't be sure he'd absorbed a thing she'd said. "On your way, you will, I'm afraid. You'll pass by what's left of his body. They—" She paused, wondering how to say it, and decided to disguise what she thought had really happened. "They burned his corpse."

His mouth took on a mulish expression. He was not going to take anything she said as the truth until he'd seen it for himself.

"All right," she said with a shrug, as if she didn't care. "Just a moment while I put together some things for you to take."

She separated out some cheese and pickles, a blanket from her bedroll, and parted with her flint, steel and tinderbox; she wouldn't be lighting any fires until she was sure the lancers were nowhere in the vicinity anyway. Fortunately, she had enough coins on her to be generous, and she handed over half of what she had.

His eyes widened. "I – I'll never be able to pay all this back, Proctor Brantheld," he stammered.

"I don't expect you to. This is a gift."

"And your clothes—" He looked down at the culottes in distaste.

"I saw some of what must have been your clothes near the fires. Use them, then you can keep mine for extra warmth at night. Or use them to wrap up that bare foot of yours." She had not found his missing boot on her way up the slope, although she'd looked.

He stared down at his feet.

"How old are you, Perie?"

"Near twelve. Da's going to buy me some fine toggery when we reach Twite. He says twelve's a special birthday. Says that's when you start being a man." His gaze hardened even as she looked.

"I'm sorry about your dad. A mile or two down the track, you are going to see something very difficult for you. You need to prepare yourself."

He didn't answer or look at her.

"Do you have other family anywhere? A home?"

He shook his head.

"If your father was a petition writer, I assume you can read and write too?"

"Course I can. Da says I have a fine hand!"

"Then you can find work, even though you're young." She handed him the bundle she had put together. "Food, money, blanket, the means to light a fire. There are several streams crossing the track on the way down, so water is no problem."

He nodded, took the bundle and turned to walk away, wincing with every step.

Blister you, Gerelda. You are going to feel bad about this for the rest of your life. She sighed. Duty. It was all about duty.

She gathered her things together and went to repack her saddlebags. Recollections of the feeling of dread and the reeky smell surfaced every now and then; she refused to dwell on them and the memory began to fade.

The lawyer woman had told the truth. It wasn't far down to the remains of the soldiers' camp, but even so, every step he took sent pain ripping through him somewhere. One foot in a shoe and one foot bare, he trudged on anyway, because none of the pain was as bad as thinking his da was dead.

Da had been his one sure rock, ever since Ma died, along with the new babe. He'd been nine, then. Da had been away, on the road. The midwife had called the Va-faith cleric and the cleric had taken the bodies. He'd watched them being buried under the trees in the grave-yard. Ma wouldn't like resting there. She'd been a town woman, his ma.

Never mind, if you'd led a good life, you got to choose where your spirit rested when you were gone. That's what the shrine keepers said, and he liked shrine keepers better than clerics, so he liked to imagine her looking out from the plinth of the old king's statue, right in the middle of the high street. She'd be watching the world go by, with the babe in her arms, that's what she'd be doing.

A tear trickled down his cheek.

He showed Da the graves afterwards when he'd come home, weeks later. That was when they started walking the roads together and he learned how to read and to shape his letters.

And now his thoughts spun without stopping, and the tears kept coming and drying on his cheeks just thinking about it.

He rounded a bend and saw the ashes on the road. Something smelled too, like a dead dog flung in a drain and just beginning to rot. Not real bad yet, more sweetish than putrid.

Dropping his bundle, he stood still for a long while, staring at the boot with the red tongue, lying there beside the charred wood of the long-dead fire. His chest heaving, he limped over to where it lay. His da's boot, no doubt about it. He stared.

It had a bit of his foot poking out the top, chopped off at the ankle. She'd said they'd burned his body. He stared some more. But if that was all they did, then why were those two big bones over there with all the flesh cut off like slices from a roast? Roasted flesh.

He stared and stared. Mostly he couldn't think. He just looked, but then something would punch into his thoughts with the impact of a man's fist, and then he'd be looking at something else, waiting for another punch, another impact.

Those cut marks, just like when you carve a roast with your knife and put a slice on your trencher . . . *Punch.*

Those bones. The length of a man's thigh . . . *Punch.*

The rib bones with the meat gnawed off . . . *Punch.*

He stood there, swaying, each punch hurting more than the last, each gasp of breath rasping into his lungs like red-hot flames.

She'd said they burned him, but she'd lied. They hadn't burned him; they'd *cooked* him. Those bones had been Da, just a few hours back . . .

Numb all over on the outside and a mess of agony within, he stood staring straight ahead of him. A long time later he realised he was looking at an oak tree growing by the track. Not an ancient oak, all gnarly and twisted like most shrine oaks, but old enough. *Va help me.*

Stepping over his father's foot, he dragged himself to the base of the trunk and put a tentative finger to the bark. A shiver shot up his arm.

Yes, I am here . . . to all who cry for help.

He heard the words as clearly as the sound of the wind rustling the leaves in the branches above. He leaned against the trunk, pressing his cheek to the fissured bark, and said, "I can't bear it . . ."

He pressed harder and harder, trying to rid himself of a burden too great to bear, of intolerable pain that was more than he could endure. He gave all he had. The boy he had been melted and shifted, losing shape and identity. Limbs hugged him, entwined him, until he was not sure where he ended and the oak began. For a moment he was safe and tears of healing coursed down his face. His mother's comfort whispered in his ears, his father's hand stroked his hair, the unseen guardian dried the tears with his breath, and he slept.

He dreamt. He saw a young man, with hair the colour of autumn leaves, and lithe brown limbs, all muscle and strength and supple resilience. Brown eyes pooled with sympathy; fingers touched his face with love.

"Am I safe?" he asked.

Safe. But Peregrine Clary, you must make a choice. You can leave and walk on, grieving alone, and in time you will forget a little, and then a little more, until the boy you are now finally becomes a man. Grief will twist your youth; bitterness will taint your adulthood. Or I can take away the worst of the pain in your heart right now and replace it with hard oak, that you may fight, for there is indeed a war to be fought.

"Who is the enemy?"

The man who caused this atrocity. The men who forgot their humanity to eat another's flesh. This you can fight, not with a sword, but with the witchery I will gift you. But beware, the battle is one you may not win. It may be in vain, for I cannot promise victory; I can only guarantee the cause.

"Who are you?"

An unseen guardian.

"But I see you."

Some say that to see the unseen is a curse. Which would you: fight or walk on?

"Fight. My father died for me. I cannot walk on."

Nothing will be the same. You will not be the same.

"I am already changed."

So be it.

By the time he woke, the dream was only a confused memory. The one thing he knew was that he was different.

And much, much older on the inside. He touched his cheeks, but the tears had dried.

An hour after Gerelda set off, it started to rain. A persistent drizzle, but sufficient to turn the track – already churned up by the horses ahead – into a ribbon of gluey mud. She tried riding, but had to stop so often to clean the mud out of the horse's hooves that she gave up and led the beast instead.

As she set up camp near a small stream that night, the clouds thinned enough to reveal a rising full moon. Even better, the rain eased off. There was no sign of anyone ahead of her, no lights showing through the trees; no sound came to her ears carried on the wind.

She ate a meagre meal, and settled into her bedroll beside the road, her sword and knife tucked out of sight on either side. Just as the last twilight vanished from the sky, she closed her eyes and drifted off into sleep.

Three hours into the night, something woke her. Quietly, she groped for her knife with one hand and edged the blanket away from her face with the other. Slowly, she raised her head. The only sound was the restless nickering of her horse, alerting her to the approach of someone. Or something. The track was in full moonlight now, and she had no trouble making out the single figure dragging his way wearily upwards. Not someone tall enough to be an adult.

She swore under her breath. Pox on the lad; what did he think he was doing? But even as she cursed, her admiration for his tenacity softened her ire.

Hang me, the boy's got the guts of a fellhound.

With a sigh, she rolled to her feet and waited for him to reach her.

When he did, he was swaying with fatigue and pain. He was, she was glad to note, still carrying the bundle. He had slung on his own retrieved clothes over those she'd given him. When she lowered her gaze to his feet, nausea rose in her gorge.

He was wearing his father's boots.

He saw her look and said, "Da and me, we have the same size feet."

With that remark, he dropped his bundle and collapsed into her arms.

5

The Lonely Exile

"Hey, you!"

Aureen halted, heart thumping. She knew the voice of authority when she heard it. Fear ensnared her, but she forced herself to turn. The two men walking towards her through the market crowd wore no uniform, but they reeked of confidence.

"Who, me?" she asked. Her question emerged as a squeak. Trying to hide her nervousness, she smoothed down her white servant's apron over her hips.

"If you are the Regala's maid, yes, you!"

She nodded dumbly.

"We want to chat to you about another one of your Ardronese servants. The Redwing woman."

She tried not to look worried. Castle guards had already questioned her so many times about Sorrel's disappearance, stupid questions about the theft of a valuable fan belonging to the Regal, which was ridiculous. Sorrel wasn't a thief, and she had not fled the castle because of a theft. She eyed the two men warily. These black-clad men were not castle guards, nor were they obviously the Regal's men. Then how did they know who she was? And worse, approaching her like this, out in the street. She had barely left the castle since the birth of the Prince-regal Karel two moons ago, and yet here they were, calling her by name.

Dear Va. Who are they then?

Her heart plunged. She'd heard whispers of men called the Dire Sweepers. Some said the Sweepers sought twin babies, in order to smother them. Others said they spirited away those with the plague; whether to cure or kill them was never spelled out. The Sweepers were everywhere, they said. They knew everyone's business. You couldn't keep secrets from the Sweepers . . .

"Where have you been?" one of the men snapped. He was the smaller of the two, a fellow with a pinched, sour face.

"Nowhere. I-I live in the castle, mynster."

"Lackwit! I mean just now. Where were you?"

She blinked, trying to make sense of what they were asking. "I-I went to pray, mynster."

"You lie. There's no shrine down there." He waved in the direction she had come from, near the riverbank.

"I'm Ardronese. I p-p-pray under an oak. There-there's one growing down by the river. I'm s-s-sorry if that's wrong."

The larger man snorted. He had a round, pleasantly red-cheeked countenance, but when he stepped closer, he towered above her, his wide-shouldered bulk intimidating. "You were friends with the Redwing woman," he said. "Have you been meeting her?"

She gaped. "I-I haven't seen her! Not-not since she left the castle."

"Where did she go?"

"I've no notion! Nor why she went, neither. And we wasn't friends. She was a handmaiden, not a skivvy. More like a – like a lady-in-waiting, from a proper family an' all. Hoity-toity, like. Handmaidens don't have aught to do with the likes of me." Her mouth dried out as she uttered the lie. Maybe that was true of most handmaidens, but she and Sorrel had slept in the same servants' bed for months. With an effort of will, she just stopped herself from nervously licking her dry lips.

"You're a midwife," the other man growled, the words an accusation.

She swallowed down a choking wave of fear. "I-I-I'm the Regala's maid." *Sweet Va, this is not about Sorrel stealing something. This is about the baby . . .*

The other baby. Princess Mathilda's twin daughter.

After the birth, Aureen had been in a fever of terror that their deception would be discovered. Then, as the days passed, she'd begun to breathe again. Perhaps they had gotten away with it. Perhaps Sorrel was on her way to the Pontifect with the child and all was well. She'd almost come to believe it.

Now the expression on the faces of these two men made her doubt. She wasn't safe. Princess Mathilda wasn't safe. Maybe Sorrel hadn't escaped to Vavala. Maybe she'd been caught, and tortured into telling the truth . . .

44

"You are a midwife," the large man repeated.

"I-I was," she admitted, "back in Ardrone. But here I'm just a lady's maid." She wasn't about to tell them she'd been in attendance at the birth of the Prince-regal. If they realised that, they'd know she could have hidden all evidence of an earlier birth that night. *Va, help us all . . .*

"What do you know about the baby this Sorrel Redwing was carrying?"

Her stomach heaved. "What babe? She didn't have no babe!"

"She visited more than one midwife before she ran off. She glamoured herself, but she couldn't glamour her Ardronese accent. She asked about twins."

She shook her head, trying to use the gesture to conceal her ragged breathing. "Good sirs, I know naught of this! Why would she go to a midwife? She weren't bearing no babe. Slim, she was. Never had no babe under her skirts."

"Yet later she had a baby with her, and tried to find a wet nurse to suckle it. I suppose you know nothing about that either? Whose babe did she have if not her own?"

"I know naught of this!" She was panicked now, and her voice was too high, like a scared child's. Around them, pedestrians stared, then quickly glanced away and hurried on as if they sensed this was not an affair they should meddle in. "Mayhap a friend of hers? She left the castle often enough, not like us maids; she could come and go. Folk like me have work to do! Half a day, I get, each moon. But the likes of her, nose in the air, money in her purse – she came and went."

"A twin it must be," the large man said to his companion. "She spirited away a twin. But whose, eh?"

Her knees almost gave way under her. *They know! Dear Va, save us all, they know!* She stared at them, unable in her terror to speak.

"We reckon it was someone in the castle. A lady-in-waiting maybe? Tell us, and you will escape punishment," the second man said. He was calm, and his voice was gentle now, cajoling. He reached out and patted her arm. "We just want the truth."

"I don't know what you're talking about!" Words began to spill from her. She scarcely knew what she was saying, knowing only that she had to lead them away from the truth. "If it was a lady-in-waiting, you think anyone'd tell the likes of me? Anyways, that night Mistress Sorrel disappeared – we was all busy with the Regala. Reckon that was why Mistress Sorrel chose that night to run away. 'Twas the night m'lady gave birth and no one was paying any attention to what Mistress Sorrel was about. The lords and ladies were in a right tizzy. The Lord Chamberlain came to attend the birthing, and the Ward's-dame, Lady Friselda, not to mention one of the Regal's physicians and others of her ladies.

"So many of them around the bed there was scarce room to move! The Regal himself came to the solar. His Grace were in the retiring room, he was, awaiting the news with his courtiers. With all that going on, is it no wonder none of us knew till morning that Sorrel'd done gone, vanished? No one noticed her go. No one knew what megrims she got in her head as made her went. That's Va's own truth, mynster." *And I pray Va will save me from my lies . . .*

The large man reached under his coat, behind his back, and withdrew a dagger. Carelessly he flipped it in his palm several times. She was mesmerised, watching the blade turn. He placed his other hand on the side of her neck where his long fingers and thumb caressed her skin. She shivered, unable to move. He raised the point of the dagger until it pricked her under the chin. She gave a single sob.

Around them, people scattered, giving them a wide berth.

He leaned forward to speak in a raspy whisper. "Last chance," he said. "Last chance for the truth."

"I told you the truth," she whispered. "All I know."

There was a long silence. A stillness that dragged on and on. She couldn't move. She felt damp between her legs, and knew she had wet herself, but it didn't seem to matter. She was beyond mortification, mired in a fear so deep she thought she would die of it.

"If you have lied," the smaller man said, and the malice in his tone was like poison, "I will come for you one day. I will see you strapped to a wagon wheel and raised spread-eagled to look at the sky above. The ravens will come to peck out your eyes. The hawks will come to tear out your tongue. And at night, the rats will climb the pole to burrow their way between your legs and feast on your privates . . ."

She was shaking so hard she thought the knife would stab her through the face. She closed her eyes and waited to die.

Nothing happened.

The fingers vanished. The dagger point no longer pricked. She waited, eyes closed, incapable of moving. Still nothing happened.

She opened her eyes. She was standing on the street, swaying. Around her people continued on their way, apparently oblivious to all that had happened, laughing and chatting. An ordinary day, sunny and warm even. The kind of day that made folk feel all was well with the world.

Of the two men, there was no sign.

Mathilda felt the colour drain from her face, leaving her faint and sick. She stared at Aureen's white features, and saw a reflection of her own fear.

She drew in a deep breath. *I am a Regala. A queen. I am more than any common-born woman and I must always appear to be so . . .*

Her thoughts raced, assessing, discarding, deciding. "You did the right thing," she said, striving for measured calm. "I commend you. These men – whoever they were – were trying to trick you into betraying us. If you had admitted anything, we would all be dead, including the Prince-regal. You were truly brave, Aureen. Perhaps, though, it would be better if you did not leave the castle for the time being. You are safer within the walls."

"Oh, I'm not going nowhere, milady! Too scared, I am. But who were they? Not the Regal's men, surely? Yet they spoke of twins! They knew so much about Sorrel. About her asking the midwives 'bout twins, and her wanting a wet nurse . . ."

"They're clever. Pox on them, but they are clever! Still, it seems they are so busy looking for the squirrel, they have not seen the bear in the forest."

Aureen looked at her blankly.

Mathilda curbed her irritation and said gently, "I think you are right. These men are Dire Sweepers, looking for twin births. The Dire Sweepers work for the Regal, so who is the last person they would suspect of hiding twins? The Regal!" *And, I hope, the Regala.* "We don't have anything to fear, Aureen. As long as we keep our heads. We are the bear in the forest, and they can't even see us because they keep looking at the smaller prey."

Aureen didn't appear any happier. "How did they know about Sorrel?"

"It doesn't matter! Someone must have told them an Ardronese woman was asking about twins and they made a connection to Sorrel. But the important thing is that no one is making that connection to the Prince-regal. And they must never do so!" The trouble was she wasn't sure that was true. Perhaps they were already drawing the right conclusions and had been attempting to scare Aureen into admitting it.

"But Sorrel escaped the same night he was born! And the next day someone saw her with a babe. How can they not see it?"

"You said it, yourself! The Prince-regal was born in the presence of the Lord Chamberlain, Lady Friselda and two of the Regal's physicians! They all saw it. One child. They will swear till the day they die that there was no twin." She shuddered. "Ugh, I'll never forget it! I felt like one of Prince Ryce's pedigree fellhounds dropping a litter with everyone watching."

"But—"

"Aureen, even if they were ever to wonder, how could they ever admit it, even to themselves? It would mean their own downfall. But there is no reason for them to doubt. We were careful. None of us will ever say otherwise. Keep your counsel and we are all safe. Do you understand?"

"Of course, m'lady. I will never betray you."

"Of course not."

But if you were tortured?

The thought came, unheralded, unwanted, and she pushed it away. "I think you should be less conspicuous for a while. I'll get another maid. Lady Friselda has been pestering me to take a Lowmian girl for so long. You can be my chambermaid for a while. No one takes any notice of a chambermaid."

Aureen looked at her, aghast.

"Only for a little while, don't worry. The less important you appear to be, the less you will be noticed. No one must know we share a secret. No one must know that I trust you with my life. You do understand, don't you?"

The look on Aureen's face told her that although she may have seen the reason behind the decision, she didn't like it one little bit. Mathilda shrugged. "Lady's maid or chambermaid – what difference does it make? What matters is that no one ever finds out. We must both do whatever it takes to make sure of that. Do you understand?"

Aureen bobbed a perfunctory curtsy. "Of course, milady."

But the words were sullen.

"Your Grace."

Mathilda used the fact that she had Prince-regal Karel in her arms as an excuse not to curtsy. Va, how she hated the ridiculous court protocol!

I lie down and fornicate with the man in his bed, and yet I am expected to curtsy to him as if I am an underling?

"I have brought your son with me, Your Grace." She walked to where he was soaking up the sun in the window embrasure of his retiring room. Several of his attendants politely backed away to give the royal couple the deceptive appearance of privacy. Karel was sound asleep in her arms, wrapped in all the embroidered and lace-trimmed gowns and blankets deemed worthy of an heir to the Basalt Throne. At least he was at last beginning to look less like a wizened prune; now more than three months old, he'd plumped out and his cheeks were fattening up. Still, she wondered sometimes at her own fierce protectiveness.

Like a mother cat ready to scratch the hound to pieces if it comes near . . .

She subdued her reluctance to hand him to the Regal and asked, "Would you like to hold your son, Your Grace?" She smiled fondly at him, her loveliest dimpled smile. Va above, she practised it often enough.

He inclined his head and she passed Karel into his arms. He held his son awkwardly, but his gaze was intent. "Is he well?"

"Indeed, sire. He thrives. How could he not, given his parentage? He eats well and has a fine set of lungs, lustily crying for his milk when hungry."

"Good, good." He peered short-sightedly at the prince. "I do believe he has my chin."

"I'm certain he has. A strong, princely jawline. Sire, shall we breakfast together this morning? It seems such a time since we dined intimately, husband and wife. I have asked the cooks to prepare your favourite dishes."

He looked up from the baby. "An excellent idea, my dear. Oh, and I have some news for you. Our ambassador at the Ardronese court informs us that your brother's wife is increasing."

She inclined her head. "Good news indeed." *And you have no idea how I hate being the last to know anything.*

Half an hour later, with Karel handed back to his nurse, with the courtiers and servants dismissed, Mathilda surveyed the food laid out on the table. "What would you prefer first, sire? Sugared pork, perhaps? Or liver braised in wine and topped with cream served on buttered pastry?" She began to offer him titbit after titbit while she chatted.

She knew it was a narrow path she was treading. Now that Vilmar's mind was no longer confused by the lascar magic of the plume he'd been gifted, he was the astute and ruthless ruler he had been before. Her charm and apparent naivety amused him, and he liked teaching her, but only up to a point. She had to read every nuance of his tone and expression to know when she was close to overstepping a line between what he thought was appropriate interest in his rule and his policies, and what he considered none of her business. The concentration involved was exhausting, but she was learning.

"Tell me more about Prince Ryce. The Staravale princess he married – isn't she very young?" She hadn't been able to attend the wedding, which had occurred shortly before Prince-regal Karel had been born. In fact, she hadn't even been asked. *How easily they forget.*

"Fifteen, I believe," he replied.

You got yourself a young bride, Ryce. I wonder if you ever think of me.

"I am not pleased with such a union," he continued. "Staravale shares a long border with Lowmeer. Ardrone thinks to ally itself with *our* neighbours."

"Oh, but Your Grace, you need have no fears of Ardrone, for is not Lowmeer more prosperous and its monarch wiser than Ardrone's? Come, my sweet, will you not try some more of these griddle cakes? They are delicious with syrup and cream."

"Well, perhaps just a little more. And yes, I regret to say that King

Edwayn appears to have lost his edge. And him not as old as I am!" He snorted. "Such a shame your brother is not showing the wisdom required of an heir." He smiled. "They still struggle to build a spice fleet to match ours."

"Sire," she said as she heaped some more bacon on to his plate, "you spoke to me once of what I must do should you not live to the time when Prince-regal Karel is old enough to rule. Va preserve that such a situation will occur! But if such a tragedy should befall us, to whom should I turn to for counsel?"

"Nollen has drawn up the papers," he said, referring to his Secretary of State. "He and Chancellor Yan Grussblat will be Karel's advisers and mentors, with the assistance of three others of my own Council, until Karel's sixteenth birthday, when he will be able to appoint his own Council. Nothing you need worry your pretty head about, my dear." He patted her hand with his long, dry fingers.

"Oh, I am sure the governing of a country is beyond my capabilities, let alone interest! I just wondered if—" She hesitated. "Oh, I am *such* a poppethead! Never mind my silly frets, sire."

He selected a piece of candied liver. "Well, we can't have Karel's mother fretting, can we? What can the problem be?"

"You did say once that not even Chancellor Grussblat knows that the Dire Sweepers' real obligation is to kill as many twins as they can find at birth. He and other councillors, they think the Sweepers' real concern is to eliminate people with the Horned Plague before they infect others. Nobody minds *that* because everyone knows it's impossible to survive the Horned Plague anyway."

Vilmar nodded, all his attention on her.

"So," she continued, daintily licking sauce from her fingers, "when Prince-regal Karel is sixteen, I will tell him all he needs to know about Bengorth's Law. He will be crowned and all will be well. But before that . . ." She frowned slightly for emphasis. "What if the Advisory Council, not knowing the whole truth, were to enact a law that might affect Bengorth's Law and somehow restrict the activities of the Dire Sweepers . . . ?"

She allowed the sentence to trail away vaguely before adding, "I thought perhaps it might be better to ensure that every law be signed by someone who knows the real situation *before* it can be enacted.

Someone with Karel's interests at heart before their own. It is hard to believe that anyone would care as much as Your Grace and I do . . . But doubtless I am being silly! Come, have you tried this? The cook told me it's something newly imported through Pashalin, from the Summer Seas. It's called choclat."

Deftly, she diverted the conversation away from politics. The seed was planted, and all she could do was hope it would germinate.

6

Perie and the Pitch-men

Gerelda took off the fire-singed boots and put the lad into her own bedroll, where his exhaustion and fatigue finally overcame his grief and he dropped into a deep slumber. She retrieved her tinder, flint and steel from his bundle and, after digging out some dry wood from inside a rotten fallen log with her knife, lit a fire. She spent the rest of the night drowsing fitfully beside it. When she woke in the morning, it was with a hazy memory of lying naked in Saker Rampion's arms after a sweet climax.

A pox on dreams, she thought. *Why can I never quite get that man out of my head? It's not as if I love him!*

He'd been her first lover and she had been his, but that had been a long time ago. Their brief renewal of both physical passion and friendship had felt more comfortable than romantic – yet was now proving surprisingly hard to forget.

She snorted and stood up, yawning.

The day had dawned damp and misty. She boiled water with a generous handful of oatmeal before waking Peregrine. As she handed him a mug of the gruel, she asked, "Why did you come back? You should have gone on, sought help and rest in the valley." She was still dumbfounded by the knowledge that he'd removed his father's boots from his severed feet. That had taken a fortitude she would not have expected to find in most men, let alone a lad of his age.

He stood by the fire and took a sip of the hot liquid before answering. "I'm not going to Twite."

"Pardon?"

He thrust his shoulders back, but when she looked into his eyes, the emotions drowning there were unreadable. He said, "I want to know why. I want to know who these haggards are. I want to know

53

why they killed my da. You be sending me away, I'll still follow them."

She stared at him, lips parted in surprise. "Have you any idea how dangerous—"

"I'm not daft." His scorn was searing.

"Ah. No, I suppose not. But I don't wear this sword for decoration, you know. I know how to use it. But you? You're unarmed. You're not even grown yet. Moreover, I have a horse." She nodded at her mount grazing in the clearing. "You don't."

He shrugged with chilling indifference. "I saw all the fires. I saw all the hoofprints. You're not going to fight them; you're just following them. I can do that. I can walk too. My da and me – we walked everywhere, we did. Tucker, that's our donkey, he just carried our stuff."

"Listen, boy, I don't want to play nurse to a cub young enough to wipe his nose on his sleeve."

"I got something you need."

"Like what?" She was scornful, but tried to sound neutral. "Nothing short of a witchery will help with this lot. These men are evil. They killed your pa without even thinking about it because he saw them when they didn't want to be seen. That's all the reason they needed. They killed without even thinking about it. They see us, they hear us, we're dead." That feeling of dread, the taint they'd left behind: she shivered.

"I can . . . taste them."

Oh, pox on't; he's lost his wits. "What's that supposed to mean?"

He paused before replying, as though hunting for the right words. The look in his eyes was coldly intense. "Summat happened to me down there, where they slaughtered my da." He swallowed and looked away, taking care not to catch her eye. "But even before that I . . . I *tasted* their darkness. The dread was like . . . was like breathing in dirty smoke. I breathed it in, and I was made . . . different. I'm not like I were."

She was silent, not knowing what to say, remembering how she'd felt, the seeping dread that had attacked her rational thought. *Blister it, what have we stumbled into?*

"Anyways, I've been gifted a witchery," he added. "Down there, by the fires."

"Va grants witcheries to adults. I'm told you have to swear an oath to Va. Or at least to an unseen guardian of a shrine. Or something like that. I've never heard of a child with a witchery."

"I didn't swear aught. I'm not a child either, not any more, but I know what I have to do. Follow them. The pitch-men. I can warn you if they're about."

She found his vagueness disconcerting, coupled as it was with determination. "Pitch-men?"

"They're as dark as pitch inside. I know I can find every one of those men who did this. I'll know 'em by their stinking pitch. They *ate* my father."

Sweet acorns. She took a deep breath. "What do you mean you can taste them?"

"Not sure I got the words to say what I mean. Bit like . . . smelling something rotten, so foul you want to gag. It's not smell really, though. Not really taste, neither. It's like . . . I feel the pitch. The dark. Here." He tapped his chest, then pointed up the track. "They went that way. Reckon there be about a hundred of 'em."

"They could hardly have gone any other way."

His bravado vanished at her sarcasm and for a moment he was just a lad, grieving his unimaginable loss. "I *need* to come with you," he whispered.

No tears, though. *He ought to be wailing his heart out, not keeping it inside. He's like a barrel with its bung jammed tight.* "I'm going to follow these men up and over the mountains," she said. "On the other side of the pass, I can take a different road. You'll be a hindrance because I have a horse to ride. I can't wait for you."

He shrugged. "I'm still going to follow 'em."

She drew in a deep breath to control her building exasperation. "As you wish. I can't stop you; it is a public way."

He nodded.

"There's a shrine further up, isn't there?" she asked.

"Yes. The Oak on the Clouds. Da and me stopped there awhiles. We should reach it this morning."

He drained the rest of the gruel and handed back the cup. This time when their gazes met, she thought his eyes looked dead. He sat and drew on the boots, wincing in pain at every move. She had to suppress a shudder. *Beggar me speechless, how had he ever found the nerve to pull his father's feet out of them?*

She bent to help him do up the laces.

The time for speed would only come once she was in a position to overtake the men, so when she mounted up, she let her horse amble. She kept her eyes on the track ahead, until she reached the first curve and could not resist peeking over her shoulder. Peregrine was trudging after her.

She continued on around the bend.

Another hundred paces further along, she reined in, her thoughts jumbled. Why couldn't the wretched dewberry do the sensible thing and just go on to Twite where he'd be safe? She didn't want to be responsible for him! Yes, he'd had an unspeakable thing happen to him, but it wasn't her fault. And she had work to do.

Leak on the fool-born lad!

Urging the horse into a walk once more, she rode around one more bend, then sighed and stopped. This time, she was more annoyed with herself than with Peregrine.

Rot you, Gerelda Brantheld. You are better than this. What a rattle-brain she was to think she could just ride away.

When Peregrine reached her side, he stopped, squinting up at her out of his puffy, scratched face, his good arm supporting his elbow on his injured side, his eyes dulled with pain.

"Can you ride?" she asked, dismounting.

"Never been on a horse. Used to ride Tucker sometimes, though."

"Well, you're going to ride now. I'll help you up, and I'll lead the mount."

If he tried to hide the pain he felt climbing into the saddle, he failed miserably. By the time he was seated, he was white-faced and shaken. He did not, however, complain. He had mettle; she had to admit that.

She took the reins and plodded up through the mist that thickened as they climbed higher. And all the while, she silently cursed the mud, fate and that toadspotted whoreson, Valerian Fox, the pizzle of a man probably responsible for all this horror, if she had the right of it. She hadn't wanted to believe it, but the evidence was growing.

Your reverence, you aren't going to like any of this . . .

She'd heard about the shrine under the lip of the pass, although she hadn't been sure why it was called the Oak on the Clouds until they emerged from the fog of the forested slopes into the clear air of mountain meadows and serrated crags. Ahead the peaks soared into cloudless blue sky, and to the right of the track were the sunlit crown and branches of the shrine-oak. The base of the shrine was still mired in ground mist melting away but slowly in the chill air. She halted, awed by the ethereal beauty of an age-old oak, floating on cloud.

She snorted. *Getting soft in your old age, Gerelda? Fobbing shrine keeper has probably been murdered.*

Although doubtless the Pontifect would disagree, she was by no means sure that a pretty oak and its guardian would save a Shenat elder of Va-faith if the men who ate Perie's father decided otherwise.

"We'll rest there awhile," she said, pushing the thought away. "The horse needs to graze and you and I need to eat something better than gruel."

"We ate here, my da and me." He paused for a moment, leading her to wonder if he had the same thought she'd had about the shrine keeper's safety. When he spoke again, it was to change the subject. "Why do you ride a mare? My da used to say owning a jenny was never worth the trouble."

"I paid for a witchery from a shrine keeper over in Staravale horse country. He made sure she never comes into season."

"Oh! What's her name? You never call her anything."

"I never name my mounts. Why should I? I know which animal I'm riding. I've had this mare four years. She's a good beast. Never lets me down."

He looked at her in amazement. "I've never met anyone before who didn't give their horse a name."

"I'm not sentimental," she said with an indifferent shrug. "I've never understood the desire folk have to name their animals. *They* don't care."

"Tucker knew his name," he said, and for a moment his composure slipped. A tear trickled down his dirty cheek and he wiped it away with the back of his hand. "He cared."

"Well. All right. Maybe."

As they approached closer and the mist dissipated, she saw the shrine building was simple, hardly more than a few pillars and a sod roof of meadow grass encircling the free-standing trunk of the oak. When they reached it, she helped Peregrine to the ground. He didn't make a sound although dismounting left him white-faced. Tying the reins to the saddle, she loosed the mare into the meadow. "What's the name of the shrine keeper?" she asked.

"Red Trefoil. Those men were here; I can taste the smudge of them. They might've killed him."

Gerelda had already noted that the ground in front of the shrine was churned up with footprints and hoofprints. She ducked under the drooping branches of the oak to step inside the building.

"Va's blessings," she called out. "Is there anyone there?"

Beside her, Peregrine gasped. "The tree! Look at the trunk."

The bark of the oak had been slashed and scored, as if several men had attempted to chop it down with axes too blunt for the task. The scarred trunk was scorched black, the bark freshly charred in places, the smell of burning still pungent. Someone also had tried – and failed – to set the tree alight.

Her heart skipped a beat. If she'd needed confirmation of the kind of men they'd been following, she had it. No one ever harmed a shrine oak. *Va rot you, Valerian Fox, if this is your doing. You are a canker on the face of the earth.*

"No need to put yourself in a fidget, lass!" a kindly voice said from above her head.

She looked up to see an old man sitting on a bough above. No, not old, *ancient*. His skin was rough as tree bark, his hands and his face as knobbled as oak galls.

"The oak will heal," he said. "And I'm not so easily slaughtered neither. Sorry to be giving ye a startle; I just popped up there in case your intentions were of nefarious inclination."

"Do you need some help to come down?" she asked, eyeing the aged fragility of his arms and legs with concern.

He laughed, a quavering cackle of mirth that just reinforced her impression of great age, and swung down unaided to the ground with supple ease. "I'm a mite chary of trail folk after the last passel of miscreants," he said, regarding her with rheumy eyes. "But ye're appearing harmless enough."

"What happened?" she asked.

58

"Evil men with A'Va-dark souls paid a visit. They thought to destroy the shrine and kill its shrine keeper. But the oak protects its own. Those seeking to harm the sacred oft end up scored with their own axes. Those seeking to burn sacred wood are in turn singed. Those seeking a shrine keeper, murder in their hearts, cannot see their quarry hiding in the sacred tree." He gave a sly grin. "It was a cheery sight to see them flee, to be sure."

"I rejoice to hear it." She eyed him cautiously, having trouble reconciling his agility with his appearance. "I've heard that shrine keepers died by the number when the Horned Death visited the Shenat Hills. The oak didn't do much to protect those holy men and women then."

The smile vanished from his face. "Evil deeds, indeed."

"I heard shrine keepers don't die of the Horned Death in Lowmeer."

"Makes ye wonder about the nature of the Death, don't it? Mayhap it was not the same plague in Lowmeer as here."

"What did they look like, these evil men who attacked the tree?"

"Birds of a flock," he said. "All of the same plumage. Grey as a storm sky. Mean men with bitter intention, speaking little, madness in their eyes and darkness in their hearts. Beware if ye share their road. If they follow anything, it is A'Va, all that Va is not." He turned his attention from her to Peregrine then, staring at him, hard. "We've met before, not a day or two past. Ye've gone all a-warpskew since I saw ye last, though. Or is it skew-warped, that I mean? Or possibly widdershins. Anyhow, ye've been touched by witchery. But it be twisted. Never seen the like, ere this. Come to think on't, never seen a young 'un your age with a witchery of any sort. Where's your da, the scribe?"

She opened her mouth to answer, but Peregrine spoke first. "Those men killed and ate him. And now I will kill them. Every one."

Pickle me sour.

While she was scrambling to think of something to say, Red Trefoil remarked, "That may well be an idea, but I doubt it's aught that ye can be doing, lad, not yet awhiles. Ye're a mite too young. Mayhap ye'd better learn how to handle a sword before you go taking on those churls. Or a bow and arrow." He rubbed his chin. "Wondrous is the Way of the Oak, lad. Ye'll come into your time. What's your witchery?"

"I feel those men," Peregrine replied. "I didn't see them, but I know where they've been. I feel the grime of them, right here." He had his hand on his chest again.

The old man tilted his head thoughtfully. "Wise men say that A'Va leaves his foul smutch on those who follow him, and that others of their ilk can see that besmirching. Perhaps ye've been granted that sight, the better to deal with them."

She felt uncomfortable as she listened. "Deal with them? He's in no state to deal with anyone! He's been to Va-less hell and back. His father was murdered and he was thrown down a steep hillside. He probably has broken bones, and he's hardly had any rest since it happened."

Red Trefoil threw up his hands. "Well, now, why didn't ye say? One of my witcheries is the gift of healing! I can't be mending bones with a glance, but I can put them in their proper place and hasten up the mending to days instead o' weeks. Come, come!"

He led them to the back of the shrine, but there wasn't much to see. Some large standing stones at one end made a sheltered corner under the roof, and the bed there, cobbled out of boughs and sacking covered with woollen fleeces, seemed comfortable enough. Peregrine sat down on it with an expression of relief.

Red Trefoil cackled. "Let me take off your shirt, lad, and then we'll have ye lying down. Ye'll feel better in the wink of a bee's eyelash when I've done with ye."

Gerelda watched as he prodded softly at Peregrine's ribs. *Good*, she thought. *Perhaps I can get on my way and leave the pesky lad here.* "Do you have any food?" she asked. "Perie will be wanting to eat soon, and I really didn't have enough for the both of us."

"Oh, to be sure. Those wretches didn't find my larder, or they'd have absconded with the lot. I've plenty of cheese and turnips, nuts and mushrooms." As he talked, he ran his hands over Peregrine's shoulders. His touch must have been gentle, because the lad closed his eyes and looked at peace for the first time since they'd met.

"He sleeps," the old man said. "He must tarry here a few days."

"I can't linger. I'm on my way to warn folk. And see the Pontifect."

He glanced at her with a nod. "Ye one of her writ-wrights? Ye have the look."

She smiled at the ancient expression he used. "I'm one of her proctors, yes. You'll look after the lad?"

"I'll see him right."

"He's obsessed with those men."

"Not to be wondered at. Don't vex yourself on't. Ye and him be tied like twins; your binding to him is as clear to me as the bark of yon oak. Ye'll meet again. And lass, if he can read A'Va's smutch, ye'll need him."

She snorted, disbelieving. "A'Va has always sounded like a hobgoblin to me, made up by folk who see boggles behind every bush in the dark."

"If ye believe in the evil done by evil men, then the name of who or what they follow doesn't matter: demon, ill, bane, devil-kin, A'Va . . . or naught at all. All that matters is that ye know 'em when ye see 'em." As he spoke, his fingers gently probed Peregrine's chest. "Ye were right. A broken collarbone and two broken ribs. They'll mend. Ye'll need him soon," he said, his voice soft, "more's the blighted pity."

7

Caged

Overwhelming terror without end . . .
  Screaming without sound . . .
Struggling without achieving movement . . .
Fear, endless fear . . .

Mathilda woke. Sweet Va, a nightmare, only a nightmare. *You are in your own bed. Breathe in. Deep. You are safe in Ustgrind Castle.*

She wasn't really bound to a wagon wheel on top of a pole, left there to die on the orders of Regal Vilmar because he'd found out she'd given birth to twins. Ryce hadn't really been there, saying, "I'll help you if you ask me," when she couldn't utter a sound because her tongue had been ripped out. He hadn't really shrugged, and said, "I'm glad you don't need me," while she tried to scream as he walked away.

The birds hadn't really come to peck out her eyes . . .

Lying still in her bed, stiff with fear, she tried to steady her breathing. It wasn't easy.

The trouble was that she was *not* safe, not really. Vilmar would indeed kill her like that or in some other cruel way if he found out the truth. If he knew she'd given birth to twins, and connived with Sorrel to whisk the firstborn away. Or worse still, if ever he discovered that it was virtually impossible they were his children anyway.

She'd never be safe. Too many people knew her secrets. Sorrel, Saker, Aureen, Ryce, her father, Valerian Fox – they all knew things that could lead her to the chopping block, or the stake, or the wheel. They all knew something that would justify her execution under the law of the land. Any one of them had the means to betray her.

Pulling her covers up around her ears, she tried to snuggle back to sleep, but her thoughts jumped from one imagined disaster to another. And always, they returned to the same question: who was the weakest link in the chain, the one most likely to snap?

The answer was always the same.

Aureen.

An illiterate chambermaid, with some experience as a midwife, but without breeding. She wouldn't have a sense of what was honourable; such people didn't. Aureen would have her price. She didn't like it here in Lowmeer. She'd been scared witless when those men had threatened her. What if she sold the secret in exchange for a passage back to Ardrone? What if Prince-regal Karel grew up looking nothing like his supposed father? Would Vilmar grow suspicious? If he did, he'd torture Aureen to find out the truth. She wouldn't be brave enough to resist even the threat of pain.

Aureen was the weakness, the most obvious point for betrayal and discovery. She bit her lip, hurting herself just thinking about it. Aureen was all she had left of her old life, the only person who understood her predicament, yet the woman was also her greatest danger.

Sweet Va, what did I do to deserve this?

No one must find out. Ever. She must fight for her son to take his place on the Basalt Throne, no matter who his father was. And if *she* couldn't be *absolutely* certain who'd fathered her son, then how would anyone else ever be sure?

Maybe it was time the Vollendorn line came to an end anyway. They were the ones who had acceded to this vile bargain, this so-called Bengorth's Law that gifted one in every set of Lowmian twins to A'Va in exchange for A'Va's guarantee that their corrupted backsides would sit on the Basalt Throne. She was *glad* she'd cheated Vilmar, and if the Prince-regal was not his son, then Va would thank her for terminating the Regal's bloodline.

Karel had royal blood anyway: hers! And by Vilmar's own admission, Bengorth Vollendorn was a usurper in the first place. She giggled. An Ardronese baby on the Lowmian throne, now that was something to chuckle about. Thank goodness Karel had been tiny when he was born, smaller even than the sister the court knew nothing about, so no one had been suspicious of the early birth.

And that horrid idea of killing twins because one of them was supposed to be a servant of A'Va . . . that had to stop too. She would stop it. Or her son would when he was old enough.

She was not a Vollendorn and wouldn't be affected by the curse that said disobeying the agreement to kill twins meant the Vollendorn line would die out. Given Vilmar's previous lack of children, it was unlikely her son was a Vollendorn, so he wouldn't die because Bengorth's Law was broken.

Besides, the Law was wicked, so it would be the moral thing not to uphold it, right? Va would protect her. She'd always said her prayers and gone to chapel. Nothing would happen to her son, or to her. A'Va was less than Va the Creator, so how could he possibly know who'd fathered her children when she wasn't sure herself? And if he didn't know Karel might not be a Vollendorn, he wouldn't know Bengorth's Law was broken . . .

Just when she'd convinced herself that all would turn out well, that she and Prince-regal Karel would be the saviours of Lowmeer, doubts jostled their way back into her skull. Why had she heard nothing from the Pontifect? What if her little Karel was a devil-kin and his sister was the innocent one? What if the Vollendorn line of succession really was protected?

Her head reeled and her stomach heaved, as they always did whenever she tried to think about the paradoxes involved.

Oh, was there ever such a horrible pickle to be in? No, don't think like that, you ninny! You are the Regala. You are a princess of Ardrone. You will not act like a child.

The Pontifect was wise and she was a woman. She would know what to do. And if one of her babies really was a devil-kin, Pontifect Reedling would affect a cure.

Va-damn, I deserve to be the mother of a Regal! It's my reward for all I've suffered.

They had sold her – Edwayn, Ryce, Fox, even Saker had been complicit – they had *sold* her to Lowmeer in exchange for a Summer Seas port, as if she were a roll of silk or a sack of spices! And as far as she knew, they weren't even using the port anyway because Ardrone did not have their spice fleet launched as yet. Consign them all to beggary, she would show them what it was to be a princess of Ardrone.

Bengorth's Law would be of no more import than soured curds thrown to the pigs by the time she'd finished.

For a brief moment she was cheered. But then another niggling thought came back, rot it – one that had haunted her since she'd borne the twins. What was it she had said in the birthing room when her daughter had been born? She'd been swept along on a wave of pain and despair, terrified that someone would hear and find out that she was giving birth to twins. She'd blurted something out about Fox. Had she said he might be the father of the children? She thought she had. Sweet Va, she couldn't remember. Sorrel had heard, but had Aureen? Had she even been there?

As hard as she tried, she could not recall the details. She'd been too exhausted, too panicked, too irrational at the time. All she knew now was that if Aureen had heard, she might tell someone. She might think it her moral duty to tell.

Oak and acorn, help me, Va . . .

Just then she heard the scrape of the chambermaid – poor Aureen, demoted to that menial task – raking the coals together to rekindle the warmth of her bedroom fire. The castle was always cold. Not like the palace in Throssel.

She sighed. Almost time to get up. As soon as she'd recovered from the births, she was no longer given the luxury of lying a-bed. The Regal expected her to oversee the care of the royal prince and keep an eye on his wet nurse, and to attend all the royal functions dressed as befitted a regala. Worse, she was expected to share his bed when he so ordered, although that did not happen as often as it had previously. The royal appendage was no longer as enthusiastic as the Regal might have wished, and often, when she was called to his bed, nothing much happened.

No, no more sighs. Subtlety. Be devious. There's more than one way to victory in a battle.

As long as Aureen didn't betray her. Perhaps she should be kinder to the poor woman. "Aureen," she said, pulling back the bed curtains to look out, "I miss the way you brush my hair at night. Maid Klara is not nearly as skilled as you are. She can fetch the coals for the bed warming in the evening and tend the fire instead, while you can attend to my hair. Would you like that?"

8

Messages

Fritillary Reedling, elected head of Va-faith, stared at the pile of coded reports on the desk in her office. The Pontifect's Palace, situated on the hill with the loveliest view in all Vavala City, was well-appointed and well-staffed with competent clerics and clerks, but nonetheless, there never appeared to be an end to the depressing litany of disasters needing her attention.

In the northern lands, rulers bickered because their share of prosperity had diminished now that Lowmian sea trade challenged the profitability of Pashalin mastodon caravans over the ice. Instead of seeking solutions, rulers blamed one another. Sometimes her ire at their pettiness left her speechless.

Then there was the Regality of Lowmeer, where the Horned Death blossomed in pockets, killing in horrible ways like the sorcerers of ancient legends. Worse even than that was the connection between the Horned Death and twins, which had led the Dire Sweepers to murder the latter at birth. When she thought of the man who commanded them, the so-called Dyer, her heart shrivelled.

Perhaps he wasn't that man from her past who haunted her – no, who *taunted* her through her memories. She'd loved him once. Va, how she'd loved him! The touch of his fingers roving over her body shivering her skin, the whispered words of intimacy in her ear delighting her . . .

Perhaps a killer of children.

No, not him. Surely not.

She had loved his gentle ways once . . .

She jerked herself back to the present and considered Ardrone instead, where Prime Valerian Fox was in open rebellion. He ignored her directives, preached against Shenat teachings which had their origin in the northern hills of Ardrone, built stone chapels where once there had been only Shenat oak shrines, and encouraged clerics and congregations to believe that the Way of the Oak was an archaic and superstitious form of nature worship that had no place in modern Va-faith. When she'd asked the King to curb his appointed Prime, Edwayn had sent a polite but dismissive reply.

Pox on the royal beef-wit!

But fiddle-me-witless, what can I do? She hadn't appointed the Ardronese Prime and she couldn't dismiss him, an irritating exception that dated back to the early days of a weak Pontificate and a particularly obstreperous and powerful monarch. If the Ardronese Prime had the support of King Edwayn, she was powerless to do anything to thwart him. Her more Shenat interpretation of Va-faith could be superseded by stone buildings and set rituals intoned by clerics who knew nothing of nature and cared even less.

All she could hope for was that Saker had influenced Prince Ryce enough during his time there as tutor to ensure the future might be different.

She leant back in her chair and stared out of the window. Even with her huge network of spies and agents, she couldn't explain the multiple sources of rot corrupting good folk, turning peaceable villagers into armed bands bent on attacking supposed enemies, changing pious men and women into malefactors. She could believe Prime Valerian Fox was the moving force behind it – but he was just one man and from all reports he spent most of his time in the Ardronese capital city, Throssel. How could he possibly orchestrate the widespread unrest, some of it violent, that was occurring?

Va-faith underplays the concept of A'Va nowadays. Perhaps we should take the idea of an anti-god more seriously. Perhaps A'Va was the origin of legends about sorcerers . . .

With a sudden rage born of her frustration, she scattered all the papers from her desk to the floor with one sweep of her arm. It didn't make her feel any better.

Sighing, she took the last letter she'd had from Saker Rampion out of her pocket. Secretary Barden had translated the code words for her, but even then its scribbled contents didn't seem to make much sense. He'd written it just prior to sailing out of Ustgrind to the Spicerie on a Lowmian ship, which was unbelievably absurd, but then he'd spoken of Va-forsaken "plumes". That couldn't be right, surely. Feathers? The idea was ridiculous. She and Barden had decided that Saker had mixed up the code.

And yet, there was Saker's witchery, his strange affinity to birds. She'd never heard of anyone else being granted such an odd gift.

These are weird times.

Turning back to the letter, she read on. He mentioned a lascar's dagger influencing events, which made her wonder – in horror – if the malignancies manifesting themselves in Ardrone and Lowmeer were a result of a sorcerous contamination from the Va-forsaken Hemisphere.

She continued to read. "The woman we spoke of once, named Redwing, is on her way to you with a child, bearing a letter from me with more detail of all this. Listen carefully to all she has to say; it is of grave import to the future of Lowmeer . . ."

Redwing. Sorrel Redwing. The glamoured handmaiden. But why would Saker send her to Vavala – with a child? *Whose* child? And more importantly, why had she not arrived in Vavala? The letter was dated seventy days ago. The woman could have *walked* to Vavala from Ustgrind in that time!

She began to pace the room, long agitated strides across the flagstone floor, the parchment crumpled into a small hard ball in her hand. She knew every word of it, none of it a help, and she could think of no logical reason why Saker Rampion would want to sail to the Summer Seas. To accept that there could be a sorcerous cause made her break into a cold sweat.

I hope you're seasick, Saker, she muttered uncharitably, and rang the bell for Secretary Barden. She started to run through the list of things she'd considered doing next, involving everyone from the numerous princes of the northern states, to Prime Mulhafen of Lowmeer, Prince Ryce of Ardrone of course, then there was the bastard who commanded the Dire Sweepers.

It was several moments before she realised that Barden was unusually tardy at answering the summons. True, his arthritic knees and considerable age did mean he wasn't ever quick, but he was usually more prompt than this. She crossed to open the door between his anteroom and her apartments. Peering around, she was just in time to see a man in the uniform of a Vavala guard on his way out, while Barden was standing beside his table with a bemused expression on his face. He was holding a small unwrapped package in his hand.

"What is it?" she asked.

He looked up. "A delivery. Addressed to you."

"From?"

"I don't know." He picked up a blade from his table and began to cut the fastenings along one side. "Waxed and sewn – and there was an outer skin as well." He indicated the remains of the outer cover on the table. "Been a long time in transit, I'd say. Resembles a dog turd left in the sun. The guards didn't know who it was for until they unwrapped that and saw your name on the inside."

"The messenger didn't say who it was for?"

"The messenger," he said dryly, "was a very large seabird with a nasty temper. It broke a finger of the guard who was untying this from its leg, and almost took out the eye of another."

A shiver brushed her skin from the back of her neck to her feet like icy fingers. Va-forsaken sorcery or Va-cherished witchery? She no longer knew.

Saker, damn you . . .

"Then I know just who it's from," she said calmly. "Give it here, Barden. Let's see what marvellous tale of his doings he has to tell this time – and it had better be good."

9

The Gaunt Recruiter

Gerelda knocked on the door of the rectory next to the Needlewhin Chapel and inhaled deeply. She wasn't disappointed; the aroma that filled her nostrils was one of baking.

The door opened almost immediately, revealing Herbrobert Cranesbill, Needlewhin's cleric.

"Baked apples," she said.

The large man in the doorway raised a questioning eyebrow.

She took a deep breath. "In . . . hot treacle sauce."

"And the spice?" Herbrobert asked.

She hazarded a guess. "Cloves?"

"Just one."

"Expensive! On a *cleric's* stipend? Really H'robert! The Pontifect would be scandalised."

"Fiddle! Nothing short of holding an orgy in a shrine would raise as much as an eyebrow of hers, I swear. Anyway, the cloves were gifted by a passing trader."

"Oh, so just bribery then?" she asked with a grin.

"Bribery?" He snorted. "To do what? Say a prayer for the fellow?"

"To cook him a sumptuous meal, I imagine."

"Ah, well. Perhaps. And I demand a price from you too, Gerelda. The name of the ingredient you've missed."

"Hmm. Knowing the cook, probably sultanas, although I can't smell them." She grinned. "It's good to see you, H'robert!"

"Come in, come in, afore the neighbours see me hugging my favourite proctor!"

She stepped inside; he closed the door and enveloped her in his enormous arms. A moment later it was the turn of his husband, Rock Speedwell. She was tall, but both men towered over her. It had always amused her these two muscular, broad-shouldered fellows with hands and feet like shovels were both named after delicate pink alpine flowers. Not for the first time she reflected that Shenat naming could be disastrous.

"We knew you must be coming," Rock said. "The Pontifect's office sent a letter here for you. It arrived last week and we immediately aired the spare bed!" He took the letter from where it was sitting on the mantel and gave it to her.

She broke the seal and opened up the single sheet, signed with the Pontifect's scrawled initials and stamped with her seal. The note was terse: "Return to Vavala as soon as possible. Don't go to Sistia." She blinked, trying to read something more into the message than it stated, and failing.

Folding up the sheet and tucking it into her sleeve, she said, "I was hoping to rest my mount a day or two; now it seems I'll have to leave for Vavala tomorrow, first light."

"The chapel can lend you a hack. There's a gelding that'll be happy to get some exercise," he offered.

She nodded, quelling her irritation at the thought of having to ride an unknown horse. And Va only knew when she'd be able to get her own mount back. Pox on you, Fritillary. "I'm afraid I'll have to do just that."

"Anyway, you'll eat well tonight. You know what Rock's like."

She did too. He'd been a baker once, until his lungs gave out. Now he just cooked for Herbrobert and himself.

"We have a lot to tell you," Rock said.

"By which you mean . . . ?"

Herbrobert gave a rueful smile. "By which we mean things we want you to pass on to the Pontifect."

Halfway through their supper, they were interrupted by a thunderous knocking at the door, followed by someone frantically calling Herbrobert's name. Gerelda jumped up to grab her swordbelt even before Herbrobert was out of his chair.

"Jumpy, aren't you?" Rock asked as Herbrobert went to the door.

"That's panic I hear," she said, buckling on the belt.

"That's the town cooper, Jemony. Phlegmatic sort of fellow usually, so you are probably right." He started to wheeze.

No sooner was the door open than the man was pulling Herbrobert outside, crying in distress, "They've taken my Taminy! He says he's going off to fight for the Faith! What does he know about fighting? He's only seventeen and can hardly hammer a nail straight, let alone throw a lance. And it's not only him neither; old Viker is there as well even though he's fifty if he's a day, and Brecher the Miller's son, too."

"Where are they?" Herbrobert asked.

"Town green. We need you, Cleric Cranesbill!"

"I'll get my coat," Herbrobert said.

She looked at Rock, who was gazing down at his plate, troubled. "What's this all about?"

"Recruiters. Right proper bastards."

"I'll come with you, H'robert," she said, taking her coat from the back of the door.

By the time both of them were ready to go, Jemony had disappeared. "Where does this rattle-brained idiocy come from?" she asked as they hurried up the street.

"Va knows! I don't believe they *think* at all. We've heard of attacks on shrines and shrine keepers, and Primordials being killed as well."

"After all that shrine keepers and the witchery-gifted do for folk? Where would we be without them?"

Herbrobert grimaced. "I know. Rock would be dead with his lungs the way they are, if it weren't for a witchery healer. What I'd like to know is who's supplying the money that entices these addle-pates in the first place, the money that buys their uniforms and their lances. Rock has a theory, of course. He reckons the money comes from those mountebanks selling spice pomanders for outrageous amounts, saying they guarantee protection from the Horned Death. He might have a point. No ordinary fraudster could fund buying the spices to sell in the first place. Spread over the past year, we've had a cartload of such peddlers dribble through here, not one of them a cheery character."

She pulled a face as they approached the town green. It was lit by pitch torches, and they soon found Jemony again.

"Does this recruiting happen often?" she asked him as she looked around.

"They usually target the hamlets and farmers," he muttered and wiped a forearm across his eyes.

"Townsfolk get riled," Herbrobert said.

Indeed, men and women were gathering in an angry, noisy bunch on one side of the duck pond. On the other side of the pond was a second group, eerily quiet as the men of varying ages lined up in orderly fashion.

"Those are the recruits," Jemony said. "My Taminy among them."

Separating the two groups was a barrier of mounted horsemen with lances and foot soldiers with drawn swords. Twenty men all told, plus a couple of archers, arrows notched at the ready. Not many to keep irate townsfolk at bay, but they were coldly unsmiling and she wouldn't have liked to challenge them armed with only a stave.

"When I tried to get to Taminy, those men threatened me," Jemony said. "I recognise one of them. He bought a barrel from me, a year back. A farmer from Cosward; less than half a day's walk from here. What the blazes changed him from an ordinary yeoman into one of them onion-eyed scuts?" He grabbed Herbrobert by the arm. "Master Cleric, what can we do?"

Jemony wasn't the only one asking; a number of townsfolk gathered around Herbrobert, each with a tale of a family member seduced by the recruiters, all begging him to intervene.

She watched as the recruits shuffled forward to present themselves to a man seated at a scribe's desk. He spoke to each in turn, wrote in a ledger, then handed over a gold coin. After receiving this largesse, the recipients assembled into rows. Once again, she counted: twenty-three recruits all told. Not many for a town this size. A lot of money though, if they were recruiting in every town and village.

The kind of money that came from selling pomanders at ridiculous prices?

Some of the townsfolk called out to their sons or husbands among the recruits; others wailed their anguish or wept quietly; some shook staves at the soldiers. But none dared to storm the line of armed men.

"I have to intervene," Herbrobert said and stepped forward. Hastily, she followed. The townsfolk parted before them. When a woman clutched at his arm, begging him to save her son from his recklessness, he murmured reassurance and pushed past her to approach the nearest of the foot soldiers.

"I'd like to speak to the man in charge," he said.

The soldier stared at him, stony-faced. The horseman behind him dropped the point of his lance until it was levelled at Herbrobert's chest.

Gerelda glared at them both and drew her sword. "Don't you *dare*," she said to the rider.

Herbrobert looked over the soldier's shoulder and yelled, "Hey, you up there behind the desk! Tell your men to let me through, in the name of Va. If you are the leader of this lot, I want to talk to you!"

"I'm going with you," she said in his ear.

"Then sheathe that confounded sword of yours. I'm a man of peace."

She hesitated, then did as he asked.

The man at the desk stood up and stared at them before replying. "Let the cleric through," he said, nodding to his men.

She grabbed Herbrobert firmly by the arm, and they slipped between two foot soldiers. One of them made a grab at her and she neatly elbowed him in the midriff. By the time he'd recovered, she and Herbrobert were already standing at the desk.

"I'm the town cleric. Cranesbill. Who are you?"

"Names are of no import to us," the man replied. "We are all agents of Va."

Herbrobert inclined his head. "*I* am that, certainly. But how are you serving Va? You're bribing young men to leave their families and their trades to become fighting men, when there is no war to fight."

"There is always a war to be fought against the enemies of Va the Creator. These men are all here by choice. There is no coercion, no bribery." He turned to address the recruits. "Men! If there is any one among you who wishes to turn his back on Va and return to the bosom of his family with his gold coin, let him step forward now without fear!"

No one moved, yet Gerelda felt a blow beneath her breastbone, the concussion radiating outwards like ripples in water. No one had touched her, the blow wasn't real, yet the ripples momentarily stopped her heart, leaving her hands shaking and her brow beaded with sweat.

He did that. His voice did that.

By the light of a torch's flickering flame, she studied his face. His gaunt features were as cold and hard as carved ice. At first she'd thought he must have been in his mid-thirties, but with a closer look she wondered if that estimation might not have been at least ten years too high. His cheeks were hollow; his eyes lacked life. No emotion, nothing to soften him, nothing that spoke of passion. She suspected all that had made him look older than he really was. He had not even glanced at her.

"For whom do you fight?" the man asked the recruits. His voice was loud, but she still heard no passionate conviction there.

"For Va!" they yelled in unison.

"Who will you fight?"

"Primordials!"

"What will you fight?"

"Shenat superstition!"

Theatre, she thought. *Staged performance from an actor mouthing lines.*

The man turned back to her and Herbrobert. "You see? Go away, you Shenat charlatan. These men are mine now and your time is done. Your world is ending. Your heresy is about to be exposed – and eliminated."

No hatred, no joy, no triumph, just cold statement of fact.

He looks . . . ill. It's not natural for anyone to be so gaunt. I wish I had Peregrine with me now. He would know who here has the smudge.

Herbrobert nudged her arm. "Taminy's there," he muttered.

She glanced at him, and guessed what he wanted. She turned her attention back to the man. "Whom do you serve in this *earthly* realm?" she asked, eyebrow quirked. "Why is there no insignia on your coats? Are you ashamed of your affiliations?"

He turned to her then, his smile cold. "When right is on your side, there's no need of symbols."

She was aware that Herbrobert had stepped away from her side, but didn't look to see where he was going. "Do you follow the dictates of the Ardronese Prime, perhaps?"

She expected him to ridicule the notion. Instead, something in his eyes flickered. She cursed the lack of good light.

He said, "Every warren of rabbits has a fox den near. Now get out of here. I have more gold coins to dispense."

Behind her, Herbrobert was arguing with one of the younger recruits. When the lad raised his voice, she heard the cleric call him Taminy.

The recruiter snorted. "Fool. Nothing the cleric says will make any difference now."

"I'm off to kill them no good witches in the Shenat Hills," the lad shouted at Herbrobert, shaking off the cleric's hold on his arm. "Evil folk who would turn us towards shrines and trees and weeds with their wicked magic."

Witches? An old insult from days long gone, a stupidity not often used. Having a witchery didn't make someone an ugly crone of fairy tales, muttering spells by the full moon.

The recruiter made a gesture to some of the soldiers. "Get these two interlopers out of here," he said.

Faced with a drawn sword, Gerelda shrugged and left. A moment later Herbrobert, still protesting, was pushed out through the ring of armed men. Giving vent to several muttered curses not usually uttered by clerics, he went to join the townsfolk, while Gerelda returned to the house to tell Rock Speedwell what had happened.

"Is there no town authority who can challenge these men?" she asked him, after she'd related what had happened.

"On what grounds?" he asked. "They aren't forcing anyone to do anything." He sighed. "Unfortunately, all this will result in a resurgence of Primordials in reaction. You know that lot – those who say Va is just a made-up figure and we should all go back to the oldest of Shenat beliefs. There's going to be trouble unless this is nipped in the bud. Soon. That's what we want you to tell the Pontifect."

"How do you stop folk from believing beef-witted fustian? How can you punish people for not believing what you believe?" *Va-damn, I'm glad I'm not Fritillary Reedling!* "That recruiter, do you know anything about him?"

He shook his head, wheezing.

"I asked him if he followed Prime Valerian Fox. He made an odd remark about there's always been a fox den near every rabbit warren. He might have just been mocking me by agreeing he was indeed a predator in search of prey. Or he could have been saying that the Fox family had lots of members."

"Of which he was one?" His wheezing increased. "Perfectly possible. The Foxes have estates everywhere. I sometimes visit my cousin over in the Marches along the border with Valance, and there's one near him. Huge place, with its own forest. Valerian Fox has been there once or twice in my cousin's lifetime. The family paid to have a chapel built in the village recently, I believe. Oh, and they've always paid the upkeep on the river ferry and the ferryman's salary, as well as that of a local roadman and his sons to keep the road from the village to the ferry well-maintained."

"Well-liked then, are they?"

He frowned. "That's the odd thing. My cousin says the Fox household keeps to itself. Doesn't mix with the villagers, doesn't disturb them, doesn't employ them. Big wall all the way around the outside. You'd think, wouldn't you, that the villagers at the very least would be indifferent. But they aren't that. They're nervous. Even my level-headed cousin. When I asked him why, he just shrugged and told me to go and see for myself. So I did. I climbed a tree and looked over the wall."

"And?"

"I was as scared as a dragonfly stuck on a frog's tongue. Don't ask me why; I've no idea. I could see the house and it was a lovely old building, surrounded by gardens and stables and so forth. Nothing unusual. I scrambled down that tree and hared off home. Mind you, that was years ago. I was only twenty or so at the time. But I tell you something, every time I've been back there, I've never had the slightest inclination to take another look."

She stirred uncomfortably. The tale reminded her of a fairy tale told to her when she was a child. A castle, enchanted by a wicked sorcerer. Anyone who entered never came out.

Dread . . . I've felt that lately too.

"Did you have any problems getting here from Twite?" Rock asked when she was silent. "Forgive me for asking, but you did seem a little worn when you arrived."

"Trouble? You might call it that." She told him all that had happened, and ended the tale by saying, "I left Peregrine in good hands. Well, I washed my hands of him might be a more honest way of putting it. He's with the shrine keeper in Needlewhin Pass."

"And you saw no more of the lancers?"

"I saw their tracks. They headed off along the high trail through the border country. I came down to Needlewhin."

He pondered that. "They could have been heading towards Valance, or even Muntdorn, then."

"Or just trying to hide themselves in the rugged hills of East Denva. What's that route like?"

"Poorly frequented. Winds its way through dense forest, an advantage to people who don't want to be seen. Gerelda, I hope you're heading towards Vavala on the morrow, because the Pontifect needs to know all this."

She nodded. "She will."

10

The Unlikely Merger

There was no easy route from Needlewhin to Vavala. Gerelda was on the wrong side of the Falvale River at a time when melting snows made the fords impassable and ferries closed operations.

"There's a bridge at the Valance border," Herbrobert told her the following morning, "and the mule track through the hill forests will get you there."

"Lonely though," Rock said. "Worse, you could run into your lancers again."

"No option. I'm in a hurry."

He started wheezing, and she exchanged a glance with Herbrobert over his head.

"Time we saw the healer again," Herbrobert said, but they all knew Rock's days were numbered. He was still gasping for breath when she rode off a little later.

By the evening of the third day, she knew she'd made a mistake. The weather had turned wet, the landscape was as miserable as dishwater, and a raging forest stream made a ford impassable. As the sun set, she tethered her horse close by and turned in for the night under her oil-cloth cover. When the rain slackened, she drifted off to sleep to the sound of trickling water.

A cloudburst woke her several hours later, followed by a jolt of thunder and a crack of lightning that left her temporarily blinded. The gelding whinnied in fear. She scrambled out of her shelter into a shock of cold rain. As she reached out a hand to seize the horse's halter, the darkness vanished into blinding brilliance. A violent thwack of thunder and the splintering of the bough of a tree came together as one mind-shattering assault on her ears.

Slammed to the ground, air punched from her chest, every bone jolted, blinded, breathless, deafened . . . She whooped in agony, dragged breath into her lungs. The air around her smelled, the tang of it sharp in her nose. She thought, *I'm dead.*

When she finally sat up, wet, dirty and gasping, she wasn't sure what had happened. Her hearing and vision straggled back as her breath steadied. The next lightning strike was more distant. Clambering to her feet, she steadied herself against the sodden bark of a tree and looked around. She was standing amongst a mess of broken branches.

Another flash of lightning illuminated the area, and she realised the gelding had vanished.

When the day dawned, she was wet and cold and there was no sign of her horse. After examining her cuts and bruises, she looked for hoofmarks, but the overnight rain had washed away all traces. No amount of whistling, calling or searching turned up any sign of the gelding, and by mid-afternoon, she admitted defeat. She'd lost Herbrobert's horse.

There was nothing left to do but walk on. A newly fallen tree provided a way for her to cross the river. She made a half-hearted attempt to be grateful for that, and for the certificate in her purse, signed by the Pontifect, which would enable the requisition of a mount and riding tackle from any cloister or chapel. She wouldn't have to walk all the way to Vavala, just to the border settlements, but vex it, that was miles away.

Another restless night in the forest, and she was on the move again at first light. When it started to rain once more, the track alternated between glutinously muddy, or as slick as ice. Her cloak flapped wetly around her ankles; water streamed from her hood and cape until the felted wool was a sodden burden. Head down, shoulders hunched against the driving rain, she fell into a rhythm of placing one foot in front of another in unthinking misery.

Va-damn, but she was missing her mare – not just because it would not have bolted far; no, she just missed its company.

She sighed. *Getting sentimental, are you, Gerelda? Going to name your next mount Daffodil or Dandelion, perhaps?*

As the day wore on, unease pricked, until her insides ached with it. The trail was too narrow, too closed in for a mule track, although every now and then she did see a footprint or the mark of a horseshoe in the mire. She plodded on, unable to be sure what direction she was heading in, because the sky was uniformly grey.

When someone yelled ahead of her, she was so sunk into grim acceptance of her cold discomfort that it was a moment before she stopped dead, jerking her head up to listen. The regular chonk-chonk-chonk of an axe on wood reached her ears through the pattering of the rain. Woodcutters working in this weather? More than odd.

All senses alert now, but feeling exposed on the track, she threaded her way through the trees towards the sounds. A horse neighed and was answered by another. The gusting wind snatched up disjointed words and delivered them in nonsense syllables. She pulled the hood from her head to hear better as the rain lessened, and was appalled to hear not just a couple of people ahead of her, but many. She dodged from trunk to trunk until she had a better view of the valley below.

There were men and horses everywhere.

She dragged in a deep calming breath. *Don't panic. You don't know for certain who they are.* They might be harmless.

Pressed against a tree, half hidden by undergrowth, she watched. This wasn't a makeshift camp set up for the night. These men had erected tents and bough shelters, built proper fire places of rocks and earth, cut and stacked firewood. She spotted lances stacked like sheaves for drying, glimpsed camp fires through the trees and horses staked out at intervals to forage. These men had been here too long to be the ones who'd killed Perie's father. These were a different group of lancers, perhaps two hundred of them. All wore coats of a uniform dark grey, although their trousers were more varied in cut and more motley in colour.

The path she had followed descended to a river, its flow too swift to cross without a bridge, a lack now being addressed. Horses were hauling cut logs; soldiers were wielding hammers and axes. A bridge was not only under construction, it was close to completion.

Va-damn, she thought in sudden realisation. *Somewhere back there, I left the main track.* It would have had a bridge. She'd been misled in the rain, blindly following footprints and hoofprints. Their sentries, if they had spotted her at all, must have mistaken her sodden figure lugging her makeshift pack for one of their own wood gatherers bringing in fuel for the fire.

Her gaze moved on, then snagged on something she hadn't noticed at first. Two bodies lying near a fire, neither wearing a grey coat. One appeared to be missing a head.

Oh, pox. Oh, blister it.

Ordinary folk, she guessed: unfortunate men in the wrong place at the wrong time. Bodgers or hoopers, perhaps, collecting wood. Or hunters. Folk going about their normal business like Peregrine's father, caught up in a larger conspiracy they hadn't even known existed.

Worse, these lancers could well be waiting for the arrival of the killers of the petition writer. If she turned back, she might just meet that second contingent of lancers face to face, and she knew what could happen then. There were those bodies down there to tell her.

Hang you for a ninnyhead, your luck has really run out, Gerelda Brantheld. Now what are you going to do?

That night Gerelda bedded down far enough away to think herself safe, and the next morning she followed the river downstream to find another way to cross. She had to admit defeat when the watercourse entered an area of gorges and high cliffs.

Thoughts grim, she retraced her steps back past the lancers' camp. She circled around outside the perimeter of sentries and rejoined the track on the other side. At sunset, she settled down for another cold night huddled into a tight ball inside her bedroll.

Sounds jerked her from a doze into alertness: horses, jingling harness, the occasional curse. Cautiously she raised her head to glimpse lights bobbing through the trees. She stayed motionless, watching. Men trudged in single file down the track towards the camp, each using a lance as a staff, most also leading a horse, some carrying lanterns. She began to count as they passed her.

Stumbling with fatigue, pushing their horses hard, they blundered through the night. Around her, the forest still dripped and trickled with water, although the rain had stopped. Every now and then a quiet rustle reminded her there were other creatures abroad. A hedgepig, perhaps, or a moldwarp digging a burrow.

The long line plodded on. She guessed they were the men who had killed Peregrine's father, and rejoiced to see how exhausted they were. It had been a long hard haul via the high-country route they'd taken. Bad weather, too. They'd been sleeping rough and hunting for their meat. And the horses? Not much grazing for them, obviously.

The last few men on foot were strung out, limping, weary. The clouds thinned a little, and moonlight made the night less grimly dark. By the time she was certain there were no more coming, she'd counted ninety-eight men and eighty-five horses, including pack animals strung together. There would soon be a crowd of tired, exhausted men mingling with the men in the camp ahead, probably strangers to one another. She gave a hard smile as she rolled up her bedding; she knew an opportunity when she saw one.

Just as she was about to hoist her pack up on to her back, she thought she heard the soft whisper of a footfall somewhere in the darkness. Jumpy, spooked by her own fears, she stayed rooted to the spot, her gaze flicking from one movement to another – no matter that it was a leaf shivering or a patter of raindrops from a tree canopy.

A little later she was certain there was someone else coming, a straggler whose tired feet stumbled and dragged through the wet leaves underfoot. She edged away from her pack and pressed her body close to the trunk of a tree.

A dark shape took form, moving slowly. She eased her dagger into her hand, although she had every intention of allowing the fellow to pass unmolested. He drew level and stopped, a short fellow in an enveloping cloak. No horse, no lantern.

She froze. She was half-hidden by the tree trunk, but perhaps he'd caught sight of her when she moved off the track. *Pickles 'n' pox, now what?*

He spoke then, and his voice quavered. "Who . . . who is that?"

She stood frozen, dumbfounded.

I'll be beggared. Perie.

He really had followed the fobbing lancers. She stepped out on to the track, hands on hips, to confront him. "What the pickled pox are you doing here? I left you at the shrine! And how the grubbery did you know I wasn't one of the lancers?"

"Well, I know you're not one of them pitch-marked men, don't I?"

"But I could have been anyone else with unfriendly intentions!"

"I suppose so. But I reckoned anyone who's not a pitch-man around here is in as much danger as I am, and that makes them a friend."

"You walked all the way here? Are you daft? Injured the way you were?"

"Red Trefoil healed me good, so I left. Followed the smutch."

"You dewberry! Why? What can you hope to achieve, one lad against a hundred lancers?"

"I already killed one."

She stared at him, stilled with shock.

"Knifed him with his own blade, when they left him behind 'cause he was sick." His tone was flat, as if he was talking about something that had no real meaning. "Then I stole his food. And his cloak."

Oh, help. He's just a child.

"They deserve to die. All of 'em."

"Well, yes, perhaps. But you can't kill them all."

"Maybe not. But what else am I supposed to do? First I was a long ways behind. Thought I'd never catch up, 'specially when my bones ached something awful. But they leave their mark behind like scat and they're real easy to find, 'specially when the mud made the going hard for the horses. In the end I was going lickety-spit compared to them. So I caught up. Why else was I given a witchery if not to hunt them down?"

He had a point. Who could understand the whys of a Va-granted witchery? "I think . . . I think you had better argue that one with a cleric, not me. For now, no more killing. Unless it's a matter of life or death. *Our* life or death, all right?"

"So what are we going to do now?"

"We?"

He was silent.

Pickle me sour. I guess it is we.

She took a deep breath and assembled her thoughts. "I want a horse," she said. "I lost mine. In fact, we need two horses. We're going to take advantage of the confusion there's going to be when the group you were following meets up with a group that's camped ahead of them. If anyone sees us, with luck they'll think we belong with the other lot."

"We're going to steal two horses."

"We are indeed," she agreed.

"I can help. I'm very good at sneaking. I always know where they are."

"Yes, that's right, you do, don't you? You taste them." She wanted to cry for him. Instead, she said, "We'll rest here a while until they sort themselves out."

"Have you got anything to eat?" he asked, sitting down on a nearby log with a sigh of relief. "I'm starving hungry."

She dug into her pack and gave him a piece of cheese and some strips of salted meat.

"What have you been eating?" she asked, watching him cram the food into his mouth.

"Stealing," he mumbled with his mouth full.

"From them?"

He grunted his assent.

"You took huge risks."

He shook his head. "Not me. You'll see."

"Right then," she said, "when we get close to any of them, you warn me. I don't want any surprises. You've got to show me just how good this witchery of yours is."

There was a short silence while he ate, then he said. "You know, Proctor Gerelda, I don't like having it very much. Makes me sick to the stomach every time I come near any of them. That filthy smutch they have . . ."

She sat next to him and slipped an arm around his shoulders. "That skill of yours may save our lives tonight."

"Then I guess it's worth it," he said, but his tone was stark.

She felt ill. Sometimes she wondered at Va. "They don't set much of a guard. This track is not used much, and they don't fear anyone anyway."

"Who are they? You never said. I heard some of this lot say they're meeting up with East Denva folk. Training, they said." He tore off another hunk of stale bread and chewed hungrily. "Trained as what?"

"Soldiers, I'd guess."

"To fight who?"

"Shenat people. Shenat beliefs." She sighed. "I don't really know, Perie. But I am going to warn the Pontifect."

"Her army can fight them."

Except Fritillary had no army.

When she was silent, he added, "I will join her soldiers."

"You and me both," she said dryly. "I'll take you with me. For now, we are going to rest right here for a couple of hours. Then we will steal horses and flee." *I just wish that was going to be as simple as it sounds.*

"I know the way," he said. "We – Da and me – we went from the Oak on the Clouds to the border ferry once a year. The turn-off is about six or seven miles back. But this path here also returns to the main track. We could go straight on across the river. There's a ford."

"Not anymore. Too wet. But there is a bridge now."

"They all be asleep except for the guards," Perie said. His tone, hard-edged, was chillingly cold.

They were a bare fifty paces from the first of the lancer's tents, but Gerelda wasn't worried about being overheard: the constant thunder of the swollen river plunging under the bridge swallowed up all other sound.

"Do they all have the pitch-mark?" she asked.

"Yes. Most be sleeping, except for the guards. I can tell you where they are." His reply was confident.

Astonished, she asked, "You can tell what they're doing without even seeing them?"

"They're pitch-men! Guards stand up, so they're easy to pick."

"I don't suppose you can sense the horses."

"No, of course not. Can tell you this though: we can't take the mounts of the men I was following. They treated them real bad. Didn't give 'em time to graze, hardly had any oats. Reckon they'd drop dead afore we got 'em another mile."

"In that case, we'll look for a couple of the others." She pointed over to her right. "There's a picket line of them that way, near the river bank. Can you get us there without being seen by a guard, or will I have to kill someone?"

"Oh, we're already well inside the ring of guards," he said blithely. "We passed through them way back."

She went cold all over. And he hadn't said anything? *Va above.*

86

"The only men we have to worry about are the two over there." He pointed. "I don't know if they're sentries. They're sitting down next to one another, like they be on chairs."

"How far away?"

"Two hundred paces."

Which would put them in the middle of the river. "Ah. Then my guess is they're sitting on the edge of the finished bridge with their legs dangling over the side."

"We could kill them and toss them in the river," he suggested. He sounded cheerful. "Easier and closer," he said.

Pox on't, a lad of twelve shouldn't be pleased at the idea of murder.

With an inward sigh, she acknowledged he could be right, on both counts. Leading horses through the undergrowth in the dark would be a nightmare, especially when they were doubtless already unsettled by the new arrivals.

Va-damn. She hated killing people. "Right. First things first. We steal the animals."

As they edged through the trees towards the picket line, she blessed the obliterating sound of rushing water and wind in the trees. The horses jostled and stamped and snorted, expressing their irritation with the wind and with one another. She ignored the more restless ones and unhitched two of the more phlegmatic, handing him one of the leads.

"Anyone stirring?" she asked Peregrine.

"No."

"Walk directly behind me." Leading the horses, they picked their way back to where they'd left their belongings. "You can stay with them," she said as she tied them to a tree. "Keep them calm. I'll be back shortly."

She returned some minutes later with pilfered oats inside a saddle-cloth. "That'll keep the two of them happy," she said, as the horses snorted and jostled to get at the grain. "I'm going to scout around for tackle and supplies. You can come with me this time. I think I know where their storage area is, but I'll need help to carry the saddles."

The men had constructed a three-sided shelter for their supplies and saddlery, using strung-up canvas for a roof and roughly cut poles and brush for walls. A corner of the canvas had worked itself loose and flailed in the wind; she jumped every time it cracked against itself.

A lighted lamp hanging from a pole made rummaging easier, but being illuminated like a whore on display did not alleviate her anxiety. She was scared halfway to apoplexy.

Confound it, what did I do to deserve this?

Food for them, oats for the horses, horse tack . . . She began pulling out odd items of food, tossing them higgledy-piggledy into her pack, then grabbed up several saddlebags and stuffed them with oats.

"Someone's coming!"

Peregrine grabbed her by the arm, pulling her down to the ground even as he hissed the warning. She fell awkwardly, spilling her load. The canvas thrashed and whipped in the wind. She ducked down between sacks and saddles, Peregrine crouching beside her. He still held her arm in a tight grip, and placed his other hand over his mouth warning her not to speak.

Time crawled by. At first she could hear nothing except the wind and the canvas against the background roar of river water, then someone swore, so close she thought he was going to tread on her. Peregrine's clamped hold tightened. She desperately wanted him to let go because with him clinging like a limpet she couldn't reach her sword.

"Leak on you, you slubbering piece of a whore's petticoat!"

A man stepped into the light. She expected him to be looking at her, but he wasn't. He was staring at the flapping canvas. "Poxy green-horns who can't tie a knot to save their lives!" he muttered, his voice heavy with sleep.

He reached up, grabbed the loose rope and tied the canvas down. She could have touched his boot, but he didn't look her way.

When he walked away, she and Peregrine both exhaled at the same time. She grinned at him, her relief exquisite. They continued to lie side by side until he nodded that all was safe again. She gathered up the equipment she had selected, then slung a saddlebag, bridle and reins across each of the saddles.

"Think you can carry one of these?" she asked.

In answer he picked up the pile. She shouldered her pack and picked up the other. "Let's go," she said.

* * *

Perie watched, fidgeting, while Gerelda saddled and bridled the horses and distributed their belongings as best she could between the saddle bags. "I'll dispose of those two guards," she told him matter-of-factly. "You are to count to one hundred, and then follow with the horses. Do you think you can do that?"

"I suppose so." In truth, he was nervous around horses. They were so much larger than Tucker.

"No supposing, Perie. This is for real. Can you do it?"

"Yes. Yes, course I can."

"Good. Where are the two men now? I can't even see them; the moon's gone behind a cloud."

"They're still sitting down. On the far side of the bridge, I reckon, facing downstream."

"Good. Let's hope they stay that way. You've been a tremendous help, Perie. I'm grateful. If anyone raises the alarm, we mount up and ride like all A'Va's devils are on our heels. We cross that bridge, guards or no guards. Understand? Hang on tight and just let your horse follow mine."

He nodded.

She hesitated, then added, "If you have to do it alone, then do so. In a fight, at the end, you are only responsible for yourself. Understand?"

He nodded, knowing she was also saying that if he lagged behind, she'd leave him. That was the way it had to be and he did understand.

Sometimes there wasn't an easy choice.

He stood between the two horses, holding them the way she'd showed him, and watched her go. Well wrapped in her cloak to hide her lack of a lancer uniform, she kept to the side of the track. Overhead, a three-quarter moon broke through the gauze of cloud cover.

Every now and then, when clouds hid the moon, she disappeared into the darkness as if she had been erased. That felt odd; he'd grown used to knowing exactly where the lancers were and what they were doing every minute of every day. They had no privacy from him, ever. His awareness of Gerelda was much more dependent on sight and smell, on his normal senses.

He switched his attention to the two guards. He couldn't see or hear them either, but he didn't need to; they were solid shapes to him. Pitch-men, oozing their thick evil. It was difficult for him to even think of them as men. They weren't, not really. They'd been contaminated, their humanity rotting from within leaving only the appearance of men as a shell, a covering, to the smutch. They still sat side by side, occasionally looking towards the other side of the river.

They don't expect trouble from this side, he thought. *Good.*

He felt no compassion for them.

They didn't see her coming.

They weren't talking to each other; they weren't doing anything except sitting there. The logs of the bridge had been spread with river sand to provide an even surface, and her footfall would have been muffled, even without the roar of water.

If they'd been sentries in any unit of soldiers she controlled, she would have been rabid in her anger at their complacency. Instead, she was grateful. She dropped her cloak from her shoulders.

The closest man caught the movement out of the corner of his eye. He started to turn as she swung at him with a two-handed stroke to the neck. The blow jarred her from wrist to shoulder, but she'd judged it correctly. The edge of the blade caught him across the throat.

Blood spurted in a black shower. He tried to draw breath but his gasping mouth made no sound. He fell sideways. She raised a boot and nudged his body forward so it slipped off the bridge into the rushing torrent below.

The second man scrambled to his feet, panicked, fumbling for his sword. She lunged at him, hoping to kill him before he could gather his wits. Unable to draw a weapon in time, he dived at her. He was a large man and desperate, and he hit her just above the knees with the force of his shoulder.

She lost her footing and came down flat on her back, hard. He'd tangled himself in his own cloak and for a moment each of them scrabbled to stand before the other could. She beat him to it by a sliver, and she now clutched a handful of the sand in her fist, snatched up from the bridge surface. He ought to have yelled for help; instead he drew his sword. She used that moment to throw the sand into his face. When he jerked back with his eyes closed, she lunged with all her weight behind the thrust. His blind parry missed and her blade went through the inadequate padding of his jack into his midriff. It ripped his stomach open as he fell. His intestines tumbled out on to the boards of the bridge as he collapsed, the weight of his body jerking her sword out of her hand. He began to scream. She stomped on his throat. The screams abruptly halted, but he didn't stop moving. His limbs jerked, his hands twitched.

Another sound behind her sent her spinning around into a crouch, but it was only Peregrine. He'd arrived with their mounts and one of them, spooked by the smell of blood and guts, was shying and pulling back. She left her sword where it was and scrambled to help him before the reins were pulled out of his hand. He had the sense to leave it to her and released his hold to lead the other horse away before it, too, was spooked.

For several minutes she battled the terrified animal while it tried to pull her arms out of their sockets as she murmured reassurance that it probably couldn't hear over the sound of the water. At last she had it standing still, trembling, and she was able to stroke its neck and whisper calming nonsense into its ear.

All the while she stared at the camp, watching for any sounds of alarm, but there was nothing. Evidently the scream of the injured man had been drowned over the roar of the river.

Once the horse had settled, Peregrine, without saying a word, handed her the reins of the second mount and walked over to the dying man. He bent to extract her blade from the bloody mess of flesh and intestines, then wiped it clean on the lancer's cloak. Before he straightened again, he casually rolled the still twitching body into the water and tossed his bloodied cloak after him. She swallowed back her nausea.

Picking up her cloak, Perie brought it back to her with her sword. "I don't think anyone could have heard the scream," he told her calmly. "No one's coming."

"Up you get, into the saddle. We're getting out of here."

He scrambled inelegantly up on to the more imperturbable of the two horses, and she took the time to adjust the stirrups for him. Once she was mounted herself, she flicked the horse into a brisk walk and thought back over the result of their evening's work. Two horses and tack stolen, two men missing, a whole lot of blood and gore on the bridge. She could have done with some rain to clean up the evidence, but the clouds were clearing, Va rot it. She didn't know what the lancers would make of it all, but she hoped their reaction would be for the first group to blame the second.

With a little luck and Va's grace, by the time the lancers realised something was amiss, she and Peregrine would have a substantial lead.

She turned in the saddle to check on him. "I'm relying on you," she said. "You tell me if you sense those bastards following us."

"I will."

"When it's light enough, we'll go faster. Try not to fall off."

"You – you could leave me behind. I mean, you have to warn the Pontifect, that's what you said—"

"Yes, I did. But I think we need you and your witchery, lad. I'm not sentimental, I just think you're more of a help than a hindrance. I'm going to get you in one piece all the way to Vavala. You are going to meet Pontifect Fritillary Reedling."

And I wonder what she'll think of a lad not yet twelve, who can pull a sword out of a man's guts without blinking?

11

The Antagonists

Fritillary Reedling woke from a confused dream about a storm, to the reality of someone banging on her bedroom door. She sat bolt upright, shocked. She couldn't remember the last time anyone had thought something was urgent enough to wake her in the middle of the night. And it *was* the middle of the night. She'd left her window unshuttered, and moonlight glowed softly through a night mist.

"Who's that?" she asked as she slipped her feet to the floor and reached for her woollen wrap.

"Secretary Barden."

Ridiculous question. The old man was the only other person with a key to her apartments. Even so, her heart was beating too fast as she crossed the floor, so she took a moment to calm herself before she opened the door.

Two people stood in the anteroom behind Barden, one a boy of about twelve or so. It took Fritillary a moment to recognise the woman with him. Shabbily dressed in muddy clothes, her hair uncombed, her face smudged, she smelled of sweat, stables and dirt.

Sweet Va. "Proctor Brantheld."

"Your reverence."

Barden was already hobbling around the anteroom lighting the candles. He was dressed in a voluminous nightgown, a floppy nightcap with a tassel and heavy woollen socks. He looked ridiculous, but she found nothing to laugh at in the expression on his face. She switched her attention to the lad hesitating in the middle of the room. She didn't know him, but a glance told her he was dirty, scared and tired enough to collapse any moment. The bubble of fear inside her chest grew larger and more painful.

"So," she asked evenly. "Do I have time to get dressed before the execution?"

"Only if you hurry," Gerelda said, her tone indicating that she was not entirely joking.

She turned to her secretary. "Barden, take this lad, whoever he is, out of here, give him a meal, or a bath, or a bed – in whatever order is appropriate to his needs – and leave Gerelda and me to talk while I dress. And send someone up with a hot drink and a meal."

Without another word, Barden beckoned to the lad and they headed out of her apartment. Fritillary stepped back into her bedroom, crossed to her washstand, bathed her face, patted it dry.

By the time she was dressed and had returned to the anteroom, it was to find Gerelda had unbuckled her sword and collapsed into the room's most comfortable chair.

"So, what's this all about, Gerelda?"

"You were the one who told me to return in a hurry."

"I don't remember saying wake me in the middle of the night."

"All right. I'll come back in the morning."

She gave a soft laugh. "Ah, Gerelda, there is no one quite like you. To business. That boy is far too young to have a witchery, but he does. What's happened?"

"I have a lot to tell you, but for now just this: the discovery that made me ask Barden to wake you. As I was coming down the valley into Vavala earlier yesterday, I heard whispers of men in Wildmadder Wood, and Perie – that's the boy: Peregrine Clary – he said he could sense folk there wearing the black smudge that shrine keepers talk about. That's his witchery."

"Ah. The one they call A'Va's mark."

"Yes. He can taste it on the air, he says. I followed his lead and sure enough, we found several hundred lancers camped out in the hills above the city. All of them wear grey coats. The ones there that we overheard speaking had Staravale accents."

Fritillary pulled her wrap tighter around her shoulders. "Several hundred? That's hardly an army. There are over a thousand guards here who are charged with the protection of the Pontificate."

"With no experience of war. The most any of them has ever done is probably discipline a drunken muleteer, or catch a cut-purse lad.

These men in the Vavala hills were a disciplined bunch, alert and hardened. They have horses and lances. By the way, they were not the only lancers we had the misfortune to encounter either, but they appeared to be the best trained."

Fritillary listened, appalled, as Gerelda went on to describe all that had happened to Peregrine and herself since she'd left Twite. "I believe those earlier men were new recruits, assembling for training. Not so the group we found yesterday. They might be here to kill you. I'm betting Valerian Fox is up to his nasty nose in all this."

"Did you know he's here in Vavala?"

"He is? Doing what?"

"Seeing me. I have an appointment with our beloved Prime tomorrow morning, at his request."

"Oh!" Gerelda gaped. "Did you already know about these lancers in the hills outside of the city?"

"The local shrine keeper sent word. Fox, of course, is not openly associated with them. They wear no insignia. I suspect he will deny any connection, if asked."

Gerelda's expression darkened into a glower. "You should consider assassinating Prime Fox."

"Oh?" She raised an eyebrow. "What do you think King Edwayn would have to say about that? And no, I am not going to send a company of arquebus musketeers to battle these lancers, either. Va-faith does not condone killing, or war. For a lawyer, you can be worryingly bloodthirsty. I cannot even accuse Fox, because I don't have a shred of evidence that he's involved in anything nefarious."

"I thought Saker Rampion found evidence when he searched Faith House in Throssel."

"Sketchy at best. Enough for *me*, true, but not enough for the King. At worst, whatever proof there was, Fox surely disposed of when he realised Saker had been there. I can't attack Fox openly. He was appointed by, and is still supported by, King Edwayn."

"The Prime is poison, and you must not keep that appointment."

"*Must* not?" It was her turn to glower, but Gerelda did not take the hint.

"Send him away without an audience. He obviously wants you to know about those lancers sitting on your doorstep. He wants to intimidate you into giving him that audience, or into making concessions – something!"

"Gerelda Brantheld, you are my agent for legal matters, not my political adviser, let alone my military one. What kind of a Pontifect would I be if I fled like a rabbit when a fox knocks at my door, especially when he happens to be the Ardronese Prime? I could not maintain any credibility if I behaved in such a craven fashion."

"Why does he come backed by soldiers?" Gerelda was waving her arms, and the smell of sweat and dirt wafted more strongly around the room. "They are a bare ten miles from the city walls. Tomorrow they could well be closer. You may be dead come afternoon."

"If Fox wants to usurp the post of Pontifect, I'd prefer he started his reign with my public murder than with my abdication of duty. He'd at least look guilty of something."

Someone knocked at the door and she rose to her feet. "That will be food and drink. You can fill me in on details as you eat. And then I trust you will have time to take a bath."

Gerelda pecked at the food and downed the better part of a flagon of cider, describing all she had found out in Ardrone and East Denva. When she'd finished, Fritillary leaned forward and asked the question that had loomed large in her mind for well over a year. "Why do these people – the lancers – leave their homes and their loved ones? Not for a single coin, I feel sure. That's just an enticement to listen. You saw them, Gerelda. How did it happen?"

"We – well, Peregrine – did overhear the lancers sometimes, talking among themselves. They never mentioned what they were doing, or why. They never spoke of home, or of anything much, except the next meal, or a sick horse, or maybe to curse the weather. They weren't *normal*. They didn't sit around the camp fire and tell bawdy stories. It was the same when I saw the ones recruited on the village green in Needlewhin. It was as if they were . . ."

"Go on."

"Ensorcelled." She snorted as though she didn't believe she'd actually said that. "Can A'Va do that?"

"Of course not. Well, not to those who follow Va-faith. Tempt, perhaps. But not turn a person into something he or she is not, no."

"Well, if you want my opinion, something did just that. Or some*one*. Like Fox."

"One man? Recruiting from Ardrone to Staravale? Gerelda, the last time I saw the Prime, he was still just one individual."

"His family is a large one," Gerelda pointed out.

"The Fox estates are large, certainly. They are administered, as far as I have been able to ascertain, by servitors. I've never actually met anyone who told me they were a member of the family. Have you?"

"Possibly that recruiter?"

"But he didn't say his name was Fox."

"No. Do you have people investigating the family?"

"I do. It is amazingly difficult to find out anything. The idea that this Peregrine could recognise these lancers intrigues me, though. I want him to meet Valerian Fox."

"You are going ahead with this meeting?"

"My only possible victory will be to make Fox look bad in the eyes of true believers of Va-faith, and I think I know just how to sow the seeds of that."

"By allowing yourself to be killed?"

She swallowed her irritation with Gerelda and said mildly, "I really don't think he's going to murder me in my own audience hall. That would make others, including King Edwayn, wonder about his ambition and his motives. Besides, I *want* to speak to him. I want to know what he's up to."

Gerelda snorted. "You think he'll tell you what he's planning?"

"It's all a matter of asking the right questions. Gerelda, I'm going to tell you something that I've only ever told two people, and one of those doesn't know everything there is to know. Have you ever wondered what my witchery is?"

"Of course! There can hardly be a person in the whole of Vavala who hasn't wondered at some time or other. The most popular guess is that you read minds, because you have an uncanny way of knowing too much."

"A lot of that stems from the knowledge I gain from my many agents. However, my witchery does help. I have the knack of knowing the general essence of someone's thoughts when they speak to me – especially if those thoughts pertain to something of importance to me.

For example, I know you are fearful for my safety. I know when you speak of Fox he worries you deeply. When you speak of Perie, you are both protective and exasperated. If you were to lie deliberately to me about anything of importance, I would know. Lies in a conversation are to me like . . . flames flaring up out of coals in the fireplace. On the other hand, if you were to let your thoughts stray to some handsome fellow you wanted to bed on the morrow, I wouldn't have a clue, because it's not important to me."

Gerelda opened her mouth to reply, then closed it again. There was a long silence before she said, "That's very . . . disconcerting."

"I agree. It's handy, because it so often tells me not only if someone is lying to me, but how important that lie is. I'll admit, though, it is a somewhat uncomfortable witchery to have. Not one I want you to mention to anyone."

"No."

"Unfortunately, Fox's mind is closed to me, and always has been. Imagine that: of all the people I have met since the day I received my witchery, he's the only one I can't read. Luckily, it seems that you have delivered just the right instrument into my hands."

"Wh—? Peregrine is not a weapon! He's a lad who's been to the deepest misery of horror and is still clawing his way back—"

"We are all weapons in this war. Why has he been granted a witchery if not to use it? I shall use your lad, in the service of Va."

"He's not *my* anything. I'm no nursemaid, but I do think he needs care. He hasn't shed a tear for his father, that I know of, not once. He has a . . . a bloodcurdling coldness that's not healthy in a lad of his age. Your reverence, that boy pulled his father's severed feet out of his boots so he could wear them. He saw his father's gnawed ribs tossed to the ground by men who ate him."

She said, deliberately cold, "Witcheries are Va-bestowed for a purpose. It is perfectly obvious to me that Va has seen to it that your Peregrine has arrived at precisely the right time."

"He is here because I endured and murdered and stole and fought to get him here. And he went through a Va-less hell on the way to become what he is. If that's Va's way of achieving things—"

"I don't want to get into a religious discussion centring on doctrinal interpretations right now, thank you, Gerelda. I want him to take a look at the Prime and then tell us what he sees. And then you and he are going to Lowmeer."

That finally halted her. She thought about that in silence, then asked, "You'd seek help from Regal Vilmar?"

"Perhaps, later. But there is another matter that concerns me first. I've had a communication from Saker, delivered in a somewhat unconventional manner. There is a possibility I will need to make a . . . a clerical visit to Ustgrind to call on the Regal and the Regala and the Prince-regal. However, I think I want you and Peregrine to look into the matter first. Then I will need to know if such a visit by me is necessary."

"You want to send me to the Lowmian court?" The look Gerelda gave her said she thought the idea was odd, to say the least.

"Oh, you haven't heard anything yet," Fritillary said. "I'm going to tell you about a set of royal twins and a compact made between the Vollendorns and A'Va. Then there's the matter of a lascar's dagger, some golden plumes and a letter sent to me by a bird . . ."

By the time she had finished explaining, half an hour later, Gerelda was looking at her as if she had two heads.

Fritillary waited.

"Let me see if I have this right," Gerelda said slowly. "For the past four hundred years, regals have been giving instructions for twin babies to be slaughtered because A'Va uses them as minions called devil-kin – a *right* granted to A'Va by those very same regals. I don't think I have ever heard of anything more disgustingly vile. Or absurd!"

"It's certainly not very plausible," she admitted. "I'll say this to you, but not to anyone else: I've always had grave doubts about the actual existence of A'Va. However, there is something . . . evil . . . going on here that needs to be investigated. I want you to look into it. With Peregrine."

As the day progressed, Gerelda tried several different arguments, but nothing she said could make the Pontifect change her mind about meeting Prime Valerian Fox. Privately, though, she had to admit Fritillary's meticulous planning would ensure she wasn't going to be assassinated, at least not during the meeting itself.

The Commander of the Vavala Guards arranged a ceremonial honour guard to line the walls of the audience hall, with every man holding his pike. Invitations had been sent to all the Va-cherished Hemisphere ambassadors, as well as to the local clergy and the local shrine keepers, not to mention all the notables of Vavala. As most of those invited had accepted, and many of them would, as was customary, bring their secretaries or scribes, the number of people present would be substantial. Some of them would have witcheries. It would take a foolhardy man or woman to attempt violence against the person of the Pontifect in front of such an audience. Even so, Gerelda was still worried.

"All it would take is one person," she said to Fritillary that morning as they prepared the details, "someone willing to sacrifice his life. A single person to shove a knife between your ribs. You fall in public, tragically assassinated by a madman – and who is the noble fellow of stature who will step into the breach, full of concern and so conveniently on hand, doubtless vowing immediate vengeance on the killer? Prime Fox. The next thing you know, the assassin is dead, Fox's lancers are on the streets of Vavala, ostensibly to keep everyone calm, and the way is clear for Fox to be elected the new Pontifect. Only you wouldn't know, because you'd be dead."

Fritillary regarded her thoughtfully, head tilted. "Sometimes I wonder just what the study of law does to a normal person's mind. Do such convoluted plots occur to you often?"

"Only when merited. And you can't tell me you haven't considered this, or something like it, because I don't believe you."

"Fox is nowhere near ready to seize power, but just suppose you're right. It seems to me we have the perfect solution. You and Peregrine will wait at the entrance to the hall. Everyone who enters, from my own personal servants and guards to every guest, must enter through the same doors. Every main guest will have to halt there momentarily for their name and rank to be announced. Peregrine can tell you if any are his pitch-hearted people. You will signal my guards to bar anyone he denounces."

Gerelda had breathed a little easier then, especially when Fritillary invited the guests to arrive earlier than the meeting had been scheduled, so that when the Prime did arrive with his staff, he'd be faced with a room full of people.

"And the other entries to the building, through the kitchens and so on?"

"Don't patronise me, proctor! Guards will be on duty. No one enters. Deliveries are dropped off and searched. All right?"

Gerelda, suitably chastened, sought out Peregrine, now well-fed and rested, and asked him if he could do his part. He looked surprised that she should even ask. "Of course," he said.

"I'll arrange to have some banners hanging from the ceiling that we can hide behind, with a slit to look through. Some of the Vavala guards will stand right in front of us, ready to help."

"I don't need to see pitch-men to know them. I hope some of them do try to enter the palace. I want them to try. Then they can be killed."

Perie, I would like you a whole lot better if you weren't so – so cold in your bloodthirstiness . . . Aloud, she said, "Prime Valerian Fox may be one of your pitch-men. If so, don't make a fuss; just quietly tell me and I shall signal the Pontifect. He mustn't have any warning that we know him for what he is. That's important, Perie. No guards will be pouncing on the Prime. At least, not yet. You understand?"

"Not really. But my da once said some men are too powerful to be challenged. Is that what you mean?"

"Yes, I suppose I do." The sick feeling she'd had in her stomach roiled.

"That's wrong. But I'll do what you say."

She stifled a sigh, which was something she seemed to do a lot when she was talking to Peregrine.

Perie watched from behind the banners and remembered another time, back when Ma and Da had been alive. A windy day, it'd been, on the town green. An older lad had given him the string of his kite to hold. He hadn't known what to expect, but now recalled how he'd felt: thrilled by the thrum of the string as it pulsed and quivered like a living thing, afraid that he might not have the strength to hold on, overwhelmed with a sense of responsibility, yet taut with excitement. That was how he felt now, as he waited – with a difference.

Now those feelings were all held under a coating of ice, and he gloried in the change. *That's part of my witchery.*

He didn't want that ice ever to melt because then he'd feel again what he'd felt when he'd seen Da's feet still in his boots . . .

On his way to Vavala, he'd grown used to pitch-men, their internal tarry darkness, the way they scared and filled him with a fog of dread, reminding him more of unthinking savage animals than reasoning men. But he could handle that, because the fear was encased under the ice, neatly imprisoned so it couldn't grab him by the throat.

He watched the guests arrive at the Pontifect's palace, and marvelled at the richness of clothes, the plumpness of overfed bodies, the painted faces, the glitter of jewels. There were ordinary people too, of course. Shrine keepers, even. One of them, a tall woman with skin like crumpled silk, walked over and stared at him through the gap between the banners. Then she winked and walked on.

"Nothing yet?" Gerelda asked.

"No. I don't understand why some of them want to wear those fancy clothes, though. Aren't they uncomfortable?"

Gerelda looked down at her plain garb. Her one concession to the occasion had been to shine her boots to a spotless sheen. "I'm sure they are. But then, *they* wouldn't understand why I prefer comfort."

"Well, it's more sensible too. You couldn't fight wearing a dress like that woman in blue over there. And you couldn't run in shoes like that man in the black and red stripes."

She laid a hand on his arm. "Secretary Barden has just signalled Fox is coming." She'd been keeping an eye on the secretary where he was standing in the entry hall, looking out towards the main entrance.

Perie felt the man's presence and winced. "Pitch-man," he whispered. "The tall man in the centre. Is that Fox?"

She nodded.

As the Prime walked past, he felt his composure slipping away. The man did not remind him of an animal at all. Fox was a force, saturating the air around him with raw power.

If he looks at me I'll die.

Gerelda gave the prearranged signal to the captain of the Guard, who would pass it on to the Pontifect. Then she glanced back down at him. "Are you all right?"

No, he wasn't. He tried to explain. "He's more than a pitch-man.

He's a . . . a . . . hole so black there's no end to it. Like looking into a well and not seeing the bottom."

She looked at him askance, dubious, not understanding any more than he did.

"Wait," he said. "There's another one coming. In the Prime's retinue."

"Can you tell who?"

The fellow was the most insignificant of all, clad in a servant's garb, scurrying on behind with his head down.

This time Gerelda stepped out from behind the banners and spoke to the captain.

It was all done very neatly. One moment the man was following the Prime's party, the next he was cut off by a group of men dressed as palace servants suddenly appearing from behind banners and tapestries. He was whisked away without anyone from the Prime's party being aware he was gone.

Perie should have felt satisfied. Instead, there was a lump in his chest that wouldn't go away.

As he strode through the throng, clearing a path direct to where Fritillary was sitting on the Pontifical throne at one end, Fox wore an expression she recognised. She hadn't seen him since the ceremony of his consecration as Prime of Ardrone, but the subtleties of his anger were familiar: the grim line of his brow, the smooth flat look in his eyes that could have meant indifference in any other man. She knew what they signalled. He was planning her humiliation, or worse. He had been outmanoeuvred, and he would seek revenge.

"I thought we were to have a quiet confidential conversation, your reverence," he said as he arrived in front of her, making no effort to soften his tone. He meant to be heard. "Instead you've turned this into some sort of market-day carnival."

"Surely it is a cause for celebration when the Prime of Ardrone comes to pay his respects to the Pontifect of Va-faith?"

"There is no respect, as I am sure you are aware."

Shock reverberated through the silence of the hall, visible on the faces of those listening, heard in their gasps.

Fritillary smiled benignly, or so she hoped. "No matter what you think of me personally, you owe respect to the position I hold." She held out her hand and followed the gesture with a sweet smile of forgiveness. "*Respect*, your eminence."

Fox hesitated long enough to be rude. Then he knelt on one knee and took her hand to kiss. His lips barely hovered over her knuckles. He didn't wait for her to withdraw her hand, but dropped it and stood. "I can give no respect to a woman who sent a blasphemer to be the adviser of a young princess. I can give no respect to a woman whose rule as Pontifect has seen the revival of the primordial heresy and so many clerics dying of the Horned Death. I can give no respect to a woman who shows her preference for the Way of the Oak over that of the Way of the Flow and who favours both of those before the will of Va and the supremacy of Va-faith over the old ways."

Everyone in the hall was standing motionless, utterly silent.

Then Fritillary rose abruptly to her feet, and there was a startled intake of breath across the room. As the throne was on a dais, Fox was forced to look up, while she appeared taller and more regal. In a trick of the acoustics, her voice carried, her words clear to all assembled.

"I am merely a humble cleric, your eminence – a woman without eminence, in fact. Just one who serves Va with humility and acceptance. If you know the way to halt the spread of the Horned Death, then how is it that shrine keepers died in Ardrone under your personal ministrations? And if I truly discriminate against the Way of the Flow, why have I received no complaints from Lowmeer, where the Flow is central to their faith? But it is not meet that we argue in this august company. We shall adjourn to my private office to discuss these matters."

She looked out over the hall. At the far entrance door Gerelda Brantheld stood. When their gazes met, Gerelda placed her hand in the middle of her chest, confirming the captain's warning a few moment's earlier.

Fritillary's heart turned over. *Leak on you, Valerian Fox, you whoreson. You are indeed one of Peregrine's pitch-men.*

"Esteemed guests," she continued, her voice calm, "refreshments will be served. Pray you, enjoy the hospitality of my household, while the Prime and I settle our differences." She didn't wait for Fox's agreement or otherwise. She swept towards the doors to her workroom, shoulders back and chin up. Her guards opened the doors and she paused there, making a gesture with her hand to usher the Prime before her. He had not moved, but when she fixed him with her glare, he shrugged and walked through the doors ahead of her. Members of his staff moved to follow him, but she signed the guards to shut the doors in their faces.

"So," she said coldly, "we can now drop all pretence, Fox. No need for you to be anything but the ambitious, conscienceless man that you are."

"What, no invitation to be seated?"

She did not bother to reply to that, saying instead, "How long do you think the rulers of these lands will allow you to build an army?"

"You will, I think, be hard pressed to prove I'm doing any such thing. These lancers amassing all over the Va-cherished Hemisphere are merely a spontaneous peasant uprising in answer to social problems and religious heresies. Why, even their particular weapon of choice, the lance, harks back to the famine riots of three hundred years ago."

"Don't take me for a fool."

He shrugged. "I admit nothing. You are the one saying they are connected to me." His lips curled up in a smile.

"You can't possibly think that either Regal Vilmar or King Edwayn will let you get away with sitting on the Pontifect's throne after an illegal invasion. In fact, the whole of the Va-cherished Hemisphere would be unhappy. The Pontifect must be seen to be impartial and peace-loving. What I'd like to know is why you would ever decide to serve A'Va."

"Now what makes you think that!" His laugh was one of genuine amusement. "A'Va? How childish you are! A'Va is surely a figment of men's imaginations. I don't serve anyone. Not even Va. It's all illusion, don't you know that?"

He leaned towards her, and, utterly revolted, she took a step backwards. For a splintered moment she felt she was breathing in flames, and her lungs were filling with something sticky, tarry, dread-filled . . .

She took another step away, and snapped back into normality. "How dare you, you filthy mudworm!"

He'd tried to do something to her, but she was not quite sure what, just that it was vile. "Get out of my sight. Leave this palace with your lackeys, or I'll kill you right now where you stand."

"You don't have that power. No one has," he said. "You don't know the first thing about me, Fritillary. You never did."

With that, he turned, thrust open the doors and walked back into the audience hall. Once again the guests parted before him like the bow wave of a ship. His retainers fell in behind him, and he was gone.

He betrayed himself.

She'd pulled his strings and he'd danced, exactly as she'd intended. She should have been glad; instead, she was aghast.

12

The Task Assigned

He mustn't be afraid. Not until his job was done, and all the pitch-men were dead, along with Fox, because he was worse than all the rest put together. Maybe when they were all dead he could live again, reclaim something of what he'd had.

He just wished he understood everything better. Right now, after all the guests had gone, and he was in the Pontifect's workroom with her, he was still trying to make sense of everything. Her secretary, Barden, was there, and so was Proctor Brantheld. Barden was one of the oldest men he'd ever seen. He limped along with a stick when he walked, and when he stopped he looked as if he had to sit down or fall over. His face had as many wrinkles as lines on a map and his voice sounded like dry leaves blown by the wind.

I'd hate to be that ancient . . .

He looked from Barden to where the Pontifect and Proctor Brantheld sat and tried to follow their conversation, but it was mostly about things he didn't understand, and people he didn't know. He felt lost.

Oh, Da, why did you have to die?

He'd never been in a city as big as Vavala before; such a place had no need of itinerant scribes and petition writers. Scribes had *shops* here. He'd seen one. As for the Pontifical Palace – he'd never seen any building as large, let alone been inside one. Why would anyone build a house with rooms so huge? Even a fairground man on stilts would not be able to touch the ceilings! So ridiculously ornate, so monstrously huge – and so cold.

His wildest imaginings had never included the idea that a lad like him would ever meet the Pontifect, surely the most powerful woman who'd ever lived, and yet here he was listening to her squabble with her agent lawyer. Right from their first meeting, he'd been disconcerted to discover that Fritillary Reedling looked so . . . so ordinary. Tall, greying, sombre, rather like someone's great-aunt.

She couldn't really be ordinary, of course. She had a witchery for a start. He wasn't sure how he knew that, but he did. And she had an air of command that made any thought of disobeying seem not only disloyal, but clay-brained. Which made it doubly odd that Agent Gerelda Brantheld was always arguing with her.

Their present disagreement concerned what action should be taken on the pitch-men surrounding the city. Gerelda wanted the Vavala guards to fight them, but the Pontifect disagreed. In the end Gerelda turned to him, saying, "Perie, tell her reverence what you sense about Prime Valerian Fox. Why did he scare you so much?"

"Because he's rotten in here," he replied. He tapped himself on the chest. He didn't even have to think about that; he knew it. "So . . . so *old* inside. He's not like us."

He wasn't sure that they understood what he was trying to tell them, because even to his own ears his words sounded a little ridiculous, and Barden was pinched around the mouth as though he didn't like the reference to being old. He struggled on, trying to explain. "You have a witchery," he said to the Pontifect.

She nodded. "Yes, that's true. So do you. People with witchery always recognise one another."

"The thing that's wrong with pitch-men? I can feel that wrong thing the same way as I feel your witchery. Only your witchery isn't bad. It just . . . is. But pitch-men feel wrong. Horrible and sticky inside, like a big tar-pit. Prime Fox is worse than a pitch-man. It's like he – he *makes* the pitch."

They were all silent. He thought even the Pontifect paled, as if his words had reminded her of something.

Gerelda said softly, "Consign Fox to a choiceless grave; the good-for-nothing scum of a man can't *be* A'Va, can he?"

"If A'Va exists," Barden said in his measured, slow way of speaking, "then surely he must always have existed, by definition. Valerian Fox's birth, however, is well documented, as are his boyhood and university days. He is forty-eight years old, the son of the Ardronese ambassador to Lowmeer at the time, Harrier Fox. Valerian's mother was a Lowmian noblewoman. She died not long after he was born."

"I've known him from our university days," the Pontifect added, "when he was in his twenties."

"Fox did mean to kill you today," Gerelda told her, frustration making her snappish. "Perie identified a servant as a pitch-man, so I asked the guards to refuse him entry. He's being questioned now, but from first reports he seems more confused and, well, stupid than anything else. Either that, or he's a good play-actor. He was trailing behind Fox's party as though he belonged to them, but when the guards intervened, Fox's secretary said they didn't know him. It's my belief that was a lie and he would have killed you if he'd been given the chance."

"Possibly." The Pontifect smiled at him. "And if so, I am indeed grateful to you and your witchery, Peregrine Clary. Gerelda, even if Fox planned my assassination, I think he had a second reason for wanting to come. He wanted to see if he could contaminate me with his, well, with his pitch, for want of a better word."

"And failed, I assume. Why would he want to reveal himself to you like that?"

"Maybe he thought he had a chance of success. A chance worth taking. After all, he must have known Saker escaped his nullification and would therefore have immediately come to me with what he knew. Fox wasn't saying much about himself that I didn't already know or guess." She shrugged. "Still, it was good of him to clarify it. One thing we should bear in mind is that as far as we know, no one with a witchery has ever joined the lancers. That is worth remembering."

Gerelda stared at her, frowning, with a peculiar expression on her face, half disbelief, half worry.

"We tell ourselves," the Pontifect continued, "that we are Va-cherished. But this contamination spreads, whether it is the Horned Death or Peregrine's pitch. In the meanwhile, Fox is goading us into acting before we know the nature of what we're fighting."

"You think the Horned Death and the pitch are the same thing?" Gerelda asked.

Peregrine shivered.

"No. They may have the same cause, though," the Pontifect said. "One kills, and the other makes such fools of the infected that they will leave their families to fight for a cause that doesn't really exist."

Gerelda fell silent. Barden, who was sitting beside her, rested his hands and chin on top of the walking stick he'd propped between his knees, as if he was too tired to hold his head up.

"Remember this," the Pontifect continued. "Clerics died of the Horned Death in Ustgrind, or so we are told. The whole of the Institute of Advanced Studies was wiped out, that's for certain. The Lowmian Prime sent that news; Saker confirmed they were all reported dead, and the cause was given as the Horned Death. Shrine keepers in the heart of Shenat hill country in Ardrone also died of the Death, or so we are told. That news came from Prime Fox. They certainly died of something."

When no one said anything, the Pontifect continued, "Anything told to me by Fox, I want confirmed. So I had agents check. No one could be found who actually saw a shrine keeper with the symptoms of the Death while they were still alive. Not one. As for the Institute in Lowmeer – it was closed to the public, so no one, not even Saker, actually saw the suffering of the clerics. Afterwards, the building and the bodies were burned."

"You're saying they died of something else? Murdered, perhaps?"

The Pontifect shrugged. "All I'm saying is that we have no evidence one way or the other. You're a lawyer, Gerelda. You know the value of evidence – look for it."

Gerelda nodded. "So, what's my task?"

"I want you to leave for Lowmeer as soon as possible. I would very much like you to go with her, Peregrine. I think your talent for identifying pitch-men is of great importance to us all. I know you have experienced a terrible loss, and you've behaved with great courage and dignity and strength of purpose. I have no right to ask you to help us, but I do. I ask you to serve Va-faith. The best way to do that at the moment is to go to Lowmeer."

"And if he refuses?" Gerelda asked.

"I will see that he is housed at one of our seminaries where he can study, if he chooses. It will be his choice, his free choice."

He stared at her, his heart thumping. His overwhelming reaction was one of relief. At last, someone who recognised the gnawing need inside him, the need to do something to rid the world of pitch-men. To get rid of that dark, tarry contamination. He didn't want to be safe; he didn't want to be a student. He wanted to find out why his father had died. He needed to know what made men kill and eat someone who'd never done them any harm.

"I'll go wherever you want," he said eagerly, and held his breath in case she changed her mind.

"I thought you would. Barden, talk to the tailor about some new clothes for him, will you? Garments suitable for every possible occasion."

Gerelda strode with Peregrine down the centre of the street leading to the docks, following a contingent of the Pontifect's guards. In the first dawn light their uniforms were colourless; in the emptiness of deserted streets their steps echoed. Behind her another ten guards marched. She'd complained to Fritillary that being accompanied by guards drew attention to them and where they were going, but Fritillary had just smiled. When a drunken band of men spilling out from a tavern laughed at them and made vulgar remarks about unwanted crims always being thrown out of the city in the dead of night, she realised why.

Damn Fritillary, she's always one step ahead of me! The guards were part of their disguise.

But still, this was rattling, dizzy-eyed madness.

She was Lowmian, but she wasn't from a noble family, and one thing she knew for certain was that she didn't want to have to deal with any court. Yet here she was, about to embark on a barge to travel down the River Ard to the port of Borage and, from there, to board a flat boat to Ustgrind. In her baggage, which she'd been told was already on board, she had letters from the Pontifect to the Lowmian Prime and to the Regala Mathilda. But she still had no idea how she was going to bring Peregrine and the Lowmian heir, Prince-regal Karel, together in the same room. Her real skills lay not in understanding court etiquette, but in the interpretation of legal documents, or in researching and uncovering the many ways that people tried to cheat one another.

Fritillary Reedling, this time you've asked too much.

At her side Peregrine said, "I've never been on a barge. In fact, I've never been on a boat, only a winch-ferry."

"Perie, I think in the next month or two you are going to do a lot of things you've never done before."

There was only one person on the wharf, other than a handful of bargees seeing to the loading: an old man, leaning on a walking stick and wrapped up against the night-time cold. By the light from the lantern beside him, he looked frail.

"Oh, beggar me speechless, is that Secretary Barden?" she muttered. "You shouldn't be here," she told him as they stepped on to the wharf and the guards dispersed to block public access to the dock. "And alone, too."

He gave a smile. "Ah, Agent Brantheld, this is the very hour when I can't sleep, and the aches and pains beg to be gently eased into their daily routine."

"The Pontifect sent you?"

"Indeed no. She would be quite annoyed with me if she knew."

"Then why are you here?"

"To ease your mind, perhaps. To offer my advice, for what it is worth."

"I could certainly do with plenty of that."

"First, why don't you get this young lad settled into a bunk on the barge? Then we will chat while the barge captain waits for the tide to turn. I believe there is at least half an hour yet."

She did as he suggested, and when she came back up on deck it was to find Barden propped up against a bollard waiting for her. Without any more preliminaries, he said, "You really must stop worrying about the Pontifect. She is quite capable of looking after herself."

"Those lancers up in the hills aren't going to go away. There will be other assassins, too."

"She knows that. Proctor, have faith in her. If the danger becomes too great, she will abandon the Pontifical Palace in order to save Vavala. She has been marshalling our defences."

She sat down on an upturned wooden bucket next to him. "Defences?"

"It's odd, but people without witchery always underestimate witchery power, simply because witchery is almost never misused."

"You have a witchery?"

"No, but I do have the wisdom that comes with having lived through some bad times. And my memory tells me this much: what is out in the world now, this blackness, this pitch that Peregrine talks about – it's always been here, all my life anyway, just not so obvious or so wide-spread. So if you're looking for its origin you have to go a long way back. I am looking through all the records we have in Vavala, but I think it would be more rewarding to look through those in Lowmeer."

"Those were the Pontifect's instructions too, but where do I start, apart from Fox's family? I gather they were originally Lowmian."

"Start there, by all means. I think you should also look hard at Dire Sweepers."

"The Pontifect mentioned them. I had the impression they were fighting on our side, in charge of eliminating the Horned Death!"

"She has her reasons, doubtless, but I am telling you, look into the Dire Sweepers. Saker thought they should be investigated, too. He thinks their allotted task is twofold: to murder twins at birth and to kill people suffering from the Horned Death. Saker met a man who could well be their leader."

"And his name?"

"Saker couldn't recall it. He only remembered that the man was noble and he often came to the University in Grundorp to oversee his family's patronage of that institution. Saker met him when he was a student. Which, I believe, was when you were a student there too. You may have known this fellow, as well. He'd be in his late forties now, if he's still alive. Saker said that in their last encounter, the man had a knife thrown into his back. He might have died."

"There were a number of university patrons, but it shouldn't be difficult to find out which one. Why didn't the Pontifect tell me all that?"

He stood up, shrugging. "I've no idea. And now I must be off before the crowds are about in the streets."

And that, she knew, was all she was going to get out of him. He had come down to the wharf for the sole purpose of giving her the information that would encourage her to find the leader of the Dire Sweepers. And in so doing, he had also let her know that Fritillary Reedling probably knew that name already – and hadn't passed it on.

"I think you are very wicked old man, Secretary Barden," she said.

"And I trust your discretion." With that remark, he picked up his lantern and hobbled away, leaning heavily on his stick.

*　*　*

113

Fritillary Reedling watched the barge leave the dock from the window of her workroom. As soon as it disappeared into the mists rising off the river, she left the room and headed out of the palace, conspicuously trailed by two of her guards.

She walked briskly, heading for the city's main oak shrine. The oak itself was the oldest and largest in all Vavala; in fact, many said it was the oldest to be found anywhere in the Va-cherished Hemisphere. Its massive main trunk was anchored not just by its roots, but also by branches that drooped from high in the heart of the tree to rest on the ground. Any one of these branches would have dwarfed the trunk of a normal oak. Above, the vast canopy spread its crown of leaves as high as the roof of the Pontifical Palace.

Over the centuries, shrine keepers had encouraged the growth of stray branches into a labyrinth of rooms with living walls and latticed ceilings of limbs and twigs. Acolytes came from all over the hemisphere to study here, just as shrine keepers came to impart their knowledge. The school, if it could be called that, was informal, ever changing as people came and went. It was said that the shrine had many unseen guardians and it was their presence that ensured order and continuity.

Fritillary halted briefly at the edge of the shade from the oak. "Wait here," she said to her guards. She ducked her head under a low spray of fresh spring growth and stood for a moment to give her eyes time to adjust to the reduced light.

Taking a deep breath, she lowered her head to look at the back of her hand.

When she raised her gaze, Akrana the shrine keeper was standing before her. No one was sure if Akrana, had once been a man or a woman; it was no longer important. Age had wrinkled and withered and twisted the keeper into a figure that was barely recognisable as human. Once Akrana must have been abnormally tall because now, even shortened by time, the rheumy eyes were still level with Fritillary's own.

"He has marked ye as an enemy." The voice that issued from between thin bloodless lips was surprisingly forceful. "Prime Valerian Fox."

Fritillary nodded.

"The so-called mark of A'Va."

She nodded again.

"There was a time afore, when there was no recognition of the existence of Va, and therefore no A'Va. The smutch had a different name then."

"Which was?"

"I was not on this soil then, but as a child I heared a elder shrine keeper given it name. The mark of hexer."

"Hexer?"

"I believe ye'd call such 'sorcerer' nowadays. Valerian was never of the oak. Bad times are a-coming, Fritillary Reedling. He can track ye now, through that mark. Ye must prepare your sanctuary so he know not where you hide. Ye must also hide the oaks . . . Keep them safe."

She felt overwhelming despair. "*How?*"

Akrana gestured her deeper inside the shrine. "Ask the unseen guardians. Perhaps . . . perhaps they know. I do not."

13

Obviation

"I don't understand, Lady Friselda."

Mathilda glanced down the room to where her gaggle of ladies-in-waiting were all gathered at the other end near the warmth of the fire, then fixed her most imperious stare on the old lady seated next to her in the window embrasure of the Regala's retiring room. It was a look that intimidated most people, but it never had much effect on the wretched woman who was her ward's-dame. Lady Friselda was far too entrenched in her privileged position as cousin to the Regal to be intimidated, and her power at court was real; she appointed all Mathilda's Lowmian ladies-in-waiting.

"Moreover, surely it is *my* decision," she added with as much acid as she could inject into the words, "to decide Aureen's future?"

"Oh, nonsense, my dear! Why would the disposition of a mere chambermaid be any concern of a Regala?"

"Because she came here as part of my retinue and she is the only remaining member of it!"

"Sweet child, why would you possibly care?" The old lady raised a single eyebrow in ridicule. "An uneducated under-servant is of no import to anyone, least of all you. If the Regal wishes her to be returned to Ardrone, as a symbol of your absorption into our Lowmian court and the cutting of your final tie to Ardrone, then of course she must go home."

Pox on you, you condescending bitch! She smiled sweetly. "Well, of course, if it is the *Regal's* wish, then so be it. I shall speak to him concerning the matter."

"Do that, my dear," Friselda said equably. "I believe His Grace has been influenced by the continued inquiry into that saucy light-fingered female you brought to court as your handmaiden. His Grace's agents, you see, are convinced that Aureen must know something she is not saying about the theft of his valuable fan. After all, put two lower-class Ardronese servants together – of course they must have been in each other's confidence. A disgrace that they were ever introduced to this court! I cannot *imagine* the upbringing that you must have endured in Throssel, my dear. I blame the early demise of your mother. How else can you have come under the influence of such baseborn servants?"

She tried not to grit her teeth. "So kind of you to be concerned. But I assure you, I have never been under their influence. And I consider the insinuation insulting."

"Oh, dear, my apologies for disturbing your sensitivities. Anyway, 'tis no further concern of yours. I believe dear Vilmar's agents will deal with Aureen before she is sent home, just to make sure they have all the information they can get."

"Agents?" She swallowed convulsively. *Va above. Not the Dire Sweepers.*

"His Grace has many agents to take care of the dishonest and the traitorous. Nothing you need worry your pretty head about, my dear."

Oh, how she itched to put her hands around that scrawny woman's neck and choke the life out of her, but her anger warred with dread. If the Dire Sweepers seized Aureen the moment she left the protection of the court, she would never reach Ardrone. They'd torture her – and they weren't interested in the theft of a fan. They wanted to know about the baby Sorrel was carrying . . .

"Thank you, Lady Friselda. I will talk to the Regal about this matter. And I will inform Aureen myself. I am sure she is innocent of all wrongdoing." Not trusting herself to say another word, she turned and left the room, leaving her startled ladies-in-waiting to follow or not as they pleased.

That evening, when they were seated together at supper and other guests were diverted by the entertainment, Mathilda raised the subject with Vilmar. As soon as she mentioned Aureen's name, she saw the furrow between his greying eyebrows twitch and deepen. Her heart sank; she knew that sign. He was displeased with her in a way that no cajoling would dissipate. He'd made up his mind.

"My lady," he said, his glower matching the sharpness of his tone, "you foolishly involve yourself in matters beyond your ability to comprehend. Do not mistake my motives here. I am indifferent to the fate of servants. One of your women, that handmaiden with the Shenat name, was evidently involved in a sorcerous attempt to influence my decisions through an unnatural artefact from the Va-forsaken Hemisphere."

He reached out to take her by the wrist with his long, bony fingers. As he continued to speak, his hold tightened. "I need to know the truth of this matter, and I will go to any lengths to find it. It is the opinion of my informants that your maid, this Aureen, may know more than she has admitted. She shall be dealt with accordingly. Do not attempt to interfere, or I shall doubt your loyalty." His hold was like a vice, bruising her skin and paining her to the bone. "I have not dismissed the possibility that this was a plot on the part of your father, Edwayn."

That had to be a silly attempt at bluff. "It was not my father who gave you the plumes you now so fear." She could have pointed out the obvious, that it was his own Lowmian trading partner, Uthen Kesleer, but there was no point. Instead, she said, "If it was indeed Sorrel Redwing who stole the plumes – and there is no proof whatever that she was ever in your solar, let alone that she knew or cared about the plumes – then surely she did you a favour!"

They glared at each other and she wondered if they'd just moved into a new phase of their pointless marriage. He had his full faculties back, but perhaps he would never forgive her for having seen him at his most vulnerable.

"True." He lessened his grip slightly. "Which is the only reason I have not taken this any further before now. But my informants press me on this matter, so I will see your maid questioned. After that she will be sent on her way to Throssel."

"As you wish," she said tonelessly and he let go of her. "Why have you not arrested Uthen Kesleer?"

"He says he had no idea of what the plumes could do."

And perhaps he didn't . . . but the real truth is that some men are too powerful and too rich to throw into a dungeon. And you never did tell the Dire Sweepers or anyone else the whole truth about the plumes, did you?

And then she had another thought. None of that worried Regal Vilmar half as much as not knowing who had the plumes now, and what they intended to do with them.

Saker had said he had them, which presumably meant they were now in the hands of the Pontificate, because she couldn't imagine he'd risk stealing them for anyone else. If ever she was in dire trouble herself, perhaps she could use that information to bargain her way out.

The Lord Chancellor stepped up then, with his tiresome wife, and the evening dragged on. She said all the right things, smiled at the right times, but the thoughts inside her head circled, and always they came to the same conclusions.

Aureen had been petrified of the men who had questioned her. Hours afterwards, her face had still been unnaturally white; her hands had still trembled. Her eyes had begged for reassurance, for a promise that she would be safe under Mathilda's protection.

I can't give her that promise.

And they will *come for her.*

"Ouch! Do be careful, Aureen. I do believe you pulled some of my hair out then."

"Oh, forgive me, milady." Aureen, looking suitably contrite, untangled the hairbrush and resumed her brushing.

Mathilda hid a sigh. Her worries had niggled at her all day, like burrs in her stockings, and it was pointless to take it out on Aureen. The truth was that she was still trying to decide what to do.

"Is there something the matter, milady?" Aureen asked. "You seem to have the megrims tonight."

She didn't answer.

"Oh, milady, I'm ever so sorry. I shouldn't pry. But I know Ustgrind is so . . . dismal, and folk here are sometimes solemn enough to sour a jug of beer! And milady's been missing Sorrel. But you have the Prince-regal, the little sweetling. I'd wish I could see more of him, but Lady Friselda says it's not 'propriate for a maid like me to have anything to do with a royal heir, for all that I brought him into the world, the darling wee mite."

"You did not bring him into the world! *I* did. Indeed, Lady Friselda is right. It's not your place, Aureen."

119

"Of course not, milady." She hung her head. "I do forget me place summat terrible. If Your Grace will forgive me impudence, has milady had word from Mistress Sorrel?"

"No," she snapped, and was immediately contrite. "No, I haven't. It is a worry, but nothing you need concern yourself with. In fact, I have news for you – good news, I hope. You are going to return to Ardrone."

"Oh, milady!" She dropped the brush in her surprise, and there was no mistaking the expression of delight on her face. "I dream about it sometimes."

Mathilda stared at her. She was *happy* – happy to leave, knowing she'd be leaving her princess alone, the only Ardronese at court. She thought viciously, *She has no loyalty to me! None! Why should I worry about her?*

Aureen glimpsed her expression then, and hung her head, biting her lip. "Forgive me, milady. I didn't mean that. I'd never leave you, truly. You're me mistress and I'll serve you as long as I'm needed. Here's me place now."

This time Mathilda gave her a long hard stare. How could she trust the woman not to betray her? If the Dire Sweepers beat her, or worse, she'd talk, of course she would! And what, she wondered, would the woman do if she did return safely to Ardrone? Once she was back with friends and family around her, would she think twice about betraying Mathilda by speaking of things that should never be mentioned?

Aureen continued to brush her hair, gently now, with soothing strokes of the brush, but Mathilda's thoughts were dark. She made up her mind, aware she was about to take the first step on a terrible journey. "Oh!" she squealed. "Look, a rat!"

Aureen whirled around to look. "Where?"

"It ran under the cupboard. Oh, I *knew* we had rats! You saw where they chewed my slipper last week." She shuddered.

"I'll call in the rat catchers tomorrow—"

"Ugh! No." She pulled a face in disgust at the thought. "I don't want dirty and smelly ratters in my solar. Go down to the apothecary tomorrow in the bailey. What's her name? Frynster Anna?"

"Frynster Annusel."

"That's right. Ask her for some poison baits. You can lay them in all the corners. But until they are all gone, I want you to sleep on the truckle next to me. Just in case they climb on my bed!"

"Yes, milady. And never fear, I'll tuck in your bed hangings real proper, so not even a midge can enter."

As Mathilda lay in her bed that night, as securely tucked in as Aureen had promised, sleep was still a long time coming.

Abandoned, she thought. *Everyone has abandoned me. Even Sorrel failed me, just like Saker.*

So much time had passed since Sorrel had left with Prince-regal Karel's sister in her arms. In all that time, she'd heard nothing. Nothing of the baby, nothing from Sorrel, nothing from the Pontifect, no word of guidance.

Perhaps Sorrel and the baby had never arrived in Vavala. Perhaps they'd died.

Perhaps it would be better if they had.

No, she mustn't think that. But, oh, it would make things less complicated. Although . . . Maybe not. She needed to know if Karel was a devil-kin or not.

She'd trusted Sorrel, and the woman had let her down. Her tears welled up, and the lump in her throat grew large and painful.

Even Aureen would like to abandon me . . . I'm sure I can't trust her, either.

Well, I'll show them. I'll show them all.

Regal Vilmar called Mathilda to his private retiring room mid-afternoon of the next day, which was unusual. When the servant delivered a message telling her she was to present herself to the Regal in his private chambers, she feared it was to tell her to deliver Aureen to his "agents".

Her one hold over him, her ability to pleasure him, was tenuous at best. She wasn't foolish enough to confuse his delight at her youthful body with love. Vilmar didn't love people; he used them. She must never forget that. Even his pride in his son was not enough to give her real power. He may have been her husband, and she was the mother of his heir, but she still addressed him as "Your Grace" and, tellingly, he'd never requested that she do otherwise.

She hurried downstairs to his solar, to find him alone, which was odd. He was sitting in the most comfortable chair in his retiring room and he indicated the hard straight-backed chair next to him. "Sit here, my dear."

She curtsied deeply, smiled prettily, seated herself and touched his hand where it rested on the arm of the chair in a gesture of fond affection. In truth, she hated the feel of his dry skin, creped with criss-crossed lines, loosely wrinkled over the bones of his knuckles, but nothing of that ever showed on her face.

Saker, I'm glad I have the memory of that night . . .

"I have spoken with the Privy Council," Vilmar said, his dry, quavery tones a match to his desiccated skin, "about procedures to be followed were I to die before Prince-regal Karel reaches his majority."

Relief flooded through her, and she did her best to stop it showing on her face. "Your Grace demonstrates to all that your wisdom and courage is unmatched."

"They have agreed that the Council will make all the decisions, but you will be the one to sign them into law on the behalf of the Prince-regal. He will be proclaimed Regal-apparent by the Privy Council on the day of my death. You follow that so far?"

I'm not a child, you toadspotted, fusty old stick. "Yes, Your Grace."

"On the same day, you will be declared the non-legislative regent. This means you can have no say in law-making, but if you refuse to sign something, it will not become law. That way, you will be able to annul anything that impinges on the integrity of the work of the Dire Sweepers, or anything which would be antithetical to Bengorth's Law. If such a situation were to arise, I suggest you tell the Council you will not sign because Regal Vilmar would not have wanted it. And, of course, you must not let them press you to do otherwise."

"No, Your Grace." She put on her most earnest face. "If this unhappy state of affairs should ever come to pass, I shall continue to serve you and the cause of the Vollendorns, for our son. You can be certain of that." Without allowing her grave expression to slip, she revelled in her internal wave of joy. The muckle-headed man was so sure women were idiots and that she in particular was a ninnyhead, he was giving her a way to paralyse the Privy Council if she cared to do so – never dreaming she would use that power to further her own ends.

He continued, "Each member of the Council has sworn before Va and Prime Mulhafen to uphold this decision and they signed a declaration to that effect. There were some protests, men who felt I should not give such power to any Regala, and least of all one born an Ardronese princess, but they were outvoted. Most were pleased that it would be the Privy Council that governed, and not just the Lord Chancellor, the Lord Treasurer and the Secretary of State, as they had expected."

He gave a self-satisfied smile, and she knew he had played them skilfully, tricking them into voting the way he wanted without them ever realising they'd been cozened.

"When those few protested, I allowed them to make an exception of any laws pertaining to matters of Lowmian relations with other lands." He snorted in contempt. "I reassured them that all that concerns you is the welfare of our son, and this will be all that you wish to protect. In other respects, you will of course be guided by them. In fact, if truth be known, you will never have to challenge them and all will be well."

She nodded and held his hand between hers. "Indeed. I have no wish to involve myself in tiresome affairs of state! Let us pray for Va's grace to grant that you live long enough to see Karel not only grown, but the father of many sons himself, and for me to be spared such matters." She allowed a slight frown to crease her brow. "Although perhaps you ought to tell me which councillors were less than . . . obliging. Just so I know who to be watchful of in the future. What do you think?"

Later, when she returned to her own solar, her mind was seething with plans. She knew now which councillors had not wanted her as regent, but that knowledge was not enough. Growing up in the Ardronese court had taught her much about how power was wielded, and she knew that here she was as weak as a kitten.

I have to know more about the court; I have to know who has secrets, and what those secrets are. The women: I must make more friends among the court ladies. I must have the Lady Friselda on my side.

Inwardly she sighed, knowing that she would have to appear more compliant and sweet-natured to impress the wards-dame.

But for power? Yes, she would do anything, and she had been far too lax up until now. That, she decided, was about to change.

One day I will rule this court and then they'll know that an Ardronese princess is not to be dismissed so lightly.

"I haven't seen no signs of the rat," Aureen said to the maid, Klara, as the two women were folding the Regala's clean linen to put away in the cupboard later that afternoon.

"Did you get the poison baits from Frynster Annusel?"

"Yes. I just put some at the back of the linen chest, under the cupboard likewise, and along the wainscoting, but there's no sign of droppings anywhere. Nary a one."

"I've not smelt them nowhere, neither."

"Just as well, I reckon. Her Grace can be real particular."

Klara smoothed out the petticoat she was holding and began to fold it neatly. "Reckon you're right. She's a snippy one, the Regala."

"And you're an impudent one," Aureen snapped. "Not for us to use language like that when talking about royal folk. Not wise neither. You could find yourself without a place here, nor nowhere."

"Well, you was the one who said she was particular! An' it's true! All this 'bout wanting you to sleep in the truckle bed now? 'Tain't right. If anyone is supposed to sleep in their mistress's chamber, it's the maid. We're supposed to wait on 'em hand and foot, and chambermaids is supposed to look after the bedroom and the bedding and the cleaning and chamber pots and such. And now she tells me I'm to sleep with them kitchen girls, while you have the truckle? What's all that about then?"

"She wants me close by, 'cause she's scared of rats. Leastways, it's never our business why the Regala wants things a certain way. Our place is just to do what she wants."

And that was the truth of it, always. She heaved a sigh and picked up the freshly laundered pile of linen to put away in the drawer of the wardrobe.

That night, long after midnight, Aureen woke. Unused to her new bed, she was disoriented and not sure where she was. Her sleep-stupefied mind struggled to make sense of her surroundings and the voice that was calling her.

Princess Mathilda.

She scrambled out of the truckle bed, her bare feet hitting the cold of the floorboards before she remembered why she was there in the bedchamber. "Milady?"

"Bring me my robe, quickly. I heard something."

The tiny flame from the night lamp was sufficient for her to find the woollen wrap draped over the bedpost. She held it open so that Mathilda could slide out from between the bed-drapes straight into its warmth.

"The rat, mayhap?" Aureen asked, her wits still befuddled.

"No, something much noisier. Not in the bedroom. Out there." She waved one hand at the door that led into the rest of her solar. Her other hand seized Aureen by the wrist, her clutch as cold as ice. "Light a candle, quickly."

"Milady, why don't you climb back into bed? You'll catch your death of cold. I'll go look." The Regala pushed her away with an unprincess-like snort. "I'm not delicate! Light the candle." She was already fitting her feet into the slippers beside her bed as she spoke. "I want to see what that noise was."

Aureen removed a candle from the candelabrum and lit it from the night lamp. "Milady, perhaps you should stay here and let me get the guard."

Regala Mathilda was scornful. "I'm not so moonish as to be scared of a noise."

Without another word, she opened the bedroom door and walked through into her drawing room. Aureen peered around her shoulder, but could see little. The fire in that room had long since died out.

"I think I can hear something in the retiring room," Mathilda said in a whisper. "You go first with the candle."

"Milady—"

"Go!"

She couldn't hear anything at all, but she obliged, almost certain it was all the Regala's imagination. Holding the candle high, she crossed the threshold, and saw one of the windows was open.

"How odd," she said. "I'm sure it was closed this evening. What witless dunce would open the window on a wet night like this? That's what you could hear, milady. The window banging in the wind!"

"Very likely. That's a relief! Here, give me the candle. You close the casement."

The window had swung fully open, and now banged against the outer stone wall. This side of the keep overlooked the castle bailey, so the walls were not as thick here, but even so, Aureen had to balance herself on the wide stone sill as she reached for the window catch. Her feet left the floor and she laughed as the wind whipped her hair every which way.

She felt Mathilda grip her ankles and wondered at her bothering to do such a thing, for she was in no danger. The sill was broad and most of her body was still inside the room. She had a brief moment of puzzlement.

When she realised her legs were being lifted, not steadied, but lifted higher and higher, she wasted a moment in disbelief. Princess Mathilda was teasing her? Then she shrieked, first in shock, and then in utter terror. Mathilda was pushing her legs, sliding her across the sill. She half turned, scrabbled at the inner side of the window ledge, tearing her skin.

Even then, she thought it accidental.

"Milady!" It was a cry for help, crying out to her mistress in her extremity. Her nails ripped and tore as she tried to dig them into the stonework, in vain.

Even in the brief whisper of time left to her as she fell the four storeys to the grassed inner bailey, she failed utterly to accept the notion that Mathilda had murdered her.

Mathilda leaned back against the wall, listening.

There was nothing to hear. No alarm from the courtyard of the bailey, nothing from inside the castle.

I'm sorry, Aureen. But they would have tortured you . . .

She closed her eyes and swallowed back the bile in her mouth. *I had to do it to keep Karel safe. I didn't have a choice.*

I'm sorry . . .

14

The Pontifect's Envoys

Prime Mulhafen was an elderly, cadaverous man and, Gerelda decided, about as different from Prime Fox as it was possible to be. His clothing was austere, he wore no jewellery apart from the symbol of the Way of the Flow, and, as she glanced around his office in the Ustgrind Faith House, she decided its lack of comforts must be a statement in praise of frugal living.

Fortunately, she and Peregrine had dressed in the Lowmian style, in plain garments of grey and white. Peregrine wore the black hat of a Lowmian burgher's son, while she'd elected to wear the neat white cap more normally seen on a well-to-do burgher's wife than a lawyer. She didn't mind; she had grown up wearing such dull clothing. In fact, she still preferred it to the overly coloured and ornate fashion of Ardrone. What she didn't like was the idea that it was not a matter of preference, but of proscription.

That thought caused her an inward smile at the irony. *I'm a lawyer,* she thought, *and we are supposed to prefer things to be orderly and planned and regulated.* The unwritten rules of convention dictating that a woman must wear skirts annoyed her intensely, nonetheless.

Right then, wearing a dark grey dress, she stood in front of Prime Mulhafen's desk, hands clasped behind her back, with Peregrine two steps behind and to her right.

Like being back at school . . .

The Prime was reading the letter she had brought him from Fritillary Reedling. Judging by the expression on his face, the contents were not pleasing him. He'd already read through the two pages once and was now perusing them a second time. When he finally raised his gaze to look at her, his eyes were troubled.

"The Pontifect informs me that I should give you every aid in your

127

research, and that I should see to it that you are admitted, with this lad here, to a private audience with Regala Mathilda. Yet it is hardly within my purview to dictate the granting of such an audience."

"I am sure that the Pontifect knows that, your eminence. This is a matter of considerable delicacy, you understand, between the Pontifect and Regala Mathilda. For this reason, she also entrusted me with another missive which I have here. This sealed letter is to be given into the hand of the Regala personally, by you. Once the Regala has read its contents, the Pontifect feels confident Master Peregrine Clary and I will be granted an audience." Gerelda held out the letter.

The Prime inclined his head as he took it from her. "Yes, her reverence says as much to me." He placed the letter on his desk, squaring it neatly to line up with other documents there. "I shall inform you of what happens. As for your historical research . . ." He shook his head dolefully. "We have an extensive library here, but it mostly concerns religious history and study. You're welcome to read whatever you will. It's a shame the Institute of Advanced Studies was burned down after the Horned Death struck. That library would have been of much more help to you."

He stood, indicating the interview was coming to an end. "The Pontifect has asked that you be lodged here at Faith House. I will have you shown to your rooms. It could be several days before I have an opportunity to pass your letter to the Regala Mathilda."

"Of course," she said, standing up. "I'm so obliged for your time, your eminence. Terrible disaster, the burning of a library, though, wasn't it? Documents are so irreplaceable. What happened?"

"The Dire Sweepers happened," he snapped. He caught himself and softened his next words. "It is their custom to burn any building which has had the Horned Death within. If the situation allows for it. Stops the spread of the disease, I believe."

A few minutes later, she and Peregrine were alone, looking around their spartan cells in the staff quarters. "Hardly luxurious," she remarked.

"Be looking good to me," Peregrine replied. "It's got a bed for a start and I reckon the roof won't leak. "'Sides, a hot bath every five nights sounds good. But Agent Gerelda, I still don't understand why we're here. I'd be of more use staying in Vavala and warning the Pontifect every time one of them pitch-men popped up his rotten head—"

"I think perhaps the Pontifect can look after herself."

"So why does she want me to see the Regala of Lowmeer?"

Gerelda waved a hand at the bed. "Sit down, Perie. It really is time for you and me to have a talk about everything. But let me explain something first. The Pontifect has not told me the whole truth. So don't blame me later on if you find out you only know a little bit of what's going on, all right?"

He nodded. "My da used to say that you should never be telling anybody everything."

"Maybe." *But damn Fritillary anyway. I hate being hamstrung by ignorance.* "Anyway, we're going to meet the Regala Mathilda because she asked for help from the Pontifect. She is worried about Prince-regal Karel. She thinks he might have been contaminated by A'Va at birth, that he was born a so-called devil-kin."

He stared at her, his eyes widening. "What's that?"

"It's a Lowmian thing. The Pontifect thinks a devil-kin contamination might be the same thing, or similar to, what pitch-men have."

He looked at her blankly. "I thought we had a fret 'bout Prime Fox having summat to do with the pitch-men. Now you be saying A'Va gives the pitch to babies? You think maybe Prime Fox is working for A'Va?"

"Possibly."

He shook his head. "No."

"Why not?"

"Because Fox would never work for someone. He *is* the pitch pit. I *told* you that. He be not at all like the folk who killed my da."

"Look, all you have to do is take a look at the Prince-regal and tell us what you see, if anything. We want to know if we need to worry about him. It wouldn't be good for anyone if there was a devil-kin, or a pitch-man, on the throne of Lowmeer one day."

"I can do that much."

"One other thing. There's another kind of black smudge too, only visible to us ordinary folk when someone marked with it steps under the protection of a shrine oak. Wicked people leave that mark on their enemies as a warning to their fellow evil-makers. You must be careful you don't confuse that kind of smutch with pitch-men."

He was offended. "I'm not that daft."

"Good. We will have to wait a couple of days for the appointment. In the meantime, I'll be working in the library, looking into the history of the Fox family and the Regal's family. What would you like to do?"

"Can I go out into the city?" he asked, his eagerness to be gone from Faith House obvious.

After considerable cajoling on his part, Peregrine was on his way out when he saw Prime Mulhafen coming the opposite way.

"Where are you going?" the Prime asked, smiling slightly. "No, silly question; you're going out into the city, as any small boy would do if given the chance."

"Yes." His voice sounded childish to his ears, but in his head he denied the idea of being young. His boyhood seemed distant and fleeting, as if it had once been no more than chalk marks on a slate, wiped away by the pitch-men who had murdered his da.

"I wanted to chat with you." Mulhafen was still smiling, but the smile looked uncomfortable. "Tell me, Peregrine, what is your witchery?"

He was about to reply, when he remembered neither he nor Gerelda had told the Prime he had a witchery. It was possible the Pontifect had mentioned it in her letter, but he'd had the impression that she'd not said much at all. "Boys of my age," he said neutrally, "don't get gifted witcheries."

"I can see you have one."

That shook him. He said carefully, "To see a witchery, you must have a witchery." *And you don't have one.*

The Prime smiled, but this time there was something heart-rending in the way he was forcing his lips to curve upwards. "You are right of course; I don't have a witchery. Nonetheless, I have the ability to see that you do. You see, Peregrine, I once had a witchery too. I had it taken away from me. Vanished, far more easily than I earned it."

Peregrine was speechless. He had no idea what he could possibly say to that.

"You do know that can happen, don't you?"

He nodded.

"I knew too. But I was young. I didn't realise that you can lose a witchery, not just for misusing it in a bad way, but for *not* using it in a good way when you should. Youth understands very little."

Probably that's because too few adults ever explain things properly.

"Will you tell me what your witchery is?"

Peregrine shook his head.

"Ah, perhaps you are wise. Be on your way." There was such sadness in that old man's tone that Perie wanted to apologise, but Mulhafen had already nodded and walked away.

Peregrine sighed. He might not have been a boy any longer, but he wasn't grown either. Sometimes it was so hard to guess what went on in the heads of adults.

Princess Mathilda sat in her retiring room with several of her ladies-in-waiting. She was supposed to be delving into the book on her lap, entitled *The Small Compendium of Court Etiquette*, but she was gazing out of the window instead. When her ladies tried to talk to her, she waved the book at them, and bent her head over the pages, but the words remained unread.

She had pushed Aureen through that very window to her death. No one had questioned the supposed suicide; no one had pretended concern. She'd got away with murder.

But she hadn't, not really. Guilt sat on her shoulder, all the time, digging its claws into her bones. All she had to do was glance out that window beside her. One glance, and the claws tightened.

Strange – at first the murder really hadn't bothered her that much; she'd done it for little Karel, after all. Like Sorrel. Sorrel had murdered her husband in revenge for her daughter, hadn't she? Anyway, it was all Sorrel's fault that Aureen's death was necessary. Or maybe the Pontifect's fault. If Sorrel had gone to the Pontifect immediately, as she'd been bidden, and the Pontifect had come to counsel her, none of this would have happened. She was the Regala and an Ardronese princess – and no one had come to help her in this dilemma. No one!

Guilt had crept up on her and now it wouldn't go away. Then there was the stupid irony of it all, prodding at her, not letting her forget what she had done, reminding her with a truth: she *missed* Aureen.

The woman had been no more than a servant, but she'd been a link to Ardrone, to her previous life. Aureen's knowledge might have been a danger, but killing her meant that Mathilda had rid herself of the one person who understood her situation. Her secret was safe, but her death left a hollow inside.

I'll never forgive you, Vilmar Vollendorn, for making what I did necessary. Never. You'll pay for it, I swear.

She waited until her ladies were all chattering at the other end of the room, exclaiming over some newly completed embroidery, then drew out the Pontifect's letter, which Prime Mulhafen had given her the previous day. She'd read it several times already, but was still puzzled. At first, she'd assumed it would be confirmation that Sorrel had reached Vavala, but that wasn't the case.

In fact, the Pontifect intimated that neither Sorrel nor the baby had arrived, although the information was vaguely worded. The letter then continued, "Do not be alarmed, Your Grace; the woman and her child are under the care of a reliable cleric, who has their best interests at heart." So, if they hadn't reached Vavala, where in all of Va's creation were they, and how did the Pontifect even *know* about them? Infuriatingly, there was no explanation.

The rest of the letter said two people – Gerelda Brantheld and Peregrine Clary – had been sent to her, and would she grant them a private audience. Neither of the names meant anything to her. She sighed, realising she'd been naive to think the Pontifect might make a trip to Ustgrind herself, even though the reason was of paramount importance, but it was some added information from Prime Mulhafen that had truly shocked her. He hadn't any knowledge of why the Pontifect had sent anyone, and he'd casually mentioned that one of her emissaries was merely a young lad.

That, she didn't understand at all.

Surely, surely the Pontifect had not told a mere *lad* that the Regala of Lowmeer had given birth to twins and one of the babies had been spirited away? By all that was oak holy, her life – and Karel's – was forfeit if *anyone* in Lowmeer learned the truth! She'd asked Sorrel to take the other twin to the Pontifect, wanting help and advice. She'd wanted to be told that there was no such thing as devil-kin; she wanted to be praised for her courage; she *needed* to be told that all was well and her secret would never be known to anyone who would ever utter even a hint of it.

A *lad*? Had the Pontifect lost her wits?

A shiver went up her spine. How many times had that horrible dream returned? *Red-eyed crows on the traitor's wheel stabbing at her eyes . . . Dearest Va, anything but that.*

Please, oh please.

Just then Lady Lotte, the boldest of her younger ladies-in-waiting, approached her, saying, "Whatever can the Prime have said to make you reread it, Your Grace?" she asked. "Is his note so obscure?"

She raised her gaze and gave Lotte a hard stare. "You can be very silly, Lotte. This is not from the Prime. It is a letter from the Pontifect, informing me she has sent an emissary. Doubtless merely a courtesy, to deliver blessings for the good health of the heir. I am giving them an audience tomorrow."

Her heart raced at the thought, but she was confident no agitation showed on her face. At hiding her feelings she was now an expert.

15

An Heir Under Scrutiny

When the herald announced that the Pontifect's emissaries were on the way to her solar, Mathilda seated herself on the Regala's chair in the reception room and bade the nursemaid to place Karel's cradle at her side. The ladies-in-waiting in attendance – ten of the chattering flock that morning – gathered around, brightly curious and ready to sharpen their relentless tongues on any breach of protocol.

Ward's-dame Friselda, the pesky woman, was the first. "Your Grace," she'd said in her most imperious tone, "should the babe be here when you are expecting the arrival of strangers? Who knows what pestilence they bring clinging to their clothing? Who knows what noxious streets they have walked down?"

If Friselda hadn't been the Regal's trusted cousin, she would have flung the wretched woman into those same noxious streets. "Surely you are not saying that the Pontifect of Va-faith is so indifferent to our well-being that she would send someone unclean into our royal presence, Lady Friselda? Perhaps you should mention such concerns to my dear husband."

Friselda, puffed up like a pigeon, glared, but it was all posturing for she said nothing more. Doubtless, though, she would carry some tale or other to the Regal later.

The guards in the gallery flung open the door and the herald announced the two envoys. "Proctor Gerelda Brantheld, Agent to the Pontifect of Va-faith, and her attendant, Master Peregrine Clary!"

Silence fell, almost a funereal hush, as the two walked forward to face her. Dear oak, what an unprepossessing couple! The woman was too tall to be fashionable, and although her face was attractive enough, she was too broad across the shoulders to be feminine. Besides, she strode into the room like a man. The lad was clumsy and coarse, wearing a sullen expression. They wore Lowmian clothing, but she had expected their garments to have been made of fine linen as befitted envoys, not ugly broadcloth more suitable for tradesmen.

Brantheld curtsied in a perfunctory, graceless fashion and the lad belatedly attempted a bow.

"Come forward," Mathilda commanded, "where I may see you better." Her heart was beating so fast, she wondered if they would hear it. Who were these people into whose hands the Pontifect had put her life – and that of her son? Commoners, surely. Not even clerics!

The woman came closer and Peregrine followed her lead. "Your Grace," she said, "we are honoured to be granted this audience."

Mathilda nodded, then she turned her attention back to her ladies, saying, "Leave us alone. You may all await my pleasure in the retiring-room."

The ladies-in-waiting obeyed, but the ward's-dame did not budge and the nursemaid moved towards the cradle. Mathilda glared at them both, asking, "Did I suggest you take the Prince-regal with you, nurse? Leave him be. And you, Lady Friselda: this visitor has come from the Pontifect with spiritual guidance for me, as mother of the Prince-regal. You may safely leave us alone." She glanced back then at Peregrine. "Although perhaps it would be best if my ladies were to entertain this young man." She nodded at Peregrine.

He shot a look of entreaty at his companion, but she jerked her head at the door. Lady Friselda inflated her chest and hesitated as if she were about to argue. If so, she then thought better of it and beckoned to the lad. "Come this way, boy." Without looking behind to see if he followed, she sailed from the room.

"So," asked Princess Mathilda after they'd gone, "come sit here next to me so that we can be truly private." She waited until the woman had obeyed before adding, "Gerelda Brantheld. What message is it that the Pontifect has sent to me through a *lawyer*?"

"Your Grace, my designation is irrelevant. I am a trusted agent of the Pontifect of some years' standing. Whatever secrets exist are safe with me, now and in the future. After all, I am – as you emphasise – a lawyer."

"And can you say the same for a boy scarcely out of a suckling's smock?" The very thought sent terror coursing through her veins.

"Your Grace, I would trust the lad with my life. Indeed, I have done so. He is no ordinary child, and against all that is normal, he possesses a witchery. However, he knows nothing of twins. If you had not dismissed him, I would have done so. He is not privy to such matters."

She took a deep breath, partially mollified. Perhaps she was safe yet. Perhaps she would survive. Perhaps there was no traitor's wheel in her future. Still, she wanted explanations. She said, the steel in her voice intentional, "I sent word to the Pontifect immediately after my travail; what has taken her so long to send you to speak to me? Were my affairs not thought to be urgent? Perhaps the Pontifect should have come herself instead of sending her lackey. Did she not realise what is at stake here?"

"Your Grace, I am sure she did. Does. But it is no easier for a Pontifect to leave the seat of her power than it is for you to leave yours. In truth, without an invitation from the Regal, it would be impossible for her even to set foot in Lowmeer."

"So what took you so long?"

"Sorrel Redwing and your daughter did not arrive in Vavala. The Pontifect knew nothing of your predicament until recently. It's my understanding that Mistress Redwing was being hunted, and her one avenue of escape was a ship. Unfortunately, the ship was on its way to Karradar. She is not yet returned."

Her consternation burgeoned. "*Karradar*? But that is almost in the Summer Seas, surely! This is rattle-brained nonsense. How could you even know she was on board? And my daughter . . ." Incredulous, her thoughts churning, she stared at Gerelda. She clutched the arms of her chair tightly, thinking she was going to faint. For almost the first time, she felt something for the girl she had given birth to, for the baby she had sent away with such desperation. "Did . . . does my child have a wet nurse, then?"

"I imagine so, Your Grace, for she was alive and well, several sennights into the journey. She is accompanied by a witan who cares for them both. It was he who managed to send a message to the Pontifect."

"A witan?" Her bewilderment suddenly doubled. The only witan Sorrel had contact with before she'd left the castle that night was Saker. "You – you can't mean Saker Rampion!"

The expression on the lawyer's face told her she was right. "Is this a jest? *Rampion*?"

Confused memories of that dreadful night she had given birth tumbled through her mind. Saker, inexplicably, had been there in the castle the night before. And if her memory served her truly, he had indicated he knew she was going to have twins. She should have demanded more answers of Sorrel, but her travail had been upon her, and nothing else seemed to matter. She and Sorrel and Aureen had been so scared . . .

Sweet acorns, what if Saker hates me? Va knows, he has reason and he knows too much about me.

Gerelda Brantheld was looking at her blankly. "Jest? No one is jesting in this matter, I assure you. Unfortunately, the Pontifect has not been able to examine the child, to see if there is aught ailing her by virtue of being a Lowmian-born twin."

Mathilda shook her head in disbelief. "You haven't explained how it is possible to send a message from the middle of the ocean. Do you think I am that gullible?"

"Apparently Witan Rampion has a witchery that involves birds. A written message was delivered by a bird."

"Saker has no witchery!"

"Your Grace, he was chained to a shrine oak tree on freezing high-country moors and survived. He now has a witchery."

She closed her eyes, trying to halt the tears that threatened. Oh, Va, how tangled the threads were becoming.

"Your Grace, the Pontifect's primary concern is the welfare of the Prince-regal. If there is a problem, it should be identified as soon as possible. This is why she sent Peregrine Clary with me. He has the ability to tell if Prince-regal Karel has any, er, issues that need the Pontifect's immediate attention."

She tried to clamp down on her emotions, but doubted that she was able to stop the horror she felt from showing on her face. "This – this *commoner* boy is going to tell me if the Prince-regal is a devil-kin?"

"Not – not exactly. All he will be able to see is whether Prince-regal Karel has been touched by something . . . corrupted. If there is no sign of such, then the Pontifect suggests checking again in a few years' time, just to make sure."

"And if he is, as you put it, *corrupted*?"

"The Prince-regal will grow up a perfectly normal child for about twelve years, possibly more. During that time, the Pontifect will find a way to cure him so the corruption never manifests itself. You have her promise on that."

"How does she know all this?"

"After he left Ardrone, Witan Rampion, together with some Lowmian clerics, was working on the matter of devil-kin and twin births here in Lowmeer."

She leaned back against her chair. A reprieve. If this woman was telling the truth. "Did the Pontifect give you a letter for me?"

"She did not dare to write down her advice in case the letter fell into the wrong hands. She told me to emphasise that Your Grace is not alone and that she will pursue this matter to a satisfactory conclusion for everyone concerned. For *both* your children and yourself. She also said you must put your trust in Va and the Way of the Oak or the Flow. There will be a solution."

"Perhaps," she said, losing her composure, "she should explain to me why Va allowed this – this abomination of devil-twins to occur in the first place."

"I am not a cleric, Your Grace. That is a question for a person who has studied such things. For now, what the Pontifect recommends is that you allow Peregrine to look at your son. Depending on what he finds, the Pontifect will make decisions."

"My daughter – is she to be examined by this Peregrine too?"

"When she returns to the Va-cherished Hemisphere, certainly."

"But only one of them will be this . . . this—" But she couldn't continue.

"We don't really know. I'm sorry, Your Grace, that we can't give you a more definitive answer at this time. The Pontifect has asked me to investigate the history of this whole question of Lowmian twins and devil-kin. That is the second reason that I was chosen for this job. I have already spent some time perusing documents kept inside Faith House. I didn't find much that was useful. The librarian did tell me that there are more books and papers and scrolls here in the castle library. I was wondering if it might be possible for me to have access to them. The Pontifect feels that answers may be found in Lowmian history."

Lowmian history.

Appalled, Mathilda froze. Sorrel knew about Bengorth's Law, of course; she'd been there when the Regal had informed her about the whole horrible deal between the first of the Vollendorns and A'Va. Sorrel was supposed to tell the Pontifect, but she hadn't yet met the Pontifect. She might have told Saker though, and he might have written it in the message to the Pontifect. Words committed to paper could damn her to the chopping block or the torture chamber. She tried to swallow back her growing terror.

So, the Pontifect might already know, but would she have told this woman about it?

Is that what this canker-worm of a female wants to research? Sweet Va, if the Regal ever finds out I told anyone, I'm dead, broken on a wheel and left for the birds to peck out my eyes.

"What else did the Pontifect tell you?"

Gerelda frowned slightly, as if the question puzzled her. "Is there something else I should know about, Your Grace?" she asked. "If we can pinpoint just how it happens, this process of subverting a twin into a devil-kin, perhaps we'll understand how to cure it."

"A cure." Her voice whispered oddly, like the steel of a blade drawn from a scabbard. *A cure for Bengorth's Law? Or just for a devil-kin baby?* She didn't dare ask.

"The Pontifect believes all things are possible in Va's name," Gerelda said, meeting her gaze without flinching.

"I'm not sure I know what a devil-kin is." She chose her words carefully. "I mean, people gossip. But really all they say is that devil-kin serve A'Va. How?"

"To separate the folk tales from the reality is one purpose of my research. One of the few things we know for a fact is that when twins are separated at birth, one of them, sometimes both of them, appear to be perfectly normal all their lives. The other often dies of the Horned Death, and possibly seeds those around him – his family, his village, his street in the town – with the same plague when he or she reaches the age of twelve or thereabouts. Unfortunately, a lot of the research evidence disappeared when the Institute of Advanced Studies was burned."

She looked down at Karel. *Twelve years . . . No, no. It's not you, is it? It's her. The girl . . . It must be.* "Was there no further message from the Pontifect?" she asked, glad to hear how calm she sounded.

"She told me to say that any transactions with A'Va are anathema to her. She believes your courage is unparalleled, and you will triumph because Va is on your side. Your line will continue, and she offers every support."

Va rot you! Did you just tell me the Pontifect has suspicions about who fathered the Prince-regal? She sat back, her fingers drumming on the padded arm of her chair as she breathed in, dragging air deep to keep her agitation from showing. *Don't be such a dewberry, Mathilda. Of course the Pontifect knows about Saker.* Fox would have told her, even if Saker hadn't – a pox on that whoreson of a Prime.

"And you want me to arrange for you to work in the castle library," she said, her voice level.

"Actually, Prime Mulhafen has applied to the castle librarian on my behalf. We are awaiting his reply. If you feel your support would help—"

"I doubt it. What reason did you give for this research?"

Gerelda gave her the faintest of smiles. "We are approaching the four hundredth anniversary of the ascent of the first Vollendorn to the Basalt throne. The Pontifect suggested that there be a celebration throughout the pontificate in honour of the Vollendorn line and their pious support of Va-faith and the Way of the Flow through the centuries. Officially, my job will be to look at the history of the Basalt Throne in order to select the highlights for celebration."

"I see." She shrugged, as if she were only half-convinced. "If Prime Mulhafen doesn't obtain consent, I will broach the matter with the Regal."

"Thank you. Now, with your permission, shall I fetch Peregrine?"

Peregrine looked around the room full of women, appalled. He felt as clumsy and as unattractive as a turnip in a bowl of perfumed roses. The ladies-in-waiting clustered around him, wanting to know who he was, why he was there, where he came from, and everything else about him and Gerelda. His hands and feet were suddenly larger than normal. He stumbled over the leg of a chair, only saving himself by grabbing the nearest of the ladies by the elbow. A flush of heat rose from his neck to his cheeks.

At a loss about what to say, knowing he mustn't betray any secrets, he stuttered and stammered over noncommittal answers. He thought he detected disapproval and suspicion.

The aroma of the room overwhelmed him; not of the perfumes, but of scents he did not recognise. Tangy smells, pleasant but not sweet. When he glimpsed a lady with a pomander dangling from her wrist, he knew he was smelling spices that supposedly prevented the plague.

Still they hounded him with questions. "You've come from the Pontifect?"

"You're not Lowmian, are you?"

"Where do you come from?"

"Why did the Pontifect send a boy like you here?"

Flustered, he said, "I was born in Sistia."

The old lady stepped forward then. "Leave the lad alone! Where are all your manners, plaguing him so?"

The other women quietened in deference to her and he breathed a sigh of relief, thinking the interrogation would stop. He was wrong. The old lady was more subtle, but just as probing. Worse, he had the idea her interest was not just curiosity. She was suspicious. Tongue-tied, in the end he said nothing at all.

When he finally heard Gerelda's voice from the doorway asking for his presence, he bolted to her side and happily shut the door behind him as he left the room.

"We want you to give your attention to the baby in the cradle," Gerelda said, "and tell us what your witchery feels."

This was the moment he'd been dreading. Ever since he had entered the castle, he'd deliberately blocked his witchery from his thoughts, determined to feel nothing of the black smutch, even if it was there, until he was asked.

She led him forward to the crib and he looked down at the sleeping child wrapped in soft wool blankets and lace, fabrics so delicate and beautiful he felt it would have been sacrilege to touch them. He lowered all his barriers and reached out with his witchery sense.

For a sliver of time, this was just a baby, smelling of milk and lavender, the picture of contentment. Then he felt it, the tendril of contamination, of foulness. It was the most delicate of touches, nothing

141

comparable to the foul heat of pitch-men, or to the deep darkness of Valerian Fox. This was just the merest breath of pitch, the softest of hints that all was not well. For one horrible moment, he was aware of a slurring, a warping, a twisting of innocence, and then it was gone. The child was just a baby, nothing more.

He drew in a shuddering breath.

"Well?" the Regala snapped. "What do you see?"

He shot a desperate glance at Gerelda.

"The truth, Perie," she said.

"There – there is s-s-something. Something not right. A touch of pitch buried deep, not yet awoken. B-b-but it is there. I am sorry, Your Grace."

For a moment he thought the Regala might faint. She gripped the edge of the cradle tightly, her eyes closed. Then she snapped them open and her gaze switched from him to Gerelda and back again, a look filled with terrible rage.

He took a step back. Gerelda clutched his shoulder in warning.

"Is he one of the devil-kin?" the Regala asked.

He quailed before her. "I d-don't know anything about devil-kin. I've never met one. All I can say is that he has a shadow within him. B-b-but right now, he's just a baby."

For a long moment, no one spoke. He held his breath, waiting . . . for what? He wasn't sure.

The Regala's grip on the cradle had slackened, but there was nothing relaxed about her. She stood, deep in thought for several minutes and neither of them was brave enough to interrupt her thoughts.

When she did straighten and stand back from the cradle, her eyes glittered with an intensity he found unsettling. Regala Mathilda may have been young, but when he looked at her he was afraid.

She said, switching her penetrating gaze from one to the other, "You hold the safety of my son, the security of the heir of the Basalt Throne in your keeping. One careless word from either of you could mean his death. So there is one thing I wish you to know: if my son suffers because you tell the wrong person or people of what you have seen or heard here today, I personally will see to it that you are locked in a cell under the ground with the rats, in the dark, for the rest of your lives. That is my promise to both of you."

The coldness with which she spoke sent shivers down his spine. She meant every word.

She continued, "Agent Gerelda, I will see to it that you have whatever you require to help you. You must be careful. If anyone suspects the kind of research you are doing, they may wonder about things that are better not wondered about. Do you understand me? The librarian answers not to me, but to the Regal and his advisers. So remember what I said. And believe me when I say I will stop at nothing when it comes to the welfare of my son. *Nothing*." She switched her gaze from Gerelda to Peregrine. "Remember my promise. I can make you regret the day you were born."

Peregrine only just managed to stop himself from shivering.

16

Breaking the Spell

Captain Lustgrader, seated at his desk in his cabin, sighed and turned his head to stare out of the stern window that ran lengthwise above his bunk. The view included the Regal's galleon, *Sentinel*, anchored on a sea as flat as bathwater.

That afternoon, the winds had been contrary as the ships beat their way through the scattered outer islands, the so-called Calves of Karradar, only to drop away to nothing once the fleet slipped into the leeward shelter of the largest of these islands. The sudden calm had ensured that none had reached the port anchorage closer to the shore. Four of the ships, including the galleon with its array of cannon, now rode at anchor several miles short of Port Karradar on the main island, Bull Karradar. The fifth ship, the ageing carrack *Spice Dragon*, was out of sight, doubtless becalmed somewhere among the Calves.

The first time Lustgrader had come to Karradar, he'd thought the islands had been named after cattle. Now he knew better; they referred to the basking bull seals and their offspring strewn like sea-washed boulders along the islands' many beaches.

As he gazed outwards, seabirds skimmed by, hunting scraps. A diverse array of boats clustered around the stern of *Sentinel* with all the busyness of water beetles on a pond. Lustgrader pursed his lips in distaste. *Leprous lot of scum, trying to sell their cloyingly syrupy fruit and their poxy light-skirt women.* Va, how he hated foreign ports! He heaved a sigh, knowing that keeping sailors away from such evils was a well-nigh useless endeavour.

In the morning, if there was a wind, he would signal for the pilot to come and guide all of them into a safer port anchorage. Once there, he would organise the revictualling of the fleet and some shore leave for the crews. No captain could keep seamen on board when there were grog houses and brothels and gambling dens within sight. Port Karradar was lawless and Va-less and far too foreign for his liking, full of Pashalin traders, lascar seamen and Ardronese pirates. The lookout had already told him there was at least one Ardronese ship at anchor. Va grant that it didn't belong to that bastard privateer Lord Juster Dornbeck, that botch of nature, with his fancy clothes and flamboyance.

He glanced down at the desk again, where the bambu lay, corked and sealed. It had been four days since he'd opened it, an effort of will that had kept him on his knees in prayer for hours each day. He shuddered just recalling how he'd had to wrestle his addiction to arrive at this small amount of detachment. He bit down on his lip, hard, until blood ran down his chin. He revelled in the pain. It gave him back his independence, his rationality.

It's time. I have to get rid of this poison. I can do it now. I must.

It would be easier once the plume was not on the ship any more, and – if he was correct in his logic – he'd worked out just how to rid himself of its compulsion altogether.

You wait, Reed Heron. My revenge on you and that whore and her baby is about to begin. You're a dead man. You'll rue the day you came on board my ship.

"Mynster Bachold!" he called.

By the time the young seaman on duty outside his door entered, Lustgrader had composed himself and was reaching for his hat. "Mynster Bachold, tell the bo'sun to ready the pinnace. I wish to visit *Sentinel*. Ask Mynster Tolbun to run up the signal flags."

"Aye, aye, sir."

With the bambu wrapped in a piece of canvas tucked under one arm and the Regal's letter in his hand, he made his way up on to the main deck. The sun was already low to the horizon, yet it was still sweltering hot. He ran a finger around his wilting starched collar, feeling the discomfort of the humidity. Midden heap of a place; he couldn't wait to leave.

While the seamen prepared the pinnace for launching, he looked to see if Reed Heron was on deck. Just thinking of the man made his heart beat faster and his stomach lurch queasily. Who was he, this factor, that he used such Va-forsaken sorcery? He ought to have had the man keel-raked or have ordered him thrown overboard en route to Karradar; instead he obeyed Heron like an obedient hound fawning before its master.

The man wasn't on deck, thank Va. He breathed a little easier and groped for his kerchief to mop his forehead. Pain in his chest nagged at him, begging him to stay on board the boat. One part of him wanted to think about the Va-forsaken feather, the same part that desperately wanted to look at it again, to stroke its colours . . .

He forced himself instead to watch the signal flags being hoisted up the mast of *Sentinel*, acceding to his request to come aboard. When the pinnace was ready, he climbed down the pilot steps so he could be rowed across a glassy sea to the escort galleon, the bambu a lead weight under his arm.

Once on board the Regal's ship, he pried his thoughts from the plume and focused instead on climbing on to the deck, on greeting Captain Russmon, on being escorted to the captain's cabin, on accepting a tot of banana brandy, freshly bought from a bumboat.

With the conversational preliminaries out of the way, Russmon remarked, "I have the cook working on this evening's meal, using some local fresh victuals. Would the Commander honour me by agreeing to grace our wardroom for dinner?"

"It would be my pleasure to try the culinary skills of someone other than my present cook. Most uninspired fellow; everything he cooks tastes the same. However, cadging a meal was not my purpose. I have more serious matters that need some discussion. Did you, by any chance, have a communication from His Grace, the Regal, just before we sailed from Ustgrind? Concerning the procurement of feathers of paradise birds?"

"As a matter of fact, yes. I found the subject puzzling, because I wouldn't have thought they were more valuable than spices, yet that is what the letter seems to imply."

"Ours is not to question."

"No, of course not. I would not presume to do so."

Lustgrader held up the bambu, still wrapped in canvas. "That letter put me in a position of some embarrassment, because I already had such a plume in my possession. It was given to me by a factor of the Company. Of course, I did not read His Grace's letter until we had already sailed. I have decided it is best that I give this feather into your keeping, as it now belongs to the Basalt Throne. By relinquishing it to you as the Regal's representative in this fleet, I hope to make it quite clear that I no longer make any claim to the ownership of this plume. Just to avoid any awkwardness, you understand. Would you please accept it in the name of the Regal and thereby witness that it is no longer my property?"

As he spoke, crunching pain spasmed inside his ribcage. He closed his eyes momentarily and swallowed, trying not to scream. Sickening grief engulfed him, as he pushed the bambu into Russmon's hands.

I am doing the right thing. I have to get rid of what has been eating my soul. I reject this foulness. It's not mine any more. I pass it to my sovereign Lord.

"Commander, are you all right?"

Russmon's anxious voice came from a distance, barely audible to his ears.

"Dyspepsia," he muttered in reply. "Gives me problems sometimes. Fusty shipboard food, you know."

Russmon clicked his tongue in sympathy. "Ah, indeed, I do know. Never mind, fresh food tonight. And as for this feather, it would be an honour to ensure its safekeeping." He frowned slightly before adding, "However, *Sentinel* is a fighting ship, and therefore not the safest place for something so valuable, should we be attacked by privateers or Va-forsaken pirates."

"Nonetheless, it is in your keeping now, as the Regal's property. With Va's grace, no ill shall befall this vessel."

"Would it be possible to see this plume? Forgive me if my request is not proper, but if I am to know what it is we must seek in the islands . . ."

"They are dangerous items. I think the Regal made that quite clear in his letter, did he not? They are not to be handled." He paused, debating. "However, perhaps it is a good idea for you to look at this one. Let me show you."

He took the gloves he had tucked into his belt and put them on, wishing he'd known the penalty of touching the vile thing before that pizzle of a factor had gifted it to him. Taking the bambu from Russmon, he eased the plume out of its containment until it blossomed free in all its golden glory. Russmon gave a sharp intake of breath. Lustgrader risked a look, dreading what would follow. Sweet oak, but it was beautiful! For a moment he was tempted to touch it to his cheek, then remembered and drew back. He no longer felt the urge to covet it, to own it.

Va be thanked. Factor Reed Heron, I am free of your sorcery. You're a dead man, you and that wanton with her ill-begotten baby.

He took a deep breath, revelling in his freedom.

Russmon stared, mesmerised by the flowing colours. "Sweet Va, I've never seen anything so glorious."

He reached out a finger to touch the feather, but Lustgrader knocked his hand away. "Watch it! It's . . . poisonous."

The captain, embarrassed, folded his arms. "Well, at least I know what we are looking for on the nutmeg-growing island. A bird as large as a cow, if it has feathers like this! It will be an easy target, I imagine."

"One would think so. I can't say I actually saw the creature myself." Carefully, he threaded the feather back into the bambu, wrapped it in the canvas and handed it over to Russmon.

"I shall lock it away," Russmon promised. "Oh, while I remember to tell you: one of my sailors recognised the flag on that Ardronese ship anchored in the bay. He says it's the coat of arms of Lord Juster Dornbeck, privateer."

"That rutting fellow? Pox on him!"

"She looks fast, that one. Well-armed, too."

"You've come across him before, I believe?" He kept his tone neutral. No point in antagonising the captain of the fleet's galleon, but he knew what Russmon would be remembering. The last ship he'd commanded had to be scrapped after Juster Dornbeck had finished with it.

"Our paths have crossed, yes."

"I wonder if we might consider being . . . er, pre-emptive this time?"

There was a long silence while Russmon considered the suggestion. Lustgrader knew he had put the captain on a spot and he was interested to see whether he would take the bait or veer away.

"The Karradar Islands are considered neutral, off limits to any acts of aggression."

"They are indeed," he agreed. "But if they can't prove who the aggressor was?"

Russmon looked at him with quick interest and leaned forward like a hound scenting prey. "Just what do you have in mind, Commander?"

Sorrel, with Piper in her arms, crouched on the weather deck shaded by one of *Spice Winds'* carriage guns, captivated by all she could see. The sun would soon descend behind the steep slopes of Bull Karradar Island, but for now the sea – turquoise, aqua, cobalt – basked in its late-afternoon glow and glinted with blinding sparks of light. Beneath the stillness of the surface, fish darted, gaudily striped or spotted, some bewhiskered, others trailing their fins in streamers.

The vessel was so far offshore the details of the port town were lost, but the mountain beyond was imposing. The folds of the land were smothered by the vegetation, the canopy of each tree slotting into its neighbours like a child's puzzle. Every so often, the trunk of an emergent forest giant would break free of this continuous green, thrusting the spread of its branches above to catch the sun.

Anchored ships, no two alike, studded the bay in front of the port, while smaller boats scurried from ship to shore, rowed or paddled in frenetic competition. A flotilla of rafts and skiffs, made colourful by their varied cargoes of fresh food and elaborately dressed women and boys, bumped against the hull of *Spice Winds* like puppies nuzzling at their mother's teats. Crewed by a motley selection of dark-skinned Pashali seamen and lascars or sweating, sun-burnt Ardronese and Lowmians, the vessels were laden with produce, now for sale in a language brewed from three or four separate tongues into an island argot. Most of the men were bare-chested and barefooted, some wearing nothing more than colourful loincloths.

The sailors on *Spice Winds* dickered with them, offering coins and trinkets in exchange for produce. No one noticed her. Glamoured into invisibility, she watched, fascinated. The air was warm and humid; sweat trickled between her breasts and soaked the shirt she wore. It was just as well that she could glamour more appropriate clothing when she wanted because, since they had arrived in warmer seas, she'd chosen to wear only a sailor's shirt and knee-length britches. Captain Lustgrader would have been appalled.

It had been a lonely voyage, prevented as she was from mixing with the crew or the factors. Piper, the little darling, had thrived, but

Commander Lustgrader had insisted everyone ignore them both; the only crew member she'd had anything to do with officially was the obliging but scruffy ship's boy, Banstel.

Glamoured, blended into the background, she'd been able to snatch moments with both Ardhi and Saker, whispered conversations often ending in argument, as she was adamant that she would leave the ship in Karradar. Saker was beside himself with worry about what would happen to her if she tried to travel alone.

"If you're so worried," she had countered, "you should come with me. It's your fault that I'm here in the first place!"

The idea that he thought it his duty to go to the Va-forsaken Hemisphere because his witchery was bird-linked was both absurd and infuriating. Why would a solution to the problems of the Va-cherished Hemisphere be found on the other side of the world?

But then, if the dagger had really changed the weather so she couldn't leave the ship . . . perhaps he was right.

Oh, the stupid weak part of her ached to have someone at her side, protecting her when she headed back across the ocean on her way to Vavala. *Don't be so cowardly*, she'd admonished herself again and again. *You must go back. It's your duty. You promised Mathilda.*

Before sunset, the floating market of boats disappeared towards the shore, but she stayed where she was, Piper still sound asleep in her arms. She watched, unseen, as Captain Lustgrader came on deck, a parcel under his arm. The pinnace was launched and he was rowed over to the galleon.

It was pleasantly cooler now, and Piper slept on. She stayed where she was, waiting for the sunset because a sun-cast shadow of her crossing the deck without anyone visible to cast it would have betrayed her presence. As the night fell, lights on the shore began to delineate the port buildings. A surprisingly large town, it sprawled along the waterfront, then scrambled haphazardly up the slopes beyond.

She dozed a while, until Saker's voice brought her awake. "Sorrel."

Piper jerked in her arms, and she turned to find Saker behind her.

"I bought you something from one of those boatmen," he said. "Here, try this."

She glanced around to make sure nobody was watching before she took what he offered. "What is it?" she asked, holding it up to see better in the dim light. It was long and yellow.

"It's a kind of fruit. Ardhi calls it *pisang*. The locals here call it a banana."

He showed her how to peel it and she took a bite. Her teeth sank into creamy flesh, and it squashed on her tongue, the delicate tang of it new and fresh on her palate. She ate it all, suddenly aware how much she'd missed fresh fruit in the two months it had taken to reach the islands from Ustgrind. She gave a sigh of pure pleasure.

"That was perfection. Thank you. Did you know Lustgrader went over to *Sentinel*? He might return soon and we can't be caught talking."

He shrugged. "I'm not worried. There's nothing Lustgrader can do to me that I can't make him undo."

"That's horrible. Don't remind me."

"Sorry. Look, I have some good news. It seems one of those ships anchored in the bay is Lord Juster's *Golden Petrel*. He will help us find a berth on a trustworthy ship going to Throssel for you, if that's really what you want."

"He's a privateer! Will he attack *Spice Winds*?"

"Not here. The Karradar Islands are neutral territory." He paused, then added, "It would be so easy for you to come with us to Chenderawasi. All I have to do is tell Commander Lustgrader that I insist you do."

She shot him a look, hoping it was enough to tell him what she thought of that idea. She wasn't changing her mind.

"All right, all right," he said, "I'll tell Lustgrader you're disembarking tomorrow."

A sailor came past to light the ship's anchorage lanterns. He nodded to Saker, oblivious to her presence. Saker leaned on the bulwarks and waited until the man was out of earshot before speaking again. "I think the sailors are getting used to me talking to myself," he said with a grin. He reached out to Piper and stroked the downy hair on her head. She was awake now, but made no sound. "She's lovely, isn't she?"

"She's wonderful, but it is getting harder to include her in my glamour. She's becoming too – too much her own person."

"You mustn't become too fond of her. You may have to give her up one day."

"Do you think I don't know that?" Instinctively, her hold tightened. "It's ironical, isn't it? I'm the only mother she's ever known, and I have no rights to her at all. And neither do you, even though you could be her father."

"We'll never know who fathered her."

"I suppose not." She looked down at Piper. "It's too late, you know."

"What is?"

"Do you think I don't care for her already?" Her laugh was half-sob. "It doesn't matter who fathered her, or who her mother was. There's not a moment of any day when I'm not reminded of my own daughter, by the sheer intensity of what I feel."

Her words stilled him.

She wanted to say something more, but choked on the memories.

"Ah," he said. "I recall you saying that no woman who has lost a child fears death, for she has already died once. You were speaking of your own daughter?"

She couldn't look at him, so she kept her gaze on Piper. "Heather. Heather Redwing Ermine." Her voice was husky, but suddenly she wanted to tell him. "Her father murdered her when she was three, because she annoyed him. She was born deaf, you see, and he didn't like that."

"Sweet Va above." His shocked whisper was barely audible. He knelt beside her, but didn't touch her.

She bowed her head over Piper and continued, unable to stop now that she had started. "I only found out much later that he'd killed her. When I realised, I tried to run, but he came after me. I pushed him down the stairs. Killing him wasn't something I'd planned, but I'm glad I did. He was going to murder me, else. I fled. The next day, at the Melforn shrine, I was granted my witchery and I met the Princess Mathilda."

There was a long silence. Then he pulled them both towards him, held them close, rested her head on his shoulder. "I'm so sorry," he said. "I'm so terribly sorry."

She felt his breath on her hair, and her heart pounded. More than anything she wanted to raise her face to his, to have him kiss her.

Fool. He's not right for you. You're lonely, and so is he.

She moved her head so she could look at him. "Are we just puppets, Saker?" As she spoke her anger built. "It's as if we're just here to dance to the tune that Va plays for us, our strings pulled by witchery and dagger magic and shrine guardians for some purpose we can't even guess! A game played by greater powers, with us as the counters on their board. I don't understand why I'm here on board his ship. I don't understand why Piper is here. I don't know why I have this witchery. You were a witan of Va, so tell me! Give me some answers."

But she knew before he spoke that he didn't have a reply that would satisfy her.

He said, "All I know is we have to try to make things better. We have to fight for what appears right to us. Sometimes we fail, and when that happens, we just have to pick ourselves up and try again."

"Do you believe in the power of prayer?" she asked, knowing he would hear her ire in the way she said the words. "Because I've done an awful lot of praying and I don't hear any answers."

He made an odd sound that was almost a laugh, as if her question amused him in some visceral, ironic way. "Well, I think it helps us. I just don't think we get the answers we want."

She started to laugh. "Oh, Va-hells, Saker. What the pox are we going to do?"

He held up a hand to silence her. "Hush, I think I hear a boat."

They both looked out over the bulwarks to where a lantern was bobbing across the water towards them, accompanied by the splash of oars. He rose and helped her to her feet.

"Probably Lustgrader coming back," she whispered hurriedly.

"Odd he didn't call Russmon to come to him."

"He took something with him, all wrapped up in canvas, long and thin."

Saker was stilled. "Oh, rot it. It couldn't have been the bambu, could it?"

17

A Second Murder

Once Sorrel had left the weather deck down the aft companionway, Saker, worried, headed towards the forward hatchway. Just then the ship's bell rang, signalling the change of watch.

At the top of the steps he ran into several seamen, including Ardhi, coming up from below. The lascar grabbed him and pulled him deep into the shadow of the sloping base of the bowsprit while the other men disappeared into the gloom towards the stern. "I've been looking for you everywhere," he whispered in Pashali.

He answered in the same language. "Where are you going?"

"We're on watch. I have to go up in the crow's nest."

"Now? Why? We're at anchor!"

"In case someone tries to sneak on board to steal something. Karradar is home to half the scum of the known world, or so the scuttlebutt says. There are four of us on watch tonight." He snorted. "They always give me the crow's nest, but I like it up there. But that's not important. Saker, there's something wrong."

"Keep your voice down. The captain is about to come aboard astern. He was across on *Sentinel*." He glanced behind, but the pinnace was coming in on the portside, while he and Ardhi were on the starboard. He doubted they'd be seen. "What is it?"

"The kris won't stay still. Look!" He pulled the dagger from its sheath, and sure enough, it writhed across his palm until he clamped his other hand over it. "You can't see the colour in this light, but it's twisting with red. That means trouble."

"Pox on't!" His dismay ratcheted up a notch. "Could it be something to do with Sorrel intending to leave the ship? I promised her I'd ask Lord Juster if he'd find a berth for her."

"I thought you could persuade her to come with us—"

154

He gave a deliberately hollow laugh. "Sorrel Redwing has a mind of her own. Not that I blame her for being disinclined to go to the Summer Seas."

"The kris wants her with us."

"Leave her alone, Ardhi. That woman has had more trouble in the last couple of years than most people get in a lifetime. And she deserved none of it."

Ardhi winced. "I don't decide these things."

"She just told me that Lustgrader went across to *Sentinel* with something long and thin wrapped in canvas. I was wondering if that might be the bambu with the plume inside. Perhaps that's what the dagger is fussing about?"

Ardhi thought about that before replying. "Taking the plume somewhere else doesn't change anything."

"It would if he was gifting it away, though, wouldn't it?" *And if he does that, my power over him ends.*

"Would he give it to the captain of *Sentinel*?"

"I don't *think* so. Oh, pox, wait a moment. If he figured out how the magic works, and wanted a way to rid himself of the compulsion without harming someone, Captain Russmon would be a good choice. The man is under his orders anyway. Cankers and galls, I don't know. You tell me."

"He's had weeks to think about it," Ardhi pointed out. "And a strong man can override its seduction. You did."

"I guess I'll find out tomorrow. I'll be able to tell by the way he treats me."

"I think you ought to get off the ship tonight."

He snorted. "It's a long swim to shore."

"I doubt they'll hoist the pinnace back on board again tonight."

"You're suggesting I steal the pinnace? Come on, you just told me there's a full watch tonight. I'd be spotted in a thrice."

Ardhi clasped his hands to his head in a gesture of helpless indecision. "And if you stay and he is no longer under your influence, he'll kill you. Saker, do you remember how angry you were with me when you realised what my gift of the plume did to you? There was a time when you would have happily strangled me. Do you think Lustgrader will ever forgive you?"

He thought about that, tried to think dispassionately about a man he'd grown to dislike. One conclusion came to mind: Lustgrader was not a forgiving man.

"He's not just the captain of this ship; he's commander of this fleet," Ardhi added quietly. "I've been a sailor for the Lowmians long enough to know that, on his ship, the captain is a king. He can kill you in any fashion that pleases him, and there's no law to stop him. He *is* the law."

"Let's not overreact. We don't even know *what* he was carrying when he left the ship, let alone what he was going to do with it. It could have been anything. And I am not one of his crew. I'm employed by the man who owns this vessel. The man who pays Lustgrader's wages. Kesleer."

"Doesn't matter. If he rids himself of the plume's witchery, you're a dead man."

"I doubt Captain Lustgrader is going to send a sailor to knife me in the middle of the night. Ardhi, if I am in that much trouble, so is Sorrel, and I can't see any way I can get her off the ship without someone seeing. I won't sleep in my hammock, all right? I'll find somewhere else, and I'll sleep with my sword."

The officer on watch bellowed Ardhi's name; Ardhi muttered something in his own tongue that sounded like an imprecation, and disappeared up the shrouds.

Saker left the weather deck, cursing to himself. He was worried; that fobbing dagger had signalled timely warnings far too often for him to ignore another. If there was trouble, he needed an escape route. *The galley*, he thought, *behind the stove. No one will think of looking for me there.* There was a small rubbish hatch from which he could wriggle through into the sea if escape was necessary.

But what about Sorrel?

Lord Juster Dornbeck came up onto the deck of *Golden Petrel* just at sunrise. Usually, if he saw the sun come up when he was in port, it was because he hadn't yet been to bed. Not this time. In the Karradar Islands, he was disinclined to drink too much, or sleep too much. In this particular island group, poised as it was between the Va-cherished and the Va-forsaken Hemispheres but belonging to neither, the watchful lived longer.

I have to admit, though, dawn does have something to recommend it. The bay looks confoundedly pretty at this time of the day.

He nodded to the seaman on watch on the poop deck. "You can go below, Dolf. Break your fast."

"Aye, aye, sir."

He let his gaze wander over the ship and still felt a familiar delight. *Beggar me speechless if she isn't a beautiful maid!*

He'd been more than satisfied with the voyage from Ardrone. *Golden Petrel* was fast and answered the helm better than any ship he'd previously captained.

He leaned on the taffrail to gaze through his spyglass at the fleet that had arrived the previous afternoon, all Lowmian ships flying Lowmian flags. He'd sent one of his small boats over there with several of his crew posing as islanders with goods to sell and they'd come back with not only the names of all the vessels, but a lot of other useful detail, like how many cannons each had, and what poundage. His master's mate, who was always drawing on a slate, or paper if he could get it, had sketched all four ships in detail for him.

Juster had studied all the drawings. A fifth vessel, a carrack, had joined them some time during the night, he noted. He'd send someone over there to have a look at that one too, but he was sure this was the first fleet sent, not by Kesleer's company, but by the Lowmian Spicerie Trading Company. It was in no danger from him now. They had no cargo to tempt him.

Later, out on the high seas, anything could happen. *Ah, Saker, I'm sorry, but it will come to a sea battle one day.*

He thought of the young witan often, and the man's condemnation of privateering as blatant piracy. Strange how they'd become such good friends when they believed in different things and had so little in common. But he'd *liked* Saker. Indeed, he'd laughed out loud when he'd heard how King Edwayn's men had gone to the shrine where Saker was supposed to have died, only to find empty manacles still attached to the tree – and no bones. The witan led a charmed life.

I wonder what you did with my rubies. I hope you're safe, my friend, wherever you are.

In the morning, Sorrel packed up everything she had, ready to leave. Banstel, the ship's boy, brought her breakfast and Piper's goat's milk in her tiny cuddy, as usual.

When the lad returned to collect her plate and mug an hour later, he said, "Message fer you from the cap'n, mistress. He says come up on deck with the babe and your things. He's sending you ashore in the dinghy."

"Oh, but I haven't spoken to Mynster Heron! He was arranging for me to— He was arranging what I need ashore."

"I'll find him and tell him what's betide, if you like, ma'am. But I wouldn't keep the cap'n waiting, if I was you. His face would sour beer this morn. Right proper foul! If you'll give me your belongings, I'll take them topside now."

There wasn't much. It was the work of a moment to wrap all she possessed – and all that Piper had – into a bundle. She handed it over and said, "Look for Mynster Heron. I'll go to the captain."

He took the bundle and left. She picked up Piper, who'd been squirming across the floor holding a toy rabbit Banstel had carved her, then gave one last look around. Hardly more than a storage cupboard, it had been her home for months; her haven where at least she'd felt safe. In contrast, what lay ahead was scarily vague; she was about to enter a world of which she knew nothing.

Piper giggled and waved her rabbit, as if she thought they were heading somewhere better.

Captain Lustgrader was standing next to the pilot ladder, waiting for her. The roped wooden steps led down to the ship's dinghy, now bobbing on choppy water at the foot. About half the size of the pinnace, it was manned by two seamen. Her bundle of belongings was stowed under the aft seat, but neither Saker nor Banstel were anywhere to be seen.

Life with her husband, Rikard Ermine, had taught her the wisdom of masking her emotions and feigning unquestioning obedience, so she schooled her face into impassivity and curtsied. "My thanks, captain, for your forbearance. May Va reward you. Would it be possible for me to bid Factor Heron farewell?"

His eyes narrowed. What she read in them made her take an involuntary step backwards; there was no mistaking the burning hatred. "I am gratified to be able to inform you that Factor Heron is chained in the brig, and there he will remain until I deal with him. You are lucky not to be there as well."

For a moment she couldn't move, couldn't speak, couldn't think what to do.

He's going to kill Saker. Va help us. Oh, Saker.

"Have you nothing to say, mistress?"

"I doubt you'd recognise the truth if you heard it, captain. My presence on your ship was not of my making. The child and I were victims of Va-forsaken sorcery, too."

He snorted, disbelieving and indifferent. "Just get off my vessel, you hussy."

She gave him stare for stare, but read nothing of compassion in his eyes. She'd never needed courage more, and never felt less brave. "And Factor Heron?" she asked.

"A dead man, mistress, as good as." He was jeering at her, reminiscent of Rikard at his nastiest. "On that you have my word, and on board ship, my word is law. As you will find if you don't remove yourself from my presence. *Now*."

She raised her chin, still locking her gaze on his. "Safe voyage, captain," she said, her voice grating roughly to her ears. "Go with Va. Temper your anger with mercy, I beg you."

He walked away without another word. She turned to look down at the sailboat, wondering how she could manage with Piper in her arms. The wind was catching the steps and dancing them against the side of the ship. She turned, searching for Ardhi, but he was nowhere to be seen.

"Lad, take the babe down." It was the officer of the watch speaking. He nodded to her and waved a hand at Banstel, who'd just arrived on deck.

"I'll bring her to you," Banstel said, then, as she handed Piper over, he added in a whisper, "The factor's in the brig."

"I know." She turned away to descend the wooden steps, clinging tightly to the rope handrail, remembering to keep her glamour of skirts even as she was grateful for the sailor's culottes she wore. As she stepped into the dinghy, she glanced at the seaman holding the ladder to stop it from drifting away from the mother ship. The look he gave her was not reassuring. His name was Fels, and she knew he'd once been disciplined by Mate Tolbun for hitting Banstel too hard and blackening the lad's eyes so badly he could hardly see out of them for several days.

Banstel followed her down, and she held out her arms to take Piper from him as soon as she'd seated herself. Fels, leering at her, deliberately rocked the boat so that Banstel stumbled just as he handed the child across. Piper startled and began to cry.

Fels laughed. "Pity you didn't drop that one overboard! Reckon there's a scent of the uncanny about you and your ill-gotten brat."

Piper halted her crying and turned to stare at him, her blue eyes wide and stark, as if she could feel his contempt. Sorrel murmured reassurance, touching her lips to Piper's forehead. Her heart was beating wildly. Saker needed help, and Ardhi was nowhere to be seen.

The second seaman was already hauling on the halyard to bring the single sail up, and she'd noticed him before too, a ruffian with a twisted scar across his cheek from a recent shipboard knife fight. He also had a penchant for making Banstel the butt of his nastiness.

Perhaps not only Saker is in trouble here . . .

These men were the scum of the crew, and Lustgrader must have been aware of that.

As Banstel was about to climb up the ladder again, Fels loosened his hold on the steps, and the lad fell back into the boat, cracking his elbow on the gunwale.

"Get on to that tiller, Banstel, you scut," Fels growled. "You're allus telling us you know how to sail, so show us! Head across wind, thataway," he added, pointing in the direction he meant. "Let's see some seamanship, or you'll be on scrubbing duty every day we're in port."

As far as Sorrel could tell, Banstel appeared to know what he was doing, but even so the two men taunted him about his skills as he took hold of the tiller and swung the boat away from *Spice Winds*. The sail filled and the boat emerged from the protection of the larger ship into a sea now chopped by the wind into white-capped waves.

The man with the scarred face was soon blocked from Sorrel's view by the sail. Fels was busy with the sheet, feeding the line through the cleat to keep the sail trimmed. He said, with a grin in her direction, "Your fancy factor's been taken care of, he has. Not coming to your rescue, pretty henny."

She sat straight and met his stare with one of her own as she clutched Piper. "I have no idea what you mean. If you have something to tell me, then say it, otherwise keep your mouth shut. If you want to scare me you'll have to do better than that." It was a lie of course; her heart was thudding under her ribs, each beat hammering home her fear. She sat rigidly still, rubbing Piper's back, thoughts jumbling.

Ardhi will make sure Saker doesn't come to any harm. Or the dagger will. And we'll be all right, Piper. I'll go to Lord Juster. He'll help us . . . You won't be hungry for a few hours and I'm sure I can buy a goat or two on an island like this. I'll get milk for you, I promise, and if I can't, well, you're almost old enough to make do on solid food.

She breathed deeply, seeking a calm place within herself. Glancing back over her shoulder at the shoreline, she studied the port, wondering if there was a jetty or a dock. It was hard to see much because there were so many small boats and barges dodging between larger ships and the shore, blocking her view.

Don't panic. Think about something else until you are in control of your fear. She'd never expected so many large trading vessels. Pashali, most of them, she guessed. But why did she have to look past Banstel's shoulder to see the port? Her heart flipped uncomfortably in her chest.

They were heading the wrong way.

She tried to convince herself there was a logical reason. Reefs they had to circumvent, perhaps. But no, she'd seen the bumboats take direct routes. So, maybe something to do with the wind. The breeze was stiff, but boats zigzagged, didn't they? *Pickle it, I wish I knew more about sailing.*

"Where are we going?" she asked, furious with herself because her voice wavered.

Fels pointed. "That island there. That's where."

She looked straight ahead. When they'd sailed past the outer islands on their way towards the port the day before, she'd been up on deck. Uninhabited, they were all little more than inhospitable humps emerging steep-sided from the sea, laden with thick green blankets of rampaging vegetation on top, decorated around the base with the occasional half-moon beach tucked in between the jagged teeth of a rocky shore.

"Why there?" she asked, fixing Fels with what she hoped was a steely glare. Her heart thumped painfully. "What are your orders?"

The man grinned at her. "The captain paid us to get rid of you and the babe. He didn't say how. Reckon he meant get out of sight and then toss you overboard, but me and Voster there, we reckoned we could have a bit o' fun first."

Banstel gasped, and his hand jerked on the tiller. The boat yawed and Fels cursed as he adjusted the sail to compensate. "Watch it, you misbegotten lout!"

"You're going to *murder* me?" Sorrel asked.

"We're going to dump you on a beach of that island ahead of us. And just mayhap we'll enjoy a little playtime with our maypoles first, eh, Voster?"

"Me nuggins are aching fit to burst."

Repulsed, striving to contain her fury, she shouted at them. "Marooned there with a baby and no goat to feed her milk, how long do you think she'll live? That's fobbing murder!" But her rage jostled with rampant terror, and she strove to quell the fear. *I will not let you do this. Pus and pustules, if you touch Piper, it will be over my dead body!*

Fob it. That's what they want.

Fels gave an indifferent shrug. "What does it matter to me? I do as I'm bid. If I don't, I get whipped, till me back's raw. And then I might die of the putrid rot. I'd rather get rid of the likes of you." His tone changed, hardening. "Us tars down there on the lower deck, we reckon you and the brat are no good. Things ain't been right since you've been on board. The captain ain't been right in the head. Reckon you're no loss."

"Dead right," Voster said in agreement.

"Well, blister that for an idea!" she snapped. "Listen, you turn this boat around and sail to that Ardronese vessel in the bay. I know the captain. For my safety he'll pay you more money in your pocket than you've ever seen."

Fels said, "Now that's right tempting, but fiddle me witless, it sounds more like a sea-monkey tale tole by a Pashali trader than the honeyed truth, don't you reckon Voster? Besides, what use is coin if Cap'n Lustgrader knows? And you reckon he won't know? The watch has got the spyglass on us, likely! Forget it, woman. There's no changing aught. Mayhap your luck'll be good, an' a passing boat'll pick you up. Afterwards." He grinned.

He turned his attention forward once more, so she glanced at

Banstel. He stared back, white-faced. Obviously he hadn't known the orders and was horrified by them. Besides Ardhi, he was the only other member of the crew she'd ever spoken to on board and he adored Piper, saying she reminded him of a baby sister who'd died of the meazle.

Neither of them spoke, and he looked away.

Could she trust him? Banstel was only a lad, and he'd be scared witless of disobeying Lustgrader.

Once Piper stopped crying, Sorrel wrapped her up and wedged her under the seat with her head peeping out and her hands free. Banstel picked up a stray seagull feather from the bottom of the boat and gave it to her. She gurgled her joy and Sorrel turned her attention to the boat's pair of oars shipped under the seats.

Please be still, Piper. Your life may depend on it.

She sat upright again, to glance at Fels. He was watching the island, adjusting the sail and pointing whenever he wanted Banstel to change direction. He and Voster had to duck under the bottom of the sail whenever the boom swung over.

Sweet Va, protect us both. I've killed before. I can do it again. For a child. For this child, this time.

Under the protection of the glamour of her non-existent dress, she reached out one foot and used it to edge one of the oars towards her.

"I can't let you do this to us," she said.

Fels laughed without looking at her. "You think you can stop us?"

"Of course I can! Come now, think, you foolish malt-heads. I'm a woman who persuaded Captain Lustgrader, against his own wishes, to take me and my babe on board his precious ship – is such a person helpless? I have powers that can persuade. I can make you jump overboard and drown yourself. Can you swim, Seaman Fels? I've heard many sailors never learn because they think it better to die quickly if shipwrecked."

He glanced back at her. For the first time he looked uncertain and exchanged a doubtful look with Voster.

Banstel spoke up then, horrified. "I doan want nobody dead! That's a babe – who wants to kill a babe? Captain Lustgrader wouldn't do that! He's a Va-fearing man, he is. On his knees every night come night watch; I seen him, all the time. And the mistress and the factor, they ain't done naught to hurt nobody!"

Fels turned on him. "You calling us liars, you bilge-rat? Keep a quiet tongue behind your teeth, lad, or we'll toss you to the fish."

Banstel, thinking the man was about to leap at him, jerked backwards and the boat yawed again before he was able to steady the tiller. The boom swung as the wind spilled out of the sail, and Fels turned to haul in the sheet.

With the attention of both men elsewhere, Sorrel quickly slipped the oar wholly free and leant it against her body, glamouring her nonexistent skirts wide to block any view of it. Banstel, his attention fixed on Fels, didn't notice. Fels was looking ahead and Voster couldn't see her because of the position of the sail.

"Your last chance, Fels," she said. "You either set course for that Ardronese ship, or you die, right here on the sea in this Va-less land. Your choice."

Fels looked over his shoulder at her, and smirked. "You ain't got neither the brawn nor the brav'ry."

She looked up at the sail, watching for the right moment. "You're prepared to risk that? You wouldn't be the first man I've killed." *Va guide me . . .*

"What you goin' to do? Knock us senseless with your wit?"

"Fels, come on," Banstel protested. "You're talking murder. I didn't sign up for no murder."

She gripped the oar tight with both hands. The wind gusted, ruffling the surface in scurries, and filled the sail. The boat heeled in answer. Fels, gripping the sheet, leaned outwards over the gunwale to balance himself against the pull.

Sorrel stood, feet wide. She dropped the glamour of her dress and poured her witchery into an image of her face. Not a woman now, but a monster of teeth and tongue, maw dripping saliva, eyes bulging and hair a twist of hissing snakes. And she swung the oar with all her strength.

Fels never saw it coming. He glimpsed her movement and turned to look, but then his horrified gaze never shifted from her face. His jaw dropped; he leaned away, the beginnings of a scream starting in his throat. That was when the paddle struck him full in the face, smashing his nose and breaking his teeth. He dropped the sheet, the line spun loose and the sail whipped free. The boom swung across the boat. Sorrel didn't see it crack Voster on the side of the head, but she heard the sickening sound of it. Fels, his balance upset, toppled over the gunwale into the water without the scream ever breaking free.

Sorrel herself had tumbled between the seats, dropping the oar. She was an arm's length from Voster. He was flat on his back in the bottom of the boat, blood streaming down his face. She knelt, checked to see that he was unconscious, then looked up at Banstel. He was still seated, hand still on the tiller, gaping at her, even though she'd dropped all pretence of her glamour. His face was so white, she thought he might faint. The dinghy was tossing in the waves, the sail hanging loose.

"I'm no monster, Banstel. It's all just a Va-bestowed glamour witchery."

He didn't move, didn't acknowledge her words.

She turned her attention back to Voster. Dump him over the side? That would be murder. Another murder.

But if she didn't do anything and he recovered consciousness, he could easily overpower her and kill her and Piper. She vacillated, feeling ill.

I am not supposed to misuse my witchery . . .

Just then the boat rocked violently, knocking her off balance again. She sat down hard, landing in the water sloshing along the hull under the seats.

She looked around wildly. The portside gunwale dipped low, shipping still more seawater on board. She tumbled towards that side as the boat tipped. Piper, unsettled, began to scream. Hands grasped the gunwale and then a leg and an elbow appeared.

Sweet acorns, Fels is still alive—

He was intent on climbing back into the dinghy.

Scrambling up, she reached for the bloodstained oar. The boat pitched still more, and she went down on one knee fighting to keep her balance. Fels' head appeared over the edge. She aimed a blow at him, but the blade slammed into the gunwale instead.

Precariously balanced half in and half out, he grabbed at it. They battled, pulling in opposite directions. Piper screamed.

Sorrel let go of the shaft. Taken by surprise, Fels slipped backwards into the water, but kept one arm hooked over the gunwale. She snatched up the second oar and stood balanced, one foot braced on the seat amidships, and leaned over the side of the boat to jab at his face with the blade, not once, but repeatedly, thrusting it downwards with a savagery she had not known that she possessed.

The first oar drifted away, but he gripped tightly to the boat with one hand while his other made ineffective grabs for the oar she was wielding. Frantic, beyond thought, she hammered him with the edge of the blade. His nose and mouth poured blood, then his cheekbone caved under her blow. Her next strike slammed into his eye socket. When she withdrew the blade, an eye hung loose on his cheek. He tried to shout, to scream, but his swollen lips, blood-filled mouth and broken teeth only allowed spluttered gurgles.

She stopped, exhausted. Dropping the oar, she knelt and stared at the battered remains of his face. Only then did she realise he was unconscious – or perhaps dead. One hand was still gripping the gunwale, fingernails hooked underneath the edge. She began to shake uncontrollably. Slumping back into the boat, she stared at Banstel. He still held the tiller, petrified with shock. Or perhaps terror. Fear of her, of what she might do.

Dear Va, am I a monster?

Piper's screaming finally penetrated their consciousness. She reached for the baby, but Banstel was closer. He let go of the tiller and, crooning, picked up the baby to cradle her in his arms where she began to quieten.

Sorrel turned back to Fels and unhooked his fingers, one by one, until his body slipped into the water and drifted away, face down. She clambered over to Voster and touched him. He was still breathing, still unconscious. Only then did she look back at Banstel.

"Wh-who *are* you? he asked, his face ashen.

She shook her head. She no longer knew. Her whole body was shaking. Her stomach heaved and she emptied her breakfast over the edge of the boat.

18

Imprisoned

The ship's brig was not designed for comfort or any possibility of escape. It was little more than an iron cage built on the orlop, the deck immediately above the hold. In addition to the brig, the orlop was where the ship's stores and extra sails were kept, an area of the ship out of bounds to anyone without a specific reason for being there. It was cut off from the decks above by a bolted hatch cover, its contents the responsibility of the ship's constable.

Saker had hidden in the galley, sufficiently worried not to sleep, but his wakefulness had not helped him in the end. When he heard the ship's constable and four able seamen searching for him in the galley's larder he did have time to slip out through the rubbish hatch, but elected instead to climb across the still-warm top of the galley stove into the seaman's mess. Once there, still undetected, he headed for Sorrel's cuddy. Four more swabbies, waiting for him at the foot of the companionway, nabbed him after a short and brutal fight in the confined space. He emerged with a bloodied nose, bruised ribs and the ignominy of being relieved of his dagger, sword and shoes. More disastrously, they'd also found the picklocks he kept in a hidden pocket of his trouser leg. They then escorted him to the brig and left him there. No one had bothered to tell him why he was incarcerated – or for how long.

It didn't matter; he knew why. Sorrel had been right: Lustgrader had realised how to rid himself of his compulsion and now he was about to exact his revenge on the man who had laid it on him.

I suppose I ought to be flattered that he sent so many men to arrest me.

Once he'd tested the lock and all the ironwork and was sure there was no way out of the brig without his picklocks, he settled down to wait. And wait. He castigated himself for not doing something, anything, after Sorrel had told him about the captain's trip to the galleon, but even now he wasn't sure what he could have done. There had been no possibility of stealing a boat undetected – and how could he have ever left her to attempt the long swim to shore?

Time passed slowly in the dark.

He could hear many of the normal sounds of a ship at anchor, but no light penetrated to his prison. If he sat still, the rats grew bold, so he stood and kept moving in order to keep them at bay. Not that it was hard to stay awake; the turmoil of his thoughts precluded any temptation to doze. Sorrel and Piper . . . Involved in this mess because of him and Ardhi. Not to mention that wretched, Va-forsaken dagger, pox on't!

At last, the dawning day was heralded by the ship's constable opening the hatch for the cook's boy to enter so he could fetch breakfast supplies from the barrels housed on the orlop. This morning it was pickled herrings. The constable supervised, ordering the boy not to talk to Saker.

"What's going to happen to me?" Saker asked.

"Nothing you'll enjoy," the man replied. "Wouldn't expect no ease into death, if I were you. The captain's plenty angry."

With that pessimistic opinion, he left with the lad, and Saker settled down to wait some more.

Patience and I, he thought disgustedly, *have never been at ease with each other.* Neither did he favour being dependent on others for rescue, and yet he suspected his only hope was Ardhi. A lascar was right at the bottom in the hierarchy of the ship's command, but that was an advantage Ardhi often exploited. Everyone overlooked a lascar. His shipmates treated him as if he were an exceptionally stupid child and not even the fact that he was teaching the factors the basics of the Pashali language altered their erroneous perception. Deceived by his apparent lack of skill at speaking the tongue of the Va-cherished, unfeigned when Ardhi had first left Chenderawasi, they were unaware that his linguistic stumbling was mostly now all an act. His accent might still be thick, but his comprehension was excellent.

Ardhi, I hope you can see a way out of this for me because, by the sweet oak, I can't see any other solution that's going to help me out of this one.

When the constable returned with other crew members to open the brig and escort Saker to the quarterdeck, the ship's bell was ringing, telling him it was only halfway through the forenoon watch. He was still blinking in the light when they came to a halt outside the captain's stateroom, where one of the guards tied his hands behind his back with a piece of cord.

A wise precaution: one of his half-formed plans had been to seize Lustgrader as a hostage for his own release. Instead, a moment later, he was pushed down to his knees in front of the captain's desk by the same tar.

Lustgrader looked up from the flintlock pistol he was holding, then laid it carefully down on the desk next to its ramrod and powder flask. "You may go," he told the guards, brushing a few specks of gunpowder from his fingers while he waited for them to leave.

Consign you to a choiceless hell, Saker thought. *I hate theatricals.* Nonetheless, he silently cursed the stench of cockroaches and rats clinging to his clothes in a foul perfume, exacerbating his irritation at appearing unkempt and barefoot before a man who wore starched white collar and cuffs.

"Well," he drawled, after noting Lustgrader's nose wrinkling with distaste, "you should have let me have a wash before desecrating your private quarters with the disgusting smell of the ship's brig. Of course, you could also have sent your sailors to scrub the place out from time to time. Oh, and if you don't deal with the rats soon, you might have a problem with your food supplies by the time you get to the Spicerie."

Lustgrader gave him a look designed to shrivel the spirit of a crewman, but Saker chose to ignore it. "Would I be right," he asked instead, "if I assumed you worked out how to free yourself of the power of the golden plume?"

"You are scum beyond contempt," Lustgrader said, his fury contorting his face. "What kind of a man chooses to serve the evil of A'Va and that vile feather? You brought Va-forsaken sorcery on board my ship! You are a traitor to our nation and a traitor to our faith. There is no fate too terrible for a leprous wretch like you."

A pox on our labels, he thought. *We're the ones who named half the world "Va-forsaken" in our unthinking hubris. We dismissed an entire hemisphere without even knowing its truths. We showed our contempt for all who live there with those words.*

Briefly he contemplated pointing out that Lustgrader now had power to coerce someone too, but decided the captain might not be aware that giving the plume away not only freed him, but also enthralled another. If so, it was probably better that he didn't know.

Instead he said, "I didn't bring Va-forsaken witcheries to our hemisphere. You did, when you allowed your crew to kill what was forbidden to them. Think on that, before you return to Ustgrind with more such feathers. The plumes could spell the end of law and order in our land."

Lustgrader paled.

"Ah, that made you think, didn't it?"

During the night he'd considered explaining that he was in the service of the Pontifect, but it would be difficult to prove. Early in the voyage, he'd feared someone on board might rifle through his papers and discover he was not actually a Lowmian bookkeeper, so he'd destroyed everything that connected him to her.

Aloud, he said, "Do what you will to me, but don't blame the woman for my sins. She had nothing to do with this." He wanted desperately to ask where she was, but resisted giving Lustgrader the satisfaction of hearing him beg. "And the child – a child is always an innocent."

There was no softening of Lustgrader's implacable malice. "I doubt that," he said. "Devil-kin is what springs to my mind when I see that hussy and her ill-gotten babe. She has already been dealt with, and her death was more merciful than she deserved. Let no one say that Lustgrader takes pleasure in torturing a woman or child."

Shock pulsed through his blood. He leapt to his feet then, his hands straining at the bonds. Lustgrader seized the pistol from the desk, and cocked it in one fluid movement.

Saker found himself looking down the barrel a bare hand-span from his face. "You lie!" *Sweet Va, please tell me he lies! Lustgrader, if you've killed them, I'll see you gutted.*

It must be a lie; Ardhi would never have let her die. The dagger would never have let her die. Fobbing hells, if it came to that Sorrel would have fought like a cornered cat; she had her glamour. *Va, tell me I am right.*

Lustgrader looked him up and down. "So I have finally penetrated your calm. Believe me, the woman is dead and that's no more and no less than she deserves."

"The child?"

"Likewise. The spawn of a lightskirt deserves no pity."

He began to shake. A black hole with no bottom had opened up and he was falling into it, emotions tumbling. The blackness closed in on him, crushing the air from his lungs. Only force of will allowed him to drag in a breath. He gasped and whispered, because a whisper was all he could manage, "Leak on you, you whoreson! You're a dead man, Lustgrader. I swear it."

No, I won't believe it. I have more faith in Ardhi and Sorrel.

"Fear not, factor. You won't live long enough to grieve, let alone kill me. You are to be keel-raked." The smugness of his triumph was sickening. "This morning, as a matter of fact. Have you ever seen that done?"

He couldn't stop shaking. His longing to put his hands around the captain's neck and choke the life out of him was so strong he couldn't understand why the bonds around his wrists weren't torn apart.

Through teeth he couldn't seem to unclench, he said, "No, I can't say I have. Keel-raking is a filthy Lowmian practice and I'm an Ardronese witan in the employ of her reverence the Pontifect." He did know sailors often died in the process.

He struggled against the cords that bound him, but sailors knew their knots.

Lustgrader lowered the pistol, but it was still cocked at the ready. "I don't care who you say you are because I doubt you know how to tell the truth. I will admit I never thought any crime committed on any ship of mine deserved such a cruel punishment, until now. Did you know that sometimes the miscreant has his head ripped off in the process? At the very least, he is skinned by the barnacles on the underside of the ship. Painful, I imagine. You will be glad to know that I don't intend to behead you in such a fashion. That would be too . . . merciful. After you've been keel-raked, you will be revived. Then we'll hang you from the yardarm, quarter your body and throw the pieces to the fish. May Va have mercy on your filthy soul." His fingers drummed on the surface of his desk as if he could not contain the rage that fuelled him.

Oh, fuck. Saker felt himself sink still deeper into the blackness of the abyss. *Oh, fobbing hells. Sorrel, please, you have to have been better at saving your own life than I am at saving mine. For your sake, but most of all for Piper's . . .*

Every thought of Piper bruised his soul, so he thrust them away. He had no notion how he was ever going to live through the day ahead, let alone escape the ship, but he was damned if he'd die quietly.

Survive. Va, show me how to survive. While there's a single breath left in my body, I'll fight.

It was hot up on the deck. The pitch-and-hemp caulking between the planking burned his bare feet, forcing him to stand on one leg at a time. He steadied his breathing and looked around. One of his escort still gripped his upper arm tightly, fearing perhaps that he would try to leap into the ocean.

From the number of men on the deck, he guessed the whole crew had been assembled to witness his punishment. As his glance shifted from one man to another, he saw a whole gamut of expressions: sympathy, anger, anticipation, indifference, dread, nausea. Several of the factors and the officers, men he'd come to know well during the voyage, refused to catch his eye. Cultheer the merchant was openly furious. The bo'sun was more nervous than angry, which was odd. He wondered if there was a rumour spreading about sorcery and his hold over Captain Lustgrader. Now that the captain was himself again, and he and Sorrel were in trouble, that was a distinct possibility.

Sorrel. She *can't* be dead.

He looked beyond them to the other moored ships in the bay, all of them closer to shore. Lustgrader had not yet changed the anchorage of *Spice Winds* to a more convenient proximity to the jetty and warehouses. Lord Juster's *Golden Petrel* was still in the bay, but too far away to be of any help. The bumboats, which had been floating around them the day before and were still flocking around the other ships of the Lowmian fleet, had apparently been warned away from *Spice Winds*.

Saker scanned the deck. No Sorrel, no Ardhi. He looked for the ship's boy, Banstel, who might have been able to tell him what had happened to Sorrel, but couldn't see him either.

Where in all the wide ocean is that wretched lascar?

He thought of dashing for the rail and plunging into the sea. But how long would he live with his hands tied behind his back? He could swim, and swim well, but he didn't like his chances of escaping when there was a whole shipload of men armed with muskets and cannons, not to mention boats, that could be sent after him.

Instead, he reached out for his witchery and began to call the birds. Surprise surged through him at the sheer number that answered. A rich abundance of avian thoughts whirled in his mind. He steadied himself, focused his mind to single out the seabirds, to call them with gentle persuasion. He was aware of huge wingspans tilting, tails turning like rudders. Water slipped from slick backs as diving birds rose to the surface in answer. Flocks of pipers roosting on the shore lifted their heads in unison in answer to his summons and took off in swirling assemblies. Sea eagles, skimmers, petrels, lumbering pelicans, elegant terns, argumentative sea gulls, those he couldn't name and had never seen: he called them all.

He bade them fly high into the sky overhead the ship. He felt their initial resistance to his call, and coaxed them to acquiescence. Some, curious, came to investigate with only a little prompting; a few came gladly, with a sense of comradeship. For a disconcerting sliver of time he viewed the world through their alien thoughts, feeling the wind through their feathers. No one appeared to have noticed the birds gathering far above, and he did not look up.

Seamen beside him prepared the hempen cordage for keel-raking. He strove in vain for detachment. They were manipulating the rope under the keel of the ship so that it could be let down on one side and hauled up on the other – with him tied in the middle. At least they were planning to haul him across the ship, not lengthwise.

He took a deep breath. He needed to stay calm and plan because he was certain of one thing: if he was keel-raked, he would die, one way or another. Which meant he had to act first. What he didn't know was how to free his hands so he could swim properly, or how he was going to get from the ship to shore by swimming anyway, not when he could be so easily seen from the deck of *Spice Winds*.

Confound the clear waters of this bay!

He closed his eyes, focused his thoughts.

When he opened his eyes again, he knew if he lived through this it would be because of trust. He had to trust Va, trust the Chenderawasi magic. Trust the kris.

He looked up, and there, on the yardarm almost directly above his head, was Ardhi.

19

The Handmaiden and the Privateer

Sorrel held out her arms to take Piper from Banstel. Trembling, his eyes wide, the lad surrendered the baby into her care. There was blood everywhere, spattered over Piper, over Banstel, over herself. Piper quietened as soon as she was in her arms again, but her stare was angry. With a defiance that seemed adult to Sorrel, she stuck a bloodied fist into her mouth and sucked.

Shocked, Sorrel stared at her. The thought that entered her head was unheralded and unwanted.

Devil-kin.

Then common sense reasserted itself. A baby sucked her fist for comfort; she was just a babe in arms with no knowledge of right or wrong – or what had just happened in the boat.

This was no time for megrims. "Head towards that beach on the island over there," she said, forcing back her nausea.

He didn't move from where he was.

"Please, Banstel."

"You-you— You were an *animal.* Or s-s-something."

"No. It was a glamour witchery, that's all. I'm just a woman with a Va-given witchery and a child, a woman who wants to live long enough to see that child grow up."

"What – what are you going to do?"

"I'm not going to hurt you. I want to dump this fellow Voster on the island. It's either that, or I kill him right now by throwing him into the sea while he's still unconscious."

"He's not dead?"

"Not yet. Will you do as I ask or not?"

He stared at her and asked again, "Who are you?"

"Nobody special. I didn't ask to be aboard *Spice Winds*. I've not harmed anybody."

"You killed Fels!"

"I didn't have much choice in that. And Captain Lustgrader condemned me to death first. Well, I'm not going to die, not now, and not here. I certainly don't want to harm you because I'm sure you're just as innocent as I am. Can you get this boat to the beach?"

"If – if I help you, the captain'll have me guts hanging from the yardarm for them mewling gulls to eat."

"No one is going to tell him what you did. You can make up any story you like when you get back to the ship. But I can promise you one thing: if you don't help me, I'll kill you. And you know why? Because to me, Piper needs to live. And for her, I'll do *anything*. Understand?"

He regarded her, wide-eyed.

"You've seen my witchery. I can kill you." *And I hope you don't realise I'm bluffing.*

He nodded and capitulated. "I 'ave to fix the sheet so's I can look after the sail 'n' the tiller at the same time," he muttered and scrambled forward to untangle the lines.

Later, while he sailed the boat towards the tiny little beach between the two rocky promontories, she kept a close eye on the unconscious Voster. When she lifted his eyelid, he didn't react. His clothing was blood drenched, but the wound on his head was no longer bleeding. Once Banstel had brought the boat up on to the sand, the two of them hauled him out and dragged him further up the beach.

"You can come back and pick him up again if you want to," she said. "If he's still unconscious, he'll never know exactly what happened to me, or Fels. If he mentions a monster, tell him it was all his imagination because he was hit on the head. Tell him I tried to push Fels out of the boat, and we both fell in and drowned."

He looked blank, not understanding.

"What you are really going to do is take me where I want to go. After that, you can do what you want."

The scared look on his face made her feel sick. "Where's that, mistress?" he asked, barely able to get the words out.

"To the Ardronese ship anchored in Karradar Bay. *Golden Petrel*."

If anything, his fright deepened at her words. "But – they say that there ship's a pirate vessel. Wicked man he is, their captain. They say he's got the evil eye and when he lays his look on you, there's naught you can do. They say he takes men to his bed, two or three at once. He's a wicked dog."

"You shouldn't believe everything you hear, especially when it's other sailors telling you a tale. I've met Lord Juster, and I assure you he's not so very terrible. Now let's get back to the boat and set sail."

His eyes widened. "You met a lord? An *Ardronese* one? A pirate? But you're just a nobody!"

She raised a sharp eyebrow at him. "Everyone is somebody, Banstel. You, me, Lord Juster, everyone. Now, head for *Golden Petrel*."

Lord Juster sat at ease in the wardroom, a tankard in one hand, a plate of tropical fruit in front of him. He was chatting to Finch Aspen, his grizzled and arthritic first mate. Juster was an aristocrat, while Finch had been born in a hovel along a shabby lane on the waterfront of Throssel, incidentals of birth that made little difference to either of them. Finch was deferential on board ship to his captain; on shore, if not on the ship's business, he regarded himself as an equal to any man, and Juster was wise enough to agree.

"The crew," Finch was saying, "don't like looking across the bay at that Lowmian fleet without being able to do something about them."

Juster took a sip of his wine. "I know, I know. Tell them to look the other way. Their time will come, once they have filled their holds with nutmeg."

"They mislike the waiting."

"Keep 'em busy, Finch."

"Them bastards are taunting us, cap'n. Some of their swabbies were onshore last night, mocking our men at the Bickles Tavern. Luckily, old Pegrim got our lot calmed down and out of there before they blew up like a busted cannon, but it won't last."

"Kesleer's second Spicerie fleet should be here any time," Juster replied. That fleet had left Ustgrind on its way to the Summer Seas before *Golden Petrel* had even been completed, and they'd seen no sign of it yet. If he had his calculations right, the Lowmian fleet of three merchant ships would soon be calling in, laden with spices. He grinned. "We'll be busy then."

The Lowmians' normal route on the way back was to sail direct from Kotabanta to Karradar, bypassing Javenka in Pashalin because the rulers there would tax their cargo. After revictualling in Karradar, Kesleer's fleet would probably try to sneak out on the tide one night, bound for Ustgrind, and he would follow as soon as the authorities allowed him to sail in pursuit. Karradar law demanded that merchantmen had twelve hours' start before a privateer was permitted to leave port.

Juster believed any Lowmian captain, once they realised the speed and the firepower of *Golden Petrel*, would heave to rather than be blown out of the water. Especially as he had a reputation for generosity to ships prepared to do so. Sinking a trader, or leaving them nothing to show for their voyage, was not in anyone's interest.

Before Finch could comment, there was a knock at the door. One of the crew on watch put his head in, saying, "Cap'n, sir, sorry to interrupt, but the watch officer requests your presence on deck."

"That's Grig Cranald," Finch said.

"Interesting," Juster muttered as he rose to his feet. "Not much happens that he can't handle." Grig was the third mate and also his willing companion in his bed, with one particularly estimable virtue: he never let his private life interfere with his duties or his adherence to shipboard discipline.

Up on deck again, Juster was even more puzzled by what he saw. A small sailboat was pulling away from the ship's side. The name on the transom, painted in the stark, unadorned lettering of the Lowmians, was *Spice Winds*. A woman was standing on the deck of *Golden Petrel*, dressed in the blood-spattered togs of a sailor, jogging a howling baby up and down in her arms.

Juster arched an incredulous eyebrow in the direction of Cranald, signalling his need of a credible explanation.

"She asked for you by name, sir. Says she knows you," Cranald said. "Lad in the boat dropped her and made off as fast as a frightened minnow."

Juster switched his gaze back to the woman. He didn't recognise her. "Knows me? I think not, lady."

She spoke then, with an authority he hadn't expected. "Introductions can wait. What is more important is that I lack the wherewithal to feed this child." Her accent proclaimed her Ardronese; the modulation of her voice told him she was someone of wealth, or standing, or education.

Juster was intrigued. He turned back to the third mate, who was looking at him expectantly. "Well, Mister Cranald, what are you waiting for? Milk for a baby takes precedence over everything, does it not? Hurry along, man! We have that goat on board; get someone to milk it. And after that, send some men ashore with a handful of coins in search of a wet nurse. There must surely be someone in need of money in Port Karradar who is also in a position to help."

An appalled expression flickered across Cranald's handsome features. "A wet nurse."

"Yes."

"Aye, aye, sir." He eyed the nearest swabbie. "You heard the cap'n! Get that goat milked." He looked back at Juster. "Does it have to be a respectable woman, cap'n?"

"Indeed she does," Sorrel said.

Juster turned back to the woman, amused. "Forgive me, mistress, for my social solecism. I am not accustomed to forgetting a face, especially one as lovely as yours, but alas, I do not recall that we have ever met."

"I am sure you can be forgiven. We have never been appropriately introduced, my lord, and you will certainly be unfamiliar with this face, which – although properly mine – is not the one which you encountered previously. You knew me as Celandine Marten, hand-maiden to the Lady Mathilda, Princess of Ardrone."

Shocked, he cocked his head, searching his memory. And then he had it: the woman who had come to the aid of Saker Rampion during the witan's court case. She'd spoken up for him. A grey mouse of a woman, demurely dressed, if he remembered correctly. Not this blood-spattered creature clad in a seaman's culottes and shirt, nor yet a woman with a head of rich dark hair, blue eyes and a face that spoke of strength and determination, not timidity.

Astonishment robbed him of speech. Was his memory really so poor? And if she was Celandine Marten, what the soused herrings was she doing *here*?

"Madam," he managed finally, "I cannot conceive of *any* scenario that would adequately explain the words you just voiced. But I have to admit that there is no way I shall ever allow you to disembark from this vessel before I have heard one!" He bowed with an elaborate flourish. "Do you think you could possibly halt the distressingly noisy emanations from that scrap of humanity in your arms long enough for me to hear such a tale?"

She smiled slightly and, while he watched, her face changed. One moment, she was a grubby, windswept woman of striking appearance; the next she was an unremarkable mousey creature, as undistinguished as a servant one passed by without noticing.

Oh, beggar me witless. A glamour. He hadn't come across anyone with a glamour since . . . oh, since he was a child of ten. There'd been an old man on his uncle's estate who'd once been a spy for the old King.

"Ah. Ah, yes, I do remember you," he said dryly. "I commend you: a picture always tells the story better than words. I still cannot imagine what brings you here, although I'm positive it must be a fascinating account. But *please*, what can we do to silence the child long enough to have such a conversation?"

Her glamour lapsed, and she reverted to her more striking appearance. He wondered if that was her true mien; she was certainly more attractive that way.

She said with a shrug, "I suspect the babe will only quieten when I feed her." Placing the child against her shoulder, she knelt to rummage around with her free hand in the bundle of clothing that had been deposited on the deck, and emerged a moment later with what looked like a tiny pottery teapot. A baby feeder, he assumed. She rocked the child, but it continued to wail.

"You are full of surprises, Mistress Marten. Is the child yours?"

"No. And my real name is Sorrel Redwing."

"Should I know it?"

"Probably not, unless you happened to hear of the unimportant murder of a country landsman by his wife a year or two ago."

"Ah." Once again, she had left him floundering for words. The name was unknown to him, but the story sounded even more fascinating. "Ah. Well. Yet another intriguing tale to be told one day, but not now, I feel. Come below; this sunshine is not a place for a baby's soft skin."

"Not yet, my lord. There is something I must tell you first."

Her tone halted him as effectively as a hold on his arm. He could read it as clearly as words on a page. She was terrified, but not for herself. Nor for the baby either. "Someone is in trouble on *Spice Winds*, I suppose," he said. Then he groaned. "Don't tell me it's Saker Rampion."

It was her turn to be shocked.

"How . . . how very astute of you, Lord Juster. Most of that tale can wait. Except you should know that Saker is, or was up to last night, on board *Spice Winds*. I have every reason to believe he may be in great danger."

Juster winced. "That man courts disaster like a wind-rover courts a breeze."

"Perhaps. Although I seem to remember a time when it was you who was closer to disaster then he."

The smile she gave contained not a little mockery, the minx.

Just then, the tar who cared for the goats arrived with a mug of milk, so he said, "Allow me to escort you to my cabin, Mistress Redwing, where you can bribe that child into blessed silence and I can hear myself think while you tell your story."

"You are a man of infinite good sense, my lord. I hope I can encourage you to extricate the witan from his present predicament. Although," she added as they descended the companionway, "he is a resourceful man, with a habit of extricating himself. Still, I'm sure he'd appreciate your assistance."

Her effrontery amused him. Dressed as she was, with the blood still unexplained, and with her station in life apparently lowly, she addressed him as if she was an equal. He was beginning to like Sorrel Redwing. A lot.

She seated herself on his bed under the stern windows and began feeding the baby from the tiny pot with practised ease. Her fearless calm fascinated him. She treated him with all the poise of an aristocratic dowager, reminding him of his formidable grandmother. He was none too sure who would win a confrontation in the unlikely event of such a meeting.

"As much as I would like to know the full story on what brings you and Saker here," he began, "I think perhaps we had better deal with first things first. What danger is Saker in?"

"The captain of *Spice Winds* sent me off in that boat this morning with several sailors who had instructions to get rid of me in whatever fashion they saw fit. I don't know what happened to Saker, but I do know that if Captain Lustgrader was prepared to murder me, he would be more than prepared to kill Saker."

He digested that with growing wonder. Several sailors? And where, pray, were they now?

Deciding this was not the time to enquire, he asked instead, "When you left the ship, where was Saker?"

"In the brig, I believe."

"Mistress, I don't know that I can help. I'm a privateer, and if I were to go over to the Lowmian fleet they might well point a cannon at my boat, and a musket at my head. They certainly wouldn't answer any questions. And any enquiry by me or my crew could make things worse for Saker, not better."

"We have a lascar friend on board. Name of Ardhi. He will help Saker if he can. He was on watch last night, so he was probably sleeping this morning and missed what happened to us. Perhaps if you could talk to him . . ."

He stared at her, and resisted an almost overwhelming desire to hear every detail of just how an Ardronese witan had ended up on a Lowmian ship heading for the Spicerie. "Wait here," he said. "Finish feeding that child. I'll do what I can."

Leaving the cabin, he sought out his first mate and found him up on the deck staring at the Lowmian fleet through a spyglass. "Finch," he asked, "can you get another bumboat over at *Spice Winds* with our spies on board? I want them to find out what's going on over there. I'm interested in a tall fellow, dark hair, dark eyes, slim and tough, handsome sod. Might be in trouble, and in need of rescue. Come to think of it, you know him: Saker Rampion."

"The witan who rescued you from falling on to the deck headfirst from the rigging?"

"The very same."

"Might be difficult getting a bumboat close, cap'n. Seems *Spice Winds* chased them all off earlier on. The lookout in the crow's nest just told us it looked as if they were getting ready to keel-rake someone." He indicated the spyglass. "Been trying to make sense of what they're up to meself."

"Scupper the scuts!" *Saker, I'll wager that's you they intend to send to scrape barnacles off the ship's bottom. What the blistering pox did you do this time? Fuck the captain's daughter?* "What d'you reckon you're seeing?"

"Can't really make it out. Summat's going on, for sure. There's a weird hornswaggling lot o' birds around the ship, for a start." He sighed. "Va-damned horror, keel-raking; makes a bloodied mess of a man. Can rip his pizzle off, for starters. Maybe the blood and flesh in the water is what's attracting them birds."

Fuck. "Get the sloop in the water, Finch. And make it quick."

"Cap'n—"

"No. Don't say it, Finch. I know. But that man saved my neck once, so if I can rescue his pizzle—! Tell Surgeon Barklee he's coming with us."

"Aye, aye, sir!"

"Oh, and get the bath and hot water down there into my cabin, towels, and that chest of women's clothing? Get it brought in too."

Once Finch and Cranald had everything in hand, he returned to Sorrel Redwing. "My cabin is yours, mistress, for the moment. I would strongly advise a bath and some clean clothes. Choose what you will from the selection I have on board. In the meantime, I will see to the health of this wormhole-skulled witan."

Without waiting for her reaction, he left the cabin, already considering how best to save a man who might just have been keel-raked.

20

Keel-raked

Saker knew that Ardhi, standing near the end of the spar, could dive or jump straight into the sea. Quickly he looked away, hoping no one else noticed the lascar's presence up there. Instead he concentrated on the birds, bringing them lower and closer. Confused and unsettled, they battled against the alien nature of their subjugation to him. Worse, as a flock of mixed species, they squabbled among themselves.

Another glance around the deck told him the rope under the keel was now in place. He turned to the sailor still clutching his arm. "How does this keel-raking work?" he asked, sounding much calmer than he felt. With his hands tied behind his back like this, there was no easy way they could pull him under the ship.

It was the bo'sun who answered, and he spoke to the sailor, not him. "Untie his wrists and bind them in front, using that." He was pointing at the end of the rope hanging over the bulwark; the rest of it snaked into the sea and under the ship. "Quickly now. Oh, and take off his shirt first."

Bile surged into his throat at the thought of his bare skin scraped over barnacles. *Va save me.* His fear made him merciless, and he imposed his will on the birds, yanking them onto a steep, downwards trajectory. They screamed their anger at the coercion, but came anyway, exuding a contradictory eagerness to please.

I hate this, he thought.

The sailor began to untie his wrists. A small porthole of opportunity was opening . . . He gathered himself for the sliver of time that was his chance.

"Take care!" the bo'sun snapped at the sailor. He took a fistful of Saker's hair and wrenched his head down to his knees. "We don't want him jumping overboard."

He swore, but wasted no effort in struggling. He turned his attention to the largest bird instead, pictured the bo'sun's bald head, and channelled the avian anger towards it. There was a rush of wings, strong beats cleaving the air, a screech and men shouting their warnings. His hands were free. The hold on his hair was gone. Blood dribbled down the side of the bo'sun's face as he clutched his head in disbelief. Saker lunged for the ship's bulwarks.

And someone tripped him as he flung himself forward. Accidental or deliberate, he didn't know, but the result was the same. He fell hard, face-down, on the deck. Someone kneed him in the back to pin him there.

Voices yelled, an appalled chorus around him.

"What the sweet cankers is going on?"

"Hang me for a haggard! What the fobbing pox are the birds *doing*?"

"I'll be beggared! They're everywhere!"

Saker focused. Slashing beaks, clawing talons, powered wings tilting across the deck like windmill blades. *Cry*, he commanded. *Shriek! Screech! Scratch! Lacerate!*

The pressure on his back disappeared and he scrambled to his feet.

Men scattered, but their fear swirled around him, interwoven with the fury of the birds. Feathers floated in the air. Above it all, he heard Lustgrader shouting orders, roaring for someone to tie the factor up, to stop the leery lubber of a quill-sharpener. "It's him doing this; it's all his fault, the factor; seize the fobbing factor!"

Saker dived for the bulwarks once more, and was tackled again. It was the bo'sun, his head still streaming blood as he shouldered Saker to the deck. Two sailors flung themselves into the fray, weighing him down with their bodies. He struggled, called to the birds. Someone snatched up the keel-rake rope and tied his hands in front of him. The birds came, ripping at the men, but other sailors beat them back with belaying pins.

He saw bloodied feathers, crippled wings, broken beaks; felt their dying, their terror, their pain. His mind screamed at them, *Fly!*

And those that could lifted into the sky to safety. Sickened at the carnage around him, at the pain and the confusion and terror echoing in his skull, none of it his, he had to force himself to rationality. He looked down at his piniomed hands, saw the rope snake away from his wrists, over the port bulwark and into the sea. He knew without looking that the other end was somewhere on the deck.

There would be no going back once it was tied to his feet.

He struggled to rise, but one of the sailors still pinned him down. Glancing sideways, he saw two pelicans lumbering about on the deck in a panic, unable to take off again from such a confined space. A sailor holding a belaying pin raised his arm, his lips pulled into a grimace as he prepared to shatter the skull of one of them.

"No!" Saker heaved away the seaman sprawled across him, and sat up calling the two pelicans towards him. They obeyed, running, wings spread to beat the air in ineffectual attempts at flight. Va above, they were *huge*. Ungainly, with beaks as long and as broad as barbarian broadswords, and swinging throat pouches as large as a fat man's beer gut . . . The belaying pin missed its target.

A massive beak stabbed at the sailor trying to push Saker back down to the deck. The man back-pedalled away, aghast. Saker picked the bird up, surprised to find out how light it was, and tossed it bodily over the side of the ship. It momentarily laboured to fly, then caught the wind and was gone. The bo'sun charged at Saker, just as the second pelican lumbered up, its beak opening like a gaping vat lid. They collided, the bo'sun tripped and the bird was bowled over.

Saker grabbed it and hugged it to his chest, soothing it with his thoughts. He flung himself over the bulwarks with the bird in his arms, but released it in mid-air as they fell. The pelican opened its wings in time to skim the surface of the sea, paddling furiously at the waves with its webbed feet until it lifted into the air. Saker plunged past it into the water, the rope attached to his hands uncoiling behind him.

Surfacing again, he bent his head to the knots on his bonds, attacking them with his teeth. He had to loose them before it occurred to someone to haul him in.

His terror mounted as, out of the corner of his eye, he saw the slack of the rope begin to disappear into the depths. Someone was already hauling on it from the other side of the ship.

Pickle it, Ardhi, where are you?

Someone – or something – splashed into the water beside him and disappeared beneath him, only to pop up a moment later a few paces away.

Ah. Think of the reeky fellow, and he appears. He had the kris clamped in his teeth.

Saker held out his hands. "Quick!"

Too late. A sudden jerk on the rope yanked him sideways and pulled his face under the water.

He twisted and thrust himself up, spluttering, gasping for air. Ardhi was stroking towards him, fast. Saker just had time to take another gulping breath, and then he was wrenched away, hands first, under the water. Towards the ship.

Too fobbing fast, Va help me.

His last glimpse was of Ardhi reaching out to grasp him – and missing.

Helpless, his arms stretched forward, head under the surface, he was dragged down. And down.

How can they pull me so fast? Ardhi will never be able to catch up! Logic, as chill as ice, told him they'd done the sensible thing and put the rope through a pulley and were hauling on it, a number of them. Beggar them, those bilge-crawling tars.

The hull loomed over his head, and he slammed into it, just getting a shoulder up in time to save his skull from taking the brunt.

The rope dipped further down. He flipped over to protect his face and stomach, allowing his back to be scraped along the hull. No barnacles, thank Va. Yet. He was going to be ripped to pieces any time now.

Thoughts scrambled through his mind, each a quicksilvered flash of knowledge layered on top of the last.

He didn't have enough air.

If he hit his head on the underside of *Spice Winds*, he could be knocked unconscious.

The only thing that could save him now would be something happening on the deck . . . like . . . birds disrupting the keel-raking.

Blood, feathers, crippled wings. More dying terns and shearwaters and petrels, sacrificed for him,

I am a Shenat witan. I dedicated myself to the way of the Oak.

With a deliberate, brutal briskness, he made his decision to accept whatever happened. No more deaths, not even of birds.

If I die, I die.

Silver light, a sinuous gliding shape, flashed in front of him. He thought it must be a sea snake, bumping into the rope. But then his forward momentum ceased. The rope tying his wrists was no longer attached to anything.

He was floating, trapped beneath the curve of the ship's hull, bumping gently against the wood. No cladding, those witless Lowmian ship-builders . . .

The Chenderawasi kris. It was swimming, right in front of him. It had severed the rope, stopped the keel-raking.

Now what? It's too late. I can't think. Air all gone.

The kris slipped itself between his hands to slash the bonds apart. He could swim now, and felt a frustrated grief. Flashes like tiny bursts of lightning obscured his sight. His ears were filled with a rushing sound as if the ocean was weeping against his eardrums. *Sorrel, what of Sorrel.* He must not die . . .

She has a witchery. She's strong and brave.

He'd run out of air. He clamped his now free hand over his nose, refusing to take water into his lungs, but had nothing left to drive his body through the water. His last coherent sensation was the comforting grip on his arm, a hand closing around his bicep. He wasn't alone.

Va?

The lights exploded in his head, his lungs ached and ached, pain was everywhere, and fear and terror and horror and . . .

Peace.

His next thought – was it immediate? – had to do with the gripping pain in his chest as he dragged in a much-needed breath. He coughed, racking coughs. He heard a voice saying in his ear in Pashali, "Can you possibly be a little *quieter*?"

He opened his eyes. Gasped and heaved, sucking in precious air. Spat out saltwater. Ardhi was floating next to the ship's planking, holding on to him. When he looked up, he saw they were on the surface, sheltered by the bowsprit. It was not much of a hiding place; if anybody looked over the bulwark at the prow, they would be seen. A temporary safety, at best.

"Thanks." One more breath, and then he was ready to have his question answered, the one that had been hammering at him ever since he'd been taken to the brig. "Where are they? What happened to them?"

Ardhi was silent.

"Tell me!"

"I don't know. When I came off duty, I went to my hammock. I didn't know they'd sent you to the brig. When I woke up, one of the tars told me you were in big trouble. He also said Fels and Voster had taken Sorrel and Piper off in the dinghy. He said they were being sent ashore."

"But you don't believe it."

Ardhi shook his head. "Not likely, is it? You know what Fels and Voster are like. Worst scum in the bilge. Lustgrader knows what they are. The only good thing was that Banstel was with them, and we know he's besotted with Piper. Saker, we have to get out of here. Now."

"Have you got the kris?"

"Of course. It swam back to me. The question is – what do we do? We can hardly wait here until nightfall, hoping no one will spot us. That's not going to happen. Yet they'll see us if we swim away."

He was silent, thinking. There would be bumboats from the shore, supplies arriving. They were sheltering directly under the ship's heads. He and Ardhi would indeed be seen sooner or later, probably sooner. Va damn, the ship's crew would already be looking out for his body.

"No suggestions?" Ardhi asked neutrally.

"Not really. Apart from saying it might be wiser for you to sneak back on board before you're missed. Did anyone see you dive?"

"I'm not sure."

"Look, I can start to swim away under the water, bob up every now and then to take a breath, hoping no one sees me. If someone does start a ruckus, it would at least give you an opportunity to get back on the ship."

He pointed to a rope, the end of which was floating in the water only an arm's length from them. Ardhi rolled his eyes. They both knew where it began: in the heads. A piece of rope was dropped through each of the two latrine holes in the decking above them, one on either side of the bowsprit. When needed, the rope was hauled up and the wet fluffed-out tip was used to wipe a sailor's arse.

Saker looked at him, and his compassion stirred. "If you leave the ship now, you'll never get back on."

Three plumes, still on board hidden in Ardhi's baggage. And the fourth not far away – but only as long as the lascar stayed with *Spice Winds*. If the fleet sailed without him, he might lose the plumes for ever.

Ardhi bit his lip, thinking.

"You know that's true. Look, I can swim to shore from here. Well, I can *try* anyway. I can use the birds to conceal me every time I come up for breath. Better still, I can go several hundred paces and then let them see me. That'll give you the chance you need to climb back unseen."

"If they catch sight of you, they'll send a boat after you. They can sail or row faster than you can swim. You mustn't be seen. Saker, it's a matter of life or death for you. You know that."

He did, too.

At that moment, the decision was taken out of their hands. Above their heads, someone yelled, "He's here! At the bow!"

Another voice replied a moment later. "The lascar is with him. I *told* you I saw someone else go into the water. Tell the captain!"

Neither he nor Ardhi hesitated. As one, they dived and began swimming underwater. Ardhi's instinct was to swim directly for the shore, but Saker grabbed his hand and pointed to the stern. Fortunately, Ardhi followed his lead; if they'd swum directly outwards they would have been easily visible in the clear water. Instead, they swam underwater alongside the ship where they couldn't be seen from the overhanging deck. Neither of them surfaced until they were at the stern. There, it was easy enough to remain out of sight, next to the rudder.

"Well, that answered your question. They know I helped you," Ardhi whispered. Above, they could hear the sailors calling to one another, organising themselves to scan the sides of the vessel, arranging to man the pinnace, which was already in the water, and to launch the longboat.

"We swim together. I'll bring the birds down onto the sea. Cormorants, gulls, pelicans. Every time we come up for breath, we come up in the middle of the floating flock. All right?"

Ardhi nodded.

But it wasn't all right, he knew that. Everything the lascar had worked for, every sacrifice he had made, his years of work – they were all for nothing if he had to leave the plumes in the hands of Lowmians.

And not so good for us Ardronese, either, he thought, his gut twisting. *There's too much power in those fobbing plumes. We'll all suffer for this.* "Ready?"

"As ready as I'll ever be."

They dived away from the ship, side by side. While he swam, he called the birds again, gentling them down onto the water in a raft of floating bodies. When he and Ardhi surfaced in the middle of the flock of mixed seabirds, he was assailed with guilt. Because of him, so many birds had died that day. Yet they clustered around him, reaching out with their beaks, tapping him gently in affection, and his guilt doubled.

"Let's move on," he said, and the ache inside him was a physical pain. Sorrel and Piper were gone; Va knew if they were even still alive. He knew Voster and Fels; everyone on board did. They were the ship's rats. The bullies who had no moral compass. And Lustgrader, damn him to a choiceless hell, must have specifically chosen them for the job.

Only one answer made sense. The captain wanted Piper and Sorrel dead.

He stopped that thought before he could dwell on it. You have to hope. You always have to hope, at least until every vestige is snatched away from you. Sorrel. And Piper. No, he couldn't think that. He wouldn't think that. Not yet . . .

Sorrel's a fighter . . . and she's clever.

For a second time, then a third and a fourth, they submerged and swam on. The birds flew ahead and alighted on the water once more where and when he asked. From within the safety of the flock they looked back at the ship to see that both the *Spice Winds*' longboat and its pinnace had been launched.

"They haven't seen us y—" he began, but before the rest of the sentence was out of his mouth, sailors lined along the rail started shouting, pointing them out to the two boats.

"I think they realised that looking among the birds would be a good idea," said Ardhi. "We might do better without them from now on."

"Better idea – we confuse the issue with lots of birds." The next time they surfaced, there were separate floating rafts of birds in all directions.

Let them try and work out just where we've gone, he thought as he looked around in satisfaction. When he glanced back at the ship again, no one was pointing at them, but his complacency vanished much faster than it had arisen. *Spice Winds* had opened up some of the gun ports and was running out the guns.

"Pox on them!" he muttered, then asked with more optimism, "Can they hit us with cannonballs? Isn't that a bit like hurling acorns at an ant floating in middle of a very large lake?"

"It would be, yes, if they were about to use the cannon. But those are the carronade ports. They intend to pepper us with grapeshot, or maybe canister shot. Effective at short range. They spray musket balls in all directions."

"Can they hit us from there?"

"Oh, yes. Let's get out of here." Ardhi didn't wait; he dived and was gone.

Saker lingered a moment. No more deaths. He sent a vague sense of unease to the birds and then snapped his connection to them, to all of them. And dived once more.

When he broke the surface again it was to hear the explosion of gunpowder. Water twenty paces away dimpled as it was peppered with grapeshot. The birds had already disappeared.

After that, it became a frantic race, one he didn't think they could win. It was a matter of which happened first: being hit by the shot or found by *Spice Winds*' boats.

21

Shipboard Reunion

"What the blistering pox was that?" Lord Juster, seated in the prow of *Golden Petrel*'s sloop, twisted around in his seat. A puff of smoke was still drifting in the air around the gunports of *Spice Winds*. "They are *firing* at us?"

"Not at us, methinks, cap'n," the able seaman at the tiller replied. "That were grapeshot, that were. Couldn't hope to hit us with grapeshot, not from this distance."

Juster considered that. "No, you're right. But I'd like to know just what they are firing at. Or whom." He sighed in a mixture of hope and worry. "Look for someone in the water."

Rampion would have escaped, of course. The impudent witan had the sneakiness of a wharf rat and the luck of an alley cat on the prowl. "Head towards wherever that grapeshot is landing. Mister Cranald, what's your assessment? Will these scurvy Lowmians risk hitting us, do you think?"

"Doubt it, cap'n," the mate replied as another cannonade was fired. "Karradar councilmen take a dim view of outside conflicts being brought into the Bay. Killing some of their own crew wouldn't shiver the Karradar Council none, but hitting another ship's boat? Deliberately?" He shook his head. "If the Lowmians want to come back again, they'll behave themselves."

"My thought exactly." Still, he was glad he'd left Finch in charge on board and brought Grig Cranald with him, rather than the other way around. If anything happened to him, Finch could take charge of *Golden Petrel*. Grig was a fine sailor, but he was only thirty. Finch was the one with a lifetime of experience of handling men.

He stood up, holding on to the mast, as several more volleys of grapeshot scattered like hail into the waves, but after that, nothing. He laughed. "Ah, we're safe. Their own boats have just joined in the search and they won't risk hitting them."

The *Spice Winds*' pinnace and longboat had separated, obviously looking for someone in the water. The birds clustering around earlier had all dispersed.

"A Karradar gold guinea," he said, "to the first person to see someone in the water!"

The able seaman in the prow spotted the swimmer before the Lowmians did, but when the man pointed him out, Juster was disappointed. It wasn't Saker.

That's a Pashali, surely. Or maybe the lascar Mistress Marten mentioned. No, not Marten. Redpoll? Redwing. Confound it, I want to get to the bottom of that story, too.

When the man saw the *Golden Petrel*'s sloop approaching, he swam towards them using an unusual swimming stroke that involved keeping his face down and bringing his arms up out of the water one at a time to drive himself forward with powerful strokes, occasionally breathing by turning his head to the side. Juster had never seen anything like it before. Weird, but effective.

And fast. Fascinating. I must try that sometime.

Unfortunately, the Lowmian pinnace was faster. A strong breeze had filled the sails and the boat was scudding after the swimmer like a shark after a meal.

"Give those Lowmian lowlifes something to think about," he told his crew. "Steal their wind. Show them how Ardronese sail!" *Golden Petrel* was a disciplined ship, where drills were a part of every day, on the voyage and in port, and it paid off in a situation like this one. He nodded to Cranald. "You take the tiller."

He sat back to watch Grig's skills unfold with seamless precision. The race between the pinnace and the sloop culminated in a clever manoeuvre that robbed the pinnace's sail of the wind at the crucial moment, followed by another that stopped the more manageable sloop dead in the water alongside the swimming man just long enough for the two crewmen to heave him in. The pinnace, trying to make up for the earlier mistake, now shot past them too fast.

The master of the Lowmian boat yelled as they raced by. "That there tar is a deserting scut! A no-good grog-blossom of a lascar! I *demand* you return him."

I know that fellow. They'd met in Karradar years before. Juster stood again. "Overly fond of the demon drink, is he, Tolbun? In that case, I imagine you'd be glad to get rid of him."

"You know the law, Dornbeck! You tell him he's ours until he is released from his contract."

He turned to Ardhi. "Did you sign a contract, my good man?"

"No. They think I not read or write. They never bother ask me sign paper." His lips were twitching as if he was trying not to laugh.

And you can read and write? Now that's interesting . . .

He turned back to the Lowmians with a bland expression on his face, shouting across to the other boat as they drew apart, "No contract. Sounds like he was a passenger, not a crewman. Tell your captain that Lord Juster Dornbeck says if the contract is produced, signed and sealed with the Ustgrind company seal, then he'll get his man returned, forthwith!"

There was no reply from the other boat as it sailed away.

"Picaroons," Juster muttered and grinned at the lascar. "Now tell me, where is that dammed witan?"

The man grinned back, pulled his dagger out of its sheath and flung it into the sea.

"Best follow that," he said, "if Factor Reed Heron is man you mean."

The only time Sorrel had heard the sound of cannon fire was to cele-brate the birth of the Lowmian heir, but she knew exactly what she was hearing when *Spice Winds* fired its carronade. The sound carried over the sea like thunder and she leapt out of the tin bath, careless of dripping water, to kneel on the bed and peer out of the windows of Juster's cabin. All she could see was the shore.

She glanced at Piper. The baby had been bathed and wrapped in some of the fine linens in the trunk delivered to the cabin, and was now asleep on Dornbeck's bed. She wasn't stirring. Grabbing up a towel, Sorrel dried herself and began to dress, flinging on clothing as quickly as she could. The trunk had contained a selection of women's attire, all of it of a quality she'd never dreamed of wearing. Even the most modest was more akin to something worn at the Ardronese court by a noblewoman's wife, not by a humble handmaiden, while the immodesty and flamboyance of several other gowns made her eyes widen and wonder just what type of woman would ever clad herself in something so daring.

Donning one of the more modest gowns, she glanced in the mirror and halted, astonished at the image before her. Her hair was wildly disordered, out of keeping with the rest of her appearance, but it was the soft curve of her breasts that caught her eye. Dear Va, she couldn't walk out on the deck of a privateer with a bodice that displayed more than it hid! Nor could she cover her shoulders with a wrap, not in this warmth which was already causing perspiration to sheen her skin.

She dug into her own bundle of clothing and brought out an item she'd carried with her everywhere: a grey kerchief with an oakleaf-patterned trimming of lace. Tucking the ends into the cleft between her breasts, she arranged it to make up for the deficiencies of the gown.

Pickle it, that would have to do. Ignoring the paints and powders she'd also found in the trunk, she found a hairbrush and dragged it through her sorely neglected tresses full of salt-encrusted tangles. Surveying the result, she sighed. *Vex you, Lord Juster, I think I'm not in the least like your usual onboard female company!*

In truth, the whole cabin was a witness to Dornbeck's extravagant lifestyle. Silk sheets and a feather mattress on the bed, paintings on the wall, lush carpets on the floor, a chamber pot of finest porcelain . . . She had never thought to see anything like this on board a ship.

Leaving Piper asleep, with pillows arranged to make sure she couldn't roll off the bed, Sorrel propped open the cabin door and hurried up on deck.

The rumbling of gunfire in the distance had ceased.

Saker was tiring.

They hadn't swum in a straight line to the shore. Once they'd been seen, they'd had to dodge by diving and changing direction, even doubling back. They'd split up too, Saker heading north-west, Ardhi north-east, so the further they went, the further they were apart.

A stiff breeze had patterned the surface of the water so they'd become harder to locate, but it also made the swim more difficult. *Spice Winds* had stopped firing at them in order to allow their boats to search, but each time he surfaced Saker was wearier. Those weeks of sailing from Ustgrind to Karradar had taken a toll on his fitness. Still, he wasn't going to give up. He took another deep breath and dived beneath the waves yet again.

Next time he surfaced, he turned on to his back and floated. He needed the rest. When the swell of a wave raised him up, he saw there were now three small boats, all uncomfortably close. At first he assumed another boat from the fleet had been launched, but then he recognised the flag at the masthead: a yellow seabird in flight on a blue background.

Va-damn. How the foaming oceans had Juster known he needed help?

There was a sudden shout from the *Spice Winds*' longboat. An extended arm pointed towards him and left no doubt that he'd been seen. Wearily he dived yet again. A fish darted in front of him, long and silver, with odd shaped gills and fins behind the head. He followed it as it turned, not knowing why. When he rose again all the boats were closer, with the Lowmian pinnace almost on top of him. He trod water, wondering just how far Juster would go to save him.

The silver fish swam up and slipped in between his fingers. His hand closed around hard, inflexible metal. The kris. He stayed where he was, wondering what it intended, not sure how best he could use it.

The pinnace glided up, and someone seized him by the hair. Tolbun, the mate. *Pox on it, I'm going to wear my hair short in future.*

Tolbun said, snidely triumphant, "That keel-raking is still scheduled for today. All your swimming was for naught, Factor Heron."

"That remains to be seen," he replied.

He had concealed the dagger in his hand, holding it under the water, pressed against his thigh. He could easily have reached up and stabbed the man, but he felt no inclination to do so. Instead, he raised his free hand and shoved the heel of his palm hard against Tolbun's nose. The man jerked back and let go of his hair.

Saker dived under the boat and jabbed the dagger point into the hull. No blade should have been able to penetrate a well-made boat, and he had no idea why he'd attempted it, but the kris always did have a mind of its own. It slid in as if the wood was riddled with ships' worm. Saker twisted it to make the hole larger, withdrew the blade and then swam on under the boat and out on the other side as far as he could go. When he popped up, he was close enough to the Ardronese sloop to recognise Lord Juster sitting forward of the mast. He waved a hand, then turned back towards the Lowmians. "Watch out, Tolbun," he called out, "I think your boat is going to sink any time now."

"You should have seen those Lowmian hornswagglers then, Mistress Redwing," Lord Juster said. "Sad sight, really. The officers sitting in the pinnace, one moment all so proper with their starched collars and hats; the next minute realising more than the soles of their buckled shoes were getting wet. The boat steadily filled to the gunwales until they were up to their thighs in water, as panicked as cats in the rain and fearfully reluctant to abandon ship . . ." He shook his head sadly at Sorrel, while giving her a sidelong look that was pure mischief. "I fear my men jeered them in the most *ungenerous* way."

She smiled, but she was having trouble feeling at ease. She and Juster Dornbeck were sitting at the table in the officers' wardroom with Ardhi, Saker, the weather-beaten first mate who had the Shenat name Finch Aspen, and the attractive third mate, Grig Cranald. It was strange not to have Piper in her arms, or at least nearby, and she kept turning around to look for her even though she knew the child was safe on the deck below. Lord Juster's men had found a woman ashore who, with a six-month-old baby of her own, was happy to feed another for coin.

"Of course, the Lowmian longboat rowed up to their rescue," Juster continued, "so none of them had time to care about us or Saker any more. We hauled a very sorry-looking witan up out of the water and scurried back here as fast as the wind would take us."

Sorrel pushed her concern for Piper away and said quietly, "You're a fool if you think Captain Lustgrader will take any of this calmly. His temper festers, and he will want his revenge. Especially if he ever finds out I'm on board your ship as well."

"Which he will soon know," Finch Aspen said, rubbing a hand through grizzled hair. "It'll be all over the port that a ship of privateers was looking for a wet nurse."

"True," Juster remarked thoughtfully. The look he gave her was far from dismissive. "You appear to have observed Lustgrader closely."

"A woman using a glamour is overlooked and hears much that was not meant for her ears."

He smiled faintly. "I shall take that as a warning. But Lustgrader won't be wanting to upset the Karradar Council. A council who, in spite of their respectable-sounding name, are the biggest gathering of Pashali rogues, Lowmian outcasts and Ardronese pirates in either hemisphere, united only by their unlimited capacity to commit fraud and semi-legal thievery. Not the kind of fellows any ship's captain wants to cross."

Sorrel dabbed at the sweat on her forehead. The room was hot, in spite of having all the windows propped open to let in the sea breeze. Ardhi, now clad in dry garments belonging to a common seaman, was the only person who looked at home in the heat. He'd tied his long hair back with a band of plaited leather and his eyes brightened when his gaze met hers. He had the loveliest smile, she decided, and wondered how he stayed cheerful in a world so foreign to him.

She glanced at Saker. He was wearing a soft linen shirt borrowed from Juster, together with a fancy waistcoat that was too large for his smaller frame and more appropriate for both a royal court and a colder climate. He was uncomfortable, glancing at her, then looking away as if he really didn't want to meet her eye. Several times she saw him eyeing her neckline. Or perhaps it was the kerchief that caught his attention.

I wonder if he remembers that he once gave it to me? Probably not.

"Right now," Juster was saying, "I think we should be frank with one another. There are far too many holes in the stories I've been hearing." He turned to Finch, saying, "Would you and Mister Cranald leave us now, Mister Finch? I'd rather you were both up on deck, keeping an eye on our Lowmian friends."

The old man wryly inclined his head and both men rose to their feet.

"My thanks for your help," Sorrel said.

"Ours too," Saker added.

Once the two men had left, Lord Juster gave Ardhi a shrewd look. "And you . . . seaman? Is it appropriate that a lowly ill-educated youth such as yourself should be present at a captain's table when secrets are discussed?"

The gleam in Juster's eye told her he already knew Ardhi was not a simple seaman, and the way Ardhi's eyes crinkled at the corners said that he knew he was being teased, not insulted. He said something in Pashali, a language Sorrel did not speak. Juster smiled and, when Ardhi had finished, Saker laughed.

Sorrel wanted to ask what he'd said, but knew this was not the time.

"Your educational pedigree aside, Ardhi," Juster said, "there are some questions to which I would like to have the answers, if you would all be gracious enough to indulge me. No one has given me an explanation that makes any sense at all of why Mistress Celandine-Sorrel Marten-Redwing was on *Spice Winds* in the first place, with – what's more – a baby that is apparently not her own, and why Captain Lustgrader wanted to kill you all. Suppose you start from the beginning and give me the entire story?"

This request was met by a studied silence. Juster looked from one to the other; no one said a word. "Saker," he said, pulling a face, "You disappoint me."

"I consider you a friend, but not all secrets are mine to share. My lord, will you take us to Kotabanta in the Summer Seas?"

Sorrel was startled. It was surely a strange question to which Saker must already know the answer. Why would Lord Juster even consider doing such a thing?

"Of course not!" Juster said, echoing her thought. "My job is here, separating cargoes from their Lowmian owners to the best of my buccaneering ability."

"Best of your privateering skills," Saker corrected.

From the way Juster chuckled, she guessed it was a shared joke. "Exactly so." He turned to Ardhi to explain. "I have letters of marque from King Edwayn of Ardrone which permit such, er, piracy. Our aim is to make sure Lowmeer doesn't corner the market on spices. Saker already knows this, so I have no idea why he thinks I would go to Kotabanta."

"I don't. Not really. And because you won't, I don't think it wise to tell you the whole tale. Some things are better not known."

"What utter bilge rot! Knowledge empowers. Information is wealth and safety." Suddenly Juster sounded seriously annoyed.

"Perhaps," Sorrel agreed, "but he's right. There *are* secrets which are not ours to tell. All I can say about myself is that it is of utmost urgency that I reach Vavala as soon as possible. With Piper."

Juster considered that in silence, then turned to Saker. "And you, my friend?"

"Ardhi and I must go on to the Summer Seas."

"Take a Pashali vessel from here to Javenka and arrange an ongoing leg from there. Do you have sufficient money?"

"Hardly. I left everything on board *Spice Winds*. I doubt Lustgrader will restore anything to me."

"So you want money as well. Sometime you must tell me what happened to my rubies."

Juster wasn't looking at Sorrel, which was just as well. Her face burned red with embarrassment. Saker had sold the rubies to supply her with the coin she needed.

"You know whom I serve," Saker said. "You know you'll be paid back."

Juster glanced pointedly at Ardhi. "Do you know who gives this witan his orders?"

"First time we meet, I tear his shirt," Ardhi said. "I saw his medallion. Mystery for me then, but I find out he's a witan. He works for his god." He frowned. "Maybe that not all true. Now I think he works more for Lady Pontifect, not so much for this god."

Sorrel, not for the first time, was impressed by Ardhi's acuity. *He understands you better than you understand yourself, Saker.* "Lord Juster," she said, "the secret I hold, of who Piper's parents are and what her parentage means, I hold for the Pontifect. You have my assurance that it is in Ardrone's interest that I reach her. I still have some money that Saker gave me. I don't know whether it will be enough."

"When I left Ardrone," Juster said slowly, "Lady Mathilda was about to marry. You were her handmaiden. Now you turn up with a baby of an age to match a baby – if there was such a one – born some nine months or thereabouts after a royal wedding. My mind is—"

"—jumping to unjustified conclusions!" Saker interrupted. "You will be glad to know that the Regala Mathilda gave birth, as is customary, in the presence of numerous court officials, to a son and heir. Piper is a girl."

"Ah. I'm relieved on that score, then. Consider it done, Mistress

Sorrel. If you need money, I will supply it. Finding a safe berth for you might be much more problematical as ships from here to the Va-cherished Hemisphere are not suitable for a wayfaring lady travelling alone. The traders who ply the route are rough and ready. It might be easier and safer to go via the Pashalin Empire."

She sent an unhappy look to Saker.

"You could go with Saker as far as Javenka," Juster pointed out. "Javenka is closer to us now than Throssel. It's not so bad, Mistress Sorrel. Pashali ships happily take passengers and look after them well. They ply back and forth regularly because Pashalin buys and sells goods here for the Va-cherished Hemisphere."

She stared at him, trying to take in all he was saying, a sick feeling rising up through her stomach.

"Once you're in Javenka," he went on, "Pashali coastal vessels would take you to the start of the mastodon caravan route on the Bay of Kzyl and hence to the Principalities over the ice cap. Very safe, and you'd find it interesting."

She was appalled. "*Interesting?* I am *not* interested in it being interesting! I have a child to consider. Besides, it would take *months!*"

"It would take you four months to get from here to Vavala anyway. Possibly six. Plus you could be waiting weeks, or even months right here in Karradar, for a suitable berth on a Lowmian or Ardronese ship with an honest captain prepared to take you as far as Ustgrind or Throssel and not treat you as the ship's whore servicing the sailors. Forgive me for my bluntness, but it needed to be said."

She shot Saker a look of angry frustration. "This is all your fault!" Standing abruptly, she dropped Lord Juster a curtsy. "Forgive my rudeness, captain. You are generous indeed, and I am truly grateful. I never had any wish to be a burden to anyone. Now I must leave you to attend to Piper."

She left the room blinded by tears, unable to decide whether she was crying with despair or sheer uncontrollable rage. *Va-damn you, Saker Rampion! If you'd kept your pizzle where it belongs, perhaps none of this would ever have happened.*

Saker slumped back in his chair, feeling as if he'd been kicked in the gut.

Juster sent him a sidelong look. "Why," he asked, "just an hour or two after being saved from a nasty form of torture, culminating in death by hanging, do you look about as happy as a mealworm on a fishhook?"

"Maybe because that's how I feel: as low as a mealworm. She's right: I'm the one who involved her in this mess in the first place. If it hadn't been for me, she'd be safe in Vavala by now, and as ridiculous as it may sound, the Va-cherished Hemisphere would be safer as well."

"Not all true," Ardhi remarked. "Much my fault too. And Va-cherished Hemisphere is *not* safe."

"She didn't deserve any of the things that have happened to her," he replied. "She has saved my life. And it has cost her dearly." Sweet Va, what had he ever brought to her in return, save misery?

He thought back at all she had done to keep him alive, from the first time in an Ardronese courtroom, then risking herself on the Chervil moors and later in Ustgrind Castle in the Regala's solar, not to mention bringing Juster to his aid just then.

"Come to think of it, she's actually saved my neck four times. And yes, you are to blame too, Ardhi. I don't know how either of us can compensate her. Fiddle-me-witless, Juster, how can we send her off on a journey halfway around the known world, with a baby and no protector?"

Juster snorted. "Sounds as if she doesn't need one. Not if she can repeatedly rescue a swordsman agent of the Pontifect! Sounds to me as if *you* are the one who needs help. She has a glamour for a start. You *did* know that, I suppose?"

"Of course I did," he snapped. He took a deep breath and added more calmly, "Would you consider giving up this particular privateering jaunt and taking her to Vavala instead, if I could give you a good enough reason?"

"There's no possible reason that could be great enough. If we lose this spice war, Ardrone will be a subject nation of Lowmeer economically, and we'll all be doffing our hats to the Regal. I *must* reduce the Lowmian profits long enough for Prince Ryce to get our new fleet in the water! Then with copper cladding on our ships to prevent ship's worm, and our knowledge of how to prevent scurvy, *we* will rule the oceans and the trade and the wealth, not Lowmeer."

"You are one ship and one man. How much can you achieve? Let's say you do catch Lustgrader's fleet on the way home. Five ships, one a fully-armed galleon. Are you going to sink them all?"

"Well, it used to be I'd steal what I could and run for home. Not any more. And I am not one man. I have the best crew afloat."

"So?"

"First, odds are that the Lowmian galleon and the carrack will not make it back from the Summer Seas. They are old, and ship's worm will make honeycombs of their hulls. If they do arrive here on the homeward journey, they'll have so much marine growth on their bottoms, they'll be as slow as grain barges going upstream. First decent storm, and they're gone.

"Secondly, the Lowmians are so determined not to learn anything from the Va-forsaken Hemisphere, they'll lose at least half their crew to scurvy and fevers. No one on any ship of mine ever sickens with scurvy, and few die of the Fitful Fever, because I know how to prevent them." He nodded to Ardhi. "Thanks to lascars, who told us about Karradar limes for scurvy, and about an infusion of the bark of a certain tree for the fever."

Ardhi nodded to Saker in agreement.

"So," Juster continued, "when they call in to revictual here, on their way home, your Lowmian fleet will have – at best – three ships and whatever's left of a sickly crew. It will be like stealing from a child. What I do then is put all their crew on one ship of theirs and let them escape to Lowmeer. I'll even let them have the cargo that's on board. I happen to believe it'd be counter-productive to impoverish Lowmeer, a philosophy your employer promotes, I believe."

Saker nodded. He'd heard Fritillary say as much.

"We're waiting for Kesleer's earlier fleet at the moment. If I have too much cargo for the ships I've seized, I pay the Pashali merchants here to deliver the captured cargo to their caravan terminus in Kzyl Bay, and it finally arrives in the Va-cherished Hemisphere on the backs of mastodons. Once we have a fine merchant fleet, we will bypass Pashalin, of course. But that's all in the future."

Saker shook his head, bemused. "That's the . . . the most curdled crazy thing I think I've ever heard. The same spice cargo goes from the Summer Seas to here in Karradar, bypassing Pashalin, then sets sail for Lowmeer, only to fall prey to you, or so you hope. It then comes back here where *you* now own it and send it all the way to Pashalin! From there it has to cross a number of Va-cherished lands until *finally* some of it ends up in Ardrone."

"And the profits end up in Ardronese pockets, don't forget that," Juster said.

"Not to mention Pashalin's," Saker added.

Ardhi said quietly, "Me, I wonder what price is paid in islands like mine."

Saker was stilled. That sounded very much like a pointed play on words, and he had an uncomfortable feeling it wasn't accidental. *Pickles 'n' hay, life is complicated sometimes.*

"We Chenderawasi folk till the soil and grow the spice trees and pick and dry the spices," Ardhi said.

He thought of the words Ardhi had spoken to Juster in Pashali, and said, "Ardhi, I'd like you to trust me. I want to talk to Lord Juster alone. Do you mind?"

The lascar rose to his feet. The smile he gave was knowing. "I hope your betrayal of secret has good result, no?"

"I would have thought you were confident," Saker snapped. "Confident that your blistering sorcery would win the day."

Ardhi shook his head soberly, the smile vanished. "*Sri Kris,* he tries, but in him, there is little bit of the Raja's regalia, so witchery is also little bit. One plume, though, has much witchery, so much more power. We lost all four plumes. I not sure what happen now. We have only the power in Sri Kris."

He turned and let himself out of the wardroom.

"Translate what he said to me in Pashali earlier, about himself," Juster said. "I'm not sure I understood it all."

"Something like this: 'Not a mere seaman, my lord, but a graduate from the world's most prestigious university. Youthful, perhaps, but a man already old with the weight of the history he carries on his shoulders. Not so lowly either, as counted by men who think birth is important, for I am the grandson of a ruler. A fool, though, who pays yet for his foolishness. You may call me a fool, then, and speak the truth; they call me *si goblok* where I come from. That means: the idiot.'"

"Ah." His expression was wry. I had the gist correct. *Si goblok.*

Delightful expression. And I suppose you know what happened to make him call himself a fool."

"Yes, he did tell me."

Juster eyed him moodily. "I'm guessing this is all about who Piper is."

"Juster, there isn't one secret. There are several. Ardhi's secret is all about feathers. Plumes of the paradise birds found in the Chenderawasi Archipelago, which is the only place where nutmeg trees grow. On board *Spice Winds* there are three such plumes that belong to Ardhi. He abandoned them to save my life today, and they meant everything to him. Possibly his life. The debt I just racked up to him is, well, huge." He ran a worried hand over his hair. "On *Sentinel*, that's the Lowmian galleon, there's another plume that used to belong to Ardhi."

"So? They are valuable . . . why? To adorn ladies' hair-dos? Gentlemen's hats?"

"All four are sorcerous artefacts. Or witchery ones, perhaps."

"Superstitious nonsense?"

"No, unfortunately, and I know that for a fact."

"Nasty. So are you going to tell me the whole story?"

There was a knock at the door before he could reply, and Cranald stuck his head in. "Cap'n, seems the Karradar Council wants to see you both. Now."

22

Secrets

Mathilda smiled at the Regal and popped a sweetbread into his mouth. "Your favourite," she said and dabbed at his lips with a napkin when saliva dribbled on to his chin. He was having trouble with his rotted teeth, so she made sure all the softest dishes coming up from the kitchens were also those most rich in creamy sauces, or made with thick gravy laden with liver and kidneys, or topped with minced oysters and shellfish.

Unfortunately, although he ate the foods wolfishly, he never appeared to have the slightest dyspepsia or imbalance of humours as a result.

He waved her away as he swallowed. "Enough, enough," he said. "It is late, and I must dress. A Regal's responsibilities are never done, my child. Would you ring for that pesky manservant of mine?"

"Of course, Your Grace. Although I really think Torjen is getting too old and decrepit to look after you properly! You ought to retire him and find somebody younger and more able."

She had little expectation that he would follow her advice; he was far too fond of Torjen. The wretched man was the one person she feared because she knew he didn't like her influence. If he were ever suspicious . . .

My plan is not working, she thought as she left the Regal's apartments a while later. *He's never going to die from a surfeit of rich food, confound him.*

Vilmar might have looked sickly, but he was like a stone pillar with a crumbling and mottled exterior and a core of tough granite. So what was she going to do? She didn't think she could stand another month of his pawing hands, his dribbling chin, his rotten breath and his continual disapproval of anything at all frivolous or fun.

I've had enough!

She might have put up with him with more equanimity if there'd been some possibility she would conceive again. Another son would make her position even more secure. However, he called for her to share his bed less and less frequently, and when he did, the result was often inadequate. He was pathetic.

Still, at least she had no cause to worry about the health of the Prince-regal. Karel was her joy, as plump and healthy as a baby could be. He'd be a fine Regal one day, and she'd be the one to educate and teach him, not Vilmar and his sanctimonious relatives and advisers.

First, though, she had to find a way to hasten his father's death.

She had no compunction about that. Why should she? He'd bought her like a gem in Goldsmith Street, without ever asking her how she felt. And afterwards? Not once had he consulted her feelings about anything. He and that canker of a cousin of his, the wards-dame Friselda, they determined who she could talk to, what she wore, what she read and what she did with her days.

Well, she'd show them. She wasn't quite ready to use rat poison yet, but it was a possibility, especially if she could persuade Vilmar to send Torjen into retirement.

Gerelda, cursing the untidy writing of a rural cleric who had sent a letter to the Regal two hundred years previously, sighed and stretched. Va, how she wished the various clerical schools had standardised handwriting conventions, not to mention spelling. Still, she was learning a lot from her research. Too much, perhaps. Sometimes it was hard to find the gems among the dross. There were clues and odd pieces of information that were building up a frightening picture, but Fritillary Reedling had been clear: she wanted proof of the Vollendorns' involvement in twin murder and their supposed pact with A'Va, or the so-called Bengorth's Law that all Vollendorn heirs were supposed to swear to before their coronation. She wanted proof of the Fox family's involvement in the kind of sorcery that could produce men like the gaunt recruiter of lancers. Unfortunately, there was one thing Gerelda was now certain about: the Vollendorns and the Dire Sweepers and the Foxes were all diabolically clever at keeping secrets. They never put anything in writing and were apparently very skilled at making sure no one else did either.

"Agent Gerelda, I think I might have found something."

She raised her head to look across the table to where Perie had been poring over a hand-stitched book. Over the past month and a half of her labours in the castle library, his diligence at his task had surprised her. She'd expected the research to bore him, but on the contrary, the library fascinated him and he was content to spend hours searching the shelves for anything that would help their task, so long as he could also spend time wandering the town. She'd worried at first that his lack of experience in a big city might make him vulnerable, but soon realised his previous wanderings with his father, not to mention his tragedy, had left him with a healthy scepticism of all he was told and a shrewd caution around strangers.

"Yes, what is it, Perie?"

"You said that we should look for mention of Dire Sweepers. Well, I found this. It's about a hundred years old, a collection of reports to the Regal. All signed by a Yan Dyer. Spelled D-Y-E-R. They're all dated and the first date is about fifty years before the last one."

"He must have been a long-lived man."

"They weren't written by the same man. Different handwriting. Might as well compare a cat and a hog."

"Ah. Now that is interesting. What are the reports about?"

"Mainly Horned Death outbreaks. Many years there were none at all. Then all of a sudden there were. All sort of hard to understand 'cause whoever was writing the reports, he didn't want anyone to know what he's talking about, 'cept the Regal. I reckon they be killing sick folk, but it doesn't actually *say* that. Just that 'their misery was brought to an end', or 'their illness terminated mercifully in a quick death'.

"Some reports have other stuff too," he continued. "About twins dying of the Death. Why would they make special reports about twins? As if being a twin was important somehow. Then every now and then, they warn about midwives and clergy, 'specially witans of the Way of the Flow, warning the Regal about them, as if witans were encouraging the spread of the Horned Death. Doesn't seem to make sense to me. Why would any of the clergy promote a plague?"

Gerelda's spirits sank. It was beginning to make too much sense to her, and she didn't like it one little bit. She said, "I don't think they would. They might, however, try to stop Dire Sweepers from killing people who weren't sick at all, and pretending it was because they had the plague."

"The Sweepers did that? That's . . . putrid."

She smiled faintly. "What makes you think these reports have something to do with the Sweepers – other than the name Dyer?"

"One was written by a fellow who mentioned how proud he was to be a dire broom, sweeping away the rot for his liege lord just as his ancestors had done since the days of Aben and Bengorth."

She sat back in her chair. Her heart started to pound. At last. Someone had made a mistake. This was the first indication she'd seen that the Sweepers dated back to the time of Bengorth's Law. She began to smile.

"Is that important?" Perie asked.

"Bless you, Perie! It is indeed. Just the day before yesterday I came across a historian's account of Bengorth's ascent to the throne and his early reign. I've been struggling with it ever since because it's written in old Lowmian. The writer mentions the names of two families who supported Bengorth Vollendorn of Grundorp in his seizure of the throne. One was a family called Voss from Grundorp. Voss is an ancient Lowmian word for a fox. One of the Fox family's largest estates today is just outside Grundorp. And the other family name mentioned is one I've heard before too: Deremer. But do you know what this man's first name was? Aben! Aben Deremer was Bengorth's closest friend. There's a noble family with the surname Deremer living in Grundorp today."

He frowned, trying to follow the connection she was making.

"Perie," she said, "you've placed the Dire Sweepers back in the same time period as the beginnings of the Fox, Deremer and Vollendorn family fortunes. If Bengorth Vollendorn wanted someone to do his dirty work, who would he turn to?"

"His best friend, Aben Deremer."

"Exactly. There's another and better connection to the Deremers, too. Not so long ago, a witan saw a man leading a band of Dire Sweepers and recognised him as a patron of Grundorp University. The Deremers are patrons of the university. It's all coming together."

"So Bengorth became the Regal. Aben Deremer founded the Dire Sweepers. And his other friend, Voss, or Fox, became a pitch-man?

An ancestor of the Ardronese Prime? But how is that possible? Prime Valerian Fox is Ardronese Shenat!"

"Well, he says he is when it suits him, but his actions don't support that. In the past family history, their personal names are neither Ardronese nor Shenat. Then they changed Voss into Fox and said they were Shenat, probably to further their ambition in Ardrone. Possibly they kept their respectable side to the fore in Ardrone, while their sorcerous activities were confined to Lowmeer. Until recently anyway."

"What do they *want*?" Perie asked, puzzled. "All of them! The Prime, the Dire Sweepers? I don't understand. They are already rich and powerful."

"I don't know. I don't know how to stop them, either. Let alone how to prove that Regal Vilmar supports the Dire Sweepers. Or what the present relationship is between Fox and the Regal."

Perie held up a hand to stop her. "Someone's coming," he hissed.

"I wish I had your hearing," she said, and she wasn't at all surprised when the library door opened and a servant stepped in to tell Gerelda that the Regala desired her presence.

It's the same every time I speak to her, Mathilda thought. *She never actually* tells *me anything*.

It was like a stately court dance they performed, just the two of them. She would probe and Gerelda Brantheld would gracefully avoid answering. She would try to trick the woman into being indiscreet, but Gerelda deftly deflected her questions, leaving her none the wiser.

The only difference this time was that Gerelda told her she and Peregrine Clary would soon be leaving.

"We're going to Grundorp University," she said, "where we have every hope there might be more written resources to help us solve your problem, your grace."

Mathilda clutched her shawl around her shoulders. "I don't know how long I can keep up the pretence of being a happy mother and attentive wife when I am so anxious, so sick with worry!" She shivered delicately. "I can't sleep properly. I lie awake, night after night, imagining the worst – imagining my lovely beautiful boy growing into a monster . . ." Her shiver became an involuntary shudder, and she was aware of the irony: her pretence was not far from the reality of her feelings.

"It is so long since I had a good night's sleep," she whispered.

"Why don't you ask a healer for a sleeping draught? I believe there are drops which—"

"How can I? I am the Regala! No one must suspect that there is anything wrong. If they know I can't sleep they might wonder why. I am supposed to be a happy new mother of an heir."

"I've heard there's an apothecary in the castle. If you like, I'll buy something from her and tell her it's for me."

"Would you?" She reached out to clasp her hand. "I would be so grateful."

"I can do that today. I'll bring it to you the same time tomorrow, if that's convenient."

She quelled the smile of triumph that hovered on her lips. "As much as you can persuade her to part with. If you are going away, I may have to make it last for months."

A flash of concern passed across Gerelda's face. "You will be careful, won't you, Your Grace? I mean, don't take too much at any one time."

"No, of course not," she said, with imperious indignation; then, when she guessed that Gerelda was sufficiently contrite, she added, "I have something else you could do for me. My Ardronese handmaiden, Sorrel Redwing. She was a friend, and then she left with – well, you know. I used to have a maid as well, whom I loved dearly and brought with me from Throssel, but she killed herself a while ago. Since then . . ." She sniffed. "I need someone I can trust. Someone I can ask to send a message for me to the Pontifect, for example. Or just someone who is not spying on me all the time! Could you perhaps ask the Pontifect if she could find me someone? Another handmaiden. If the Pontifect sent someone, then my horrible old ward's-dame, the Regal's cousin, would have to allow me to have her."

"I can ask, certainly. I think it would be an excellent idea."

A few minutes later, when Gerelda had gone, Mathilda relaxed and allowed herself a triumphant smile. Even a lawyer wasn't a match for her when it came to manipulation.

23

A Prince Goes Hunting

Prince Ryce, only son of King Edwayn of Ardrone of the House of Betany, moaned in his sleep and kicked off the last of his blankets. In his dream, he'd been unable to build the King's fleet in time for a summer sailing, but the ships left port anyway, possessing only one sail apiece. Even worse, their hulls had no protection against ship's worm. In his dream, the fleet sank, not from ship's worm but because spice beetles in the cargoes ate holes through all the hulls – and everyone turned on him with their blame and their fury. He tried to explain that the lack of copper on the outside hull would not have protected the ship from nasty little things burrowing through from inside, but no one listened.

For some inexplicable reason, he was on board one of the sinking ships, and he'd ended up being pulled into a rowing boat by Regal Vilmar, who berated him for selling him a wife who wasn't pure and then beat him with an oak branch. After that, equally inexplicably, Mathilda appeared riding a horse through the waves and yelling that Prime Valerian Fox was an evil fox with horns. Only the horns weren't like those of a goat or cow; they were the type of horns the heralds blew to signal an important occasion . . . and they were summoning up an army of soldiers with the plague.

He woke, sweating, breathing hard, into the silence of his bedchamber. No horns. No crash of waves, or an indignant sister. And, thank Va, no blasted Fox looking down his supercilious nose and making cutting remarks for which he could only think of suitable replies hours later.

The nightmare was over, but the fear remained.

He groaned just thinking about the horror of all the things going wrong in his waking life. Despite Lord Juster Dornbeck's help with obtaining copper cladding, and despite Saker Rampion's help with sourcing wood for the ships, the Ardronese fleet had not yet sailed. Lowmeer was far ahead of Ardrone in the race for spices. His father was furious and blamed him, which was grossly unfair as in the beginning the King had been the one who wouldn't listen to advice about the importance of a merchant fleet.

None of that, though, would have mattered so much if only Edwayn had still been the ruler he once was: decisive, far-sighted and a good judge of men. Instead, aged only fifty, his mind seemed to be disintegrating.

The worst thing is the way he turns to Fox, Ryce thought. *And I can't understand why!*

He rolled out of bed and considered going into the marital bedroom that adjoined his. But no, he was too agitated for desire, even with Bealina, as pretty as she was. He wished she could be more of . . . a companion. Someone he could talk to, as well as fuck. But Princess Bealina, so blistering young and over-awed, never had much to say about anything. And he was too tired and stressed to encourage her.

My fault. I should take the time to make her feel more at home.

Still, maybe she'd be more mature and confident now she had a son. He grinned with pleasure. A father! He'd secured the continuity of the Ardronese monarchy, and he was only twenty-two. Prince Garred of Ardrone, as lustily healthy as ever a baby could be. It felt good.

He walked to the window. The garden below was still in darkness, but the first dawn light was tingeing the sky. Outside the garden wall he could hear drunken singing. From their choice of songs, he guessed it was a group of young noblemen on their way home from a night of carousing and lovemaking. Not long ago, he would have been one of them. Now, though, that old life of his offered no enticement. Not even the new chambermaid with her come-hither smiles and her blouse deliberately loosened at the neck could tempt him these days.

He frowned thinking about her. Odd, really. Not long ago, a woman so obviously lascivious and ready to play would never have been allowed on the palace staff, but things were different now. The palace chatelaine had died, and the palace steward had suddenly descended into senility. After that everything had begun to change. The new staff were lax with their underlings.

The distant crying of a baby stirred him. He would have liked to go to his son, but there was no place for him in the nursery. He sighed, and decided to return to his bed.

Later that morning, after talking to the King, he walked down to the stables to enquire after the health and fitness of his hunters, and sent his pageboy to fetch Sergeant Horntail.

Ryce had been only a lad of twelve when the King had made the sergeant head of his son's personal guard. At the time, Horntail's duties had been mostly preventing a reckless young prince from breaking his neck doing something stupid. For years, he'd resented having his activities curtailed by the man and resented that Horntail had reported all that his young charge did to the King.

Gradually, over time, their relationship had changed. Horntail had begun to rescue the prince from the worst of his excesses without telling King Edwayn, until now – somewhat to the surprise of both – Ryce was actually asking advice from Horntail before he did something. More often than not, he followed it, too.

The sergeant came to a halt in front of him and, as was proper, bowed. "You wanted to see me, your highness?"

"Have you heard? The King wishes to go hunting tomorrow morning, early."

"Will you be in attendance?"

"Yes. The master of the hunt will be preparing all that is necessary, but I wanted to inform you that I intend to take you and all your men with me. Please see to it that they are all suitably mounted."

"It will be done, your highness." If Horntail was surprised, he didn't show it.

Ryce looked around to make sure no one was in a position to overhear their conversation. "I want you and your men to be especially vigilant during the hunt."

Horntail nodded. "Of course. Is there a particular reason?"

At one time, he would have considered that question an impertinence. Not now. "The King has not hunted for a year and barely rides a horse any more. But that's not the only reason for my concern. Many of the King's personal guard are not men of . . . experience. There have been so many deaths lately, and those who replaced them . . ." He let the words trail away because he had nothing specific to say. You couldn't level accusations when the only reason you had was something as nebulous as "I don't like them".

"As you say, your highness. After the number of unexpected deaths among the King's guard, it was hard to find local men of experience."

Horntail packed a wealth of meaning into those few words, enough to make Ryce feel sick. He asked, attempting to sound unconcerned, "Do you know anything about the new men?"

"They don't talk to us. Keep to themselves, they do. I did hear a . . . whisper that at least one came from a Fox manor."

Ryce's stomach turned over. "Ah. Horntail, whispers *interest* me. For example, I can't help wondering what prompted the King's desire to hunt tomorrow. A whisper that ended my curiosity on that matter would be welcome."

"I'll bear that in mind, your highness."

When Horntail strode away sometime later, after they'd discussed the specifics of the hunt, Ryce was tempted to call him back, to tell him to take care of his own hide. He resisted the temptation, but when he thought of Horntail suffering an accident his fear burgeoned.

Returning to the barracks where his men were busy with their morning duties, Horntail drew one of them aside. "Orlo, am I right in thinking your sister's son is the King's cupbearer?"

"Aye, captain." He snorted. "Right proud the family is of the lad, too."

"And so they should be. Just as we are proud to serve the Prince. Not everyone has the right set of innards to be a soldier, Orlo! But listen carefully. I have an interest in what – or rather, in *who* influenced the King's decision to go hunting. Find out if the lad heard aught on that matter."

"Aye, sergeant."

"Good. And remember, Orlo, watch your back."

The man nodded soberly. They all knew there had been too many deaths among the King's men, and Horntail's ruling for the Prince's men was strict: no one went anywhere alone. Ever. When one of the Prince's guard went home to visit his wife, two guards loitered at his door.

* * *

For the first time in his life, Ryce did not enjoy a hunt. The drumming of the hoofs around him, his mount rising to jump a fallen log, the blare of the horns, the yipping of the fellhounds scenting prey, the musty stink of a fox den: all the sights and sounds and smells and action that had once made his blood rush with the intense joy of living – suddenly they meant something different. Danger to his father. Fear for his King. Horror at the thought of how his life would change if his father died now, here, this day, in this place.

He didn't know how to make sure King Edwayn lived through the day and his fear lurked behind his every action, in every word he spoke, with every thought he had. So many things could go wrong. Edwayn and the huntmaster would be in the lead, vulnerable. Everyone knew where the King's favourite hunting route was; everyone knew which part of the woods they would enter. The forest was thick. An assassin could throw a spear or loose an arrow and never even be seen. Riders split up and scattered through trees pursuing different prey; a skilful huntsman among them could kill more than a pig and remain undetected in the resulting confusion.

And what about an unfortunate accident? A boar could turn on a rider without warning; a horse could put its foot in a hole or fall at a jump; some idiot could do something stupid that resulted in another coming to grief. Once King Edwayn had been able to look after himself; now he was ageing, slow, sometimes confused.

Ryce tried to stay with him throughout the hunt, but the King's guards prevented his approach. He could never decide if it was done deliberately, but when some of them lagged behind, they slowed him down until several times he lost sight of Edwayn completely. To his unspoken relief, when he did catch up halfway through the morning, it was to find his father in fine fettle, speckled with blood, surrounded by his hounds, and boasting of the first major kill of the day, a half-grown boar.

"See," the King roared at him, shaking a blood-stained spear in triumph, "there's life in this old royal hound, and don't you forget it."

"I never doubted it," he replied, grinning to see his father not only unscathed, but also brimming with vitality. He dismounted and doffed his hat to place it on his breast in salute. "Not old father, but honed. Age has merely seasoned you."

"Then let us celebrate!"

Edwayn tossed his blood-soaked spear to the nearest guard, clapped Ryce on the back and called for his spare mount. "Beck's Field, men! Ale to quench your thirst, food for your empty bellies. Maybe this afternoon will produce a boar with bigger tusks."

Servants, busy since the day before, had transformed the meadow bordering the forest, known as Beck's Field, into a gathering ground fit for a king. Colourful tents flying royal flags and courtiers' standards surrounded a central area of trestle tables laden with food and drink. Ryce, even accustomed as he was to the feasts served to hunt parties, was taken aback by the opulence of the trappings and the sumptuousness of the provender.

The King was in fine spirits; for a while he appeared to be his old self. He joked and jested, ate heartily and ribbed Ryce about being too slow on his horse to keep up with the hunt. "You missed the kill!" he chided. "What kind of a hunter are you?"

Ryce smiled and joked and hoped his father would let the afternoon hunt continue without the King to lead them, but wisely kept that hope unspoken. *I'm learning*, he thought.

When some of the older courtiers joined the King, Ryce withdrew, unnoticed, to take a look at the morning's kill, already being skinned or plucked and dismembered at the far end of the field. No one had brought in a deer yet, so the boar was still the largest of the bag, but there was a good selection of hares, pheasants, grouse and squirrels. He spoke with the butchers, then returned to the tables to eat and drink.

The feast was almost finished when he looked up from his platter of jellied fruit to see Prime Valerian Fox ride up. His appearance was an odd mixture of austerity and wealth, dressed as he was all in black, yet adorned with ostentatious gold jewellery. He ignored Ryce and dismounted to bow to the King.

Ryce gritted his teeth. The man couldn't have come for the hunting; killing animals for sport was not considered appropriate for a cleric of Va-faith.

He watched the Prime greet the King and chat to him, doubtless congratulating the monarch on his hunting success. His bow was graceful, his smile charming. The confounded man never seemed to age. His face was unlined and his hair without a trace of grey, his body as lithe and supple as a cat's.

"Your highness."

He turned to see Horntail standing at his shoulder. "Yes, sergeant?"

Horntail leaned down to say quietly into his ear, "The question you asked yesterday, about who influenced the King to come a-hunting." He nodded to where the Prime and the King were being served wine by a lad dressed in the palace livery. "Me sister's son."

"And he said—?"

"The Prime."

"Speak to him again when you have a chance."

Horntail nodded. He didn't need to be told that Ryce was interested in what the Prime was saying to the King now.

Still later, when the King announced that he was returning to the palace, but hoped the hunt would continue without him, Horntail again materialised at his side.

"Anything?" Ryce asked.

"They spoke of the hunt. An amiable conversation, according to the lad. The King said he would not hunt in the afternoon, otherwise his royal arse would trouble him for a sennight; the Prime laughed. 'Twas all."

"Glad to hear it. I will return with the King. Tell your men and instruct them to keep clear of the King's guards. We don't want any arguments."

"Quite so, your highness." Horntail's expression was wry; there had been some not-so-amicable encounters between the two troops of guards over the past year, for all that the sergeant had attempted to rein in his men.

Ryce walked over to where King Edwayn was chatting to the Prime, the Master of Hunt, Lord Dashell and several other huntsmen.

"Nursemaiding me?" the King asked, his eyes flashing in his annoyance, when Ryce told him he would ride back with the royal party.

The Prime stepped in, saying smoothly, "Oh, I'm sure he was only showing his concern for his father, as any dutiful son ought."

"I do not need his concern," Edwayn snapped. "I am the King, not some senile old man, and I'll thank you to remember that, Ryce. This is a royal hunt, and your presence is required when I am not in attendance."

Ryce tried to keep his expression blank. "Of course, sire. I did not think." *Damn you, Fox.*

"It would be my pleasure to accompany you, sire," Fox said, "if you will permit."

"Of course," Edwayn agreed, and waved Ryce away.

He bowed and withdrew to tell Horntail of the change in plans, fear for his father's safety growing. The King's party would contain all the older huntsmen, or anyone bruised or injured by falls, plus a few others whose horses had taken a tumble. The younger, fitter men would remain to continue the hunt.

Am I worrying over nothing?

He didn't know. He didn't even know what made him feel so fearful for his father's safety. He had nothing tangible to hang his worries on, no evidence of plots or assassination attempts. He had no ambitious cousins or uncles with an eye to usurping the throne. In fact he had nothing but a growing hatred of Prime Fox, prompted – as far as he could see – by a baseless unease that seized him every time he was in the Prime's presence.

It had started the day father told him about Mathilda's supposed ravishment. It had been compounded by his realisation of how much the Prime had enjoyed bringing Saker down. The supposed perfidy of a cleric ought to have grieved him, but Fox hadn't been grieved. He'd been pleased.

A pox on you, Saker. You ought to be here. Va-damn, he missed the witan.

24

Alliances Under Scrutiny

When Saker, Juster and Ardhi left *Golden Petrel* to appear before the Karradar Council, Sorrel expected the worst. She spent the time with the wet nurse, the woman's six month old son and Piper, but her mind was in a turmoil of dread. What if the men never returned? What if the Council had them imprisoned for sinking the longboat from *Spice Winds*?

She need not have worried. When the men returned several hours later, they were laughing.

"The Lowmians had been called as well," Saker explained. "They complained about us to the Karradar officials, demanding that Ardhi and I be forcibly returned to their ship – only to find themselves in trouble with the Council because they had fired their carronade without permission!"

"Even worse," Lord Juster added, "Lustgrader sent Tolbun to negotiate instead of coming himself, a tactical error the Council interpreted as arrogance." His grin broadened. "The real truth is the islanders find my activities more lucrative to them than Kesleer's. I pay the godowns handsome fees to store my privateered goods. Moreover, Pashalin merchant ships have been coming to pick up those cargos, paying their port fees and buying their provisions. Docklumpers and bumboat owners earn more wages. So, the islanders are more worried about upsetting me than they are about upsetting the Lowmians."

"Without the Lowmians, you wouldn't be here with all those benefits for them," she pointed out.

"No one said the Council was a *logical* bunch of reprobates," he replied. "Anyway, Mistress Sorrel, it all went well. The Council said that if Ardhi and Reed Heron wanted to jump ship in Karradar, that was fine with them. No one mentioned you at all."

"Moreover," Saker said, "when we asked for our belongings, the Karradar Council said we were entitled to them and instructed the Lowmians to hand them over!"

"Don't hold your breath that you'll get anything of value back," Juster said.

"I want my sword. It's Pashali steel, a gift from a Pashali trader when I was a young witan on duty up on the northern borders."

"And I want the rest of your story," Juster said. "Come on down to my cabin." Without waiting for an answer, he headed for the forward companionway.

"How is Piper liking the wet nurse?" Saker asked before he turned to follow.

"She adores her," she replied. "I feel quite put out. It's only for while we are here in Karradar, though, so I suppose I should make the most of the rest I'm getting!"

Saker smiled at her, then followed Lord Juster.

It was Ardhi, standing beside her, who commented, "No one replaces loving mother."

"But I am not her mother." The truth of those words almost choked her.

"Yes, you are, in every way that matters, no?"

Something clenched in her chest, as tight as a closed fist. Sweet Va, one day she was going to have to give Piper up. She *was* going to lose her. First Heather, then Piper. How would she ever bear the agony a second time around?

She turned her face away, not wanting him to see her pain.

"She's happy because you love." He struggled to express himself while she looked at him in surprise. "I admire you," he added. "You have courage, kindness, heart, wisdom. I'm sad because you meet me and bad things happened to you." He gave an exasperated grunt. "My words tangle in your language; I'm sorry. My Pashali speaking much better."

"They – your words were exactly right." *Only it was Saker I wanted to hear say them. Now, how silly was that?* She started to smile, her heart lightening, and was grateful Ardhi had cared enough to say what she needed to hear. "It seems I must learn Pashali. We'll be on the same ship to Javenka, as passengers. Perhaps you can teach me?"

His answering smile lit up his face. "Yes! I teach my language too, if you want. Journey long. You can learn much." He paused, then added in his own tongue, "*Kami perlu berteman.*"

"What does that mean?"

He grinned. "One day you can tell me."

"Oh, that's not fair!"

He relented. "'We both need a friend.'"

She smiled back at him. "I think you'll soon have a friend on this vessel. While you were all ashore, I met a sailor called Iska. He's a lascar too, from the Summer Seas."

He shrugged carelessly. "Oh? You call us both 'lascar' because we come from the same seas. Summer Seas are vast. Many, many islands, many languages. Word 'lascar'? That means nothing to me."

He turned and walked away.

Oh vex it. I hurt his feelings. You are a ninny, Sorrel.

It was dark by the time Saker had finished telling Juster his adventures since they'd last met. The remains of their evening meal littered the desk in the captain's cabin, although in truth, Saker had not eaten much. He'd said very little about Piper, but he'd omitted nothing else of importance.

Lord Juster swirled brandy in a goblet of blown glass and shook his head in disbelief. "If anyone else had told me this tale, I wouldn't have believed a word of it."

"If I hadn't experienced much of it, I wouldn't have believed it either." Saker took a sip from his own goblet, thinking how typical it was of Juster. He may have been on board a ship in a foreign land, but he still surrounded himself with his luxuries.

"So, Piper is the twin sister of the heir to the Basalt Throne."

Saker spluttered over his brandy. "What?"

"Oh, come now, Saker. It's obvious. Did you really think I wouldn't guess? Why else would Sorrel have a baby who's not her own? Let me see if I have it right. Princess Mathilda gave birth to twins. Sorrel, at the Princess's request, spirited the firstborn away because of Lowmeer's superstitions about devil-kin twins."

Saker said nothing.

"Just as well Piper was a girl. You want my opinion? There's no such being as A'Va. But I think there's a good chance that the Prime of Ardrone, the oh-so-despicable Valerian Fox, is in the service of something or someone not remotely connected to Va. I'd call it sorcery."

Saker waved a hand in acknowledgement.

"But that's not all," Juster added. "We have sorcerous plumes and daggers that swim and alien witchery and pox knows what else, and, according to Mistress Sorrel, a possibility that Fox fathered the heir to Lowmeer." He shook his head. "On one level, all this sounds absurd. But on another – do you know how *worrying* all of it is?"

"Indeed, which is why I have told you. Will you consider either taking Ardhi and me to the Summer Seas, or alternatively will you take Sorrel to Vavala? The Va-cherished Hemisphere could well be in jeopardy from two threats from different sources. I don't know which is the greatest danger. I do know that *I* don't have any choice. Va-forsaken magic is sending me to the Summer Seas, whether I like it or not. I also know that it must surely be important the Pontifect deals with the whole problem of Piper and her brother to ensure that the devil-kin never sits on the throne of Lowmeer. I'm asking for your help."

"I'm already doing what I do best. And if I understand your story correctly, it appears to me that Sorrel or Piper – or both – is being drawn, by magic, to the Va-forsaken Hemisphere. At least, that's what Ardhi believes, right?"

"Yes. Rot it, Juster, I don't know what I should be doing. Sometimes I feel Va-forsaken myself! I struggle constantly against this Chenderawasi magic, and I remain caught up in its web. Will you help us?"

"Have you any idea what you're asking of me?" He sipped his brandy. "I can be a rake and a sot and a rogue, but I take my duty to my country and my liege lord seriously. I would have to disobey the orders of Prince Ryce. Because of the stupidity of King Edwayn, the cupidity of his advisers and the avarice of Ardronese merchants, I am all that is standing between Ardrone and financial disaster.

"You're right. I am trying to do the impossible, one person attempting to halt a rolling ocean comber by flinging this vessel in front of it. But if it weren't for me, every time someone in Ardrone or the Principalities bought a stick of cinnamon or a single clove bud, or a dried nutmeg – in fact, any spice at all – the money they spent would go direct to

Lowmian coffers. And people *would* buy because they are terrified of the renewed outbreaks of the Horned Death, and they believe in an unfounded rumour about spices as curatives, a tale probably being fed by minions of A'Va, or Fox, or Lowmian merchants, or someone equally unscrupulous."

"I understand that. But I believe what is facing Ardrone is worse. If a devil-kin ascended the Basalt Throne, or if Lowmeer gets its hands on these magical plumes, Ardrone and the other nations of the Hemisphere will suffer. And if *both* of those things came to pass – Juster, it could be catastrophic. It could mean war for generations."

"Perhaps. But how can I be certain what to do when even you aren't sure? You don't really know what's going on. For instance, it's perfectly possible that neither of the twins is a devil-kin. Piper looks and behaves like a perfectly normal baby to me."

"And what about the plumes?"

He shrugged. "Their power would be curtailed if everybody knew that accepting one as a gift was the pathway to being a slave."

"You don't know what it's like being offered something so bewitching. It has *power*. Regal Vilmar was a victim. He made a fool of himself by obeying every suggestion of Uthen Kesleer, a ruthless, greedy merchant. Sorrel says it was the gossip of the court, although they didn't know the cause, of course. Then, once he is free of the compulsion, what does he do? He decides to get as many of those plumes as he can so that he himself can misuse them! There is something diabolical about this sorcery. We have to stop it getting to the Va-cherished Hemisphere. And if that means going to the Va-forsaken lands, then that is what I will do."

Lord Juster sat still with a thoughtful expression. Saker was silent, hoping that the more Juster considered it, the more alarmed he'd be. However, in the end he shook his head. "I'm sorry, my friend. I have my orders and my inclination is to obey them. My expertise is not necessary to you, or to Sorrel. I will arrange for you all to get as far as Javenka with someone I trust."

Saker rose to his feet. "I see. Thanks for the brandy. And thanks for coming to my rescue once again." Rueful, he smiled. "I do appreciate it. I'll tell Ardhi and Sorrel."

"I *am* sorry."

"Not half as sorry as I am. Sorrel is going to be furious because I've spoken to you about Piper."

"Tell her the truth: I guessed. The secret is safe with me. For ever." As he stood, he asked, "Do you really think it possible Valerian Fox could have fathered the Lowmian heir?"

"Possible, yes. But how can we ever be sure?" *And how will I ever know if I did?* That was one thing he had not told Juster; he was too embarrassed. With that thought foremost in his mind, he left the cabin.

The cloud-darkened night sky was starless and as black as printer's ink. The only light came from the candle lanterns hung at the sides of the ship, one green, one red, and two clear-glass lanterns, one on the prow and the other over the stern. Although the ship was still and quiet, sounds spilled across the water from the port: music, laughter, revelry, a barking dog, all the sounds of a town backed by the strains of a forest orchestra. The sawing violins of insects, the drumming of frogs, the clicking and thrumming and wailing of a night-time world Saker couldn't begin to comprehend.

The humidity in the air was velvet against his skin as he walked the length of the deck. He nodded to the officer of the watch midships, but the two tars also on duty, one on either side of the deck, continued to scan the bay. In a place like Karradar, even a length of worn rope had value beyond its initial cost, and thieves were always ready to take advantage of the careless or unobservant.

He'd come topside, restless and tense, unable to sleep despite his exhaustion. Enclosed in the stuffiness of the lower decks, he'd been unable to free himself from the events of the day.

Coming so close to an unpleasant death does that to you, I suppose.

When he found Sorrel on the foredeck looking over the bulwarks, he assumed she'd suffered the same ache of restlessness. The lanterns didn't offer much light to the deck, so he couldn't see her features, but he knew her anyway by the ambience of her witchery. When he came close, he heard the soft swish of silken skirts. Juster, he assumed, had given that dress to her. The thought, instead of amusing him, annoyed him; his reaction exasperated him in turn because he didn't know what prompted it. What did it matter that Juster had given her clothes to wear? He should be glad!

Earlier, he'd found it difficult to gaze at her face, when the curve of her shoulder and the low-cut gown enticed his gaze. He'd never seen her look so alluring, so lovely.

And don't you forget, she loathes you. Although she *had* been wearing the kerchief he'd given her.

She turned her head when she heard his footfall. "Saker."

"Yes."

"Come, look at this. The wavelets breaking against the sides of the ship – they glow!"

She sounded light-hearted, charmed by what she saw. Earlier that day she'd killed a man, brutally and bloodily, and he'd heard the horror in her voice when she'd finally recounted the story to him. Now he could only wonder how much of that she had really managed to put behind her, and how much she was feigning her pleasure at seeing something trivial, if pretty.

Joining her at the bulwarks, he looked over the side of the ship. Rippling waves crinkled as they broke against the hull, sending out radiant ribbons of blue. It was as if a breeze puffed across the water, painting an effulgence on the surface as it passed: a lustre that expanded, then contracted, then vanished, only to return with the next breaking wavelet.

"Luminescence," he said. "The Lowmians say those are the lights of A'Va's seagoblins."

She laughed softly. "And you? What do you say it is?"

"An integral part of the Way of the Flow. Another of Va's gifts to the world." He thought she smiled at him then, but couldn't be sure in the dark.

"The perfect answer when one is a witan."

"Not a witan any more."

He watched her as she turned back to look at the sea and startled himself by his awareness of her proximity. Her skin, flushed with a rosy sheen by the port lantern, made him swallow convulsively. A single pearl of sweat edged down the hollow of her neck, gleaming blood-red, and he followed it with his gaze until it disappeared under the neckline of the gown into the valley between her breasts.

He clasped his hands behind his back. "I-I need to apologise to you. What happened to you today? I feel responsible. I should have protected you. I should have treated what you said about Lustgrader going over to *Sentinel* with more seriousness. When I consider how you and Piper came so close to death . . . No, I don't even want to think about the possibility! I wasn't there when I should have been. I'm deeply, deeply sorry."

"It's past. Forget it. He's not the first man I've murdered. I did not regret the first, and I'll not dwell on this one either."

"Then you are braver than me. I don't think I'll ever be able to forget it. I certainly won't forget your courage. You saved Piper today as well as yourself and you did it alone. I don't even have the words to tell you how much I admire your strength."

She turned towards him, her face now illuminated by the meagre light of the starboard lantern. "I learned once before what I am capable of, and that was just for the memory of a little girl. Today I found how much more I am capable of for a living child. You should be wary of me, Saker. Or glad because I'm a woman capable of getting to Vavala all by herself." She drew in a deep breath. "Lord Juster is not going to take us where we want to go, is he?"

"I'm afraid not."

"And you're going to leave me in Javenka."

He felt himself redden and was glad she wouldn't be able to see his shame. "I'm sorry."

"I must go below and make sure that Piper is still happy with the wet nurse. I worry she may not have sufficient milk for two babies." She expelled a sigh. "It's odd, there were so many times before when I would have liked to have handed her over to someone else just so that I had some time to myself. Now that I do, I worry all the time, and feel guilty. I even feel jealous! How silly is that?"

She'd changed the subject, and he was disappointed, left feeling there'd been so much more to say – and the chance was passing them by.

"I don't think it's silly at all." He wanted to keep her there, just to talk, but nothing sensible came to his mind.

She said good night and walked away, her tread firm on the deck. He stayed where he was, but his anxiety did not dissipate. He could still feel the bruises and cuts on his back from being scraped under *Spice Winds*; his shoulder muscles ached from all the swimming and his skin was red and sunburned, but he knew none of that was the cause of his restlessness. Guilt. It was guilt. Guilt because he failed Sorrel and Piper.

And the birds, dear Va, what of the birds?

Shame stalked him along with the memory of bloodied feathers. He was Shenat, and all life was sacred to him, never to be taken heedlessly, never to be squandered. So many of those beautiful seabirds had died that day because he had called on them. Did he have that right?

Behind him, as if he was reading his mind, Ardhi spoke. Confound the man; he moved with the stealth of a cat and the Pashali words rolled off his tongue so much more easily than they did off his own. "So many birds died today. Their deaths haunt you, don't they?"

"I felt them die. Every terrified torment." Their fear and pain had clawed furrows into his memory. Those scars were for ever, he knew that now. "They were wild and free and so – so right."

"You learned something today that will stand you in good stead in the future. Do not forget the lesson."

In spite of the evening's warmth, he shivered. There was warning in Ardhi's words. "Don't be so damned sanctimonious! Tell me instead: what do we do now? We don't have any of the four plumes. It's unlikely that Lustgrader will send across our kit bags. If he does, he'll search them first and he'd steal the plumes. The plume that's in Captain Russmon's hands on *Sentinel* is lost for ever anyway."

"For ever is a long time."

His heart lurched at his tone. "Ardhi, you've seen the watch set on those ships. There is no way you can board without being seen. Don't try it."

"Captain Juster is not going to take us to the Summer Seas, is he?"

"No. We will have to make our own way on a Pashali ship."

"And the cost of such a passage?"

"Lord Juster will lend the money, for all of us. Sorrel comes with us as far as Javenka. After that, she will go overland with Piper."

"Ah." He nodded, but more to himself than to Saker.

"Have you met the other lascar on board?"

"He is from Serinaga Island. He does not even speak my tongue. In fact, he is a little frightened of me. We Chenderawasi have a reputation."

"For the life of me, I can't imagine why," he said dryly. "I think I will turn in for the night. It has been a tiring day."

As he walked away, leaving the lascar on deck, Saker's unease increased. He knew he needed to write a letter to Fritillary Reedling. It could be sent with a trader by sea and then overland to Vavala. But what the pox was he going to say? How could he possibly explain everything to her satisfaction? Something told him Ardhi was still sure that either Piper or Sorrel, or both, were destined to end up in the Chenderawasi Islands.

Va-damn, what a tangle we have woven around ourselves.

25

Attack

For want of something better to do, Ardhi turned back to watch the luminescence in the water. It reminded him of home, and night-time swims in the lagoon; poignant memories of Lastri emerging from water that left a momentary glow on her naked breasts and thighs . . .

One of many things better forgotten. He had no future, and certainly none with the woman he once thought to wed.

His train of thought was broken by the sound of voices coming to him across the water, too close to be from the shore. There was laughter and drunken cursing, a splash of an oar in the darkness. Sailors, he assumed, coming back to their ship from a night onshore. There were six or seven ships anchored in the Bay besides the Lowmian fleet and *Golden Petrel*, all Pashali merchantman. Odd, though, it sounded more like a very Lowmian swearword he'd heard. Still, nothing to say a Pashali ship couldn't have Lowmian crew. But why no light?

Over his head the lookout in the crow's nest yelled out to the officer on watch, saying he thought the sounds were off the starboard bow. The officer shouted as he ran forward, calling out to the unseen boat to stand well clear. Both of the swabbies on watch scurried towards the prow as well, one of them grabbing a boathook on the way in case he had to fend off a boatload of drunken tars.

Ardhi was about to go to their aid when instinct kicked in. There was something wrong. Even drunken sots didn't set out to row or sail in the pitch dark without a light. Besides, every seaman knew the correct configuration of the mainmast, port and starboard lights of his own ship. There was no way anyone would mistake *Golden Petrel* for a Pashali merchantman. Nor did Pashali seamen swear using Lowmian curses.

He went cold all over. He raced towards the stern and stuck his head down the aft companionway, bellowing for Lord Juster. Then he ran on to the taffrail, looking out into the darkness towards the outer islands. There was nothing to see. He couldn't tell where the bay ended and the islands began; there was no difference between water and land and a cloud-dense sky.

But his panic would not subside. *This is a trap, a distraction; they want us to look forward not behind.* He lifted his head looking upwards to the lookout on the mainmast. "Crow's nest! Look astern, look astern!"

"Aye, aye, sir!" Fortunately the lad hadn't recognised his voice, and assumed the order came from someone who had the authority to give it. "Naught there, sir!"

Pickle it, it was so splintering *dark*.

And then he saw: alarmingly close, more of the eldritch light of the luminescence. It ran out on either side of a central point, two silent, beautiful bands of glowing light forming a V shape. It was coming nearer. Then he knew.

"Captain!" he roared, turning from the railing towards the ship's bell. "On deck! Now!"

He yanked the rope attached to the bell, a moment later the man in the crow's nest yelled, "Boat! Dead astern!" and then the ship was in an uproar. He dived back to the stern rail as the first man pounded up the companionway from below. He could see it now, the boat stirring up the luminous blue as it cleft the water with its prow, gliding in silence like a bat on the hunt. A dark sail, a dark-clad crew, a small vessel full of menace, all suddenly illuminated by the flickering candlelight of *Golden Petrel*'s stern lantern.

Time seemed to slow. Everything he saw etched itself on to his mind's eye; his comprehension lagging a sliver of time behind. Captain Juster was there, issuing orders. Beside him, Finch was loading a pistol and the master's mate was lighting a taper. The gunner's mate was swinging the small gun on the quarterdeck, trying to lower its muzzle to aim at something already too close. The captain leant over the bulwarks and barked an order for the boat to identify itself. When there was no immediate answer, he yelled, "Veer away, or we'll put a ball through you!"

"*Spice Winds*!" Ardhi cried, recognising the ship's dinghy and the officer on the prow. Tolbun. Behind the Lowmian mate, a tar was lighting the wick attached to something round.

Blister it, a shrapnel ball.

"Shoot him!" Juster snapped at Finch.

A splinter of a moment to do something, anything . . .

Ardhi whirled, bent, grabbed the handle on the nearest fire bucket, wrenched it free of its stand and flung it, water and all, at the boat.

Too late.

Even as Finch's lighted taper touched the powder in the flash pan of his pistol, even as the bucket left Ardhi's hand, the first of two shrapnel balls smashed through the window of the captain's cabin. The second followed the first through the hole in the glass.

Ardhi's effort to fling the bucket wrenched his arm and precipitated him halfway across the taffrail.

The force of the explosion inside the cabin below him blew out the rest of the windows beneath the quarterdeck and lifted him upwards, spinning helplessly, all the air driven from his lungs.

The last thing I ever see . . .

A stupid thought in his head as he flew through the air above the ship, and the scene below unfolded in a series of glimpses, each vivid, intense, detailed. Captain Juster and first mate Finch were flung across the quarterdeck as the planks beneath their feet burst upwards, carried on an explosion of light. The gout of fire from Juster's cabin showered the Lowmian dinghy with a burning rain of debris and shards of twinkling glass. The surface of the sea ruptured with blue-fire luminescence spreading outwards. The sound that shattered the peace of the night was so great he thought his head would burst.

A burn flashed across his body, charring his clothes, singeing his eyebrows and frizzling his hair, only to be immediately drenched with seawater coming from storm-raja knows where. He crashed down, unable to breathe, blinded by the light, deafened by the sound, crushed by the weight of his fall.

He wasn't in the ocean.

Utter silence.

Complete darkness.

The gradual return of his senses. Pain first, everywhere. Sounds returning, heard through a ringing in his ears. The wailing of men in agony, the shouting of enraged sailors. The crackle of flames, the sizzle of fire mixing with water. Smells: fresh blood, burned flesh, smouldering canvas, singed hair.

Little by little his sight cleared. He was lying on his back on top of canvas, staring upwards at broken lines. And above that, the side of the ship loomed.

Curse it, that's Golden Petrel. *And I'm not on board!*

He groaned and tried unsuccessfully to ease himself upright. His head ached and spun. He was looking at what remained of the mast of the dinghy, and he was lying on what was left of its sail. He guessed the *Golden Petrel*'s gunner had managed to fire a lucky shot through the mast, splintering most of it to smithereens.

When he moved his head, red-hot pain shot down his neck and left arm. Pox. He'd taken a splinter into his shoulder. He yanked it out. With infinite care, almost passing out in pain, he edged himself into a sitting position and found himself staring at Banstel, the ship's boy from *Spice Winds*, crouching low with his hands clamped over his head. It took him another moment to realise that he and Banstel were the only two people in the dinghy, or rather, the only two who were conscious. Another man was draped over the prow, half in and half out of the boat. He appeared to be still breathing. Tolbun was nowhere to be seen.

Wincing in pain, Ardhi groped to see if he still had his kris and breathed easier when his hand closed over the hilt. He raised his gaze to look at *Golden Petrel* again. The dinghy was drifting away, and the distance between the two vessels was increasing. The fire at the stern of the ship was burning still, supplying enough light for him to see by, but it looked as if it was under control. Relief swept over him, although he doubted there was much of the captain's cabin left.

His next thought clawed away the relief. *Sorrel.* Sorrel: she hadn't been still using the captain's cabin, had she? He tried to think, but his memory was dancing this way and that, none of it at his bidding. In his desire to get back to *Golden Petrel*, he almost leapt into the sea, but stopped himself when his head reeled and his left arm wouldn't cooperate.

"Banstel," he said, gritting his teeth with pain, "are you badly hurt?"

"Not much."

"Row us over to the ship."

The lad shook his head. "They'll kill me."

"I won't let them."

Banstel looked disbelieving.

"Refuse, and me, Ardhi, will kill you. Row!"

Banstel's eyes widened in astonishment at his tone. "Aye, aye, sir." Scrambling forward, he fumbled to extract one of the oars from under the tangle of canvas, halyards and sheets.

"What happened to other men? I saw Tolbun and another." His head was aching, and he was having trouble sorting out the sequence of events.

"Don't rightly know. Them pirates shot at us. Mate Tolbun and Mynster Baak, they got blowed into the water. Reckon they couldn't swim." He jerked his head at the body in the bows. "An' he got hit then, I reckon. He's still breathing though."

"Lustgrader has an empty head. Even attack successful, Karradar men get very angry."

"Cap'n was right proper mad at you 'n' Factor Reed Heron. Real furious with Heron." Banstel stepped over Ardhi to rummage for the second oar under the torn canvas. "Guess he figured no one'd ever prove what really happened. We was supposed to do it all quiet-like, use one of them slow-burning fuses to blow up the stern off from under, rudder 'n' all. Cap'n said it wouldn't go sky high till we was safe back on ship. That was the plan. But then you seen us and Baak lit the fuse too soon. You was supposed to be looking at them others in the bumboat off the bow. They was port layabouts Mate Tolbun paid to make a noise. Cap'n reckoned they'd get the blame."

He fitted the oars into the rowlocks. "Please, Mynster Ardhi, I just does as I get told. Nivver wanted to hurt nobody."

"I know, Banstel. Mistress Sorrel said you helped her. Now row us to the ship."

Juster schooled himself to an outward appearance of calm. "Finch! Report."

"Fire's out, cap'n. The lady is still structurally sound. No damage to the rudder; the explosion was all upwards and outwards. Could o' been much worse. Lost the outer wall and windows to your cabin and most of the furnishings, alas. The decking above will need rebuilding. We've fished up that rat Tolbun's corpse from the drink. He took a splinter through the heart."

"Good. Bring him on board. We'll need to show it to the Council. We've got the Lowmian dinghy on board now, too. There's another Lowmian seaman and their ship's boy, both alive."

"Enough proof to sink their damn fleet with the Karradar Council, eh?"

"I certainly hope so." He suspected that Lustgrader had never considered his attack would end up being such a fiasco. He gave a grim smile; he would make the Lowmian pay for that miscalculation.

He turned to where Ardhi sat on the deck with blood dribbling down his face from a head cut. He was pale, clutching his left arm tight to his body. More blood soaked the cloth of his jacket at the shoulder. He was surprisingly composed as he watched what was happening up on the fo'c'scle. Juster followed his gaze, thinking he might be concerned about Saker who had suffered some minor cuts and bruises, but it was Sorrel who had his attention.

Now that's interesting. "Ardhi, I owe you my ship and probably my life. I was in my cabin when you yelled the warning and I could well have died then and there. My gratitude, and my thanks."

The lascar looked up at him. "You saved me from the Lowmians!"

"Then let's say we are even. The surgeon will take a look at that shoulder of yours."

He looked around for Surgeon Barklee, but he was still attending to the bo'sun's mate who was lying on the deck in a pool of blood. Even as he caught Barklee's eye, the man shook his head. "Sorry, my lord," he said. "Too much blood lost. He's dead, rot those fobbing canker-worms of Lowmian scum."

Young Norbert had been barely eighteen. Juster's rage roiled once more. Va, but he would get his revenge for this death. He signalled Barklee over to attend to Ardhi. "The man's in pain for all he'll hide it," he murmured. "Give him some tincture of opium when you fix that shoulder. Fix him before you bother with that Lowmian seaman with the lump on his head."

Once he was sure that everything was being attended to, he marched off to look at the damage to his cabin himself.

Someone had lit a lantern there, and what he could see by its light almost broke his heart. He stood stock still, taking it all in.

The windowed rear wall that had once projected out over the water was missing, and so was the decking immediately above that section, which had once been part of the poop deck. Everything that remained was either scorched, sodden, broken, or pitted with shrapnel. Sobered, he acknowledged there was no way *Golden Petrel* was going to sail anywhere without repair. And he'd been right; had he been in the cabin when the shrapnel balls exploded, he would have died.

"I'm so sorry, Juster."

He turned to find Saker had followed him.

His hands balled into fists. "I think I want to strangle you. Lustgrader was probably after your arse rather than mine."

"Quite likely. Which is why I'm sorrier than I can say."

"At least your damn lascar saved my ship, not to mention my mother's darling."

He looked blank, so he said, "*Me*, you canker worm. I was down here when Ardhi bellowed for me to come up on deck. If it weren't for him, my hide would have as many holes as the ship has scuppers."

"Ah. Yes. I'm glad the noble hide is still wholly whole, rather than just holey, then." He ran fingers through his hair and added sombrely, "Ardhi is a valuable friend to have."

The next day, after a blissfully long and painless sleep, followed by an excellent meal, Ardhi met Saker, Finch and Lord Juster in the officer's wardroom. There was a gaping hole where all the windows had blown out, and a smell of smoked wood and salt water permeated everything, but the room itself was otherwise intact. Already there were sounds of ongoing repairs being made to the captain's cabin next door.

Ardhi seated himself at the wardroom table, wincing. His shoulder felt as if shards of glass had been jammed into the bone, and the rest of his bruised body was not much better. Sorrel, sitting opposite, gave him a strained, white-faced nod. Juster had already told him she had spent much of the night keeping watch over him. He smiled his thanks.

"To bring you all up to date," Juster said. "Finch and I questioned the ship's boy and the wounded Lowmian tar Ardhi delivered into our hands last night. Their tale was illuminating. We persuaded them to recite it to the Karradar authorities, who objected quite colourfully to the violation of their neutrality. They have ordered the Lowmian fleet to leave. None of those particular ships are to be permitted to return, ever. So their ill-considered attack has cost them dear."

"Insanity," Finch muttered. "What the blithering blazes could have prompted Lustgrader to order something so daft?"

Saker shot a warning glance at Ardhi, indicating he wasn't about to enlighten the first mate. *We made a mess of things, you and I, Saker*, Ardhi thought. *Between my* sakti *magic and your decision to use it, we brought an astute and experienced ship's captain to the brink of madness.*

He suspected Saker was wracked with guilt about it, but it wasn't a sentiment he shared. Lustgrader had sent his tars to kill the Raja Wiramulia, bringing to an end the reign of a wise ruler long before he had time to impart his skills and knowledge to his heir.

"To put what I just said another way," Juster continued, "my prime target, the one that would have the greatest wealth in cargo because of the capacity of the holds of its three fluyts, is about to sail out of the harbour never to return. Which will make my task of finding them on their return journey from the Spicerie a great deal harder." He didn't look happy.

"They still go Summer Seas?" Ardhi asked, straining to keep the hate he felt out of his voice. "Not home to Lowmeer?"

Juster snorted. "With their tail between their legs like a beaten cur? Lustgrader would never do that! If he did, the merchant Uthen Kesleer and Regal Vilmar Vollendorn would dice him up as fish bait."

Finch frowned. "Long journey home for his fleet from the Summer Seas if they don't call in here. They need water and fresh food."

"They could hug the mainland coast," Saker said.

This time it was Finch who snorted. "The Glacier Coast? Easy to see you're no sailor! Almost every ship that's tried that found themselves holed by icefloes and bergs, or battered to death by storms."

"Certainly they'll have to take on water on their way back," Juster said, "but they could do that by sneaking into one of the Calves of Karradar and finding a stream. They could hunt there too, for fresh food, and hope by the time anyone from Port Karradar realised they were there, they'd be gone. Anyway, that's not our concern."

"They did hand over your baggage, yours and Ardhi's, as we demanded," Finch said to Saker. "But Ardhi says there are things missing."

Saker looked at him then, and he stared back, knowing the witan would assume the plumes were gone. Neither of them had expected anything else. The stab of pain he felt in his chest was as real as the ache in his shoulder, and twice as agonising to his soul. All he had worked for, all he had fought for, and it was out of reach.

His hand fingered the bone hilt of his kris, touched the fine carving that marked it with patterns. *Wiramulia's bone and his blood and the filaments of his regalia . . .* Would it be enough? He'd gambled everything when he'd dived off the *Spice Winds*.

"My sword?" Saker asked Finch.

"It's here."

The smile Saker gave was an indication of how much store he put by the weapon, even though it had no *sakti* and its damask was so plain. *Saker, whatever I have done, it was for your witchery, not your sword hand.*

"And . . . and *Golden Petrel*? Can you repair it here, captain?" Saker asked.

"*Her*, not *it*, you ignorant lubber. I've arranged for Karradar carpenters to help our ship's carpenter. They will start work immediately on the repairs. It's costing me a fortune to make it a quick job. I'll have to persuade people to part with their seasoned timber already earmarked for other things. And as for glass, they say they can persuade townsfolk to take out their own windows if I offer them enough."

"All of which will amount to a small fortune. Va only knows how we'll recoup it," Finch said sourly.

"Maybe Va doesn't, but I do," Juster told him.

Finch's sour expression didn't alter. "Catching a few ordinary Lowmian traders between here and home won't refill our coffers in a hurry."

"I've just had worse news than that. The earlier Kesleer fleet, the one that left Ustgrind last year: it's been sighted on its way back home through the Calves of Karradar. And *Golden Petrel* is too wounded to do a thing about them. They'll be long gone on their way home to Lowmeer before we are ready to sail again." He pulled a face that summed up his disgust, then added, "Which is why, as soon as we have a seaworthy ship once more, we are sailing for the Summer Seas."

There was a startled silence.

It was Finch who broke it. "Who's been sipping at the bilge-water?" he growled. "'Cause summat's rotted your brain, m'lord!"

"You are looking at a privateer in a rage, Finch," Juster said. His tone was pure steel. "I intend to stalk Lustgrader's fleet all the way to the Spicerie, wait until they've bought and paid for their spice cargoes, seize all three fluyts, sink the galleon and the carrack – if they haven't already foundered – and sail my own spice fleet all the way back to Throssel, as a present for my prince and my king."

Saker stared across at Ardhi, his frown thunderous. Ardhi had a good idea why; he was blaming the *sakti* again, upset because he was supposed to be a peacemaking witan, not part of a vengeful exercise in privateering. The woman he served would not like it.

Ardhi smiled at him. He doubted if *sakti* had anything to do with Lord Juster's decision and he didn't care one way or the other. All he cared was that they would be sailing for the Summer Seas. The Spicerie wasn't the Chenderawasi Archipelago, but it was close.

Saker knew Juster's idea had advantages: they could be sure that Sorrel would have a safe passage to Javenka and he and Ardhi would be heading in the right direction. Perhaps Ardhi would have a chance to retrieve his plumes. And in the end, Saker could possibly return to the Va-cherished Hemisphere aboard *Golden Petrel*.

Yes, for him and Ardhi and Sorrel, Juster's madcap idea was definitely one that had plenty of advantages. But for Juster? It was a huge risk. The journey to the Spicerie and Chenderawasi and the return to Throssel would take over a year. It meant risking storms and pirates, the diseases that thrived in the warm climes of the Summer Seas, and the sometimes unpredictable hostile local rajas.

Saker waited until he and Juster were alone before probing some more. He didn't have to dig too deeply: Juster was willing enough to explain.

"Did you know that Lustgrader's ship's boy didn't want to go back to *Spice Winds*?" he asked when he came across Saker watching the crew clean up the mess that had been the aft deck.

"You mean Banstel's still on board?"

"He is indeed." Juster took a swig from the flagon of wine he was holding before handing it across to him. "Apparently he's more scared of what Lustgrader would do to him. It seems he was already in trouble with the captain. After he brought Sorrel here, he went back to get the second swabbie from the island. Once on *Spice Winds* again, Lustgrader showed his gratitude by blaming Banstel for everything that had gone wrong. The bastard said he was going to whip the lad. Fortunately it was postponed because of everything that happened, but Banstel felt sure it was still in his future. I promised him a berth and a cabin boy's pay, and he's decided to stay."

"He's a good lad, as far as I know. But he is Lowmian. He might be persuaded to change sides again, so watch him."

"You have a jaundiced view of humanity, my friend."

"I'm a cleric. And a spy. Believe me, I've seen everything, in spite of my tender years."

"He told us more about Ardhi's plumes."

"What about them?"

"Lustgrader searched Ardhi's kitbag. Stole his money and three golden plumes hidden in a piece of wood."

"Bambu. It's hollow."

"Bambu, wood, whatever. Lustgrader immediately rid himself of the feathers by sending them across to *Sentinel*."

"Ah. I think I can guess why."

"Then please enlighten me."

"The galleon is the Regal's vessel. The others all belong to the Lowmian Spice Trading Company. I think Lustgrader is gifting the plumes to the Regal."

"Why?"

"It could just be because they scare him to death. More likely because the Regal has ordered him to obtain plumes, and he'd rather hand over the responsibility of them to the captain of the Regal's ship. There's also the possibility that he thinks that will put Regal Vilmar under a spell to him in the future."

"That last is what I thought. And that is why I've decided to go after Lustgrader. I reckon when you gifted one to Lustgrader he spent too much time fighting the coercion. It drove him insane. Or at least made him irrational in his risk-taking. Those plumes are poison, Saker. Evil things, full of Chenderawasi sorcery. I want them to stay where they belong: in Chenderawasi. And that, apparently, is exactly where the Chenderawasi want them too."

"So . . . you want to help Ardhi bring them back to his island."

He nodded. "And revenge on Lustgrader would be so . . . *nice*." His smile had a grim edge to it. "I'll do it because I am now convinced it is in the interest of Ardrone. I will take you all the way to this island of Ardhi's, if that is where Lustgrader is going, and I'll make sure the Lowmians don't hunt these confounded birds too."

Saker gave him a hard look. "You're not fooling me. Lord Juster Dornbeck is not really doing this for me, or Ardhi, or even for his liege lord."

Juster gave a bark of laughter. "No. You're right. Most of the time I'm an easy-going hedonist privateer. But this same privateering captain has cracks in the sweetness of his character. And when they open up, they reveal a man who can, alas, be vengeful. *They tried to sink my ship*. My beautiful lady!"

Saker was silent.

"I'm doing this because I'm furious. I don't want to hear anything from a witan about forgiveness and compromise. I'm out for revenge, and I intend to get it."

26

A Prince, a Prime and a King

Niggled by his worries, Ryce had no interest in the remainder of the hunt. Still, he was pleased with the afternoon's success: five deer, another boar, several braces of game birds brought down by the archers, and sufficient hares to have exhausted the hounds. Unfortunately, the last kill of the hunt, a fine stag, had led them a merry dance, and the hunt ended later than he'd wanted. They wouldn't be home until after dark. Still, the last part of the ride would be along the main Throssel road, and the clear skies meant there'd be plenty of moonlight.

They left most of the retainers behind on Beck's Field to butcher the kill and load the carts. Even the hounds would remain there with the houndmaster until they were rested enough to return the following morning, along with the grooms and the extra horses.

As he set off down the track that led from Beck's Field to the main Throssel road, Ryce counted those with him: ten huntsmen, courtiers with their attendants numbering about thirty-five all told, and the twenty men of his guard. Everyone was tired, but mostly content. It had been a good hunt: no one seriously hurt, no horses permanently maimed, and a good selection of wild meat for the palace kitchens.

Horntail, as usual, had divided the guards up, half in front, half behind. The cart track was only wide enough for two abreast, and Ryce was happy to ride alongside Lord Anthon Seaforth, an old friend of his.

"Good to see the King so active and in good spirits," Anthon remarked. "There's been too little good cheer of late."

"Too little to be cheerful about," Ryce said.

"And you with a lovely young wife and an heir? Shame on you!"

He had something he wanted to ask Anthon to do, and he wasn't sure how he was going to introduce the topic. It'd be pointless to hint.

Give him a hunter between his knees and a pack of fellhounds at the kill and Anthon wouldn't notice if it rained fish and blueberries.

Ryce decided to be blunt. "I heard yesterday that another shrine was burnt up north in Shenat country."

Anthon frowned. "Primordials?"

"No, not this time. It was those grey-clad fellows no one knows much about. Some say they're the agents of Va-faith, but a recent edict from the Pontifect said that's a lie."

"Ah, yes. Prelate Masterton read it out loud last chapel day. Something about them actually out to destroy the unity of Va-faith. Reckon that's true?"

"The Pontifect isn't reckless with her accusations. If she says they want to destroy belief in the Ways and kill folk with witcheries, then it's true. There was a hellish row about that edict, though. Fox didn't want it read."

"And Conrid Masterton read it anyway? That was brave."

"Masterton was appointed by the Pontifect, not the Prime. Pox on them, these grey-clad wretches, they are a nasty lot. A horde of thugs wrecking our peace and our unity, and supplanting it with something else, using violence. Three years ago, if you'd told me that was going to happen, I'd have laughed in your face."

"You aren't exaggerating, are you, your highness?" Anthon shot him a worried glance. "I mean, most people don't believe in what this rabble is spouting forth, let alone consider joining them. Your grey horde will end up looking as silly as drunks in a gutter."

"I wish I could believe that."

"But it's all up in Shenat country, on the borders, isn't it?"

"Is it?"

Anthon looked shocked. "Well, I'm sure the King's Company can take care of it."

Ryce rolled his eyes. He had little faith in a force of three thousand men led by a handful of impoverished noblemen who regarded the job as a way of getting paid for nothing more than holding a few parades on special occasions.

"What does King Edwyn say?" Anthon asked.

"It's a religious matter the Prime should settle."

"And the Prime says?"

"That there isn't a problem. Anthon, your cousin Beargold – he's an officer in the King's Company, right?"

"Yes. Useless muckle-top. Gambles away his pay, that fellow. Family doesn't have much to do with him these days. The silly laggard is always wanting to borrow money."

"Have a word in his ear, will you? Tell him to bring the men in his corps up to top-notch fighting readiness. They need to know more than how to polish their shoes and wear bright red coats to parades."

Anthon looked thunderstruck.

"I mean it, Anthon. In fact, go to all ten company commanders, and tell them – confidentially, mind – that I'll quadruple the allowances of those in charge of the top three corps six months from now. We'll have a competition to determine the winning corps. Swordplay, archery, fitness, horsemanship, arquebus, the lot. Prize money for the top individuals too. Tell them to keep it quiet, though, as it's going to be a surprise for the King."

"You'd do that?" He blinked. "Out of your own pocket?"

"Yes, and you'd better hope that their fitness for combat is not needed before then."

"Pickles 'n' pox, you *are* worried! Tell you what, I'll match whatever money you put up."

Ryce grinned. "Knew I could rely on you."

"You bastard. You hooked me deliberately!"

Just then they rode up on Horntail, who had pulled his horse to the edge of the track. "A word, your highness," he said.

Ryce nodded to Anthon to drop back, and Horntail took his place at Ryce's side. "What's the matter, captain?"

"Not sure. Maybe naught. Just seems too quiet. No birdcalls, no squirrels. And the horses up front smell something that's making them restless."

He tilted his head, listening, momentarily ashamed that he hadn't noticed anything amiss. He watched the movement of his horse's ears and concluded that Horntail was right. Turning in the saddle, he opened his mouth to ask Anthon to pass a warning back to be on the alert, but the words remained unspoken. The scream of a horse ahead of them, followed by shouts, made any warning superfluous.

"'Ware!"

"Look up!"

"Archers in the trees!"

Beside him, Horntail bellowed, "Flee! Everyone for himself!"

Time only for a random thought: *Rot it, everyone has their bows unstrung . . .*

An arrow thwanged past his head, clipping the top of his ear. He ducked, reached to draw his sword. Horntail viciously snatched the reins out of his hands and flipped them over his horse's head. Then the sergeant raised his horn to his lips and gave a single blast.

"What the pox do you think you're doing!" Ryce bawled at him, flinging himself forward in a vain attempt to grab the reins back.

Horntail took no notice. He was already hauling the Prince's horse away from the track and into the trees.

Another arrow slammed into Ryce's saddle above his knee. A third took a chunk out of his horse's mane, which sent the animal flying through the undergrowth with scant attention to its own safety. A volley of arrows bracketed him, one clipping the heel of his boot.

Sweet Va, they're everywhere! He kept himself tucked in low over his horse's neck. Fury swamped his terror. "Fuck you, Horntail! Let go!"

But if the sergeant heard, he took no notice. Ryce leaned forward to reach the reins, but all he achieved was to pull Horntail halfway out of the saddle. When it was clear the man was determined not to let go even if he fell, Ryce relinquished his hold.

The arrows stopped coming, but Horntail's pace never slackened. Bushes beat at the legs of their horses as they twisted through the trees at a reckless pace. A low branch nearly swept him from his saddle. A few paces further on, only his quick thinking saved his knee from being shattered against the trunk of a tree.

Not wanting to alert the attackers to where they were, he stopped yelling. His rage was undiminished. *I'll kill him. I swear I'll skin him alive.*

At last the mad bolt slackened and he was able to wrench his reins from Horntail's hold and manipulate them back over the head of his mount.

He drew his horse to a halt, gazed back over his shoulder, searching for movement, for any sign of the attackers. The undergrowth stilled behind them; nothing moved. He couldn't even be sure which way they had come. Somewhere in the distance, men and horses screamed. Dying. He swallowed back vomit and turned once more towards Horntail.

"How *dare* you!" In his anger he could barely force the words through his teeth.

The sergeant pulled his mount around to face him. "For the safety of my prince I'd dare anything. Even disobedience."

"Your duty is to obey me!" His hands shook with rage. "I could see you dead for your treason."

"Ten years back, my King bade me keep his son safe, whether it cost me my pride, or my honour, or my life, and that's what I've done this day."

"You caused me to desert those under my care! You caused *me* to lose all honour this day. And you lost your own, indeed. How can I ever lead men when they've seen me desert them? They saw me flee a field of battle. Run away, like a craven coward."

Thinking to return to where the ambush had taken place, he pulled his horse around. There was nothing to be heard now. The dying had been silenced.

"It's over," Horntail said. "I saved your life. Whoever they were, it was you, my prince, they sought. The only living will be those who fled. We were surrounded by archers in trees loosing arrows. What could we do, any of us? Our bows unstrung, our arrows mostly already loosed once today and in need of refletching! They had us caught like pigeons in a net for plucking, about to have their necks wrung."

He closed his eyes. Breathed deep. Patted the quivering neck of his mount.

Blister the hedge-born vassal; he was right. "You deserted your men," he said finally.

"Aye."

"A dark moment for us both, then."

"Aye."

Horntail pointed a finger. "If we ride towards the setting sun, that way, we'll get ourselves out of this cursed forest before dark, methinks."

He looked over his shoulder. "There must be wounded men back there. We have to go back."

"I blew the horn. It was the signal to scatter and flee. My men will have obeyed. They will regroup, what's left of them, and help any who are still alive."

Anthon, I pray you are one such . . .

"Your highness, I'm sorry, but I can't allow you to ride back."

"Can't *allow* me, Horntail? Since when does a sergeant give orders to a prince?"

"Since he was appointed by his king, your highness."

Sick at heart, he nodded his reluctant agreement. Perhaps this would be what it would be like to rule. Not to be a hero, but to be wise. "Let's get to the road, then."

They urged the horses on. Twice they had to dismount and lead them, picking their way down slopes and up hills. They didn't speak again until they'd emerged from the forest. Grimly, he looked up and down the deserted road, now barely visible in the gloaming.

He was desperate to get help, but the horses needed to be walked, and he knew it. He curbed his raging impatience and said as they continued on, "Who were they, Horntail?" Va, he sounded piss-weak.

"I've no idea."

Think, you ninnyhead. Marshal your thoughts. You're a prince! "It was a clever ambush. Good place. They chose their spot well."

"Aye. Well executed. They were accurate with their arrows."

"Well trained, then. What makes you think they were after me? Why not the King?"

"If they'd wanted the King they'd've known the likelihood he wouldn't be hunting all day. They would have waited for him earlier."

He thought about that. "They knew where to wait, and when. Someone told them."

"Reckon you could be right, your highness."

A traitor.

But why? Why me? Tamping down his anger, he considered coldly the little they knew. "To train men, you need space and privacy and time. A large estate somewhere."

"Money to spare," Horntail added.

The horses paced wearily on. "Privacy," he said at last. "That's the key. Secrets don't last long usually. Some chambermaid working at his manor house would have a relative working in the palace, or a stableboy would blab to his sister at a neighbouring property. That's the way things work, especially when something unusual is going on. People talk."

The King always knows what I'm up to. Or he did, in the days when he cared to listen.

He looked across at Horntail. "So, possessing estates no one's ever invited to visit, a man of wealth whose servants don't mix with others – we all know who fits that description. All we have to ask, in fact, is what's changed."

"What's changed? His confidence. Prime-poxy-Fox now thinks he can attack the King's heir – and get away with it."

It was an effort to unclench his jaw sufficiently to speak. "We will see about that!"

For a time, they paced on in silence. To Ryce, the night had a dream-like quality to it; a feeling of being intensely alive hand in hand with knife-edged fear. A moonlit road, tired horses, shadows dancing as the wind tossed the trees, two men from different walks of life suddenly closer than brothers.

"Witan Saker Rampion warned me," Horntail said. "He said Fox moves with men who serve A'Va. So I found out all I could about the Prime."

"I've heard his staff are not even Ardronese."

"Heard that too. The Fox family has at least one estate in every country of the Va-cherished Hemisphere. Their staff? They move from one estate to another. You're right, visitors aren't welcome. They never mix with their neighbours. Ask about who lives there, and no one seems to know."

"Does Valerian have a family?"

"There's vague talk of a son. Or possibly sons."

"He's married?"

Horntail didn't know.

"Cousins, brothers, uncles, aunts, grandmothers?" Ryce asked. The wind cut through the cloth of his hunting coat, and he shivered.

"No one talks of them. It's almost as if Valerian Fox is the only Fox alive."

"That's . . ." The only word that came to mind was *chilling*. "But why would the Prime want me dead? Of what possible benefit is that?" He sighed. "No, don't bother answering." The answer was obvious. When he became King, he'd rid himself of Fox. If he died first, though, the Prime would have a chance to control a regency for Prince Garred on King Edwayn's demise. The thought was nauseating.

"Saker warned me too," he said. "He thought Fox was financing a movement against the Shenat and the Primordials and was eyeing the Pontifect's throne. He wrote me a letter from Lowmeer after his nullification."

"You still hear from him, your highness?"

"Not recently."

"A clever man." Horntail gave a grunt that was half-laugh. "I wasn't surprised when I heard he hadn't died up on the Chervil Moors. He has the ear of the shrine guardians, that man. You could do worse."

"Worse?"

"For your own Prime one day."

He snorted. "We joked about that once, but Saker's not made for a desk in Faith House or leading chapel prayer. I will talk to the King about getting rid of Valerian, though. Let's pick up the pace."

As they rode on, Horntail's mouth was a grim line surrounded by the grizzle of his beard.

Pox on't, Ryce thought, *I hope Lord Anthon Seaforth is still alive.*

"Brigands, that's all."

His father stared at him after uttering those dismissive words, his frown drawing his unruly eyebrows together; his eyes, small and sunken now with age, still able to make him feel like a schoolboy hauled up for teasing fellhound pups. "The reports I have this morning say you did not disport yourself honourably."

"You would rather I were dead?" Ryce asked, not bothering to conceal his bitterness.

"I would rather I had a son to be proud of!"

"Fifteen men died there yesterday. All of them feathered with arrows shot from men in trees. They had no chance to flee. Thank Va, Lord Seaforth was not among them, nor Ser Raknen Marchbury. But Lord Benford's youngest son died, and so did Lord Telman's nephew. The Earl of Fremont's grandson had to have an arrowhead dug from his thigh, and who knows if the witchery healer will be able to stop it turning putrid. The rest of the dead were their attendants, four of the huntsmen and four of my guards."

"And how many of the brigands died?"

"None that we know of."

"You should be ashamed."

"How could men with swords cut down men peppering them with arrows from the trees? You should ask who's behind this. Who has the resources? Who has the men? Who has the manor lands to train such assassins?"

"Brigands! Born bad and brought up to fight and rob honest men. Such scum have no need of training."

"Sire, have you heard a word I've said?"

"Do you call me a fool? What are you trying to say, Ryce? Who are you wanting to blame for this?"

"Prime Valerian Fox, that's who!"

"How dare you? How *dare* you! Valerian is my one true friend. I am fed up with your casting aspersions on an upright man of Va, who has the interests of this monarchy and this nation at heart! *My* interests! The one man who stands with me against my enemies."

"*What* enemies?"

"Have you forgotten who killed your mother?"

The words robbed him of speech. He stared at the King, at a loss.

"Shrine healers and their fobbing witcheries! They killed her."

"She died of childbirth fever." He knew that much. He even thought he remembered something of the day she'd died.

"If I'd prayed to Va, I could have saved her! Instead the Prime, the *Shenat* Prime I inherited from my father, told me to go to the Shenat healers and to pray at the King Oak, and I did. I did all he asked. I prayed and prayed, and they sent their witchery healers – but still she died!" He drew in a ragged breath, his chest heaving as his hands clutched at the arms of his chair and his fingers clawed around the carving. "She was all that was good and beautiful and loving, and she died because Fox was not yet the Prime of Ardrone." Spittle dripped down his chin, unheeded.

"Father, you can't know that—"

"I ought to have married again. I ought to have fathered more sons . . . but I never could find a woman worthy enough to be a queen such as your mother.

"Get out of my sight. Go to the chapel and bow down to our one true deity, lest you follow in my foolish footsteps that led to your mother's death! We were led into wrong paths by the wickedness of the Shenat. Witches all!" He clawed at his eyes, as if he could destroy what his inner eye was seeing. Blood-stained tears runnelled down his cheeks.

Aghast, Ryce reeled away, then turned and fled, calling for the King's manservant to attend him.

27

Murder Most Royal

This was *so* infuriating! All she needed was for Torjen, the Regal's manservant, to make the trip up the spiral stair to her bedchamber to tell her Vilmar was waiting for her below.

But night after night, he never came.

She had everything prepared. Vilmar's signature was on the Law of Succession amendment with reference to her regency if he died while Karel was a minor. She had procured the sleeping draught through Gerelda and she had a backup of rat poison. Her new chambermaid slept in the cuddy, not on a truckle bed. Best of all, the glazier who came to fix a loose window pane in the retiring room had unwittingly provided her with a solution to another problem. On her request, he'd provided her with some soft grout, a horrid oily and smelly ball of it, but she knew just where she would use it. She now kept it wrapped tight in a piece of thin cambric torn from an old kerchief, which she hid in the drawer of her escritoire along with the sleeping drops in their tiny bottle and the poisoned pellets in a pill box.

A whole moon passed, and although Vilmar seemed to regard her fondly enough when they met in public, he never sent for her. When the next moon-month came and went, she began to despair. There was no point in her descending the stairs herself; she had no way of opening the door into the Regal's bedchamber from the inside. She didn't want to have to use the main staircase because that would mean being seen by the Regal's guards at the door to his solar.

Fortunately, Torjen – his narrow face pinched with disapproval as usual – did eventually knock at her chamber door one evening to tell her she was required within the hour.

She rubbed her body with perfume, liberally applied, then selected the most elaborate of her nightgowns. Her maid, Klara, helped her into it, then brushed her hair. She surveyed herself in the looking glass, then dismissed her and the chambermaid, saying, "You may both retire for the night. I will not require you again."

"Oh, but—" Klara began.

"I shall be most displeased if either of you are here when I return," she said sternly. "You need a good night's sleep, both of you. Off with you, right now."

She waited until they had gone, then fetched the grout, the sleeping drops and the poison. She slipped them all into the pocket of her mantle, lit the single candle on the candle holder and set off down the spiral staircase. Just before reaching the open door at the foot, she left the grout, still inside the cambric, on a stair tread.

When she entered the royal bedchamber, the Regal was seated in one of the hard-backed chairs at the table in the corner of the room. He was already in his nightgown with a rug over his knees. With a languid wave of his hand, he dismissed Torjen who had been urging him to put on his bed socks.

"You look very nice, m'dear," he said, but as the words were drawled in bored tones and accompanied by the most perfunctory of glances, she doubted it was anything more than an attempt at courtesy.

She dropped a curtsy and crossed to his side, putting on the sweetest smile she could manage. "How may I serve you tonight, Your Grace? 'Tis a little chilly in here. Would you like me to massage your back or rub your feet? Or shall I warm you in bed, perhaps?"

He ignored her words and picked up a piece of parchment from his lap. "This letter arrived from my ambassador to Ardrone. It contains news which might be of interest to you, but I was debating whether it is fit for your ears."

She blinked in surprise. Rarely did Vilmar mention his correspondence to her. "Not ill news, I trust." Her heart thumped uncomfortably fast as she seated herself in the second chair at the table, glancing at the open bottle of wine and his empty goblet.

"Judge it as you will." He looked down at the sheet of parchment he held. "It seems the King and his heir have had a falling out of considerable consequence. Prince Ryce blinded his sire and then fled to his northern estates."

"Don't be ridiculous." She blurted the words without thinking. "Prince Ryce would never do any such thing."

Vilmar snorted. "Of course, you would defend your family. However, my ambassadors are not in the habit of lying to their liege lord."

"No. No, of course not, Your Grace." She tried to appear contrite rather than stunned, but it was difficult. The idea was ludicrous. "Has – has he lost his wits then, Your Grace?"

"It seems that way."

She had no idea what could have happened in Throssel, but she was certain the ambassador had been deceived. *Still, I can make the most of this.* She flapped a hand in front of her face, panting. "Oh, my heart is jumping so! I think perhaps a glass of wine . . ." She reached for the open bottle on the table, but there was no clean glass. "Might I use your goblet?" she murmured.

He waved a hand in assent, so she filled his empty wineglass, sipped a little and then sat with her head dropping, holding the goblet below the level of the table where he could not see it. She leaned over, her hair flopping forward to further block his view. With one hand she pulled the bottle of sleeping drops out of her pocket and poured a generous amount into the wine. She stoppered the phial once more and slipped it back.

"Prince Ryce is the fool I thought him to be," the Regal was saying, his smug satisfaction obvious. "And Ardrone is finished as a rival to our wealth and power."

She swallowed her anger and smiled wanly. "I'm sure you're right, my liege. I am deeply ashamed of my own blood. That my brother should behave so badly – it is inconceivable!" She stood up and placed the glass in front of him. "I think this wine will go to my head. Let me massage your shoulders, and we perhaps can turn our thoughts to more pleasurable things . . . ?" She moved behind him and started to rub his shoulders with gentle fingers. "Sip your wine and relax."

He almost fell asleep in the chair after finishing only half the glass. Hurriedly, she urged him into bed. He was asleep the moment he laid his head on the pillow. She tried to wake him, but he was gently snoring. She flung what remained of the wine in the glass out of the window then returned to the bed, looking down at him.

Once he might have been a strong man; now he just looked pathetic, with sunken eyes and shrunken thighs, his hair thin and patchy, his shanks spindly, his dry skin sagging on his frame. She put on his bed socks and nightcap, then pulled up the bedclothes. He didn't stir.

She picked up the ambassador's letter and read it all. There was some more detail about the argument between her brother and her father, and an attack on Ryce during a hunt, but no detail that explained how the King had been blinded or why Ryce was blamed. She frowned over it, but try as she might, it all seemed nonsensical. At least the ambassador made it clear where Ryce was; he'd gone to his own estates in the north. That in itself was odd – his southern properties were much more congenial. His castle in the north was fortified, a cold and bleak place by all reports. The kind of place a man might go to if he feared for his life.

She dropped the letter back on the table, shivering, then walked to the door into the dressing room, where Torjen was nodding off in one of the chairs, waiting for permission to go to bed.

"The Regal sleeps," she said. "Please draw the bed curtains and dampen the fire. Then you may go to bed."

She didn't wait for him, but left the door open and retreated to the stair with her candle. Quickly, before Torjen had entered the bedchamber, she picked up the grout in its wrapping and rammed it inside the well of the lock in the door jamb. When she pulled the door closed, the thin cambric ends were flattened between the door and jamb. The deadlock on the door was unable to click into place, but she knew that if Torjen looked at it, he would think it properly closed.

Back upstairs in her own bedroom, she was glad to see she was alone. Quietly so as not to wake the chambermaid, she paced back and forth across the room trying to make sense of the news from Ardrone, and failing miserably. Va, how she *hated* being helpless and uninformed.

Well, that period in her life would soon be over. She'd make sure of that.

She waited until after she'd heard the midnight tocsin, then picked up her candleholder again and returned to Vilmar's bedchamber. When she pushed the door, it swung back open with minimum resistance. She pulled the kerchief out, and the grout came with it, leaving no sign that anyone had tampered with the lock. Leaving the door open, she placed the candleholder and the kerchief on the lowest step and crept into the room.

It was in near darkness. There was a little moonlight filtering in through the thick glass of the window and a dim glow from the dampened fire, but that was all. If Torjen had left any candles burning, they had since guttered. The only sound was that of the Regal's noisy breathing from behind the curtains of his bed.

She crept over to the door to the dressing room, to find Torjen had left it ajar. Listening at the gap, she could hear him snoring in the room beyond. With infinite care, she closed the door and retreated to the stairway to collect her candle. This she took to the table between the bed and the window. She opened up the curtains around Vilmar's bed to let in a little light and picked up one of his many pillows.

Apparently she had not given him enough of the sleeping draught to kill him. She regarded him dispassionately as he lay on his back, mouth open, snuffling. Then, climbing up on to the bed, she knelt with a leg on either side of his body. He still did not move.

"They say," she said softly, "that you murdered your first wife. She was Ardronese, and royal, related to me, but you killed her because she didn't give you any children. Well, neither did I, Vilmar Vollendorn."

He didn't stir.

She shrugged and placed the pillow over his face. Pressing it down with her hands, she lay on top of him, spreading her weight over his face and upper body to make it hard for him to move. She expected him to struggle, and prepared herself. He moved under her, trying to turn his face sideways. His legs kicked, but his movements were feeble, the faint attempts of a drugged man to escape a fate he was incapable of recognising. She maintained the pressure long past its need.

When she lifted the pillow, he was silent, his breathing stopped. His mouth sagged open. She reached out to pick up the candle and brought it to his face. His eyes were open, and he was now staring at her with a blank, sightless gaze, quite lifeless.

She stared back.

"That," she said, "was no more than you deserve, Vilmar Vollendorn. What price your Bengorth's Law now? How many have *died* just to keep a Vollendorn backside on the Basalt Throne?"

His eyes did not blink.

She smiled at him. "Let me tell you this: the next arse that sits there has not a drop of your blood. So much for the supposed power of A'Va." She tapped him on the nose. "You should have put your faith in Va."

Wriggling off the bed, she stood at his side to replace his cap on his head, rearrange the pillows and straighten the bedclothes. Then she leaned forward to close his eyelids. With one final check to make sure she had left nothing behind, not even a drop of candle grease, she closed the bed curtains.

After padding across to reopen the door to the retiring room where Torjen still snored, she left it open just a crack, then returned to the spiral staircase. From there, she took one last look at the room. All appeared to be in place. She picked up the grout, pulled the door shut behind her and, smiling, made her way back to bed. No one could point the finger at her; the Regal had been asleep when Torjen drew the curtains around the bed, and the closed door to the spiral staircase meant that she could not have returned.

She would sleep well that night.

She woke the next morning to the news of Vilmar's death.

No one suspected a thing. The court was plunged into mourning and she was the only person truly ready for it. She had long since laid her plans to divide and rule the Council of Regency, and knew her success depended on her alignment with her son so that any disagreement with the Regala would also appear to be disloyalty to the Princeregal. She had already been playing one off against another while the Regal was still alive.

With Lady Friselda, she didn't even bother to be subtle. The first time she met the ward's-dame after news of the Regal's death, the old woman was pale-faced and red-eyed. Mathilda could almost feel sorry for her. Almost.

"You've never liked me," she said briskly. "And I have resented your interference between my husband and me. One thing I have admired, though," she added after the first sentiment had time to register, "is your loyalty to my beloved husband."

"I always supported my cousin," Friselda said.

"I understand he paid you an allowance, as well as supplying you with your well-appointed solar."

Lady Friselda inclined her head. "That is so."

"In return, you acted as his spy."

The old lady said nothing.

"I imagine you might find retirement from court both boring and a pecuniary embarrassment."

"Possibly." The words were emotionless, but her eyes were haunted.

"I know your loyalty will now lie with His Grace's son. Perhaps you would therefore be willing to allow that our aims match: we both want the best for him and for his reign."

Friselda's gaze sharpened with hope and Mathilda knew she was about to snare her first real ally. *All one has to do*, she thought, *is find out what a person fears most, and what they need most . . .* "At the moment, I can't see any reason for you to retire from court, Lady Friselda. We have a funeral to organise. And after that, a coronation."

After which you will be my spy among the court women.

28

Returning to Javenka

*T*hink, Ardhi. You have to stop her. You can't bask in the sun and expect the *sakti* to do it for you. You know this place. There has to be a way . . .

He was standing at the helmsman's shoulder guiding him through the tricky entrance as *Golden Petrel* slipped into Javenka harbour in the last hour of sunshine. He ought to have been concentrating on the task at hand; the entrance was a narrow passage between age-old forts glowering from rocky outcrops on either side, their cannon a hint that it might pay to be a courteous visitor.

He glanced at Lord Juster fidgeting beside him. "What's the matter, cap'n?" he asked softly. *Is your reliance on a barefoot, dark-skinned lascar to negotiate a safe passage troubling you?*

"Are you sure we don't need to ask for a local pilot?"

"I'm sure."

Juster stared grimly ahead. "I came here as a cabin boy when I was twelve. We used a lead line to sound the depth then."

"Not necessary."

"How can you be sure we have enough water under the keel? You rake her bottom, and the keel-raking I mention then will be yours, not *Petrel*'s."

"I know passage." He wasn't about to admit his knowledge was theoretical. He'd never actually brought a ship through the entrance himself, but he had stood at the shoulder of a helmsman and watched the rocks slide by before.

"Saker said you came here to study." Juster's jaw was tight, and the clasped hands behind his back were white-knuckled.

"That's right," he agreed. "Helmsman, steady ahead. Two beacons on hill, one high, one low. Keep lined up, understand?"

"Aye, aye."

"Dead languages, divinity and philosophy?" Juster asked.

"Actually, navigation and pilotage, astronomy, cartography and hydrography." Not knowing the words in Ardronese, he used the Pashali ones instead, but a blank look told him Lord Juster's knowledge of the language did not stretch that far.

Probably just as well.

Think, Ardhi. How can you stop Sorrel disembarking here? You have to be clever about this.

They passed the forts safely and the passage opened up into a large expanse of water surrounded by hills on which the city was built.

Skies above, it's beautiful. I was so happy here. And so ridiculously young. "Best we anchor in front of harbourmaster's building." He pointed it out. "They will send someone to talk to us."

"Why?"

"They do this for all ships. Tax you. Want to know what you want. Maybe harbourmaster himself come. Best Lord Juster be polite."

"Lord Juster is always polite, Ardhi," Juster said. "Finch, give the orders aloft."

Saker, who had been scanning the harbour with the ship's spyglass, now turned to address Juster as the sailors began hauling in the sails not yet furled. "Remember what happened to Lord Denworth's fleet here. They were held to ransom. Pashalin didn't take kindly to the idea of merchant ships bypassing the mastodon caravan routes."

"I know, I know. But we aren't a merchantman. They should be happy to see a privateer." Juster grinned. "Our presence on the high seas encourages overland trade. Can you see any of the Lowmian fleet?"

"No."

"We'll catch up with them in our next port of call," Juster said.

Kotabanta, Ardhi thought. *Where he thinks he'll get his revenge.* His gut twisted. He knew that port even better than he knew Javenka. *Sands, how I hate this. Your half of the world brings little but trouble to mine, Lord Juster.*

He glanced over to where Sorrel was pointing out the scenery to Piper. He doubted she'd heard a word. She was focused on the city, and there was tension in her stance and an ache in her voice that told him she was appalled by what she saw. He remembered the first time he'd laid eyes on Javenka himself, remembered the suffocating fear of knowing he was going to be alone in a place so vast, so alien.

I have to stop her.

No longer needed by the helmsman, he moved away from the helm to her side. "All will be good," he said as the ship slowed and the crew prepared to drop anchor. "I promise you."

Her look told him what she thought of his foolish platitudes. She'd already done all she could to make her onward journey as safe as possible; he admired that. She'd spent hours each day with either him or Saker learning Pashali. She'd weaned Piper. She'd kept herself fit by practising the moves of silat, the warrior's way, that he'd showed her, and by climbing the rigging when the weather allowed. She had muscles now, and a body that was lean and hard. The whole time she'd been on board, she'd continued to use her glamour to cover the clothes she actually wore: men's culottes and a sailor's cotton shirt. He wondered if she knew that he – like Saker – could see through the glamour. He was sure she never guessed how much he loved the way she looked in those men's clothes, how much he admired the tan of sun-darkened skin, the litheness of the way she moved now, the ease with which she climbed. She stirred him the same way Lastri had stirred him, but he took special care never to show it. There was no point.

Now, just looking at her, he knew how terrified she was, and how determined to overcome her fear. He said gently, "I don't break promise."

"How can you possibly know Piper and I will be safe all the way to Vavala?" There was no mistaking her derision. "You won't be there."

"You are both under protection of Chenderawasi."

She flicked a scornful glance his way, and it hurt. "Go away, Ardhi. I wish I'd never met you. It's your wretched Chenderawasi sorcery that did this to me in the first place."

Sialan! Damn it, she knew how to twist his gut with guilt. He wanted to touch her cheek, tell her he would always protect her if he could, but assurances were useless. Hiding his pain, he effaced himself.

He climbed aloft to help furl the last of the sails as the anchor splashed into the water, wincing as his shoulder pained him. It still ached from where the shaft of splintered wood had lodged itself, chipping bone from his clavicle.

When the other tars returned to deck, he stayed up there, swung his arm to loosen up the muscles while the dusk crept from the shadowed bay to the streets canyoned by the buildings of the city.

Four years, more or less. Four years since he'd left Javenka and the long downward spiral had begun. He'd been happy here, full of youthful optimism, revelling in the joy of learning, in the challenges of the new. His mentor, Istanel, had called Javenka the most learned city of the civilised world; perhaps he was right.

Certainly, by comparison, Ustgrind was drab and lacking in intellectual stimulation, while Throssel was grubby and full of inequities. But this? Javenka was the City of Glass and Learning, each quarter intimately known to him, and appreciated.

Across the hilltops known as Javenka-on-High, the last rays of the sun glinted from oblong windows like a line of fiery hearths. The building sprawled along the crest was the Library, founded a thousand years in the past by a woman and her crippled brother.

It was there he'd forged relationships with his teachers that had opened his mind to the world. Istanel's words echoed in his memory: *Pay attention, Ardhi; back home you might have safely paddled your canoe in the lagoon, but you need to study mathematics if you wish to explore the oceans!*

Below Javenka-on-High was Javenka-the-Midst, tumbling from the centre of learning to the flatland. Here, rows of conjoined shops and tenements were squeezed apart by tortuous winding lanes and stone stairs. Steps, so many steps, so many wild foot races, and irate citizens berating the racing students for their reckless, drunken ways.

Tiny alleyways, tiny taverns, tiny rooms in narrow houses, it might have appeared impoverished, but for the glass. Magnificent, boldly coloured glass: thick crystal balls, rough glass panels, delicate blown-glass ornaments, statues with fragile glass insets, tinkling wind chimes of vibrant translucent baubles.

He'd lost his virginity in Javenka-the-Midst, to a town girl, a dark-haired merchant's daughter intrigued by the idea of a student islander in her bed. For a while, they'd loved and laughed and then . . . parted, bored, knowing they had nothing more than their temporary needs to bind them.

Go home, Ardhi, she'd said. *Find someone who understands your life and where you come from.* So he dreamed of Lastri instead.

Below the Midst was Javenka-the-Face, a narrow strip of wealth and prestige bordering the bay. The massive private and public buildings here were decorated with glass mosaics and linked by broad roads, public squares and gardens.

The central hub of the bay was Javenka-the-Port. The five humped islands in the bay, connected by boardwalks to each other and to the mainland, formed the beating heart that enriched the city, pumping the blood of trade and gold and spice along its arteries. The main boardwalk was an engineering miracle, large enough for drays pulled by oxen, tough enough for the heaviest cargoes, a thoroughfare passing over eight bridges to the wooden docks. And ah, those docks: enough berths for twenty-five full-sized merchant ships at any one time.

Everything and everyone a ship could need was found on one of the five islands or along the boardwalk: chandlers and chart sellers, warehouses and godowns, coopers and hoopers and ropemakers, carpenters and sailmakers and blacksmiths. Here, a captain or a ship-owner could hire a docklumper or a buy a chronometer, sign on a ship's boy or a helmsman, arrange for a cargo to be sent to Karradar or Kotabanta, and auction spices or wool bales or the ballast bricks from his ship.

Lastly, there was Javenka-the-Bay: the water road of the daylight hours, the market of the night, where boats and barges and packets and ferries plied from one shore to the next like water beetles scurrying across a pond, or lingered after sunset to service the anchored houseboats, the floating brothels, the drug dens and gambling flatboats. Constantly on the move were other small vessels: the dhows of itinerant fortune tellers and money lenders and medicine sellers; the budgerows belonging to the abortionists and drug dealers and thieves.

Ardhi watched as the last light of the sun died and the lanterns were lit. Javenka did not sleep at night; it thrived, it hummed, it sang. Like a panther, it was beautiful and languid in the sunshine, yet dark and mysterious and dangerous by night.

Half an hour after the last light faded from the sky, the harbour-master's boat glided up to the pilot steps and several men climbed up to be greeted by Lord Juster, Finch and Saker. Sorrel had already gone below. Quietly, he descended and made his way across the deck to the prow and the ship's heads. The latrine rope that dangled there was slimy, but it was the quickest and quietest way for him to enter the sea without a splash. He swung himself over the edge of the head, grabbed the rope and let himself silently down into the water.

Two hours later Ardhi was knocking at a familiar door. How often had he knocked just this way, rapping on the panelling between the brass studs, wondering just what sort of a reception he would receive? Too often, especially when he'd been in trouble. He'd been so young and foolish then.

The voice that bade him enter was familiar too. Authoritative, with just a hint of a quaver that spoke of increasing age. He stepped inside, closed the door behind him and hesitated to allow his eyes to adjust to the light of several candelabra after the darkness of the passageway. He then placed both palms flat to his chest and inclined his head deferentially to the man seated behind the table in the room.

Confound it. From old friends, he'd borrowed dry clothes and the band to wind a turban – necessary as a sign of respect, for no one went bareheaded before their superiors – but in his hurry he hadn't wound it tight enough and the headgear was in danger of falling down over his eyebrow. He straightened slowly, careful not to dislodge it.

"Mir," he said. He used the hereditary title against all usual custom. Inherited status had no place within the university hierarchy, but he wanted to signal that his was not just the visit of a past student to his teacher. He was coming to Istanel because his mentor was a member of the ruling house of merchants.

Istanel rose to his feet, a courtesy he never would have extended to a mere student. "Well! If it isn't the Datu's grandson from Chenderawasi." His gaze swept over Ardhi, lingering on his feet before returning to his face. "It is always a pleasure to see a past student, although it seems we never did manage to teach you to wear shoes, Ardhi."

"A small failing, Mentor Istanel, I assure you."

"What brings the heir of my old friend back to this place of learning? I trust the honourable Datu is well?"

"It has been several years since I saw my grandfather, but the last time I was home he was still in good health." *If furious with me, with a fury beyond rage* . . . He would never see him again, he knew that. "The ship I travel upon called into port and I wished to pay my respects."

"A short visit then?" Istanel waved a hand towards an empty chair and reseated himself. "Tell me what has come to pass. I heard of the death of the Raja, and rumours which were even more unsettling. Rumours about a former student."

"A rumour does not always speak the whole truth."

"Indeed not. I believe the death of a Chenderawasi Raja is a complex matter, especially when his heir is too young for his regalia. I know how the governance of your island is structured, and what the death of a Raja means. Oh, do not look so shocked, young Ardhi. I was once, after all, a navigator and helmsman. I sailed once with your grandfather. He took me to Raja Wiramulia's court. As a result of that visit, and without betraying a trust, I persuaded my family not to pursue direct trade with the Pulauan Chenderawasi except under very strict rules of conduct."

"You know our . . . secret."

"All of it. And I have protected it, as have a few other privileged members of our guild of merchants over the centuries. The rumours I hear now are troubling; fortunately, though, somewhat garbled."

"I would ask another favour of you. Call it . . . call it the request of a condemned man."

"Condemned? You, the Datu's heir?" He raised a surprised eyebrow. "Such as you are not condemned lightly."

"No. Nor was my crime a light matter, for all that it was a result of foolishness. However, no man condemned me, nor yet the Rani. It is the *sakti* that has decreed my fate. It needed sacrifice. Successful in my quest or not, I die when I return."

Did Istanel's face change colour then? He thought so, although with such a dark complexion, it was hard to be sure. "It is my choice to go back. And I ask a favour of you in the hope that my sacrifice may ensure success."

Their gazes locked, and it was the old man's that broke first. He looked down at his own hands and fiddled with one of his rings. "My knowledge of Chenderawasi *sakti* is minimal, but I understand it is powerful and not easily thwarted." There was a long pause before he looked up again to say, "Tell me what you need, Ardhi, and I will tell you if it is within my power to aid you."

"Have you seen Ardhi?"

Saker, emerging on to the quarterdeck after breakfast the next morning, blinked, taken aback by the irritation in Juster's tone. "No. I haven't seen him since last night."

"Nor has anyone else, apparently. He was supposed to be on watch this morning, didn't turn up and can't be found."

"That's . . . odd." A shiver prickled up his spine.

"Exceedingly. No boats have approached the ship since the harbour-master came last night. So if he went anywhere, he swam."

"Why would he want to do that? He would have been going onshore today anyway, wouldn't he?" He didn't like the sound of this at all.

"I am giving everyone shore leave in shifts, yes. At least I am once we get a berth. What the Va-less hell is he playing at, Saker?"

"Blessed if I know. He's certainly familiar with Javenka. I imagine he still has friends here. I asked him to help me find a passage to Vavala for Sorrel, but that could have waited."

"And he agreed?"

"Of course. Well, he was reluctant for Sorrel to go. I think he said something like, 'If it's necessary.'"

"I trusted the wretch. Maybe I shouldn't have done. Tell me, what was it he said to me yesterday, when he spoke Pashali?"

"He listed the subjects he studied at the Library."

"Which were?"

"Navigation and pilotage, astronomy, cartography and . . . hydrography, I think it was."

"You're not jesting, are you?"

"No. Neither was he."

"Pox on the bastard! I've been sending him aloft like an ignorant tar when he could have been using the astrolabe and plotting our course?"

"I did tell you he'd been a student of the Library."

"I thought that meant he'd been dabbling in native witchdoctory or Pashali alchemy or something!" He took a breath to calm himself. "What in all the foaming oceans is hydrography?"

"Something to do with mapping the ocean and navigation, I believe. You know what the problem is with us folk from the Va-cherished Hemisphere, Juster? If someone doesn't speak our language well, we think they are ill-educated and stupid. A grave mistake. Believe me, I've had to rethink my attitude towards Ardhi several times. And I don't believe we know one quarter of what there is to know, even yet."

"Well, that's obvious, isn't it! Neither of us expected him to go for a paddle in the middle of the night."

"Captain, sir?"

Juster turned to look at the speaker. "Yes, Costel?"

"There's a boat approaching. Came from the harbourmaster's jetty."

Juster nodded and waved him away. "Now what? How much d'you bet this has something to do with a missing lascar? Come with me to see what all this is about, Saker. Your Pashali is a long way better than mine."

"You should have come to my lessons on the way here."

"Tush! A classroom is no way to learn anything. Most of what I've learned has been in a tavern. Or in bed. Lovers make the best teachers."

"I fear my dedication to learning has its limits."

"Never mind, a Pashali gentleman I met in Karradar gave me the direction of a certain lady living in Javenka-the-Midst, ravishing by all reports. We could make her acquaintance—" He halted then as Sorrel and Surgeon Barklee emerged from below decks.

"She's a darling," Barklee was saying. He was smiling down at Piper in his arms as she pulled at his beard and chortled. "Reminds me of my own cherubs. Two little darlings, I have, one about this age when I left." He carried her over to the taffrail to watch a passing bumboat laden with fruit and vegetables.

"What's happening?" Sorrel asked Saker.

"Boat coming in from the harbourmaster," he said, "and Ardhi has vanished."

"No, he hasn't," she said, after glancing over the bulwarks. "He's sitting in the harbourmaster's boat."

He was too. Saker frowned. Va-damn the fellow. What trouble was he in this time?

A few minutes later one of the harbourmaster's subordinates was speaking to Lord Juster on deck, having declined an invitation to go below. "Two messages from Notable Xanathra," he said, referring to the harbourmaster who had not been on the boat. "Your berth is ready on Sorzrava Island, dock six, bollard two. Money to be paid in advance, amount as already agreed, when you tie up."

Juster looked at Saker, who quickly translated.

"Thank you. And the second message?" Juster inquired.

They all expected it would have something to do with Ardhi, who had come on board behind the Pashali official and was now standing a pace or two away.

"When you leave," the official continued, "everyone is to be on board. No one is granted permission to disembark in Javenka."

Juster looked puzzled. "I'm not sure I understand you," he said, with Saker translating. "We wish to replenish our supplies, and my men would value shore leave—"

"That is not a problem. You misunderstand. It is just that all who arrived on board yesterday, must depart on board. Everyone, including the woman and the child. Otherwise your ship will be impounded and you will not be permitted to sail."

Juster looked at Saker, perplexed. "I'm still not sure that I understand. Saker?"

"He's forbidding Sorrel and Piper to take the overland route," he replied. "If they don't sail with us when we go, none of us get to leave."

For a moment Juster stood, unmoving. Then he turned back to the harbourmaster's representative, his back rigid, his voice as flat as a plank of wood. "These instructions: they come from the harbourmaster?"

"Yes. But you must understand, the harbourmaster is subordinate to the Council of Merchants and Scholars, headed by Mir Alda Attaranzi." The man bowed. "My message is delivered."

Having heard Saker's translation, Lord Juster, never a fool, inclined his head. "Convey our greetings and thanks to the harbourmaster." He watched the man descend once more into the boat, saluted him, then took two steps across the deck to Ardhi, seizing him by the arm and almost lifting him off his feet. "Who is Mir Alda Attaranzi?"

"Mir is title. Like 'Lord'. Attaranzi is big merchant family. Alda is . . ." He searched for the correct word. "Head of that family."

"Patriarch," Saker suggested.

"Yes. Patriarch. Attaranzi family rule Javenka, hundred years already maybe, so family patriarch is like Regal."

"And," Juster continued through gritted teeth, "would you like to explain how this Mir Alda got to hear about the existence of Sorrel and Piper?"

For a moment Saker thought Ardhi would not reply. Finally, though, he said quietly, "It was necessary. Piper and Mistress Sorrel must go to Chenderawasi."

At Saker's side, Sorrel gave a sharp intake of breath and clutched at his arm, her fingers digging deep.

Juster glowered at Ardhi. "And you have very cleverly made it so that it is impossible for them to do otherwise. Get out of my sight, before I toss you overboard – attached to an anchor!"

Ardhi walked to the companionway and disappeared below decks. All Saker could think of was how dignified his exit was, as if he was neither ashamed nor proud of what he had done. He had the resignation of a man who knew there had been no alternative. Not for him.

Juster looked from him to Sorrel. "You could get off the ship glamoured, Mistress Sorrel. Are you still able to hide Piper under your glamour too?"

"Not really. She's too big. Besides, I can't stop her from crying or babbling at a crucial moment." She bit her lip. "But that's irrelevant surely? The official as good as told you they'll search the ship to make sure I'm on board when you leave."

Neither of them had a reply to that.

"I'm going to throw Ardhi overboard one dark night between here and the Spicerie," Lord Juster muttered. "I command this ship, and he just betrayed his captain. A sailor on board who cannot be trusted is a danger to everyone."

"You don't mean that," Saker said. "You're no murderer."

Juster gave a bark of savage laughter. "You jest! You – the man who scolds me for being a privateer? I've killed more innocent sailors than I care to think about, just as any soldier does for his country. Ardhi will just be one more on the list."

"His Va-forsaken dagger is likely to do something to prevent it, and you might be the one yelling for help in the middle of the ocean."

They all thought about that, then Sorrel raised her chin, looked from Juster to him and back again, and said, "We have no choice. I will go to Chenderawasi with you."

Troubled, he wondered if she was relieved or despairing.

Releasing her clutch at his arm, she added, "This sorcery of Ardhi's – it's powerful. No matter what we do, Piper and me, we always seem to be pushed towards Chenderawasi. I'm becoming more scared of resisting it than I am of acquiescing."

A visceral fear punched at his heart. *What don't we know?* "This business with the harbourmaster? It doesn't sound like sorcery to me," he said. "It sounds as if Ardhi went to some of his friends and put pressure on someone higher up the ladder. Good old-fashioned influence. Using one's friends in high places."

"Perhaps," she agreed, but she looked no happier.

"If you think this Chenderawasi sorcery is so powerful," Juster said slowly, "that's all the more reason you should try to escape from it."

"Are you trying to be fair and give me every chance to change my mind?" she asked.

"Never could resist a beautiful lady."

"Neither a lady, nor beautiful," she said with her usual prosaic composure. "I *like* Ardhi. He obviously doesn't think he's taking me and Piper into danger. In fact, I would feel more in danger if I try to fight this *sakti* of his."

Juster took a deep breath. "I think you ought to talk to Ardhi, Mistress Sorrel. I think you have more of a chance at charming information out of him than we do. He likes you, and he adores Piper. The more we know, the better armed we are. And is that her I hear crying?"

"It is indeed. I left her with Surgeon Barklee, but as much as she charms him, I imagine there's only so much of a wailing babe he's willing to tolerate." She gave a rueful smile, but there was a lightness to her step as she turned and walked away. Or did he imagine that?

Juster said, "He's not immune to a pretty face any more than you and I are."

Ardhi? He certainly wasn't talking about the surgeon. He felt a pang of jealousy, followed closely by a jab of guilt. He had no more rights to Sorrel's friendship than anyone else. Blister it.

"Tell you one thing, Saker. We are getting out of this port as fast as we can victual and turn the ship around. I've already had quite enough of Javenka and we haven't even set foot on the ground yet."

29

Gerelda and the Dire Sweepers

As Gerelda hurried along the cobbled laneway near their lodgings late one afternoon, her sopping skirt flopping around her calves like an over-enthusiastic wet puppy, she wondered why she'd once loved this town of Grundorp a scant seven years earlier when she'd been a student.

Because she'd been in love for the first time? Perhaps. Strange to think of that. She and Saker were friends now in a way that they'd never been then. Then they'd been discovering the joys of nights between the covers and the joy was all encompassing. Nights snatched, in secret and in defiance of university rules which decreed a celibate decorum, had an intensity of pleasure that was hard to find again.

With weather like this, no wonder we stayed indoors so much.

A passing cart splashed mud over her boots and skirt and more rain sifted down. Oh, how she wished Lowmian convention allowed her to wear trousers! She stopped for a moment to wrap her cloak more tightly, but no matter what she did, she couldn't keep the bottom of her skirt dry and her hat was inadequate. She hurried on.

Above the street, as if to add an extra coating of gloom to the grey weather, bedraggled black drapes of mourning flapped wetly from window poles. They'd been erected in honour of Regal Vilmar, who had died in his sleep several sennights past.

"Are you Gerelda Brantheld?"

Startled, she stopped, blinking through the drizzle. It was a man who'd asked: tall, middle years, well-spoken and well-dressed. He moved his right hand slightly to draw his cloak back so that she could see the sword buckled at his side. Blue unsmiling eyes regarded her without expression from below the dripping rim of his hat.

He wasn't alone. Two more men were standing behind him, both broad-shouldered fellows clad in the nondescript black of retainers.

The hair rose on the back of her neck.

"Who's asking?" she enquired, wondering if she ought to run. There was no one else nearby and she wasn't wearing her sword.

"You don't know who I am?"

She looked him over, taking in the polish of his black leather boots on the way. You could tell a lot from a man's boots. His were well looked after, a good fit; bespoke probably. "No, I can't say I do," she said. "Should I?"

"Yes. I think you should, seeing you've been asking a great many questions about me around the university, even researching my family in the library."

Hells. "I've done a lot of research lately, I fear," she said, giving him what she hoped was a bright, unworried smile. "If your family is a prominent one, then doubtless I have encountered your name. Could you be more specific, please?"

He wasn't amused. "Lord Herelt Deremer."

"The Deremers were indeed prominent in early Lowmian history." And damned secretive after that.

"I have a carriage waiting." He indicated the end of the street where a black coach was drawn up.

Black coach, black horses. Theatrical bastard. He must have given some pre-arranged signal because the equipage began moving towards them.

"I'd like to take you for a drive."

She scanned the street once more. It was growing dark and most people had already headed indoors, except for several pedestrians at the far end. "My mother always counselled against such boldness. We can talk here."

"It is raining and I prefer to be comfortable."

"I'm rooming right here." She indicated the building next to where they were standing.

"I know. And you have a lad waiting for you there. He's going to have a long wait, I fear."

Fob it. She looked up to the window of the room they had rented and thought she saw a face behind the distortion of the cheap glass.

"He might be better off forgetting he ever met you," Deremer continued.

That doesn't sound good. She thought of running and turned her head slightly to see what his two servants were doing. They had moved close enough to grab her.

"Don't think about it," he said and this time rested his hand on the hilt of his sword. The carriage drew up alongside them and she recognised the Deremer crest on it, carved wood embossed with gold portraying a mythical serpent. One of the retainers opened the door, and Deremer gestured for her to enter.

She snatched the only chance she had. She dived into the coach, wrenching the door out of the lackey's hand as she passed to slam it behind her. Leaping through the coach interior, she reached out for the door handle on the other side.

There wasn't one.

She sighed and sank down on to the seat.

Deremer opened the door once more and climbed in. "I'm not a fool, Lawyer Brantheld," he said. "It would be a grave mistake on your part to think so. I should also like to point out that your young companion is at the moment free and unmolested. Should you prove recalcitrant, that might change."

She inclined her head, but kept silent. Her heart beat uncomfortably fast. The carriage door was closed, leaving them alone, and after a moment they began to move. Leather blinds drawn over the glassless windows made an interior lamp necessary and one had already been lit.

"Have you nothing to say?" he asked. "Aren't you interested in where we are going?"

"If you want me to know, you'll tell me. If you don't want me to know, a question won't help."

"True. So let me tell you what I know about you. You are a lawyer and you are employed by the Pontifect. You are particularly interested in the Dire Sweepers, devil-kin, twin births, the Horned Death and the Fox family. And the Deremers, which latter interest is your undoing."

Va-damn, is there anything he doesn't know?

The carriage rattled over the cobbles and swayed as the horses picked up speed. She listened for anything that would tell her where they were headed, but there was a tiresome monotony to the sound of cobbles under the wheels, and little else to be heard.

"Your misfortune," he continued, "is that you have connected my family to the Dire Sweepers."

This is becoming worse and worse. "Whatever makes you think that?"

"I have a lot of spies, and I pay them well. Sometimes years pass, and I never hear anything from a spy. And then . . ." He made a vague gesture with his hand. "Over the past month I've heard a lot about you and your activities at the university, your research in the library, your lad out on the streets listening at corners."

"So?"

"In the past, whenever someone made a connection between the Deremers and the Dire Sweepers, they usually disappeared. For ever."

"And nowadays you have conversations instead of murder? How civilised of you!"

"Oh, make no mistake about it. I'm a killer. We all are, we Sweepers. I assume you know that much. We kill the innocent along with the guilty for the greater good."

She said nothing. Inside her stomach was churning. A man who thought the greater good justified any means scared her senseless.

"Do you know why we did it?" he asked.

Past tense. Interesting.

"Because your liege lord asked it of you."

"Partly. The Deremers helped Bengorth usurp power. Thanks to the support of a whole line of Regals, my family went from being obscure landholders in Grundorp to being the richest dynasty in the whole of Lowmeer. Thanks to a policy of secrecy and assassination, we are also one of the least well-known. Naturally it has been in our interest to keep the Vollendorns on the throne ever since. But there's more to it than that, as I'm sure you have found out."

"Perhaps. If you are so murderous, why are we talking?"

"There has been a change of late."

Yes, and one you wouldn't like one little bit. The Regal is dead. You've lost your patron and your paymaster, you weasel.

He was sitting opposite her, leaning back against the soft black leather of the studded upholstery. Now he leaned forward. She resisted an impulse to cringe. He said, "The Regal is dead and a fox has gone mad. I'm sure you're aware of these things."

She didn't speak. The sound of the wheels changed, rumbling hollow; they must be crossing the Ust River bridge.

"Do you know what it is like to be raised as I was raised?" he asked. "To know from the time you are ten or twelve that your life's work is to kill. To murder cleanly and humanely, but without hesitation. To kill babies, one of whom you know is innocent. To kill anyone who knows too much, or finds out too much. I killed my first child when I was thirteen. My induction. Had I failed it, my uncle would have killed me. I followed in illustrious footsteps: my father and uncles, my grandfather, my great-grandfather and his father. Back in a line of Deremers to the time of Regal Bengorth. Murderers all. Men – and women too – who kept a great evil at bay by being efficient killers and spies. If the thought bothers you, think of us as an army, protecting the populace. No different from a real army. We came to terms with killing, just as soldiers must."

Beggar me, having heard all this, there's no way he's going to let me get out of this carriage alive. "I appreciate your, um, consideration in letting me know why you are going to kill me. You must know lawyers love information."

"Not to mention your love of sarcasm?" He looked at her with narrowed eyes, a thoughtful, considering look. "We're not going to progress far if we aren't honest with one another. Let me point out first that those men you might think were my servants – the coachmen, those two retainers up on top in the rain – all three are Deremers. All are armed and all are Dire Sweepers who have spent a lifetime in the service of the Regal."

"By murdering babies."

"Amongst others. What I'm trying to say is this. You cannot escape with your life and freedom unless I wish it. You will die today if I wish it. You have one chance at life."

"And that is?"

"To listen and to be honest."

I'm dead. "Go on."

He leant back against the upholstery again and was silent. She decided the look in his eyes was more bleak than cold. Herelt Deremer was not a happy man, or even a satisfied one.

"Let me tell you a story," he said at last. "At the end, you can tell me if I have my facts right."

She inclined her head.

"I think Regal Vilmar was worried he would die before his son reached the age of discretion. So he confided in his Regala. He told her of Bengorth's Law. A stupid decision of a man who'd lost his edge and who'd already been behaving oddly, one assumes because of the failing acumen of age."

She made a non-committal sound.

"The Regala was alarmed and sent a message to the Pontifect, perhaps via a handmaiden who disappeared under odd circumstances, or perhaps some other way. It doesn't matter. The Pontifect sends you to find out what's going on. At the same time, a small segment of Va-faith clerics do their own investigation." He tilted his head. "Am I right?"

She shrugged. "Go on." *At least he doesn't appear to know about Mathilda's twins . . .*

"The Dire Sweepers murdered the clerics, and covered up their activities by blaming their deaths on the Horned Plague. Their academy was burned to the ground, taking with it any proof. What we Sweepers didn't know then was that Bengorth's Law had already reached the ears of Fritillary Reedling. A clever and ruthless woman, as I'm sure you know. I have a great respect for her. Did you know we were friends once?"

Fritillary and the head of the Dire Sweepers? She had a hard time believing that. The muscles in her face hurt as she tried not to show emotion.

"I believe," he said, "that she sent you to find the identity of the Dire Sweepers and to kill the Regal."

"*What?*" Astonishment jerked the word out of her.

"You are surprised that we know? As I said, we have many spies. We know you went to Annusel, the apothecary in Ustgrind Castle, asked and paid for a large amount of a sleeping draught just before you left Ustgrind."

"Then you must also know that was a long time before the death of the Regal!" She swallowed back bile as the implications of his accusation seeped through her shock. "I have problems sleeping and I asked for enough to last me a while."

"And can you produce some of that now, if we were to look in your room? And I already know the answer to that."

The bastard. "I wasn't in Ustgrind when Regal Vilmar died. I was here. There are plenty of witnesses to that."

"Oh, I'm sure you didn't do it yourself. It had to be someone close to the Regal. The Regala, in fact. Someone who could hand him a drink without his suspecting a thing. And guess who saw the Regala immediately after buying the sleeping draught? Gerelda Brantheld."

Mathilda murdered the Regal? And I gave her the means? The murdering bitch! The Pontifect will pin my hide to her door. No, wait. Maybe he's making this up. Feeling faint, she closed her eyes, but her mind was racing. Unfortunately, it appeared to be racing in too many directions at once. *Think: why are we having this conversation?*

Perhaps he wanted her to testify against the Regala in a Lowmian court. Perhaps the Deremers, or Lowmian nobles generally, wanted to control the Prince-regal themselves and rid themselves of an Ardronese Regala. Testify, and then conveniently die.

"There's a manservant called Torjen who has his suspicions about the Regal's death," he continued. "He has spoken to Prime Mulhafen of his fears. And, of course, we have our spies on the Prime's staff."

Oh, Va. Gerelda, you didn't guess half of what you should have guessed. She certainly didn't like the idea that she'd been manipulated by Regala Mathilda. She opened her eyes. "This is ridiculous," she said.

"I have you exactly where I want you, Gerelda Brantheld. You could be tortured and executed in a particularly drawn-out and vile manner, alongside the Ardronese Princess, if I so wanted."

"Do I detect a note of reluctance?"

"Perhaps. Suppose you tell me what you know about the so-called Bengorth's Law."

"And if I were to say I know nothing?" *Hells, he really has me over a barrel.*

"I wouldn't believe you," he said. "No matter. Let me tell you what it is. Bengorth's Law states that the Vollendorn line will prosper and the land will thrive if the Regal gives A'Va the right to own the body and soul of one of any pair of twins born in Lowmeer."

"Have you any idea how ridiculous that sounds?"

"According to the story handed down in my family, A'Va used to demonstrate his power to regals through one of his devil-kin. Minions. My ancestor, Aben Deremer, saw people killed by supernatural power and was convinced by what he saw, hence my family's involvement. Bengorth asked him, Aben, to help curtail A'Va's power by setting up the Dire Sweepers to kill twins."

"Thereby denying A'Va his minions. Do you really believe such twaddle?"

Lord Herelt looked away from her to raise the blind on the carriage window. "It's still raining," he remarked.

She glimpsed the railings of the Ust River bridge before he let the blind drop. That was odd. She could have sworn they had already crossed the river.

"So, Gerelda, do you have anything to say?"

"Herelt," she said, dropping his honorific as he had hers, "if I'd been around in Bengorth's time, and someone had told me that story, I would have laughed and told them not to be so gullible. Lawyers like statements backed up by facts. Especially when there are supernatural elements. I'm more inclined to believe in sleight of hand than A'Va."

"And yet I assume you believe in witcheries."

She smiled slightly. "You have me there. But then, I've seen proof of witcheries again and again. What do you personally believe is the reality of Bengorth's Law?"

"As a child my father took me to see what happened after the devil-kin's demonstration to Vilmar on the day of his coronation. I saw the remains of the dog forced into a fire by the stare of a devil-kin. Vilmar was shaking like a leaf in the wind, but it wasn't just his obvious shock that impressed me. It was the awful darkness left behind in that room. I don't know how to explain it, but believe me, in that moment, I was fully prepared to believe that A'Va existed and that one of his devil-kin had been there. It was like looking into an absence of light and decency. I believed then."

Past tense again. "If A'Va is so powerful, how is it that he has allowed the Dire Sweepers to exist, thereby diminishing his potential army of devil-kin?"

He gave a half-smile.

"Well, well. *You* don't believe in Bengorth's Law," she said, certain she was right.

"Not any more. At least, not in the A'Va component of it. I think it was just a way to fool a long line of regals into not looking hard enough for what was really going on."

"So what *was* going on?" When he didn't immediately reply, she said, "You still killed twins." *And you scare me more than anyone else I've ever met.*

"Devil-kin twins who spread the Horned Death are real. They do have to be stopped. What we *didn't* know was the devil-kin were only a small proportion of all twins, that in fact much of the killing we did to stop the spread of the Horned Death was unnecessary. We were fooled into it. It never had anything to do with A'Va."

"So where do the Horned Death and the devil-kin come from?"

"Sorcery."

"Does all this sound as bizarre to you as it does to me? Bengorth's Law makes no sense! It never did." The coach gave a sudden lurch and she had to put a hand out to stop herself falling sideways. "It makes even less sense to me if A'Va doesn't exist."

He smiled, and she knew then that they had arrived at the point he'd planned for when he'd seized her. He leant forward again, and his voice dropped. She had to strain to hear over the sound of the wheels.

"I can tell you two things. The Fox who started all this, Ebent Voss, was the instigator of it all. He was the one who prompted Bengorth into seizing the throne and who prodded my ancestor into founding the Dire Sweepers. I know those things because Aben Deremer wrote it all down in our family history. And my family histories also tell me Ebent Voss lived to be a hundred and thirty-eight years old. When he died, the family changed its name. Several hundred years later they started to hint at Shenat origins. I'm not sure why, but it might have had something to do with the fact that the head of the family always seemed to be long-lived."

"And Shenat shrine keepers are long-lived."

"Yes. Better to hint at Shenat longevity than to have others hint at sorcerous reasons for your ability to live a long time in good health."

"You think all the Fox patriarchs were sorcerers."

"Yes. At least, I think they have a great deal in common with the old stories about sorcerers."

She stared at him. A hollow feeling burrowed beneath her breast-bone, aggravating her nausea. *Sorcerer. The tar-pit who contaminated.*

He reached up and knocked on a hatch in the roof. It was opened and they were showered with water drops before a face appeared in the gap.

"Take us back," Deremer ordered. The hatch closed and the carriage rumbled on.

There was a long silence after that. She wanted to ask a hundred more questions, but this was not the time. Deremer had brought her to this moment for a purpose, and he wasn't going to tell her anything more. Not yet.

Finally she took a deep breath, straightened her shoulders and said, "All right. What do you want me to do?"

"I want you to pack up, take that lad of yours, and return to Vavala. I want you to go straight to the Pontifect and set up a meeting between me and her."

"That's all?"

He gave a wry smile. "That's not going to be easy, you know. Do you think I haven't tried by more normal means? I am hampered, of course, by my reluctance to put anything in writing that might impli-cate me in a crime. There is nothing that Fritillary would like more than to see the Dire Sweepers and my entire family dead and forgotten. You have to convince her that her real enemy is Fox and we have to combine to bring him down."

"An unholy alliance," she murmured.

"Exactly. She must understand that she is going to lose unless we combine forces. Tell her that in the past ten years, Valerian Fox has learned how to use his sorcery for something other than extending his life and he is prepared to bring the world to the edge of perdition to further his ambitions. Do you understand? I am prepared to meet her with all the proof I have gathered. Not much, I will admit. You, the lawyer, will say most of it is circumstantial. I'm seeking another piece of the puzzle now, which I hope to have in my hands by the time I speak with her."

"Where do you want to meet?"

"That's another difficulty. Until I am convinced she will not have me arrested, tried and executed for my crimes, we have to meet where

I am safe. Here, in Lowmeer. Borage perhaps, seeing it's a border town. I realise that won't be easy for her, but it is one of my conditions."

"And what do you bring to the table, Lord Herelt?"

"An alliance, use of my armed Deremer retainers, access to all my knowledge and my solemn promise to disband the Dire Sweepers once we've rid the world of Valerian Fox. Tell her . . . tell her I'm tired of killing babies."

Was he telling the truth? She couldn't be sure. "How do we contact you if I set up the meeting?"

"Send a letter to Deremer Manor here in Grundorp and a copy to Deremer House in Ustgrind. I'll get the message."

"All right. I'll leave for Vavala tomorrow. But hear this: unless you can explain the connection between twins, the Horned Death, Fox and Bengorth's so-called Law to her satisfaction, I think she'll kick you straight down the stairs. You haven't really *explained* anything."

They sat in silence while the coach returned to their starting point. It took a surprisingly short time, confirming her thought that they'd travelled in a circle, crossing the river twice.

One of the servants dismounted and opened the door for her. She left without saying anything more, and neither did Deremer, although he raised a black gloved hand in salute.

Perie was waiting for her on the doorstep.

"I saw the carriage take you away. I ran after you, but I couldn't get a whiff of smutch, so I let it go. Figured you could look after yourself."

"Good lad. None of that lot are pitch-men then?"

He shook his head. "They're clean. So what did they want?"

Clean? Sweet Va, he killed babies. "Someone wanted to talk to me. We leave for Vavala in the morning."

As she turned towards the lodging house, a strong smell of cooking drifted from its kitchen into the street. Such an ordinary smell, as if everything was normal and the world was just as it always had been. Boiled beef and cabbage and the smell of rain, university students hurrying by with their caps jammed on their heads, and the wind battling even to flutter their heavy felted cloaks . . .

But nothing was normal. Not any more.

All she could think about were the things Deremer had *not* explained.

30

Devil-kin

"**Y**our Grace."

Mathilda sat bolt upright in bed. For a moment she could not have said why; then the horror hit her. A man had spoken to her, and the voice was one she did not recognise. No stranger should have been able to enter her bedroom in the middle of the night, least of all a man.

Aghast, she groped for understanding. *How was this possible?* He stood by her bedside, inside the enveloping curtains. All she could see of him was a dark form, an outline. Battling terror, she opened her mouth to shriek for help, but the urge was suddenly stifled. She felt as if she was shrouded in something that would not allow her to utter a sound, or make any move. The air around her felt as thick as molasses.

He said, "You will not scream. Not that anyone would hear anyway."

She sat, speechless, choked by dread.

"You knew I was coming," he said. "Regal Vilmar told you to expect me. You may speak now, if you wish."

Lowmian accent. Highborn, at a guess. Her voice, barely audible, trembled past her lips. "Who-who are you?"

"A devil-kin, obedient to my master, A'va. I've come to hear your oath on behalf of your son. Tomorrow is his coronation day, but he is too young to understand what is required of him. So you must make the vow and see that he fulfils it as he grows up. If you don't, the Vollendorn line will end with his death in childhood. Do you understand?"

She could see him now. He looked to be no older than she was, neatly dressed. His lower face was shrouded in a scarf. There was a strange eldritch light glowing around him, greenish and horrible. It smelled with a faint tinge of rotting fish.

"D-d-devil-kin," she stuttered. *No, this can't be true. Keep calm. If*

*he was really a minion of A'Va, he'd know that Karel is not a Vollendorn.
But, oh, that foul smell, that strange light.*

"Take me to your son," he said.

She wanted to refuse – yet she rose, reached for her wrap, picked
up the night lamp. His voice compelled her forward. She preceded
him out of the bedroom and crossed the reception room to the nursery
at the far end of her solar.

Karel. *Sweet Va, protect him . . .*

"Go on," he said. For some reason she expected him to sound
amused at her inability to resist his words, but he wasn't. He sounded
weary and ill. Even so, his voice insinuated itself into her head, and
she complied with his commands, giving him the obedience of a mar-
ionette dancing for a puppetmaster.

"I want to see him. Now," he said.

*Please, Va, don't let him be a carrier of the Horned Death. Anything
but that . . .*

She opened the door to the nursery expecting the nursemaid to
awaken, but the woman asleep in the bed did not stir; nor did Karel
in his cradle. "If you harm him," she said, "there is no place in this
land you will be safe. None."

"You can threaten," he said, indifferent, "but you can't hurt me, can
you?" He regarded her with a chilling lack of feeling. "Why don't you
try? You hold a lamp; set fire to my clothing, if you can. Or perhaps
you can try waking your nursemaid."

She tried. She strove to shout, to throw the lamp at him. Her mouth
worked soundlessly, her hands fluttered weakly. The nursemaid slept
on.

"Strange, isn't it," he said, glancing in the woman's direction. "I
suspect she rouses at the first whimper of a babe, yet you could scream
her name right now and she would not hear."

"What are you going to do?" She shook with terror, but it wasn't
for herself. Not any more. It was for Karel.

"I am going to show you my power and then you are going to recite
the oath that is Bengorth's Law. Look at your son, Your Grace. Hold
the lamp so you can see his face."

She did as he told her, and the flame flickered and danced as her
hand trembled.

"Watch his cheek," he ordered. His tone was as frigid as an Ustgrind winter's day.

He was a lovely child, Karel: plump and handsome, able now to gurgle and laugh and reach for things; old enough to sit and play peek-a-boo . . . *I love him*, she thought. *I love him as I have never loved anyone before. Nothing must happen to him. Nothing.* "What are you going to do? Touch him and—"

Before she could finish her threat, a sore began to spread across the child's cheek. His eyes popped open in shock, and he wailed, a wail of heartbreaking surprise and agony. The sore bubbled and reddened in a patch the size of a thumbprint.

"Stop it!" she screamed at the devil-kin.

With one hand he plucked the lamp from her hand, afraid perhaps that she would drop it. His other hand, he waved over the child's face. Abruptly the sore stopped spreading and the wailing diminished into hiccupping sobs. The nursemaid did not waken. Mathilda grabbed Karel up out of his cot and put him against her shoulder, uttering soothing words, jogging him up and down.

"He feels nothing now," the man said. "I have taken away the pain. The blemish, however, will be his for life. A reminder to you, and to him one day, that he must adhere to Bengorth's Law. Do you understand?"

The look she gave him was pure hate, but he was unperturbed.

"Do you understand?"

She nodded. Tears trickled down her cheeks as she patted Karel's back and his sobs gradually ceased. The nursemaid had still not woken.

"Put the child back in the cradle, and kneel on the floor at my feet," he said. "Note, I do not force you to do this. This you must *choose* to do, in order to save your son from far, far worse."

Shaking, still silently weeping, she did as he asked and slipped down on to her knees.

"Repeat after me: 'I take this oath in my son's name. I swear that he will uphold Bengorth's Law. Prince-regal Karel, about to be crowned as Regal of Lowmeer, will grant one in each pair of twins born in Lowmeer to A'Va as his devil-kin. In return, A'Va grants that Lowmeer's prosperity will continue, and that the Vollendorn line will sit on the Basalt Throne and prosper likewise.'"

She repeated the words. Her voice quavered a little, but the words did not falter.

"Close your eyes," he said.

She did so, but then thought better of it and opened them again, only to find she was alone apart from her son and the nursemaid. The lamp burned on the floor beside her. She scrambled to her feet.

Pox on the toad-spotted churl! Her rage surged, white-hot and all-consuming. *You will regret this, whoever you are and whoever sent you here. As Va is my witness, I swear it.*

She picked up Karel again, crooning to him and cuddling him tight. The nursemaid woke then, sitting up in alarm and then in horror. "Your Grace! Did I not hear him cry?"

"Someone broke into the solar," she snapped at the woman. "Quick, go fetch the guards! I found an intruder leaning over the cradle! He scratched Karel."

They would find no one, she felt sure. Alone with her son, she whispered her promise to him.

"You will never hear of Bengorth's Law from me."

31

Privateers in Serinaga

Even though Saker had hated the plan from the beginning, he found it hard to believe it had gone so horribly wrong so fast.

He'd agreed to it because Sorrel had said she'd go without him if she had to, and the thought of her endangering her life had tied his insides in knots. Besides, after all the planning was in place, he'd thought it was just possible that they might succeed. There was Ardhi's climbing witchery to get them on board the Regal's galleon, *Sentinel*; Saker's own witchery with birds to supply a diversion; the dagger to find the plumes; and Sorrel's glamour to hide her while she stole them.

Yet now here he was fighting for his life on *Sentinel*'s gun deck with gouts of roaring flames bursting through the planks and licking up the masts, while Ardhi was hanging upside down in the rigging, and Sorrel . . . ?

Sorrel was nowhere to be seen.

If only he could go back to where this insane scheme had been hatched, and put an end to it then, back to that moment four days earlier, on the deck of *Golden Petrel*, when Juster had begun to formulate his idea . . .

They'd all been there at the time: Juster, Ardhi, Saker, First Mate Finch, Third Mate Grig Cranach and Sorrel, grouped near the helmsman, Forrest.

"That is Pulau Serinaga ahead," Ardhi said, pointing. "Serinaga Island. With high mountain." He waved at all the land off to starboard. "Many smaller islands. All same *pulauan*." He looked at Saker. "Archipelago: is that correct word?"

He nodded.

"Kotabanta town, that's the capital of the whole archipelago?" Juster asked.

"Yes. On Serinaga Island. Archipelago all under one ruler, Raja. He live in Kotabanta." The wind tugged at his long black hair, and he reached up to tighten the twist of cloth he wore to keep it tidy. "This Iska's land, not mine. Want to know more, you ask him."

"Send someone to get Iska," Juster told Grig.

Their first sighting of land, an amorphous blue band in the distance, had now revealed itself as a series of hills behind a coastline pock-marked by beaches and inlets. To Saker, it all looked conjoined, but once Iska was there, he laughed at that idea and said it was an illusion. The coves and bays they saw were often the entrances to the straits and channels between the islands and rocky outcrops.

"Wind is good," Iska said, addressing Juster. "Can reach Kotabanta tomorrow."

Juster grunted, his frown more grim than pleased. "Could the Lowmians have bypassed Kotabanta altogether and gone straight to the Spicerie? Or on to Chenderawasi?"

"Lowmians always come Kotabanta first," Iska said. "They not want upset Raja. Everyone must pay Raja money for sailing through his islands. Not pay, and Raja find out? He make things difficult for trading."

"Raja of Serinaga has very many war canoes," Ardhi remarked. Iska shot him a glance and nodded in agreement.

"Maybe the Lowmians have already paid up and gone?" Juster suggested.

He is being deliberately contrary again, Saker thought. The captain hadn't forgiven Ardhi for making a fool of him in Javenka, and it rankled that he had to rely on the lascar's navigating skills to sail the Summer Seas. He'd been forced to place the safety of his men and his ship in the hands of a man he no longer trusted.

"Not easy," Iska said. "Ships come, must pay fee, must visit Raja. Usually wait many days. Much . . . what the word? Properness?"

"Protocol," Ardhi said.

"So, Lowmians still there, in port," Iska finished.

Juster gave another grunt and sent Banstel, now his cabin boy, to fetch the map of the coast. In Javenka, he'd bought charts of all the archipelagos of the Summer Seas. Both Iska and Ardhi had vouched for their accuracy, which was comforting as they had to wend their way through islands and reefs scattered across the sea like a random throw of knucklebones in a children's game.

I never knew the world was so large, so complex.

Sorrel came to stand beside him while the others looked at the chart. "It's another world," she said. "Not just a different land, but another way of living. Look at the shape of the boats drawn up on the beaches. I've never seen anything like them. I like the expressive eyes they have drawn on the prow too! See all those thatched houses on stilts, built over the water. Why, I wonder? And the sand – how is it possible for sand to be so dazzlingly white?"

He glanced at her. She was carrying Piper on her hip in a cloth sling that Ardhi had made for her. The child peeped out of it, and his heart turned over when she smiled and waved her hand. Against all odds, she'd thrived on this voyage, enslaving them all with her charm.

She can't be a devil-kin. Not Piper.

But then, if she wasn't, Prince-regal Karel Vollendorn was . . . Or maybe it was all a lie.

Banstel returned with the chart, placing it on the binnacle and weighting it down so it wouldn't blow away.

"Which is your island, Iska?" Juster asked.

But maps meant nothing to the old lascar and he ignored the chart to point ahead of them. "That one." It was left to Ardhi to identify the island on the chart.

"I've promised to return Iska to his village," Juster said to Saker. "In return, he is going to help us find a way to sink *Sentinel* in Kotabanta harbour."

Iska grinned and nodded.

"You can't cause trouble in Kotabanta!" Saker protested, horrified, as Juster attempted to match up the coastline with the chart. "What about Princess Mathilda's marriage treaty? The Raja here granted Ardrone a concession area in Kotabanta at Lowmeer's insistence. If we upset the Raja, we might lose those rights. Neither King Edwayn nor Prince Ryce would be happy with you then, and irate merchants will make firewood of your ship when you return to Throssel." *Not to mention that Mathilda's sacrifice would all be for nothing.*

Juster sighed heavily. "None of my crew is going to tell anyone back home, believe me. If they did, they know what I'd do to them. And they'd certainly never sail with me again."

Finch guffawed. "They not be in any state to sail with anyone again."

"We will be sneaky about this. No one will know we are to blame," Juster continued. "We sink *Sentinel* in Kotabanta, which will give us a better chance of seizing their fluyts later when they are laden with spices. It's the galleon that has all the firepower, you see. Besides, if we sink it while it's in port, the sailors will have a better chance of survival."

"And just how do you intend to do that," Saker asked, "without the Raja and the Lowmians knowing we are to blame?"

"Who will tell them?" Juster replied.

Everyone immediately looked at Iska. The old lascar grinned. "Cap'n and me, we make bargain already. He take me my island, give gold. Iska rich, island rich. My people, we not like Raja. Much tax."

Juster continued, "Iska's island will supply the boats, we dress as fishermen, we sneak into the harbour and sink *Sentinel*. We escape back to Iska's village where we've anchored *Golden Petrel*. We then sail away under cover of night to Chenderawasi, without paying our respects to the Raja. If he doesn't know we've been here, he won't be upset with us."

Saker glanced to where Ardhi was standing. The lascar's face was blank of expression. Behind him Sorrel had blanched, her arms wrapped protectively around Piper.

"I doubt anyone thinks that's a good idea, cap'n," Finch said, stroking his chin through his beard.

"It will rely a lot on Iska," Juster admitted.

"The regalia is probably on board *Sentinel*," Ardhi said, his voice as without inflexion as his face was without expression.

"Exactly," Juster said. "And you want them back."

There was a long silence while everyone considered the bargain Lord Juster implied: *We'll get the plumes back for you, if you help us sneak into the harbour and sink the ship.*

"Rot it, Juster," Saker said, "this is madness! Do you think no one will know we are here?" He pointed at the shore. "Those villagers there have already seen us!"

"They are simple farmers and fishermen, not the Raja's men! Do you think they can differentiate between us and a Lowmian fluyt? Am I right, Iska? And you may not have noticed, Saker, but the flag we've been flying from the masthead since land was sighted is a Lowmian one."

Of one accord, everyone looked up. Fluttering half-heartedly from the cross-trees, as if it was ashamed to proclaim itself, was the standard of the Vollendorns.

Saker was appalled. "You can't do that!"

"I just have. In fact, as a privateer, that is considered perfectly acceptable behaviour. Rules of conflict apply. If someone reports our presence, it will be Lowmeer that is blamed."

He continued his protests. "What if Iska's people are blamed for sinking *Sentinel*? We'd be using their boats."

"Hundreds of such boats here," Ardhi remarked. "Every island got fishing villages, and fishing boats all look alike in the dark. Just which islanders will Lustgrader – or the Raja – blame?"

"Ardhi right," Iska agreed. "Raja not know who. Maybe he not care who. Not his ship sinking. Not his men die. Right?"

"All the same, I can't be a party to this," Saker said, horror seeping through him as he remembered that the only reason Juster had legitimate letters of marque was because – while imprisoned in Throssel – he had warned the privateer to leave the city before they were revoked by King Edwayn.

The wheel turns, he thought, *and sooner or later it runs over you.* He tried to be reasonable. "Juster, you'd be sinking a ship in a neutral port, one King Edwayn sold his daughter for as if she was a commodity. The price paid for this port was horrendous, and you want to risk everything achieved by the Princess's sacrifice?"

"Sacrifice? She's now a Regala! A queen. It's what she was born to be. I think we've had this conversation before, Saker."

He turned to Ardhi, seeking support. "Are you prepared to go along with this insane idea?"

"Yes. If the captain says we get the plumes from *Sentinel* before sinking her."

He opened his mouth to argue, but Ardhi interrupted. "I know how to do this. Difficult, but we can." He folded his arms, a gesture that made his next words a clear challenge to Juster. "I go on board first. Get plumes before you blow hole in ship."

"Agreed," Juster said amiably.

Saker looked at Sorrel again. She'd heard every word. Her gaze was steady, but he saw contempt written there, contempt for a man she thought couldn't rid himself of his infatuation for a Princess who'd used and discarded him.

You're doing me an injustice, Sorrel.

It was shame that made him want to defend Mathilda, not affection.

The land smelled unfamiliar to Saker. He inhaled, tried to name the aromas and had to admit defeat. "What can I smell?" he asked.

Ardhi didn't even have to think, but rattled off a list. "Charcoal kiln burning mangrove wood. Red hot peppers stirred in pan. Coconut milk, simmering hot, with *belachan* – dried shrimp paste. Crushed pandan leaves; we use those in cooking. Chempaka flowers . . ." His voice caught and died away to a whisper. "Lastri used to put them in her hair."

He put a hand on Ardhi's bare shoulder. "The aromas of home, then."

"Yes."

Ardhi, with Iska's help, had piloted *Golden Petrel* into a secluded bay, hidden from all passing vessels. A small fishing village, Iska's birthplace, was ranged along the banks of a tidal stream. Open boats, short-masted and squat, were tied up at a ramshackle wooden jetty, while canoes with a strange extra piece on one side were hauled up on the sandy beach of the bay.

Iska had already gone ashore, alone, and had not yet returned to tell them what his village thought of Juster's plan to borrow a boat from them.

Villagers had, however, lined up along the shore to stare at the strangers come to visit. Several boys had already swum out to the ship, as naked as the day they were born, their wet brown faces split with huge grins as they clung to the anchor rope and flicked the hair out of their eyes.

Bare to the waist, barefoot and wearing an islander's sarong he had procured in Javenka, Ardhi could have been their older brother. He waved and spoke to them in the trading tongue of the islands, a polyglot mix of Pashali and local words.

"You know these waters that well?" Juster asked with a tinge of disbelief.

"All Chenderawasi boys learn to sail to Serinaga with our traders. Part of growing up." He pointed to the sailing boats on the island. "Our boats like that. Two masts, two rectangle sails. Called *prau*. We bring nutmeg, mother-of-pearl shells and pearls to Kotabanta. Take back cloth and metals. I sail here many times from when I was twelve until I leave for Javenka."

"You are full of surprises," Juster said sourly and went below to wait. Ardhi just grinned.

"Damn it, how the pox do you manage to keep smiling?" Saker asked in Pashali.

He shrugged and replied in the same language. "Either that, or howl to the winds. I'm as good as dead, Saker. I may as well laugh as cry."

"You're almost home now. If we get the plumes back tomorrow or the day after, your troubles will be over."

"The Raja will still be dead, no matter what I do, and I have yet to pay the full price." Saker thought he wasn't going to add anything more, but then he said, "My mistake was not just telling the Lowmians about the paradise birds, you know. It was to bring the ship to Chenderawasi in the first place. I didn't know what they were like. We'd dealt with Pashalin sailors, and they respected us. There are customary laws in place which regulate the way we interact."

"So you thought the Lowmians would be like them?"

"My studies at the Javenka Library led me to believe our insularity was both stupid and dangerous now that other ships were coming from your hemisphere to ours, when in truth it was I who was both stupid and a danger." He snorted. "I thought if we allowed the Lowmians access to our islands, we would have more wealth. Then with that wealth, we could have more control of our own destiny." He shrugged. "I was so wrong. I didn't understand the first thing about how your world works and yet I trusted your traders."

"We can't bring the Raja back, but we can try to fix the rest."

"Not for me."

"You can't know that."

"Ah, but I do, Saker. I do." The catch was back in his voice, and it brought a lump to Saker's throat. *He's become my brother, and I care.* Remembering the day they'd first encountered one another, he shook his head in wonder. Who would have thought?

When Iska returned, it was with a proposal from the villagers, and to Juster's amusement, it was the village women who had determined the terms. Apparently they objected to spending much of their time weaving new palm-leaf sails for fishermen's boats. They wanted canvas sails for the village's three fishing *prau*.

When Iska relayed this offer back to *Golden Petrel*, Lord Juster grumbled. They carried spare canvas for a reason: it could be needed for their own repairs or replacement sails at any time. In the end, he capitulated, saying, "Tell them we accept. New sails and extra canvas. Get some measurements and we'll get the sailmakers on to it. We can replace the canvas we use by stealing more from *Sentinel* before we burn her."

"A pox on you, Juster!" Saker said, thoroughly exasperated. "Ardhi and I just want to sneak in and sneak out with the plumes before you burn the ship – but there's no way we can *sneak* carrying canvas. You're making things more difficult for us."

"That's your problem. If it hadn't been for you and Ardhi, getting rid of the galleon could have been done much more easily. I would have been quietly waiting for it near Karradar when it finally limped up like a sick cow. Your problem, you fix it, Master Witan!"

"How the beggary are we going to get sails out of their sail locker without raising the alarm?" he asked Ardhi when they were alone.

"I know the layout of *Sentinel*. I helped with the stowing of cargo. There's a platform amidships that can be winched up with a capstan. They use it to bring cannonballs up from the armoury to the gun decks, as well as heavy things like new sails or butts of water."

"And you found all this out when you were stowing cargo?"

"Of course. We used the same capstan."

"Hmm. If we winched sails up, we could bring them as far as the main gun deck?"

Ardhi grinned. "Yes. And guess what's on the gun decks."

"Gun ports." He started to smile. "Which can be opened."

"Noisy things, capstans, though."

"Especially in the middle of the night in an anchored ship."

"Crew sleep in the bow, officers aft," Ardhi said. "But we might need one of your diversions. And we'll need more men. You try lifting a sail and shoving it out of a gunport."

Exasperated, he ran a hand through his hair. "Pox on't, we need to think about this."

The following day, Sorrel, Saker and Ardhi discussed Juster's decision in the officers' mess. Ardhi, with the aid of a chart of Kotabanta on the table, had just described the anchorage in some detail when Sorrel said, looking at Saker, "I'm going with you."

"Where?"

"To *Sentinel*."

He stared at her, puzzled. "What do you mean?"

"I would have thought that was clear enough. I-am-going-with-you-when-you-board-the-*Sentinel*. Ardhi agrees I should."

"To do what?"

"To use my glamour to steal the plumes, of course. And stop glowering at Ardhi."

"Don't be ridiculous. Your job is to stay here and look after Piper."

"No, it's not. Anyone can do that. Surgeon Barklee, for example."

"You can't be serious. You aren't a fighter!"

"Well, I might dispute that. Ask Banstel to tell you what happened to Fels. However, it's not my intention to fight anyone. That's the whole point of having a glamour. I can avoid trouble, and not be seen doing nefarious things like stealing feathers. Of *course* I'm going with you. It's a logical solution."

They stared across the table at each other, and it was he who was at a loss. The idea seemed so hare-brained he couldn't believe he had to argue her out of it. "This is a man's job."

"What is?"

"Fighting!"

"I just told you. I don't intend to *fight* anyone. I'm going to use my glamour. It should be easy enough: I'm going to take Ardhi's dagger, which will lead me to the plumes, just as it did for you once, I believe? I will steal them, bring them back to the *prau* and wait for you *men* to finish fighting everyone. I can't see that I'll be in any danger. You might be, though. Shall I object to that?"

"Please, Sorrel, don't be silly."

"No, *you* stop being lack-witted! If you used your head instead of clinging to your ideas about who fights and who doesn't, you might ask yourself why I am here in the first place – if not to use my glamour!" She folded her arms and pursed her lips.

"You could be here because of Piper," he pointed out.

"She could be here because of *me*. And that makes a lot more sense than the other way around. Piper is either a perfectly ordinary baby, or she's a devil-kin; either way she's no use to anyone!" She paused, then added softly, "Except to those of us who love her."

For a moment they just stared at each other, unable to speak. *Loving a child is easy*, he thought, *but loving her so much you want to protect her from everything . . .*

"I can't afford to be worried about you while we're on board *Sentinel*," he said at last, only realising after the words were out of his mouth that they weren't anywhere near the ones she wanted to hear.

"Then don't be," she snapped.

"For crying out loud, you'd have to climb up a rope on to the deck from a boat bobbing in the water—"

"I once climbed out of an upstairs window on to the limb of an oak tree high above the ground, lashed by rain on a wild and windy night, all the while wearing a dress! How many *men* could do that, I wonder? And thanks to Ardhi's training, I can do anything that you can, Saker Rampion."

She turned on her heel and left the room.

Ardhi peeled himself away from where he'd been leaning with his back to the wall. "She's right. You're wrong."

"You do have a precise way with words sometimes, Ardhi. Don't you *care* about her? She's here because of your confounded *sakti* magic."

"I care enough to allow her to make her own decisions."

"I care enough to want to protect her! How will you feel if she is hurt in this attack on *Sentinel*?"

"How do you think? But I also believe that everyone has the right to their own decisions."

"That's ludicrous coming from you. It's your *sakti* preventing us from making our own decisions!"

"If there is one thing I understand, Saker, it's that the contamination is coming from your half of the world, not ours. Things went wrong for us when the Lowmians came and killed our Raja and stole the plumes of his regalia. The regalia of his line is what holds the *sakti*. And it is the *sakti* that protects us."

"And that *sakti* could very well hurt us Ardronese because of what the Lowmians did. It hardly has our interests at heart. After all, it has dragged us to this side of the world against our will!"

"How do you know that is not in your interest?"

"You can't think your witcheries are concerned about *our* welfare! Tell me, are you of the Raja's line, Ardhi?"

The lascar gave a strange smile, part amusement and part something else he couldn't put his finger on. "No. But I do know our *sakti* is not evil. And you do have evil in your hemisphere, for I felt it, several times. A deep and dark . . . thing that has been growing and biding its time."

Saker gave an exasperated grunt. "I hate it when people speak in riddles. What thing?"

"If I knew, I'd tell you. All I know is that both you and Sorrel and Piper have all touched this evil in your lives. It endangers you all."

He involuntarily closed the fist on his right hand, as if that could hide the black smutch that was probably still in the centre of his palm, even though he could not see it. He felt the blood drain from his face. Sweet Va, what if the *sakti* of Chenderawasi could sense that and wanted to destroy the three of them because it thought they were contaminated?

His next thought was no happier. He knew he was besmirched, but how could Sorrel and Piper be involved?

Oh, pox on't.

What if Piper is Fox's child?

No, not that. Anything but that!

32

Thieves in the Night

Nudged by a gentle breeze, the *prau* crept across the bay, prow cleaving an ocean as dark as the cloud-thick night sky. Somewhere out there was the treaty port of Kotabanta, safe haven for Ardronese ships because Mathilda had paid the price for it, but it was well after midnight and the town slept, wrapped in darkness. If there were wharves or jetties, Saker couldn't see them.

He glanced around at the others in the boat, but there was nothing to see there, either; they were all no more than dusky shadows on a slate-grey background. He knew the six sailors from *Golden Petrel* now resembled local fishermen, just as he did. They all wore clothes borrowed from Iska's village. Ardhi had showed them all how to fashion twists of cloth into headbands to keep their long hair tidy. Everyone was barefoot. They'd all been chosen for their dark hair and eyes and the deep honey-coloured skin common among the Shenat. They might not have been quite as dark-skinned as the islanders, or as short in stature, but he suspected no one would notice that at night. All were under orders not to speak except in a whisper. There must be no hint that they were from an Ardronese vessel. Striving to have their boat appear to be a local fishing vessel, they had not even used the new canvas sails.

Juster, fair-skinned and tall, with long hair the colour of ripe barley, could never be anything except what he was: a man of the Va-cherished Hemisphere. After long argument, he had pulled a black knitted cap onto his head and agreed to stay seated in the *prau* with the helmsman, Forrest.

Ardhi wore his own Chenderawasi garb. He was seated in the prow, giving hand signals to Forrest at the tiller as he guided them. Saker didn't need to see him to know the lascar held himself like a cat gathering itself to pounce: alert, almost crackling with coiled tension, unafraid, so very alive.

The tenth occupant of the *prau* was Sorrel. He hated her being there, but he'd been overruled – by Juster, by Ardhi, by Sorrel herself. She sat next to him, calmly composed, her hands folded neatly in her lap. She was dressed as a fisherman too, barefoot, with the kris in its sheath stuck through the cloth belt. When she turned her head to look at him, he thought she smiled as she bent forward to whisper in his ear. "This is for Piper. I feel it in my bones."

He bit back the first words that came to his tongue. He'd finally realised – dunce that he was – that his desire to protect her was not only unwanted but annoying. Instead, he closed a hand over hers and said, "Come back safe."

"You too."

Resisting the urge to say more, he removed his hand and turned to watch Ardhi instead.

At first, the lascar's skill in the dark had seemed uncanny, until Saker realised he was using the position of the port leading lights to guide them. They approached head on to *Sentinel*'s bowsprit, almost invisible to anyone on watch. There wasn't much wind, and their progress was slow.

The helmsman, Forrest, had done well. Four days back, he'd never seen a *prau*, but there wasn't much anyone could teach him about the wind and the waves and how to coax a craft into doing his bidding. He brought the boat to a gentle halt under the projecting bowsprit.

They were out of sight of any sailors on the main deck, but were now illuminated by the bow lantern hanging from the bowsprit, and it cast enough light for an alert sailor on one of the other ships of the Lowmian fleet to see them.

Luck . . . or bad luck. He tried not to think about that. Sometimes you just had to hope.

Ardhi seized the rank-smelling rope dangling from the port latrine hole. Even hampered by the bundled rope ladder he carried over his shoulder, he hauled himself up faster than Saker would have thought possible. A moment later he'd altered the position of the bow lantern so that it no longer shone on the *prau*, and immediately afterwards the rope ladder came snaking downwards into the boat.

Forrest grabbed the end and hooked it under the boat's gunwale. Saker climbed up to join Ardhi, clambering from the wooden rungs on to the tiny prow foredeck in front of the forecastle. Here the wall of the crew's forecastle quarters cut them off from a view of the rest of the ship, but they were standing in the lantern light right where anyone might come to relieve themselves during the night.

"All's quiet," the lascar whispered in his ear. "No one on watch in the bows, no one in the crow's nest."

No sooner were the words out of his mouth than there was a roar close to Saker's ear, an eruption of sound so loud that he jumped away in panic. His sword was halfway out of its scabbard before he realised the ear-splitting snorts and grunts were just someone snoring on the other side of the forecastle wall.

Ardhi grinned at him.

He pulled a face at the lascar before leaning over the bulwark to signal all was well to those in the *prau*. The next two men up had been selected to deal with the watch. Once they were on deck, all four of them climbed the steps to the forecastle deck. From there they overlooked the waist of the ship to where the aftcastle, topped by the poop deck, sat at the stern of the galleon. Beneath them, the snoring rumbled on, interspersed with grunts and breathy whistles.

The decks were dimly lit by three brass lanterns. The green and the red of the starboard and port signal lamps did not cast much light, but the stern lamp of clear glass illuminated the poop deck and one of the men on watch. He was leaning on the aft bulwarks, looking out over the bay.

Ardhi, with his sharp eyesight, was the first to spot the second man on watch, seated on one of the deck cannon amidships. "Diversion," he whispered.

Saker nodded. He'd been preparing for this since sunset. Every Lowmian ship now had seagulls quietly perched in the rigging. Focusing on a single bird sleeping on *Sentinel*'s mizzenmast, he woke it and prompted it to swoop silently over the head of the man on the cannon, close enough to brush his hair with a wingtip. Startled, the man yelped and leapt to his feet. The bird flew up to the poop deck, clipping the head of the second man on watch. It then sat on the taffrail. Both Lowmian sailors turned their heads to stare at it.

Ardhi and the two sailors ran noiselessly down the steps into the waist of the ship. Ardhi dealt with the man there, wrapping an arm around his head and twisting his neck sharply. The violence was silent, quick and deadly. The others ran on up the steps to the aft deck.

It was all over in moments. Saker saw the bodies slump, without a sound from either of them. He mouthed a silent prayer for the dead, but didn't watch while the bodies were tucked away out of sight in the scuppers; he was already retreating back to the foredeck. Leaning over the bulwarks, he signalled for the rest of the men and Sorrel to climb up on to *Sentinel*.

Sorrel had practised climbing a rope ladder on *Golden Petrel*, and she scrambled over the bulwark with nothing more than his helping hand under her arm. He led her up on to the forecastle deck, where she took Ardhi's kris out of its sheath and placed it on the palm of her hand. The golden threads in the blade writhed and glowed.

One by one, the remaining three sailors from *Golden Petrel* passed them. The last man carried the rope ladder. They joined the others amidships and Ardhi led them down the aft companionway to find the sail locker.

Sorrel remained unmoving until the dagger turned on her palm of its own volition. It pointed towards the stern, telling them the plumes were somewhere in the officers' quarters. Her form shifted, quavering. She faded out around the edges, rather like water soaking into something porous as she glamoured herself. She could never entirely hide from him, but even so this uncanny ability to change before his eyes unsettled him.

She descended to the waist of the ship, the kris pointing her unwaveringly aft. He followed, but not closely. Her safety lay in her glamour, not with him. His job was to nip any problems topside before they roused the whole ship. From now on, she was on her own.

He watched her halt for a moment to hook open the door that led from the main deck into the officers' quarters before disappearing inside. He could still see the glow of the dagger lighting her way, and then that, too, vanished.

On deck, except for the snoring in the forecastle, all was quiet. Eerily so, considering all that was happening. No one was hailing them from any of the other ships of the fleet. No one had noticed the absence of the two dead men. No one had noticed the presence of the *prau*.

Maybe Va was on their side. Or was that a presumptuous assumption? *Blister it, Saker; you think a hanged sight too much!*

There was still another hour to go before the next change of watch when the dead men would be missed. By that time they'd all be gone and the ship would be on fire – or they'd all be down in the brig.

Time crawled by.

No sound came from the officers' quarters. Nothing from below, either. He'd hear the capstan when they started it up, wouldn't he? But no, nothing bar the lapping of waves against the hull, the half-hearted rustling of a flag at the masthead, the soft creaking of timber as the ship moved in the gentle breeze, the uneven grunts and squawks of the snoring sailor.

Va, how long should he wait before he started to worry?

They'd agreed that the first step was for Ardhi and the sailors to locate the sails and load up the platform, but that they wouldn't start the capstan until Sorrel had a full ten minutes on board to find and retrieve the plumes. But who was to say when ten minutes had passed? None of them had a clock.

There: a sound from below decks, a rumble. Not the capstan, though. It was the sound of a gun carriage being wheeled away from its position in front of a gunport on the deck immediately above the orlop. He winced, waiting for someone to hear, to come to investigate. He flattened himself deep into the shadows close to the door Sorrel had entered.

Nothing. No alarm, no sound of anyone hearing something amiss and coming to look.

Another sound, fainter this time. The creak of an opening of the gunport, or of someone fumbling as they propped it open. That was Juster's cue to paddle the *prau* to the hull on the port beam, ready to receive the stolen canvas, so Saker wasn't surprised to hear a faint splash from the port side a moment later. Still no reaction from any of the sleeping crew of *Sentinel*. Nonetheless, every sound rang in his ears like the retort of an arquebus.

You're as skittish as a colt in a thunderstorm . . .

Maybe the ear-splitting intermittent snoring was Va-sent. If the men were used to sleeping through that, then softer sounds would be ignored.

Sorrel, hurry up!

And then it began: the rumble of a small capstan turning. A steady sound, not something to waken a man in a panic, but for a man already awake? Another matter entirely, surely!

His sword slid from its scabbard into his hand. He tensed, waiting for the alarm to be raised.

Nothing happened.

The capstan halted. Everything fell quiet. He was just beginning to breathe again, when he heard the squeak of a door, or perhaps a hatch cover. Men speaking. Not from the officers' quarters, but somewhere in the bows.

Oh, pox, whatever you do, don't start up the capstan again . . .

He ran quickly across the midships and up the steps to the forecastle deck. He saw no one, but could still hear the voices.

"Tell you what it was: old Pult and his blasted snoring. That's what you heared!"

"Him? I wake up when he *stops* snoring!"

He expelled the breath he'd been holding. It was just two men on the foredeck, peeing into the bay. Nothing to worry about – yet. Perhaps it had been the sound of the capstan that had woken them, but they hadn't realised it. Even as he listened, they returned to their quarters. The snoring continued unabated. He stood still until he heard a door close and was certain the men had returned to their hammocks.

When he moved again, it was to look over the bulwarks. By the faint red glow cast by the port lantern, he saw the boat nestling close to the hull. A bundle of canvas was being lowered into the stern from the open gunport directly overhead.

But where was Sorrel? There was no sign of her!

He turned away and started down the steps to midships, just as Ardhi appeared at the top of the aft companionway, on schedule to tell him they were all ready to leave *Sentinel*. Which meant two shrapnel balls had already been set with their slow burning fuses. They had less than ten minutes to leave the ship before it blew up.

He'd no sooner had that thought than deep within the bowels of the vessel the world changed. One moment he was raising his hand to acknowledge Ardhi, the next he was cartwheeling through the air, struck by a rush of wind so strong it was a solid blow to his body. Light blinded him. Heat shrivelled his skin. Noise burst in his ears, bruising rather than being heard.

Va-damn, he thought. *I'm dead.*

33

The Death of *Sentinel*

When Sorrel left Saker, she was glad he didn't follow her. He had to learn she could and would care for herself. It was time he acknowledged that her glamour was her protection and that she had become more and more skilled in its use as time went by.

I can do this, she thought.

It was even darker away from the open deck, but the glow emanating from the dagger, although faint, was sufficient. Four doorways led off the companionway, one on either side and two at the end. The dagger guided her to one of the end doors. Someone was lying on the floor in front of it.

You are not visible. You are just part of the wooden panelling. You cannot be seen . . .

She padded up to the recumbent shape, trying not to wonder if the dagger's light was glamoured into invisibility too. In the end, it didn't matter. The person on the floor was a lad of twelve or thirteen, and he was sound asleep. A ship's boy, she guessed. Indignation welled up inside her; what kind of a man demanded that a lad sleep on boards like this, just to be at his beck and call in the middle of the night?

Resigning herself to the necessity of stepping over him in order to enter the room, she reached out to unlatch the door. Only then did she notice there was a line of light showing underneath it. It was hardly likely anyone would have fallen asleep with a lamp or candle lit; she knew enough now about shipboard life to know no one was careless with a flame.

She stood still, listening. Nothing. No snoring, no deep breathing, no sound of movement. She didn't have time to waste. With precise, careful movements, she lifted the latch on the door and eased it partially open. She stepped over the sleeping lad, but halted in the doorway.

The part of the room she could see was compactly furnished, every inch put to good purpose. A braided dress-coat and a loden cloak hung on the wall to her right, with the tricorne hat of a naval captain on top. A sea chest occupied the floor space beneath. A sword belt, scabbard and sheathed sword lay on the lid. Next to the chest, a wash-stand was bolted to the wall, holding a basin, jug and wooden shaving-kit box in its recessed niches. On the stern wall the bunk, neatly made up, ran the length of the cabin under the aft window.

She paused, then pushed the door open further. No reaction. No movement, no sound, no angry voice demanding who was there.

Nothing happened.

Glancing down at the kris on her palm, she saw the blade pointed to the area behind the half-opened door. Behind her the sleeping lad had not stirred.

She didn't push the door any further open. Instead, she leaned forward to look around it.

The source of light was a brass lantern hanging from the ceiling. On the far wall of the cabin there was a desk and chair. A man, presumably the captain, was seated there in his shirt sleeves, his back to her. All his focus was on what he was holding with gloved hands.

The plumes.

Four of them, gorgeous, luxuriant billows of colour and movement and shifting light. They flooded the cabin with the power of their attraction, their fascination. It was an effort to think, to tear her gaze away.

How was she ever going to seize them and escape?

Stay calm, that's the first thing. She stepped inside, reached behind her and gently closed the door. Breathing deep, she checked her glamour, relaxing to ease its blending into the new surroundings. She looked down at the kris, but it was just a dagger lying on her palm. Even the glow had faded.

The captain did not turn. He just held the plumes and gazed at them, enraptured. The two pieces of bambu were on the desk. She was barely two full paces away; unlike Juster's spacious cabin, this one was tiny and cramped.

She ran choices through her head.

Seize the plumes, forget the bambu, and run. Once out on the deck,

Saker could fight for her while she ran down to the opened gunport. The rope ladder would be there for her to reach the *prau*. But how would she break the captain's hold on the plumes? If she ripped them out of his hands, she might break the shafts. If she touched the captain, he might realise he was being tackled by a real person, not an apparition. He might see through her glamour.

Hit him over the head with something first? She looked around to find a weapon. There was nothing useful, except the sword, a chamber pot and the shaving box. She cursed the austere frugality of Lowmian culture.

Run him through with the sword. Or the dagger. Definitely a better solution than hitting him with a shaving box. Except she didn't trust herself to succeed in killing him cleanly and silently. There was that lad outside the door . . .

Stop dithering, woman! Use your wits! Deception. What was a glamour but a deception?

She spoke, in a soft, seductive whisper. "Put them down. They are not for you."

He froze, then dropped the plumes and whirled around, almost falling out of his chair. He looked straight through her. Standing, he hesitated and took a pace in her direction. She side-stepped nimbly, backing up against the bed out of his way and adapting her glamour as she moved. He opened the door and looked out. The ship's boy was still asleep across the threshold. He closed the door, frowning. For a moment he stood there, looking at the desk.

She was terrified. The cabin was too small. He could walk straight into her before she could dodge him.

Returning to his desk, he sat down again. She flattened herself against the wall beside the door, so that if he opened it again, she would be behind it. "Put them away," she whispered. "Put them back in the bambu."

This time he didn't even look around. "No. They are mine!"

"They belong to your liege lord. Put them away."

"They are so beautiful . . ."

"They will bewitch you. Put them away."

He sat still, with his back to her, trembling. "Who – who are you?"

"A servant of Va, who commands you."

"I can't see you."

She adjusted her glamour. "Then look."

He turned. This time he saw a woman, ethereal, fascinating, demurely clad in Lowmian clothing but, or so she hoped, so beautiful her beauty would appear otherworldly.

He stared, jaw dropping. She changed the glamour again, fading the image into the wall behind her, vanishing before his eyes.

"Put the plumes away," she whispered. "Leave them inside the bambu on your desk and go to sleep. All will be well."

He was weeping now and trembling like a leaf.

Va, I hate this.

Still he didn't move.

Are my ten minutes up? Move, you clay-brained man!

Any more of this and she'd be the one trembling. She clasped the kris in her hand, ready to stab him if he didn't move to obey her.

"Yes," he murmured. "Yes, lady." He turned away and picked up the larger of the two sticks of bambu.

Va, he was so slow!

And then success was ripped away from her.

The ship jolted under her feet. The door juddered, the floor tilted. She staggered. Lost her hold on her glamour. A flash of light dazzled her from outside the windows, left her blinking, disoriented, followed by an assault on her ears that made her head ring with noise.

When her senses returned, she was leaning against the wall and the captain was half sprawled across the desk. Outside someone was screaming. Glass littered the bunk from broken windows. The captain levered himself upright, blinking. She reached within herself to re-assemble her glamour, but she was shaking so hard she couldn't seem to grasp her power.

The captain stared at her in bewilderment. The door flew open, and the ship's boy was standing there, his mouth opening and closing, his eyes wide with terror. She did the only thing she could think of: she changed her glamour into the appearance of a ball of fire.

The lad shrieked.

The captain plunged past her, grasping his sword as he went, the plumes forgotten. He and the lad disappeared down the companionway.

She snatched up the four feathers from the desk and dived out of the cabin. Halfway down the passage, she realised that she no longer held the kris. She plunged back again, saw it on the floor and scooped it up. She flew out onto the deck, into a Va-less hell of heat and flames and noise.

Right in front of her, Saker and the captain were fighting, which struck her as ridiculous when there was a gaping crater in the middle of the deck. Flames spiralled upwards from the hole in scorching gouts, licking at the shrouds and furled sails. The main mast was slanted at an odd angle.

Ardhi was – incomprehensibly – hanging upside down over her head, one foot trapped in a tangle of rigging and ropes.

Saker screamed something at her. She didn't hear the words, but she didn't need to; she knew what he wanted to tell her. The ship would blow up once the flames reached the magazine where all the gunpowder was stored.

Somewhere, in the midst of her terror and panic, a rational, cool part sorted through the scene and made decisions. Saker must look after himself. Ardhi couldn't. She needed to get the plumes safely to the *prau*. It would be on the port side; that had been the plan.

She looked away from Saker to meet Ardhi's gaze. He too shouted something she couldn't hear and once again that rational calm part told her he needed the kris. She had no idea how to throw a knife, but she also knew it didn't matter, not with the kris. She tossed it to him and, without even watching to see if he caught it, she ran for the port bulwarks.

The *prau* was there, but not against the hull. It had moved away by several lengths. Now it was Juster shouting at her, Juster's words that were lost in the hideous roar of flames, vanished into the crackling of burning timber, the sizzling of fire doused in water and the screaming of men. She climbed up on to the bulwarks, knowing she must jump.

She didn't know how to swim.

The water was littered with debris. Perhaps, if she grabbed something floating . . . Her terror overwhelmed her. She clung to the shrouds with one hand, gripped the plumes with the other, and searched for the courage to leap into the sea.

In the end, it was the flames that scared her more. She held the plumes high above her head and jumped.

For Ardhi, everything had gone according to plan at first. They'd opened the gunport, loaded the canvas on to the platform lift, run up the steps to the lower gun deck and wound the platform up from the orlop deck using the capstan. The alarm had not been raised, and they'd had time to carry the canvas to the open gunport and lower it into the *prau*.

That was when Hawthorn, one of *Golden Petrel*'s seamen, lit the fuses on the shrapnel balls with the lighted smoulder he'd brought on board in his tinder box. He and Ardhi then left the others to wriggle out of the gun ports and down the rope ladder. The plan was for Hawthorn to return to the orlop and deposit the balls where they'd do enough damage to cripple *Sentinel*, yet give the crew time to abandon ship before the magazine blew. At the same time, Ardhi was to head on up to the main deck to inform Saker it was time to go.

He emerged on to the open deck through the aft companionway to see Saker crossing the waist from the forecastle. The next thing he knew he was upside down in a tangle of ropes, swinging above the deck. His head was packed with noise, which was odd because he couldn't hear anything else. When his vision cleared and he was no longer seeing red blossoms exploding into yellow, he decided he was still alive. It took him a few moments longer to conclude that the grenade balls must have exploded too soon, deep under his feet, and the force of the blast had shot him up into the shrouds.

He looked around, blessing the fact that his foot was entangled. Otherwise he would have fallen back down into the fire, or dropped headfirst on to what was left of the deck. His immediate problem now was to leave the ship before the flames below reached him and cooked him like a hen on a spit. Reaching up, he clasped some of the ropes above his head and felt for the dagger he'd been wearing as a replacement for the kris.

It was missing.

Holding on tight, he attempted to free himself by wriggling his foot. Unfortunately, a heavy tangle of rope and lines was dragging the loop around his ankle as tight as a hangman's noose. Splinter it. He was going to die up here.

He smiled grimly. Maybe that was better than dying on the blade of the Chenderawasi kris, which would have been his fate soon anyway.

All would be well as long as Sorrel had found the plumes.

Twisting around, he surveyed the deck. One good thing: with the fire blazing out of control, there was sufficient light to see everything. Saker had evidently survived the explosion too, because he was now intent on skewering Captain Russmon with his sword as the two men battled on what was left of the deck. By the look of it, he had run his blade through one of *Sentinel*'s officers first, if the bleeding body on the deck was any indication.

Just then, Sorrel shot out into the open, the regalia in one hand, his kris in the other. She looked up at him. He shouted to her to throw him the kris. He was doubtful she could have heard his words over the roar of the fire, but she tossed the dagger to him anyway. He grinned at her, but she was already leaping towards the bulwarks, still clutching the Raja's regalia.

All four plumes. May the blessings of the Chenderawasi follow you, Sorrel, all the days of your life.

The dagger flew true, turning through the air until the hilt slapped into his waiting palm. He used it to saw through the rope that trapped him, hauled himself up higher, away from the leaping flames. Swarming up one of the braces attached to the foremast, he reached the fore topmast yard. Once there, he knew he was safe. He ran out along the yard and dived off the end.

It never occurred to him to wonder if Sorrel could swim. In Chenderawasi, everyone could.

This is madness, Saker thought. *I don't want to kill this man.* Captain Russmon ought to have been ordering the abandonment of the ship, not fighting a duel.

At least Sorrel was safe. He'd seen her run past him to the bulwarks. Juster would look after her.

His next thought wasn't so sanguine: would Juster stay close to *Sentinel* when there was burning debris raining down? Of course he wouldn't! If the *prau* wasn't there, Sorrel was jumping into the sea. And Sorrel couldn't swim.

The thought terrified him. When a piece of burning wood fell near his feet, he grabbed it up and thrust it between Russmon's legs. The man jumped backwards. Instead of taking advantage of that mistake to run the captain through, Saker turned and fled. Sword in his hand, he vaulted the bulwarks.

On his drop into the water, he glimpsed a hand raised above the surface holding tight to four billows of golden feathers. He plunged down feet first through a sea turned red by the glow of fire, and Sorrel was there, staring back at him, her eyes wide with panic, one arm ineffectually thrashing the water into bubbles, while her other hand grasped the shafts of all four plumes in a tight fist. He grabbed her around the waist with one arm and bore her upwards. His other hand still held tight to his sword.

When he surfaced, he shoved the weapon back into his sea-filled scabbard.

She spluttered, coughed up water, gasped some more and then asked, "Did the feathers get wet?"

He stroked her face, pushing her hair away. "I doubt it matters. Birds don't mind the rain."

She coughed some more, stared at him, and then her lips twitched and she gave a weepy laugh. Another explosion rocked the ship and a wave washed over them. She yelped and he began stroking for the *prau*, towing her after him.

"You have to learn how to swim," he yelled.

She ducked as a piece of burning debris just missed them. "Another time perhaps?"

A moment later, a rope snaked across the water from the *prau*. Just as they were grabbing for it, Ardhi appeared as well, churning through the waves, and the three of them were hauled on board together.

Dripping, singed and exhausted, Saker had to clamber over the pile of canvas that was taking up most of the area near the stern in order to reach a place to sit. He glanced around those onboard. Hawthorn was missing.

"What the fuck happened?" he asked one of the other seamen as Juster gave the order to set the fobbing sails and get the fobbing hell out of there.

The man shrugged. "Don't rightly know. Hawthorn must've dropped his smoulder into a butt of gunpowder. Or maybe the grenade ball was faulty, or the fuse burned too blistering fast. Reckon he was blown to specks and shreds, poor bastard. Rest of us made it out of the gunport." He grinned. "Vetch here was the last. He was blowed out like a cannonball, straight into the boat. Ended arse up in the cap'n's lap!"

Saker looked over at Sorrel. "Are you all right? Were you burned?"

"Scorched a bit, but nothing much." She looked back at the burning ship. "There'll be plenty who aren't so lucky."

"Not as bad as it looks," Juster said cheerfully. "The explosion was amidships; no one has quarters there. Look, there are boats all over now, picking men up."

It was true. Boats from the Lowmian fleet were coming to the rescue. As the wind caught the sails overhead and the *prau* picked up speed, what was left of the gunpowder in *Sentinel* blasted the galleon into the sky in a massive ball of yellow light. Even as they gaped at the red billows of flame and fiery ash in the aftermath, a crack of sound assaulted their eardrums and a blast of wind sent the *prau* skimming as if before a storm.

Saker bowed his head to recite the prayer for the dead. "May they who have died this day find their rest in the quiet of Va's creation, at peace with the world, as part of the land and sea, oak and wave, to live again within every creature that walks this way in days to come."

Everyone gave the traditional response. "So be it, verily."

Saker looked over Sorrel's head to where Juster sat.

"Ten Karradar golds," Juster said, meeting his gaze without flinching, "to every crewman here, and double to Hawthorn's widow. You did a fine job, all of you."

Innocent men died today, Saker thought. *And I played a part in that.* It wasn't the first time, and he guessed it wouldn't be the last, Va help him.

34

Dyer's Dilemma

When you've damned yourself to eternal darkness after death, what can the torture of one more man possibly mean?

The answer was nothing. Not for him, but still he felt the weight of guilt. Of horror at his own existence and of what he was doing.

I suppose, though, right now torture means the whole world to you, Master Fox.

Herelt Deremer regarded the prisoner in front of him with as much objectivity as he could muster. Mostly, though, there was hatred, and perhaps just a tinge of compassion. Theddor Fox was young, after all, and he'd never had much of a chance to be anything except what his father chose, until one night a month previously when he'd gone to sleep in an inn and woken up the next day chained in a Deremer dungeon. No one had touched him since he'd been chained there in a standing position with his back to the rough stones of a wall, mostly in the pitch dark, in his own filth.

He must have been in shock, although no one had actually heard how he felt about it. His jailers had all worn wax plugs in their ears when they'd attended to his basic needs. Herelt needed information and he suspected the only way he was going to get it from a sorcerer while staying safe himself was to starve him into a state where he had no strength to call upon to coerce anyone.

The time had now come to take the risk. He nodded to the two jailers he'd brought into the cell with him. With their ears stoppered, they were there to rescue him if the need arose.

"How do you feel, Theddor?" he asked.

The man raised his head to look at him. It was an effort. His eyes were dulled, his cheeks sunken. His hair was falling out and his flesh had melted away from his bones.

Well, the next moment will tell.

"Food," Theddor mumbled. His gums were bleeding and his tongue looked sore.

Herelt assessed the impact of the words. A slight tug and a vague feeling of uneasiness, a mild compassion for his hunger, but no real desire to bring this man a meal. He allowed himself the ghost of a smile. *I think we have you now, Master Fox.*

"You can have as much as you like to eat soon. But first, let me tell you what I know."

"Release me."

"You have no power over me. Your sorcery is not going to work in here. No one is going to feed you until you've answered some questions." He made himself comfortable by leaning against the wall and folding his arms. "My name is Lord Herelt Deremer. I suspect you know who I am. I know that your father is the sorcerer Valerian Fox."

He could almost feel sorry for Theddor, who was still blinking in the lamplight, frowning in a confused way, so weak he was finding it hard to keep his head raised.

I wonder if the lack of food has affected his ability to think clearly?

When Theddor finally forced out some words from between his loosened teeth, he said, "I need food."

"I know you do. In fact, you are starving to death. You are too weak to coerce us, so don't try. We need information and we won't give you anything to eat until we have it. Your choice. Do you understand?"

"You're a dead man, Deremer. My father will slaughter every Dire Sweeper in Lowmeer." The words were whispered and halting, which made them sound more pathetic than defiant.

"If you think your father cares about you, you're deceived. Rumour tells us Valerian Fox has a number of sons, all between fifteen and twenty-five years old. What he *hasn't* ever told any of you is that the more you use your sorcery, the shorter your life will be. You've been ordering men to join the lancers, but each man you coerce is weeks cut from your lifespan. Because that's the way sorcery works."

"You're a liar. My father is still vigorous!"

"Ah, yes, but he knows how to use his sorcery to revitalise his life, doesn't he? I'm sure you know that."

"Of course I know that!"

"But he's just never bothered to tell you how it's done, has he? And I can tell you why."

Theddor looked at him in befuddled silence, perhaps wondering if he'd already said too much.

"Don't worry, my friend. You haven't said anything I didn't already know."

Herelt waved to one of the jailers and the man opened the cell door. A smell of hot food wafted in from succulent chunks of beef topped with dumplings, swimming in thick vegetable gravy. Herelt's younger brother, Evern, brought in a plate of it, heaped high, and placed it on the floor just short of Theddor.

"You can have it all, if you answer my questions. I won't let you go, but you will have all you want to eat, and you'll be moved to a more salubrious cell. My promise, as a Deremer."

He wasn't sure that Theddor absorbed all he said. The young man couldn't take his eyes from the food; nor did his tongue stop licking his lips.

"It's beef, Theddor. Imagine savouring it on your tongue . . . the tantalising, luscious flavour of it. Cooked so slowly that it melts in your mouth, thickened with carrots and turnips and spices. Imagine relishing the creaminess . . . I feel sure there's spices in there. Can you smell them, Evern? Coriander, perhaps? Oh, that aroma . . . !"

Theddor leant against his chains, trying to reach the plate with his extended foot.

"I think I can tell you something you don't know," Herelt continued, keeping his tone casual. "It's only a guess, but I think I'm right. Your father won't explain to you the details of exactly how he extends his life, because he's afraid if you knew that, you might kill him. Just as he killed *his* father. He's doomed you, Theddor, all of you, when he asked you to use your coercion to raise fighting men for his cause."

"He'll tell me, when we've led our men to victory. When he rules the whole of the Va-cherished Hemisphere! He *promised*."

"Whether you're alive then, rather depends on me," he said. "The word of a Deremer, Theddor – I won't kill you if you tell me all about twins and the Horned Death." He dipped a finger into the still-warm stew and wiped it, still dripping, across Theddor's tongue. The prisoner closed his eyes, his desire and need so great that Herelt grimaced.

"Come now, Theddor, if you eat, perhaps you'll be able to work out how to use your sorcery to break out of here. At the moment, there's one thing for sure: you have no resources to tap into sorcery at all. Tell me what I want to know." *And I hope you are befuddled enough to believe that.*

Evern picked up the dish and helped himself to a spoonful. "Ohhh, that is delicious. I reckon it's too good for him."

"He'll get it if he wants it," Herelt said. "But I'm certainly not going to stand here all day waiting. By all hogs and galls, this place stinks!"

"We can try asking another of Fox's sons," Evern suggested. "After all, we have several of them now." That was a lie, but Theddor had no way to know that.

"Good idea. All right, let's go. Bring that dish with you."

Evern's expression brightened and he bent to pick it up.

"No!"

"What?" Herelt asked, as Evern took no notice and lifted the dish to breathe in its aroma.

"I'll tell you. I'll tell you everything I know. Just let me eat something—"

"Give him a small sip, Evern," he said, "just the one. As a demonstration of our good will."

It took an hour of probing, of questions and cajoling, of threats and promises. And with each answer, Herelt's sense of urgency grew even as his sense of his own worthiness disappeared. By the time Theddor's story was finished, Evern sat with his back to the wall and his hands over his face.

When he was sure he had all he needed, Herelt unchained one of Theddor's arms and gave him the dish of food. "Enjoy it," he said. He hauled his brother to his feet and pushed him out of the cell.

With a jerk of his head, he indicated the two jailers were also to leave. Once they were all outside he made a gesture to one of them to take out his wax plug, then said, "Kill him. Use the pike. He's too dangerous to live."

"Now, my lord?"

"After you've put that plug back in your ear."

He watched as the man did as he was asked without a twitch of expression.

A true Dire Sweeper, he thought. *Damn us all to perdition.*

Theddor didn't look up until the jailer was swinging his pike at the side of his neck. His eyes just had time to widen, then he fell against his chains, choking, as blood spurted and the bowl of food crashed to the floor, spattering what was left of the beef and gravy into the mess in the straw at Theddor's feet.

"But, you said—" Evern whispered, staring white-faced from Theddor to him and back again.

He snorted. "Evern, the Deremers *have* no honour. Not any longer. The one thing we used to be so proud of is what we should have been most shamed by. By the time we've finished, the Deremer name will be reviled, and not one of us will be alive."

He looked back at Theddor. "Check that he's dead," he ordered. "Pity about the beef."

35

Ardhi's Secret

Juster gave the orders: they would not stop in the Spicerie. They threaded their way through the pattern of islands, as far as possible offshore, even avoiding the fishing *prau*. When the winds dropped and they were becalmed, he had crewmen row the pinnace and the longboat to tow the ship.

"I think he wants those plumes of yours off *Golden Petrel* as soon as possible," Saker remarked to Ardhi.

For Sorrel, the days seemed endless. It was approaching a year since they had left Lowmeer, and she was tired of the confinement of a ship. When she could, she spent time with Ardhi, learning the language of Chenderawasi, on the assumption that anything that helped her communicate would in the end help Piper. She'd thought that the closer they came to the islands, the happier Ardhi would be, but the reverse was the case. As the days rolled by, he became more taciturn.

He'd told her all about himself and the death of the Raja. "And now I'm doing it again," he told her. "Bringing another ship from another land to my people with your guns and your greed."

Golden Petrel had a draught too deep for the river where the port buildings of Bandar Ruanakula lined the bank, so Ardhi piloted them safely through one of the breaks in the reef into the deeper end of a lagoon. The anchor splashed down, sending minnows darting through water as clear as glass. The light of late afternoon was luminous and warm, the sunset to come already promising a glory of colour-stained clouds along the horizon.

Pulau Chenderawasi. One large island in a chain of islands strung through the ocean like pearls and emeralds scattered in a sapphire sea: some rough cut and rocky, others smooth and flat; some draped with exuberant tropical growth, others trimmed and cultivated and thick with nutmeg trees. The air was heavy with the floral fragrance of the delicate bells of nutmeg flowers.

When Ardhi identified the aroma for them, there were tears in his eyes.

Safely within the confines of the reef-edged anchorage, they awaited the arrival of an official from the town. They could see some of the port buildings built on stilts over the water, with the curving prongs of roofs soaring up towards the sky at either end, like the horns of a new moon. From what Saker could see of them through the ship's spyglass, they were elaborately carved and painted, while the palm thatching was plaited in intricate designs.

Guilt stung Saker. *And we call places like this Va-forsaken? What ignorant dewberries we are!*

At his side, her hair blowing around her face in a dark halo, Sorrel stood watching a romp of otters on a white sand beach. She was wearing one of the silk gowns she'd obtained from Juster, but in the heat of the day she'd not tried to cover the low-cut bodice with her kerchief; she'd glamoured it instead. His breath caught in his throat, shocking him, and he had to look away. *She's Sorrel; she's nothing more than a friend.*

"It's so lovely," she said, speaking of the island, but then added in a whisper, "It scares me to death."

"If you're frightened, I think I should be petrified."

She gave him a puzzled look.

"You're normally so brave about everything," he explained.

"You jest, surely? I've not felt brave since – since my daughter died. Not for a moment. Although . . ." She paused, searching for the right words. "I suppose at first her death made me careless of living, because living doesn't matter as much if you don't love someone. I wasn't scared so much as indifferent." She looked along the deck to where Ardhi was holding the child in his arms, pointing out the otters to her and telling her what they were called in his tongue. "But then," she said softly, "Piper came along, and I had a reason to live – without ever being certain I could keep her safe. She calls me *Ibu* now. It means mother in Ardhi's tongue."

Her words awoke an ache inside Saker.

How often had he loved anyone? His family, not at all, except perhaps for an idolised vision of an absent mother – which was a lie, anyway. Fritillary Reedling? Respected her, perhaps; admired even, but loved? She wasn't a woman who invited love. Gerelda, yes, for a time, but that had morphed into affection. Affection of a kind too, for Juster and Ardhi.

But Piper? Her, he loved. Real, unquestioning love. Perhaps it had a purity about it, because he sought nothing in return. She may have been his daughter; she may not have been. Her parentage was no longer relevant.

Mathilda. He'd loved her so much once, but the person he'd thought she was had never really existed. He'd replaced the reality with a dream, an illusion.

Sorrel . . . Back in Serinaga, when he'd seen her leap into the sea with the plumes in her hand, he'd felt his world cracking and been afraid it was about to shatter. She could have drowned so easily. The tide might have swept her away. She'd known all that when she'd jumped – and she'd leapt anyway. When he thought of all that could have happened, his breath caught.

Asleep, he sometimes dreamed of taking her to bed with an ardour so passionately unbridled it shocked him to acknowledge it even to himself. Awake, he remembered Sorrel knew everything about his irresponsible, immature idiocy with Mathilda – and was embarrassed.

Hang you for a ninnyheaded dunce, Saker Rampion.

"Saker," she asked, "what do you fear most?"

"What this *sakti* Chenderawasi wants of us. It dragged us here for a reason."

"I worry if it wants Piper especially."

"We'll know soon, I suppose. That's what—"

The lookout in the crow's nest called down to the officer on watch, telling him boats were putting out from the port.

Ardhi came up then, to hand Piper over to Sorrel. "I not sure what will happen now," he said. "Many things can change." He gave a wistful smile as Juster joined them. "It's been years since I sailed away from Bandar Ruanakula."

"I hope they're happy to see you again," Juster said drily.

"They will be happy to see the Raja's regalia home, yes. I doubt they smile to see *me* again. I was dead to all here before I left."

322

He didn't know what he could say to that.

They watched the approaching craft. The first was a small decorated *prau* without a sail. The remaining four were all long war canoes, each paddled by twenty men arranged in twos. They sang a rhythmic song as they came, to match the beat of the paddles that they dug savagely into the water. An extra man in the stern managed a sweep.

Intimidation? Saker wondered. *Or respect for a visitor?* He was glad he was wearing his sword.

The *prau* was paddled by four men, all bare-chested, wearing sarongs of colourful cloth. Seated cross-legged in the centre was a middle-aged man. He was formally dressed in a suit of cloth, with matching cloth elaborately folded into winged headgear. He had three attendants with him, one of them a woman. Everyone on the *prau* had a sheathed dagger thrust through their cloth belts, including the woman.

As they came closer, Ardhi said, referring to the middle-aged man, "That's my eldest cousin. I glad to see he still alive."

"You have a large family?" Saker asked, and felt guilty because he knew so little about Ardhi's life. Did he have brothers? Sisters? Were his parents still alive? He didn't know. Perhaps it was his fault for never asking, or perhaps Ardhi's for being so secretive and private about his affairs.

Even then, Ardhi did not answer the question. "He's an important man here in Bandar Ruanakula." He thought for a moment. "*Walikota.* The head of the town?"

"Mayor," Juster said.

"Mayor, yes. It's honour that he comes to you, Cap'n Juster. You give him the gift."

Juster nodded. He was following all Ardhi's advice and had already prepared a present of embroidered silks and a set of steel knives. "How do I address him?"

"*Tuan Sri.* It is a title of respect. His name is Imbak, but do not use it. Speak to him in trade Pashali; he is fluent."

Saker glanced around. The crew were all on deck, dressed in their best garments, respectfully silent. A shade of silk had been stretched over the central part of the deck in anticipation of visitors, and the stuffed chairs from Juster's cabin had been brought out, laid on a

Pashali carpet, all items purchased in Javenka to replace those lost or damaged in Karradar.

Finch said in his ear, "I hope all those fellows in the canoes aren't coming on board."

"They won't," Ardhi assured him.

Finch hadn't thought Ardhi would hear what he said, and stirred unhappily. "They look as though they'd gladly eat us for dinner."

"And they probably think your sailors will shoot us for any feathers we happen to have," Ardhi said, without looking at him.

"Maybe you're right at that," Finch said, rubbing his whiskered chin in mild embarrassment. "But I'm still going to tell the men to be on the alert."

Ardhi shrugged. "I'm sure the islanders are also alert."

As Juster turned his attention to the *prau*, now arriving at the foot of the pilot's steps, Ardhi said quietly to Saker, "Just make sure Captain Juster tells *Tuan Sri* Imbak that all four plumes are on board. Best you don't mention me."

Saker frowned. "Can't you tell him yourself?" he asked. But Ardhi had already turned away.

What the pox is going on?

The tension rose several notches when the dignitaries came on board, especially as the canoes – with their speed and chanting continuing unabated – began to circle *Golden Petrel*.

Definitely intimidation.

Juster greeted the arrivals with Chenderawasi words Ardhi had taught him. One of the dignitaries introduced the mayor, then the woman and the other man. "We are the mayor's advisers," he said. "We represent the Datu of the South."

Ardhi whispered a translation of this to Juster, after which Juster continued the conversation in Pashali with Saker at his shoulder in case he didn't understand something.

The gifts were given and received, the guests were seated, drinks were served. Saker sweated as the meeting progressed. It was hot out there on the deck, but he thought it was more the tension that caused his discomfort.

The hairs on his neck were prickling, and he knew why: *Tuan Sri* Imbak – in fact all of the visitors – had ignored Ardhi. *No, more than that. They looked straight through him, as if they couldn't see him. It's as if he doesn't exist.*

The woman in the group could not tear her gaze away from Sorrel and Piper, who were standing in the shade of the mast, and that also made his skin prickle. He hoped it was merely the interest of one woman for another, or just fascination with a pink and white baby, but something about her blazing intensity made him doubt that.

Hatred? Shock? Fear? He couldn't be sure. She was dressed in a wrapped sarong, and a top that left her shoulders and arms bare, except for a necklace of gold studded with shells. Her hair was grey and elaborately bound and decorated with gold pins at her nape.

Although she wore a kris, Saker didn't imagine it was anything but ceremonial, as she was elderly and had only climbed the pilot's steps with aid. Barefoot. None of them wore shoes.

Remember, Saker, he told himself. *That doesn't mean they are poor or stupid. Ardhi was sent by his family to study at the Javenka Library.*

Juster was listening more than he spoke. Every now and then he glanced at Saker with a slight twitch of his eyebrow, and Saker would translate. Mostly, though, Juster knew what was being said, and it wasn't particularly friendly.

"The last time a ship like yours came, our Raja was slaughtered," had been Imbak's first words after the initial greetings.

"We are from a different land to that previous vessel. Our land is called Ardrone," Juster replied, giving a previously rehearsed reply. "That last ship, and the men who were left behind, were from Lowmeer. We are not Lowmians, just as you are not from Seringa or the Spicerie."

"Why do you come here?"

"To return the four plumes of the regalia of Raja Wiramulia to his son, Raja Suryamuda."

There was an audible intake of breath from the three advisers, but not a muscle moved in Imbak's expression as he replied, "There is one on board this vessel who must perform that task in person." He did not, however, look at Ardhi.

"It will be done."

"Any other reason to visit Chenderawasi?" Imbak's tone was not encouraging. In fact, he had not smiled once.

"We are in need of fresh food and water. For which we can pay. With gold or coin or goods, as you prefer."

"Water is free. Food – you can negotiate with our merchants in the town. That is not my concern. My concern is that you leave and not return."

"That is our intention. However, it is my understanding that the Lowmians do intend to return, and soon. They left their factors here, to buy and store your nutmeg."

"Alas, they died. Fever took them. They were sickly men."

Juster, startled, looked at Saker.

Saker's stomach lurched. "You heard it right. He said they died of fever. I think he's lying."

"However," Imbak continued unperturbed in Pashali, "we have the nutmeg and mace they wanted to buy. Perhaps you would be interested in the purchase? We were going to sell the crop in Kotabanta as usual."

"Would you be interested in bartering for a cargo of baked building bricks?" Juster asked.

"Bricks? I do not understand this word."

Ardhi translated, but Imbak remained impassive as if Ardhi had not spoken.

Saker's fingers curled.

Juster repeated the Chenderawasi term. Imbak turned to his advisers and there was a whispered conversation in their own tongue. While they spoke, Juster gave one of the sailors an order to bring up a couple of the bricks from the ship's ballast. Saker knew he'd been intending to sell them in Karradar once he had his own plunder to use as ballast, but it mattered little where he divested the ship of a valuable commodity, as long as there was equivalent weight to replace it. If the nutmeg didn't weigh enough, they could always make up the difference with water.

The bricks were brought, the four Chenderawasi examined them and declared themselves well satisfied with the quality. There was a short discussion on the quantity, and once Juster assured them that the plumes would indeed be returned, a preliminary bargain was struck, with the understanding that details would be confirmed by traders in the town.

"After that," Imbak said, "your ship will leave and never return."

Juster bowed his assent.

Tuan Sri Imbak rose to leave and the others followed suit.

The woman took the opportunity to approach Sorrel. She did not smile or greet her, but laid her hand on Piper's head. Piper broke into a happy smile and reached for the woman's necklace of shells. The woman caught her hand and then stepped back in shock still holding the child's fingers. She spoke then, but the words were too rapid and passionate – more hissed than spoken – for Saker to understand. The lady withdrew her hand as if she'd been bitten and walked away to join the others as they left the ship.

Juster stood ramrod straight at the bulwarks, watching the *prau* and their chanting canoe escort vanish into the gathering dark of twilight.

"What did she say?" Sorrell asked Saker. "The expression – did you see the way she looked at Piper?"

"I didn't understand her either," he replied as the sailors began to dismantle the shade and put the chairs away. "But she was shocked." He shrugged, trying to sound unconcerned. "Perhaps because she'd never seen a child with blue eyes before?"

Juster turned to them then. "I want to see you, Ardhi, and you, Saker, in my cabin. Now."

"I'm coming too," Sorrel said. "No one is leaving me out of this." She handed Piper over to Surgeon Barklee, and followed them without waiting for Juster's assent.

"Don't try arguing with her," Saker advised. "You'll rarely win."

"You could say that I am fed up with other people deciding my fate," she said. There was no smile to take the sting out of the words.

Once in his cabin, Juster turned on Ardhi, louring over the lascar like a thundercloud. "You have not been telling us the whole truth. I felt as though I had a hand tied behind my back out there."

Ardhi shrugged. "We from different sides of world. We can't trust each other, cap'n. You think I tell whole truth, then you're a fool. And I don't think you're a fool."

"Who are you exactly, and why did those people not even *look* at you? You said that Imbak fellow was your cousin!"

"He is. And I know the woman since I been born. My grandmother's closest friend." He sighed. "In Ardrone, Lord Juster rich nobleman, and Ardhi of Chenderawasi common tar, swabbie, lascar. Here, Lord Juster is maybe enemy of my land. Here, I grandson of nobleman. My kin, they think Ardhi is traitor, worthy of traitor's punishment, traitor's death. But still grandson of the lord – Datu – who rules part of Pulauan Chenderawasi. My loyalty to my Datu, then my Raja. Not to you. Not to Saker. To none of you. My . . ." He hunted for the right word. "My duty is to Chenderawasi. To these islands, to my Raja. To my people."

Va-damn, Saker thought. *That's the longest speech I've ever heard him make.*

Juster's narrowed eyes fixed Ardhi with an unwavering stare. "What happened to the Lowmian factors who were left here?"

"I cannot know answer to that! They were alive when I left Chenderawasi. They were building nutmeg godowns. *Spice Dragon* left before anyone in Bandar Ruanakula knew about death of the Raja. I left later, ten days after Raja Wiramulia killed. Factors still alive. That is all I can tell you."

"All right, I understand that," Juster said. "You can't know what happened. What do you *think probably* happened? Did they die of fever? Or were they murdered?"

Ardhi raised his chin belligerently. "You tell me. If *prau* filled with Chenderawasi traders sailed into Throssel, killed King Edwayn for his regalia, then sailed away leaving people behind to trade, what you think would happen to them?"

There was a long silence.

"Why," Juster asked finally, "did Captain Lustgrader sail away? He should have known what would happen to the factors once the Chenderawasi discovered the Raja had been murdered by men from *Spice Dragon*."

"He had no idea Raja Wiramulia was killed – until I arrive in Serinaga. I told him. Even then, he not want to believe his men kill anyone. They denied it. They were Lowmians; I just a lascar. Who you think Lustgrader believe?"

Sorrel broke the silence that followed. "I don't care who you are, any of you. I want to know what that woman said about Piper. I want to know why the Chenderawasi *sakti* brought Saker and me here. And I want to know *now*. I want to know if Piper is in danger."

Everyone looked at her. Then Juster started to laugh. "Aren't we a fine passel of turnip-head sailors! Mistress Sorrel has put us all in our place. That's the real question, isn't it? Why are we here? Was it your *sakti* manipulating us, Ardhi?"

He sighed. "You – Sorrel, Saker – you not told me all truth about Piper, so don't be angry I keep secrets. The woman, Sri Sariah, she has healing *sakti*. Like healer's witchery. That *sakti* told her something evil is in Piper. She told you to go home where you belong and take that evil thing with you."

Sorrel, stricken, stared at him and began to shake.

Ardhi continued, relentless. "I believe in truth of Sri Sariah's *sakti*. If she saw something in Piper, then it is there." He reached out and touched her hand with the tips of his fingers, adding with sudden tenderness, "Courage, Sorrel. Perhaps that is why the *sakti* brought you here."

36

The Song of the Chenderawasi

Saker knocked at the cabin door.

For a while he wondered if Sorrel was going to answer, but then he heard her muffled, "Come in."

When he stepped inside, she was sitting on the edge of the bunk with Piper asleep beside her. She looked up as he entered.

"I will claw and tear anyone to death with my bare hands before I'd let them take her," she said. "They'll have to eat my heart out first."

He closed the door behind him. "I'm sorry."

"Sorry? About what? Is that all you can say? You're *sorry*?"

For a moment he thought she was going to launch herself at him in attack. He held up his hands, palms outwards.

Her breast was heaving; her breath came in gasps. It was hot in there, too hot. He stepped across to the window and opened it. The sounds of a tropical night drifted in: unfamiliar songs and unidentifiable chattering – yips and wails, clicks and trills. Insects, goatsuckers, toads, animals? He had no idea.

"I failed to protect one child," she said. "I will *not* fail this one."

He sat next to her on the bed. "Sorrel, please don't think me uncaring. Never that. I don't give a damn if she's my child, or Fox's or Vilmar's. To me, she's a daughter, and I love her. I won't let them kill her. I'd die first, too." He mustered up a faint smile. "But we don't know what the *sakti* wants. It may be to *help* her. I'd really rather all three of us came through this still alive, all right?"

"It might not be true. Maybe the woman was wrong . . ." With a suddenness that caught him unawares, she buried her face in his chest. "Piper is the devil-kin!" she cried, her words both muffled and agonised.

"Ardhi says we must take her to the Raja tomorrow. We will go with him when he takes the plumes back."

"Saker, what if—?"

"No," he said flatly. "I won't let it happen, and neither will Ardhi. Three of us, together – we won't give up."

She looked up at him. "I could walk away if that would save her. But I will never allow her to be slaughtered like – like an injured animal."

"Look, I talked to Ardhi, and this is the way he interprets what happened to us back in Lowmeer. The dagger and Piper first came together on the docks in Ustgrind. Up until then, the *sakti* was only influencing my life, because it wanted me to help Ardhi to locate and steal back the plumes. Then, once Piper came in contact with Ardhi, the dagger recognised that there was something wrong with her, and that's when the *sakti* started to react to interfere in your life. Not to kill her, or you, but to bring her here."

"How could you know what it wants to do? Have you told Ardhi about her being a twin and—"

"I've not said anything. But both Ardhi and Juster heard the rumours about devil-kin and twins. Juster is no fool. He guessed Piper was Mathilda's child. I think we have to tell Ardhi the truth. But let's deal with that later. Right now we have to think about tomorrow. Ardhi believes the new Raja, Raja Suryamuda, is too young to help. However he possesses *sakti*, by virtue of his regalia. I don't really understand what that means, but Ardhi says the decision about whether and how to help Piper would be made by Raja Wiramulia's widow. She is the sole regent for Raja Suryamuda, and I suppose that means she has access to his *sakti*."

"He's just a child?"

"Well, he's certainly young. Ardhi's not giving me the details, but their *sakti* is gifted more directly than our witchery. Something to do with being of royal blood. Those gold flecks in the kris blade were from the regalia, the handle is carved from Raja Wiramulia's bone and the metal contains the last Raja's blood as well."

"Ugh." She stood and began to pace the cabin. "This is all so . . . strange. Why would Piper matter to the dagger, or to anyone here?" Her pacing slowed. "If she's the devil-kin, then Prince-regal Karel is not. If he'd been the devil-kin, it might have mattered to the Va-forsaken Hemisphere, because he'll be a monarch who commands a fleet." She looked down at Piper, her expression softening. "But a girl with no apparent legitimacy, no known parents, no status – she's a powerless nobody! Why would anyone as far away as this care if she was a devil-kin?"

"Not entirely powerless." He bit his lip, remembering bodies flung on to a death cart. "She might wreak havoc on the people around her when she's older; she might kill people through the Horned Death."

"But why would any *sakti* from Chenderawasi care about that?"

"I haven't the faintest notion."

"You don't think these people can, I don't know, see the future or something?"

"Ardhi's never hinted at anything like that. He says that if Sri Sariah is right, and there is something wrong with Piper, then her best chance is that the *sakti* can do something about it. He says it might be her *only* chance. I think we have to trust him. So tomorrow morning we go to meet the Raja."

"And he lives in Banda Ruanakula?"

"Apparently not. Nor, by the way, does Ardhi's family who come from another town in the south. The Raja moves from place to place at different times of the year. At the moment he will be up in the mountains above Banda Ruanakula. We have to walk there. Ardhi suggests that we leave at dawn. Just you, me and Ardhi. He's been quite clear to me that he won't take anyone else."

"I suppose that's to be expected. After all, look what happened to their last Raja. There's a road?"

"Just a walking track. There's not even a city up there, or so I understand. Just the Raja, his family, his attendants and his warriors."

She looked mystified. "Some sort of stronghold . . . like a castle? Accessible only by walking? Pickles 'n' hay, Saker. This is becoming odder and odder."

"Remember that old saying: 'Yours is not the only way to cook a stew. It may not even be the best way'? We are in a different world here, and its ways are not ours. Ardhi said tomorrow we will see things we must never tell to others. He also said at the end of the day we can give wings to our thoughts, or they can stay tethered, so to wither and die."

She rolled her eyes. "I hate riddles!"

He laughed, but it had a hollow sound. "I don't think he meant it to be a riddle. More of a warning."

"And if you don't come back?" Juster asked. "How long do I wait?"

Saker, who had been watching Ardhi and other sailors readying the pinnace for launching, grimaced. "Ultimately, that has to be your decision."

"I don't relish being caught in a lagoon when the Lowmians arrive. Are you sure they were only going to send one ship here, while the others sail to the Spicerie?"

"That was the plan, last I heard. *Spice Winds* was coming straight here for the nutmeg. The fleet would reassemble in the Spicerie when Lustgrader was finished here."

"They are going to know just who sank *Sentinel*, aren't they?"

"It's possible. I fought Captain Russmon on deck, by the light of a fire – he doesn't know me, but he might have seen enough to know I wasn't dark-skinned enough to be an islander. And I think he saw Sorrel too, when she crossed the deck with the plumes. She wasn't glamoured then." He sighed. "I pray he won't mention it to the Raja of Serinaga, or if he does, the Raja will dismiss it as a lie. Otherwise King Edwayn will be upset with you. *Very* upset. Of course, Russmon might be dead."

Juster studied the lagoon, frowning. There were four or five gaps in the reef, but only one entrance that could be negotiated by a ship as big as *Golden Petrel*. "Anchored here we're like insects trapped in a bottle. Once we have off-loaded the bricks and have the nutmeg on board I want to get out of here."

"We hope to return this evening. Ardhi says it will take only two hours coming back downhill."

"Oh, we won't finish loading today. There's also water and supplies to obtain. Look, Saker, if I sight the Lowmians, I'll take the ship out of the lagoon, but I'll hang about offshore for five days. Light a fire on the beach as a signal if you want to be picked up."

"I appreciate this, Juster. All of it."

"And I'm sorry I've not been my usual jaunty, wittily entertaining self." He sighed. "Things I don't understand make me edgy."

"I suppose I should be telling you to pray to Va for guidance, or something similar."

"You should indeed. How remiss my ship's cleric has been!" Juster looked at him curiously. "Why don't you?"

"I'm no longer sure I believe in Va."

Amusement danced in his eyes. "And you a Shenat witan? The oaks will wither! I never thought you'd become an unbeliever."

"Of course I'm not an unbeliever! How could I be? I'm one of the few people who's *seen* an unseen guardian! Spoken to her. Or a representation thereof. The Way of the Oak is true and real, I *know* that. And I'm steadfast in my belief of Shenat ways. Nothing could change that either. Our truth is to hold our lands and its people sacred, to maintain a balance between all aspects of life. Whether there is a deity or whether it's just a truth expressed as a Way matters little to me any more."

Juster raised a questioning eyebrow. "You think Va is irrelevant?"

"I've come to think the concept of Va was just a way to bring us all together, all peoples across the Hemisphere. A good thing, I suppose, although it made us arrogant of outsiders. But if we want guidance and grounding, it is better to go to shrine keepers and shrines, not to seek Va in our prayers. Va is notoriously bad at answering and I've never seen any evidence that such an entity exists."

"You have an infinite capacity for astonishing me, Saker. However, it is far too early in the morn for philosophical soul-searching. Such is much more appropriate after several goblets of brandy. Tonight perhaps." He turned to give orders to one of the tars on deck. "Go below, Tedli, and tell Mistress Redwing that we await her."

When he turned back to Saker, there was a faraway look in his eye: part amused, part sad. "Now *there's* a woman, Saker. If I were a marrying man, I'd be considering matrimony as a step worth taking."

Saker, astonished, stared at him.

Juster smiled. "You doubt it? She's desirable; beautiful even, at least to men who appreciate the etchings of strength and courage and tragedy in a face, rather than just neatly packaged features. But Sorrel is more than her face and her figure, as well you know. You oughtn't pass your opportunities up, Saker, when you meet them."

"She wouldn't have me. Believe me."

"Have you asked?"

"I don't have to."

He turned his attention to the distant tree-dense slopes they were going to climb. Above the topmost ridge, he glimpsed a movement in the dawn-tinged sky. Something large, high enough to catch the first rays of the sun.

"They don't have dragons here, do they?" he asked.

Juster laughed. "Not that I've heard. Talk to a Pashali, now . . . their folktales are full of talking sky serpents. Here's Sorrel. You want to get this expedition of yours under way?"

The trees towered, festooned with growth and propped up at the base by buttress roots as impressive as the stone ones of Throssel chapels. In the shade, the forest floor was damp and verdant and earthy. Vines looped from branch to branch and creepers on tree trunks insinuated their way upwards, striving for a glimpse of the sun. The world here was green, but Sorrel glimpsed other hues too: plum-coloured fungi, sulphur-bright mushrooms, lichens as lushly tinted as ripe apricots.

Everything appeared too large to her – ants as big as caterpillars, millipedes as long as her forearm, armoured beetles the size of mice. A butterfly the size of a starling flew past, its wings flicking iridescent blue with every beat. When Ardhi stopped at the edge of a river to cut a length of bambu, she was surprised to find the plant grew as tall as a house. He threaded the plumes inside to protect them and grinned at her. "I feel much better with them safe from damage," he said.

Further on, as she plucked thorns from her leg, she decided this forest was far from benign. Beauty had sharp teeth. The rainforest was a place of extraordinary grandeur and delicate perfection, but there were snakes and prickles and blood-sucking leeches, and oh, it was so *humid*.

She ran with sweat. Her clothing was wet, her hair sodden. Dear Va, even her feet perspired! The tree canopy met overhead, but the shade made no difference. Occasionally they crossed a stream, and she plunged into the water, blessing its cold purity. Then, all too soon, the perspiration would be soaking her again.

An hour after they'd started, Piper began to howl and wouldn't stop, no matter what any of them did. They took it in turns to distract her every way they could imagine, to no avail. Sorrel, dismayed, thought

335

her temper was prompted more by rage and indignation than discomfort, for there was no sign of a tear.

"She wants to crawl and play, not be carried all the time," she said as her own patience frayed around the edges.

Ardhi's expression told her he disagreed.

"If you've something to say, say it instead of pulling faces at me," she snapped, too angry to even try to use his language. Immediately she felt guilty. He'd done his best to entertain Piper.

"All right," he said, speaking Pashali. "I will. Piper senses trouble ahead, trouble for her. She's struggling against it, trying to make you turn around."

She stopped dead. Saker, walking behind her along the narrow track, almost trod on her heels. In her arms, Piper still screamed and fought. "Fiddle it. She's a baby; she can't even know where we are taking her, let alone why!" Feeling utterly helpless to succour the child, she wanted desperately to cry herself.

"Perhaps not, but the . . . the contagion within her knows."

She looked over her shoulder at Saker, indicating she had not understood the word Ardhi used. When he translated, she growled, "Piper's not a disease!"

Walking upwards again, her vision blurred by tears, she stumbled over tree roots.

"Let me take her," Saker said.

She relinquished Piper, who still fought to escape her carrying sling.

Inside, terror roiled her stomach. *Piper, forgive me, it's for your own good.* Even as she had the thought, she wondered if it was true.

They swapped her from one person to another, but there was no relief from her relentless screaming until some three hours later when she finally fell asleep in Sorrel's arms, hiccupping. The silence was so welcome, she felt guilty all over again.

A short time later, they crested a granite-capped hill which had a view back down to the lagoon and Bandar Ruanakula. Far below, *Golden Petrel* could have been a toy on a painted background. The ocean outside the reef was dotted with sails, but as far as they could see, none were large enough to belong to any ship of the Lowmian fleet. They'd climbed high enough for the air to be cooler and she ran fingers through her hair and tousled the wet strands so they could dry in the breeze.

"Look up ahead," Ardhi said. "That's where we're going." The path wound down again into the trees of a valley and out of sight, but he was pointing across the quilted canopy of the rainforest to a nearby ridge. For a moment she'd thought the ridge was capped with limestone half-overgrown with creepers and other vegetation, then realised the outcrops were ruins, the tumbled remains of stone towers and walls. An ancient castle perhaps, or a temple.

"No one can *live* there," she muttered. "It's just a heap of stone blocks!"

He didn't reply.

In the distance, a bird began to sing. Piper stirred and whimpered, but didn't wake. The song started softly, every note as pure as crystal, one following another until there was a cascade of sounds falling into the valley like droplets of rain. Each note was perfect, and each was part of a perfect whole. The glorious tune enveloped her senses, until she wanted to weep at the beauty of it.

Just when she thought she could not stand any more, that it was too much to bear, the song halted in an unpleasant discord. She gasped again, this time to draw breath. Somewhere she had stopped breathing.

"That was a . . . love song," Saker said. He sounded awed. "It's a young male practising a courtship song."

She was about to ask how he knew, then remembered his witchery.

He added, "Sadly, I don't think a female bird would be very impressed. He knows he didn't sing all the phrases correctly and he made a mess of the ending. He thinks the adult birds will laugh at his attempts, and he feels embarrassed."

She stared at him, incredulous. "You once told me that birds never do much thinking about anything, except eating and fighting rivals."

"This is not Ardrone, and these birds are not Ardronese."

He was subdued. Perhaps it was fear. No, not Saker. He always seemed so fearless. Awe, then.

"Watch," Ardhi whispered. "Watch."

They both turned to look across the valley again, their gaze soon drawn to the remains of one of the towers of the ruin. Age-old bricks appeared to have been suddenly gilded.

"Chenderawasi," Ardhi murmured. "You are about to see something not given to many. Remember this, for it is my . . . my *caridaum*."

Another word she didn't know. She gave Saker a glance.

"A Pashali word. A sort of lament of premonition," he said, paling. "No, that's not quite right. Something that you see or hear that reminds you that your death is imminent."

The shock of his words was still reverberating when she saw the golden patch on the ruins launch itself into the air, like a dragon of legend. For one wild moment she thought that was what it was, a fearsome winged animal. But no. Although it was surely twice the length of a man, it was a shimmering bird, not a dragon, and much of its length was in its tail. It spread its wings and soared, and as it soared, its feathers thrummed with harp-like notes so loud they carried across the valley.

She saw its underside as it rose, lifting on an updraft. A golden body rippled into a blush of vivid red, only to change to purple before fading into gold again in waves, starting at the throat, washing downwards to the tip of the tail.

And oh, the tail . . . Plumes so glorious she would never have words to describe them. Much larger than the feathers Ardhi now carried. The outer ones curled stiffly like wires to the side, the middle ones spread and contracted rhythmically to match the alternations in colour.

Sweet Va, the bird was not only changing its colour as it flew, it was playing music with its feathers.

It dipped, effortlessly, coming closer. A wingtip rose as it banked to reveal its upperside. An iridescent collar flared green, flattened and faded. Each change in hue heralded an increase in the tempo of the music as plumes vibrated. The creature passed them several lengths away, oblivious to their presence, but close enough for her to see single feathers trailing behind the back edge of each wing and others from the centre of its back, feathers that shivered in song like plucked lute strings.

When the thrumming reached a crescendo of sound, the bird contorted, throwing its head back and flipping its tail high to meet the wings raised over the back. The sound cut out abruptly. For one magical moment, the bird hung in the air in silence, a golden ball. Then it plummeted down, wings extending, straining for control, the wind streaming through its feathers to produce an eerie blending of chords.

She gasped, sure the bird would crash into the canopy below, but at the last moment it flattened out, skimming the trees, then disappearing into the foliage. She looked down and saw she had clutched Saker's hand, her grasp tight. Quickly she let go.

"That was a full-grown male bird," he said. "Those were the courtship rituals, but he wasn't really trying to win himself a mate. He was demonstrating to the younger male bird, the one that sang, how it should be done."

"Mocking him?" she asked.

"Not exactly. More like boasting. The younger bird has to learn by watching the other males showing off. That, I suppose," he added, addressing Ardhi, "was one of your paradise birds. The ones you call the Chenderawasi."

"Yes," Ardhi said quietly.

Sorrel turned on him in a fury. "Your people kill such divine creatures for their magical feathers? How could you!"

He turned to her, horrified. "Never! How could you even think that!"

"All birds moult and replace their feathers, at least once every year," Saker pointed out to her. "We don't kill our geese for goosedown, do we?"

"Oh. Oh, of course. I'm sorry, Ardhi. That was stupid of me. I was just so . . . enthralled. The idea that anything so glorious could be hunted – it's unimaginable."

"I wish it were. But that is what the Lowmians want to do," Ardhi said. "And perhaps your Ardronese tars too, if they had the chance. I've heard your court ladies dress their hair with bird plumes."

She exchanged a look with Saker, knowing he was as appalled as she was – because it was true.

"Come, let's move on before Piper wakes and starts her crying again," Ardhi said. "Remember, you must open your minds to all you see if you want answers to your questions. You must not try to change anything because you disagree with it. Chenderawasi . . . is other."

37

The Other

*O*ther.

    Blister it, that single word summed up the place they stepped into.

Other. Not just another hemisphere, but another world.

Ardhi had led them into the ruin through a crumbling stone archway. Human hands had built that, at least, but once inside the roofless ruined walls, it was clear that something else had been involved since the building had crumbled.

Sorrel's immediate impression was one of chaos, of nature run wild in unrestrained exuberance, watched over by gigantic painted stone statues of vultures. They glowered at her from equidistant pedestals along the remains of the outer walls.

Prickles ran up her spine as she tried to absorb everything – no, not everything, *anything*.

A slight movement caught her eye and she turned to take a better look at one of those statues. A vulture had turned its head to regard her with a single unblinking yellow eye.

Va-damn. Not a statue.

It wasn't a vulture either, but a living black and orange bird vaguely reminiscent of the flying bird they'd seen, but without the long tail plumes or the range of colour. A duller, more trimmed version. Claws, brutal things curved like scimitars with honed edges, dug into the ancient stonework. Va, the stone *crumbled* under its grip. As she watched, it unsheathed a spur from between two hard projections of bone along the back of a leg. The sound was worryingly similar to that of a sword being pulled from a scabbard.

She shifted her gaze from bird to bird; each was alive, and there was nothing friendly in their eyes. Something told her they were waiting for an order to tear them – or any human intruders – to pieces.

Va help us, Ardhi has betrayed us. Oh, Piper . . .

"They want us dead," she said, certain she was right.

"No, not – not exactly," Saker said, and his tone was more wonder than fear. "They are warriors, yes; but they are a guard of honour. Look at them. They are protecting their monarch's abode."

"What abode?" she asked. There was no building apart from the ruins that she could see.

"Saker is right," Ardhi said. "These warriors failed to protect Raja Wiramulia, arriving only after he was shot. Had they been there at the forest pool, those sailors would have been ripped to pieces."

She swallowed, still keeping a wary eye on the birds. "Do they – do they eat human flesh?" she asked.

"No, of course not!" His revulsion was intense. "But they can certainly kill us."

Saker's right hand had dropped to his sword hilt, but he didn't draw it. "We won't give them cause."

"Can you . . . Can you control them?" she asked, thinking of his witchery.

"I doubt it. They are not normal birds, believe me."

She was prepared to believe that much. Who'd ever heard of birds being guards? She tore her gaze away from them to glance around the ruins. If this was a guard of honour, where was the Raja? This place had none of the trappings of a royal building. It was a ruin, for Va's sake!

The roofless interior was festooned with bambu structures and intricate rattan weaving. Flowers and ferns grew everywhere. It all appeared unplanned and arbitrary, yet it reminded her of something. She groped for the memory and found it: Lady Friselda had ordered a huge cage built in the Regala's garden, with peacocks and Pashali parrots inside. A bird cage, filled with perches and swings and toys for the parrots . . .

This was a gigantic playground for birds. The bambu was for perches. The decorations here were living flowers, mostly orchids in an array of colour and shapes that was staggering. The wildness about them belied the idea that this was the work of a human gardener, but they *were* planted.

She shivered, appallingly aware that she and Saker did not belong here. They were the aliens, not the birds. "Who built this, Ardhi?"

"The Chenderawasi," he replied, but as he used the same word to describe the islanders, the birds and the magic, it was no answer at all.

"Look how intricately everything fits together," Saker marvelled in a whisper. "No nails. Just knots and notches, as if they are carved to fit . . ."

She let her gaze drift around the structures curving across from wall to crumbling wall, all adorned with plants and flowers, creepers and vines. She thought of the intricate weaving of the garden bird nests she'd used to show to Heather. She looked back at the spurs on the closest warrior bird. As if in answer to her enquiring gaze, it unsheathed its spur and stretched its leg and wing on one side. The leg spur was matched by another on the bend of the wing. Each was a formidable weapon.

Or maybe a tool.

"Oh, rattling pox. They built all this," she whispered. "Saker, the birds built it all. Not the original ruin, but everything else."

He regarded the birds. None of them had moved from their individual perches, or made a sound. He turned to Ardhi. "What are they waiting for?" he asked. "What are *we* waiting for?"

"The young Raja," he replied, "Raja Suryamuda, and his mother, the Rani Marsyanda. Because of his youth, she will speak for him. She will address you, Saker. Do not shame me. Address her as *Tuanku Putri*, 'your royal highness.'"

Saker repeated the words.

"Yes. Just remember all I have said. I trust your heart. Your understanding. Listen carefully, because her face will tell you nothing. Nothing at all. Yet the voice you hear can say many more things than words."

Another confounded riddle, she thought.

"I might do better if I knew all that you know," said Saker.

Ardhi shrugged. "Take Piper into your arms now. The Rani or Raja might have to touch her."

As Saker turned to take Piper, Sorrel was washed through with the cold of fear. She'd been struggling to understand the Pashali words Ardhi was using, some of them still foreign to her, but she suspected that Ardhi had just implied that she had no more role to play here.

No, she thought. *No one dismisses me so lightly, not where Piper's welfare is concerned. No one. And I don't care a fig if this woman is a fobbing Rani . . .*

Though she allowed Saker to take the still-sleeping child, her determination on that point did not waver.

"Stay here for a moment," Ardhi said.

He walked towards the centre of the ruin, moving under the strange woven canopy with its many blank spaces, until he was in the centre where there was nothing at all above. The warrior birds swivelled their heads to watch, their yellow eyes unblinking.

Sorrel, seeking a way to keep herself from panic, studied the bambu that had been used to fashion many of the structures, noting the way each piece was seamlessly joined, one fitted into another so tightly it could have been the work of one of the finest carpenters of Throssel or Ustgrind.

Master craftsmen. Was it possible? Could birds cut the bambu in the forest, carry it here and craft all this? She suddenly felt certain they could. "Those warrior birds perched up there – are any of them female?" she asked Saker in a whisper.

He shook his head. "I think females don't have spurs. I'm wondering if these are more like . . . eunuchs. No, that wouldn't be right. I think I mean non-breeding males."

Before she could say anything more, a bird dropped down into the space above Ardhi and perched on one of the bambu crossbeams. A cascade of tail feathers spread out in a fan, and then closed to hang like the soft folds of a chiffon curtain. It was beautifully coloured, but still not as gorgeous as the courting bird they'd seen.

"The young male," Saker whispered. "The one we heard singing."

This bird was closely followed by another, larger, but not as ornate. *This one is a female*, Sorrel guessed. *They must be some kind of pets of the Raja.*

The second bird was dark, the feathers sheened with a rich purple, its neck swathed in a ruff of white, its head crowned with red. Its tail was only a third of the length of the one on the bird they'd seen performing the courtship ritual. Black eyes, ringed with red, regarded them. Ardhi knelt and lowered his forehead to the ground. Beside her Saker stood so still for so long staring back at the female, she wondered if he was mesmerised.

She wanted to ask him why he was transfixed, but something held her back. Ardhi, still kneeling, started to speak in his own language. And he was addressing the bird – *as if it understood*.

Even then she was slow to understand. Saker was the one who could talk to birds – sort of – not Ardhi.

When the truth hit, it swamped her.

She warred with the idea forming in her mind. *It's impossible.*

Then: Sweet cankers, what purblind muckle-tops they'd been. This was why the *sakti* of the Chenderawasi had pushed and guided Saker to this point in time. This was why Ardhi had acted the way he had. This was why the path the dagger had chosen had led them to this place, to this moment.

So that Saker Rampion, who could speak to birds, could communicate with the ruler – or his regent – of the Chenderawasi Archipelago.

The Raja of Chenderawasi was – and always had been – not a man. Indeed, not human. A bird. No, there had to be a better word. These weren't just birds. Avian. They were Avians. The Raja Wiramulia's regalia weren't plumes of some long dead bird to be worn by the ruler on a hat; they were plumes ripped from the Raja's own breast as he lay dying. The Lowmians really had killed the Raja, without realising what they'd done. They'd thought to slaughter a bird, and had killed a king instead.

Sorrel fell to her knees, not so much in abeyance, but more in shock at realisation of just how far she was from all she had ever understood.

How dare we call these people Va-forsaken? We don't know the first thing about them!

Sakti.

The magic of the Chenderawasi Islands. Governed, or so Ardhi had hinted, by the Raja. *Sakti* planted in the dagger through the Raja's regalia and the Raja's blood.

And he, Saker, had missed the obvious: the *sakti* was in the plumes because they had been *part* of the Raja. As much an element of Raja Wiramulia as the blood in his veins and the bones of his body. The

Raja had not been human, any more than his heir was, or his consort. And these "birds" were not really birds. They had many bird-like features perhaps, but they were also creatures of intelligence and of magic.

The glimmer of understanding had begun to cast its light when he'd heard the song of the Raja Suryamuda. He'd understood the young bird's confused yearning as clearly as if he had used spoken words. But it wasn't until he'd come face to face with the Rani Marsyanda that he fully understood. When he heard inside his head not the nebulous thoughts and appetites of a bird as he was accustomed to hearing them but the articulate words of a queen spoken with royal imperiousness.

At first, she spoke not to him, but to Ardhi, and he guessed she was using the language of the islands – yet he heard her words inside his mind as if she spoke in Ardronese.

You have returned. So many seasons to complete your appointed task. More than just words, too. Saker felt the contempt in her sneer.

Ardhi kneeled and touched his forehead to the ground. "I regret that it took so long, *Tuanku Putri.*"

You have brought back the regalia?

"Yes, *Tuanku.*"

Show me.

Carefully Ardhi extracted the plumes from the bambu and laid all four on the ground. He then stepped away from them.

The Rani inclined her head towards her warriors, and four of them dropped to the ground, each to pick up a plume and fly away with it.

You have performed your task. I believe your blood is forfeit elsewhere. Understand that this was not my request.

Ardhi remained where he was, his head still bowed, his acquiescence written in his posture.

Pox on that, Saker thought.

And these strange people with their pale skins? she asked. *You have brought them here to pay for their crimes?*

"These are not the people who killed the Raja Wiramulia," Ardhi said. "They helped me return the plumes to you. They have a request."

Her disbelief was obvious to Saker. Her crest flared in incredulity, the red flashing iridescent as it opened. *You want them rewarded?* Her rage crackled through the words in his head. He bit his lip and curled his fingers tighter on the hilt of his sword while he waited for Ardhi's answer.

He had sworn not to kill any more birds with his actions and the idea that any of these glorious creatures would die on his blade made him feel ill. But then, he had pledged to protect Sorrel and Piper.

"No," Ardhi said. "Not rewarded. They ask for no reward, although they have suffered much to be here, and risked even more to help me return the plumes."

You trust *these pale creatures? After what the others did?*

"These are not from the same island, *Tuanku Putri*. Those others are dead long since."

By your hand, I trust.

Ardhi inclined his head.

So why are they here? Will they bear witness to the dagger's execution of its bearer as an empu *decreed?*

The snide satisfaction in her words made Saker want to cry out a protest. He subdued the impulse. *This is not my world.*

Ardhi continued, with a stoic calm Saker found astonishing. "If I may be permitted, I will tell you a story of this man and the woman and how they have danced the steps of the *sakti* of the kris and the Chenderawasi, that you may judge what is to be done."

A bird cannot smile. Instead, the Rani raised her head to the sun, and settled her crest low to her crown. *We always love a tale. Proceed.*

The second bird, her son, sat quietly, watching them all with intense interest like a lad striving to learn a complicated lesson.

Ardhi spoke Chenderawasi, and made no concessions to Saker's imperfect knowledge of his tongue, but it didn't matter; Saker didn't need to follow the story. He'd lived it.

Sorrel clutched his arm and whispered, her lips barely moving, "What's happening?"

"Ardhi is telling her who we are, and why we are here. Can you hear her when she speaks?"

She shook her head.

"I can. She's inside my head. It's weird. It sounds to me as if she's speaking our language; but I think Ardhi hears the same words in his own tongue." He took a deep breath. "This *sakti* of theirs is so powerful."

"I'm scared."

He looked around at the birds lined up along the top of the ruins. No, not birds. Avian warriors. Heads cocked, eyes unblinking, they were watching and listening to Ardhi's tale, just as intensely focused as the young Raja.

"I think Ardhi is under some sort of death sentence." Her hand tightened around his upper arm as he explained, his whisper as soft as her own, spoken with his lips almost touching her ear.

"We can't let Ardhi be murdered!" she protested.

"How do we stop it? Ardhi apparently acquiesced to this, years ago, before he even left Chenderawasi. He's hinted at this before, but so obscurely I didn't realise what he was saying."

"What about this Raja? Surely he has the power to change this death sentence!"

"I don't know. I'm getting the impression from his random thoughts that he's still very, very young in years. Like a – a six- or seven-year-old would be to us."

When he glanced at her, he saw she was biting her lip, hard, as if pain was the only way she could control her anxiety.

"Sorrel, we can't assume we know anything here."

Raja Suryamuda began preening himself as he listened to Ardhi, stroking feathers with his beak to put them in order, continually raising and lowering the ruff around his neck and spreading and closing his magnificent tail. Fidgeting, Saker thought. *Like a bored child.*

"Has he said anything to you?" she asked. "The Raja?"

"No. I catch his thoughts, just as I do our own ordinary birds. But his are more coherent. More . . . human. But childlike."

He eased Piper into a more comfortable position. She was sound asleep, still exhausted. *I'm sorry, little one. We are trying to help you. We just want to keep you safe.*

When Ardhi finished relating the story of how the *sakti* had inter-vened to bring all of them together in Chenderawasi, the Rani switched her gaze to Saker. *Why should this child's future matter to me?* she asked him.

He didn't have to ask if she would understand him. He knew she would. "I don't know, *Tuanku Putri*," he replied and he couldn't keep an edge of anger out of his voice. "Ask your Chenderawasi *sakti*. We are here because the plumes or the dagger – or both – made sure we came. That is all I can say."

She looked at Ardhi. *And this is true?*

"Yes, *Tuanku Putri*."

She dropped down to a lower perch with an elegant agility, so that she was on a level with Saker. *Bring the human child here*, she ordered.

He stepped forward until he was close enough for her to touch Piper, all too aware of the weapons she had at her disposal. Although she did not have spurs on her legs, he knew the vicious curve of her beak or the claws on her toes could have ripped his throat out.

When she bent to touch Piper, he saw there were two hooks on the bend of her wings. She used these like pincers, and gently picked up Piper's arm at the wrist. Piper stirred, murmuring her unease, but she didn't wake.

The Rani laid the arm down again. *You're sure our* sakti *wished this child to come to our lands?*

He felt her mystification. Her anxiety.

"We wondered if it was Sorrel it wanted," he replied, "but I think in the end it pushed Sorrel because of Piper, not the other way around."

The Rani nodded, and he was taken aback because the gesture was all human. *I believe you are right*, she conceded. *And I think I know why, but you have not told Ardhi the whole of the truth, have you?*

"No. There were secrets that were not mine to divulge."

You will tell me. There was no hint of compromise in her words.

"If – if that is necessary for Piper's well-being."

Give the child back to this Sorrel woman.

He did as she asked.

Sorrel, pale-faced, took her wordlessly.

"Courage," he whispered. "She wishes to speak to me. In private, I think."

She nodded. She didn't have to tell him how hard this was for her; he knew.

The Rani tilted her head to look at Ardhi out of one dark eye. *Stay here with this woman. I wish to speak at length with this man.*

Ardhi bowed his head. The look of devastation on his face was one that Saker hoped he'd never see again, from anyone.

Follow me, the Rani said.

Typical royalty, he thought. *Va forbid that they make requests, or deliver explanations. No, they just give orders.*

Feigning the meekness Ardhi had shown, he followed her as she left the ruins. She flew while he walked, stumbling over blocks of stone overgrown with creepers as he tried to keep up without the benefit of a path. Fortunately it wasn't far. When he caught up with her, she had alighted on a rock at the edge of a cliff.

Sit here beside me, she ordered. The stone she indicated was at the edge of a dizzying drop, overlooking another tree-crammed valley; her perch was higher. Beyond the next ridge line, there were further glimpses of ocean and beyond that, more islands. At least, he thought, they'd never run out of timber to build in this land.

He sat and dangled his legs over the drop, hoping she didn't take it into her head to push him over the edge.

She ruffled her feathers. *Tell me what secret it is that you keep – the one that concerns the child.*

"Her sire could be one of three men. She is a twin and her brother is the acknowledged heir of the Regal – the Raja – of the land called Lowmeer. This Regal has ordered his men to fetch more Chenderawasi plumes back to his land."

Are you one of those three?

"Yes."

She bent down to take his hand between her wing claws. She held it for a while, her eyes closed, then released him. *You do not have what ails her. If she was contaminated by her father, and not her mother, then you are not that man.*

"What ails her is *inherited*?"

Oh, yes. That is certain.

"Do you know what it is?"

I have met it before.

"Here, in Chenderawasi?" He hoped he didn't sound as incredulous as he felt.

Yes.

"Can you cure it?"

There is no cure. The wisest thing to do is to kill her. Leave her here, and I will see that it is done. Tell the woman any untruth you please. It is kinder for her not to know. Her love for this child is obvious.

He swallowed back bile, his mind screaming his negation of her words. "What – what is wrong with Piper?"

She will grow up to kill. But I think you know that.

"That wasn't my question."

She was born a sorcerer. All I can tell you is how it happens – happened – here, in the past. But first, this twin of hers. He must also have inherited this sorcerer's blood. You say he will one day rule in the land responsible for murder of my life mate? Her words were as hard as fired steel.

"Yes."

Then he must also die. And if the present ruler is the one who sired her, and he is to blame rather than the mother, then he too must die.

"I – I believe it was another man."

The man who marked you.

He jerked in surprise. That remark had caught him off guard. He looked down at his open palm, expecting to see the black smudge had manifested itself again, but there was nothing. He raised his gaze to meet hers, trying to accustom himself to only ever looking into one eye of hers.

Oh yes, little man. I can see the mark. Whoever marked you did so in order for his flock to recognise you for what you are.

Her tone was patronising, and he felt himself bristling. "What am I?" he demanded.

His enemy. I would not be here talking to you were it otherwise. She leant forward again, and this time she used the hooks on her wing to turn his hand palm up. *My* sakti *enables me to see this. Because you have been marked as a sorcerer's enemy, I have trusted you.*

"We are playing with words. And words will not solve my problem – or yours."

My problem? He heard her contempt, and her crest opened up, flaring with colour.

"If these children are sorcerers," he said, "then tell me it does not worry you that one of them will one day rule the nation that covets the spices of this island and the plumes of the Chenderawasi. The nation whose warriors slaughtered Raja Wiramulia for his regalia without even knowing of its power."

She lowered her head until her beak was on a level with his eyes, a clear threat. *That is why you will kill these children. And the parent sorcerer.*

He shrugged, as if indifferent. "And by 'we', you mean Sorrel and me?" He snorted. "The sorcerer, perhaps. But neither of us would ever be allowed anywhere near his son."

She ruffled her feathers and was silent, thinking.

"*Tuanku Putri*," he said, "I think we need to stop playing games. You need to tell me all you know, so that I have the weapons to fight. To protect my land. To protect your land. And I will, if I have the right weapons." When she said nothing, he added, "You win more arguments with your mind than with your claws, or your warriors. I need information about this evil you feel in this child. I need to know its nature."

She gave him a long, hard glare with her one black eye. He stared back, yet he still missed the instant when she decided to act. One moment she was as still as the stone she stood upon; the next she flew at him. He had a brief vision of her wings opening up, wider across than he was tall, then the soles of her feet slammed into his chest. He fell backwards, hard. The breath was driven from his lungs. Pain radiated from his back where it had been bruised on the uneven rocks.

Before he gathered his wits enough to realise what had happened, the sharp points of her claws on one foot pricked his skin deep enough to draw blood. The other foot she then planted – with a shade more care – across his face. A claw rested on each eyelid, while the long back talon was locked under his chin.

All I have to do is squeeze, she said. He couldn't see her face, but he heard her satisfaction. She relished his helplessness. *Do not reach for your blade, pale man.*

Cautiously, he slitted open his eyes. "Why would I? I want your help, not your enmity."

If you ever betray us, you will be blinded and your male organs ripped from you. Do you understand?

He almost nodded, decided that would be foolish beyond measure, and whispered instead. "Yes, *Tuanku Putri*."

She released her hold on him, then flapped once to return to her perch on the rock. She fluffed her wings and folded them neatly over her back. *A reminder of what I can do. Of what I am prepared to do if you misuse what I am about to tell you.*

Damn her for a harridan. She had intended all along to give him what he wanted. He inclined his head. "There will be no misuse. Nothing you tell me will be used to hurt the Chenderawasi."

Good, she said.

Even before she began, he knew it'd be a story that would change the way he viewed his world.

38

Rani Marsyanda

Sakti, Rani Marsyanda told him, came from the land. All things in the Chenderawasi islands were interconnected, dependent on one another: land, reefs, sea, forest, animals, people, the Chenderawasi Avians.

No one part of Chenderawasi could survive without the others, she said; their lives were intertwined and their deaths linked. Why else was there only one word, Chenderawasi, for their land, for the people, for the Avians? What was important was to maintain balance. The greater the balance, the greater the health of the land; the healthier the land, the more power it had at its heart; the more power there was, the more *sakti*; the more *sakti*, the more they had to use to mend any ills that came their way.

"What you've described is the same as our Shenat beliefs," Saker murmured. "Your *sakti* is similar to our witchery."

Who grants your witcheries? she asked.

Once he would have replied "Va", without even thinking. Now he said, "Shrine guardians. We call them the unseen guardians."

He heard her laugh the same way he heard her words, in his head, but her real laugh had no sound. It manifested only in her crest, which changed colour to the deepest purple rippling with iridescent waves of gold as she raised it around her head like a halo.

He was fascinated.

Unseen? she said. *Forgive me, I find the concept amusing. We are visual creatures, never unseen! However, if your invisible guardians bestow your witcheries, doubtless they can be equated with us on one level. Of course,* she added with what she obviously thought was unassailable logic, *they cannot be truly our equals if they are not also royal.*

He schooled his face to neutrality.

All sakti *comes from the sun, the soil and the sea. We are merely the . . . the channel. Passing it from its powerful origins into a usable – and limited – form. Doubtless your unseen guardians do likewise.*

He thought about that. "I'm not sure what they can do. Certainly, when they gift a witchery, it is limited. And it can be taken away if it is misused."

She nodded. *That is normal here, too. The gift of a plume, as Ardhi was given, was an exception given in exceptional circumstances. Even gifting a few wisps of a plume for a* sakti *kris is a gift that has to be earned. What you have to comprehend is that we Avians do not use* sakti *ourselves.*

Saker felt as if she had struck him a blow. If they did not use *sakti*, how then could they cure Piper? "But – I don't understand. You surely are using *sakti* to talk to me?"

We have certain inborn talents which we can use. Use of language is one of them. The growth of the regalia plumes is inborn within some families. Those who grow such plumes are deemed royal. The plumes have power, and we can gift a few wisps to Chenderawasi men and women to use. But we ourselves? We cannot use them.

When Saker frowned, she gave an example. *We do not heal, for instance, but we can gift part of a plume to a human, who can use the power in it to heal others. Power must always be limited, because unlimited power always ends up as an evil.*

"Ardhi seemed to think you could help us," he said.

She snorted. *Your words are spoken without thought, like water gushing from a spring! Did no one tell you to have all the facts before you jump to conclusions? Giving help and curing are two different matters. Let me finish before you interrupt so rudely again.*

He inclined his head respectfully. Pox on't, he would have loved to have listened to her and Fritillary have a conversation.

We are not birds, she said, *no more than a dolphin is a fish, or humans are chattering monkeys. We are Chenderawasi! Males of some family lines have* sakti *in their bones and their blood and produce plumes which gather* sakti *with each growth. Our Rajas must always be such a one.*

I wish to tell you a tale from our history, which may help you. It took place over five hundred years ago, by your measure of time.

Saker kept his mouth shut and listened.

The Chenderawasi – she meant the Avians, not the people – had a tradition of placing the bodies of their dead in caves high in a cliffside, deep in the mountains of the main island. In fact many Chenderawasi Avians, when they realised they did not have long to live, flew there in order to die.

This was also the place where they took their moulted regalia plumes, if those plumes contained unused *sakti*. They believed this was a place inaccessible to humans, and therefore the regalia, and the power within, was safe.

Over the centuries, this graveyard had thus become a repository of an immense concentration of unbound power. Ordinary plumes rotted, but the regalia with *sakti* lasted for generations and was under no one's control. Left alone, the *sakti* would gradually seep back into the earth, from where it had come.

Their ancestors never dreamed any man would want to disturb such a sacred place, she said, her narration faltering under the weight of her grief. Those ancestors were wrong. While lost in the forest, a hunter – she referred to him simply as Vile Man – observed a funeral procession flight of a recently deceased Chenderawasi Avian, as the bier was carried into the cliff caves by a flock of mourners.

Avarice drove him to find a way to enter the cave. Knowing the power of the plumes, he intended to steal some of them. Once inside, he was exposed to so much unbound *sakti* that he couldn't help breathing it in, absorbing it through his skin, swallowing it along with the water he drank from the pools in the cave. Probably that was unwitting; he would not, after all, have been able to see the *sakti*.

He stole some plumes and made his way back to his village, where he began to plan. Gathering similar like-minded villains around him, he had gained so much power he could coerce others and seize power in the islands. The outcome was devastating. There was war. War between villages. War between clans. Chenderawasi Avians were hunted and killed. Whole villages disappeared. People were subjugated and enslaved, used and abused.

The tide was finally turned when an *empu*, a blademaster, allied himself and his apprentices with a flock of the remaining Chenderawasi. Together they developed a way to fold the barbs of a Chenderawasi regalia plume into a kris. Whoever owned such a weapon was not so vulnerable to coercion, and the daggers themselves used the inherited wisdom of Chenderawasi *sakti* to guide their owners.

Even so, the Rani said, *it took many years to bring peace back to the islands and to return all the lost plumes to their rightful place. Now, of course, we have other ways of hiding and protecting the regalia of the dead.*

She fell silent while Saker sorted through all she had said. Eventually he remarked quietly, "That's not the whole story, is it?"

She sighed. *It was more complex than that. Which brings me to your problem. The child you call Piper.*

His heart turned over in his chest. He and Sorrel would have to make life and death decisions about a child they both loved. How was he ever going to tell her that? He had no idea. He murmured, more to himself, "A devil-kin."

No. I think your devil-kin have a different origin. From what Ardhi said, that sounds like a working of sorcery, and an imperfect one at that. A sorcerer, though, is someone else. Something worse. Something evil. I know you don't want to believe that anyone can be born evil, but they can and are – if they are birthed by another such.

Sweet Va. This had just gone from desperate to impossible.

The Rani continued, elaborating on the story she'd just told. The Vile Man had not been born that way. In fact, once he found the unbound *sakti*, he could have used it for good. Another man or woman might have, but not him. He was a man who always chose the corrupt way, the way he could satisfy his lusts with no regard for others. His motivations were revenge for perceived slights, the absorption of power to command others, the accumulation of wealth, the need to indulge his compulsion to hurt and mock. Once he'd absorbed the *sakti* that was unbound within the caves, it was his choice how to use it, and that was the way he chose.

He became a sorcerer, not so much by choice, but because he was the kind of man who was corrupted after imbibing too much raw power. It changed him physically, allowing that corruption to pass down to his children. He marked his friends with a black smutch, and marked his enemies with a different black mark.

My ancestors fought them, she said. *Ardhi's ancestors fought him. Eventually he was destroyed. They thought they had solved the problem.*

"But?"

He'd given birth to other sorcerers. They grew up. They killed with impunity, and now there were five of them, not one. It took us a hundred years to root them and their children out and rid ourselves of the blight they had caused. You must kill this child, Piper, and her brother. They are not human. They won't have choices, not when they are grown. They will be what they were born to be.

Saker's horror burgeoned with her every word. He wanted to deny the truth of all she said, to attack her logic, to prove her wrong – but he couldn't find the facts to refute her, and she was relentless.

If you want to know the source of your sorcerer's power, then look to his past, or his ancestry. Somewhere, sometime, someone who had the seeds of wickedness within him imbibed too much of your witchery, perhaps by accident, perhaps deliberately. That person, or those people, are the cause of the plague Ardhi told me about, the source of your devil-kin. And every sorcerer must be killed before you will be safe again.

He whispered, "I cannot kill a baby. Any baby. Especially one I love." *Especially when I once cared for her mother.* "Nor can I ask Sorrel to stand by while this child is murdered." *By the oak – not when she had her own daughter foully murdered!* "This is against all I ever believed in. I would jump off this cliff, right now, rather than do such a heinous thing."

She stared at him, unspeaking, and his silence lengthened into a mute appeal he did not know how to voice.

With unexpected suddenness, she flung herself off the cliff, dropping into the valley before spreading her wings to catch a wind and coast across the canopy. He stood and watched and envied her the gift of flight. When she curved back towards him, he shouted at her, his rage ripping the words from him. "Damn you! There has to be a better way!"

She ignored him and flew on. He watched and then, when she turned back and coasted past him once more, he cried out to her again. "Don't you believe in your own *sakti*? The kris and your plume – they sent us here! Why? *Why?*"

Our sakti *doesn't want to be used for ill! It happened with the Vile Man, and it will do anything to prevent it happening again.*

"Then why didn't it kill Piper back there in Lowmeer? The kris – I saw it fly through the air and stab a man in the back. It did that to *save* us! If it had done nothing, then we could all have perished. But it *saved* us with a deliberate act against another."

She circled the valley again, flying so far away she was only a speck against the canopy. It was fully a quarter of an hour before she returned and came in to land. She smoothed down her feathers, raised and lowered her ruff, then fixed him with a single red-rimmed eye.

I don't know why. But you are right. There must be a reason. I will call together the heads of all the Families. Take the child and go back to your ship. We will speak again when we have decided what is the best solution. If there is one.

"And Ardhi?" he asked.

His death was not something we required. That was the decision of the empu, *the blademaster. It takes time to make a blade of power and Ardhi didn't have time to wait. So the* empu *used the power of sacrifice. He built a Chenderawasi kris using the promise of a life to awaken the* sakti *in the plume barbs. That life was Ardhi's. The choice was Ardhi's and he made it freely. He must take the kris back to the blademaster and fulfil that vow.*

"And if he doesn't?"

She shrugged her shoulders in a very human gesture. *I don't know. I doubt even the blademaster knows. But it doesn't matter anyway; Ardhi will do it whatever we think! Do you not know him? Why do you think I did not insist on his punishment? Because he punishes himself in far worse ways than his Raja or I could ever impose. Every day that he lives . . .*

Despair soaked his thoughts. *Beggar me speechless. She is as hard as rock.* "He has to kill himself? Or does the blademaster have to kill him?"

Ask him. Now take the child and the woman and Ardhi, and go back to your ship. We will have an answer for you the day after tomorrow. Whether it will be the answer you want, I don't yet know. We will meet you after sunrise. Not here; at Batuguli. Ardhi knows the place.

"Sit down," Sorrel ordered Ardhi, pointing to the wooden signal-flag locker. She was perched on the other end of it, while Saker was seated a pace away on the hatch cover near the mizzen mast. "We want to talk to you about not dying."

"I'm a crew member, remember? I have work to do—"

"I haven't seen you swabbing a deck since we left *Spice Winds*," Saker remarked drily. "And I distinctly heard Juster give you the rank of third mate after you sailed us safely out of Javenka."

"And don't officers have things to do, too?" Ardhi waved a hand at the lagoon. Boats of varying shapes and sizes bustled between ship and shore, laden with bricks in one direction, bringing back supplies and spices in the other. The woody musk aroma of fresh nutmeg and mace in the air overwhelmed the smell of the sea and the forest. Sorrel suspected it was seeping into the seams of the ship and would remain with them all the way to the Va-cherished Hemisphere.

Ardhi glared at Saker. "I'm the only person on board who speaks the Chenderawasi language fluently. I'm the interpreter."

"They can manage without you for a bit," Saker said.

"We really need to talk to you about not dying," she added. The two men had been speaking in Pashali, but she decided to stick with her own language. She needed all her powers of persuasion.

"You can't change what has been agreed," Ardhi said, but he did sit down nonetheless.

She wanted to put her arms around him, to tell him they both cared too much to see him killed. Far too much, if she was honest. Instead she leaned over and placed Piper in his lap, where the child hauled herself up to stand in order to pull at his head band.

"Addi!" she said happily. "Addi!"

Tears gathered at the back of Sorrel's eyes, but she blinked them away.

It was the day after they'd been to meet the Raja, and even though all of them were safely back on board ship, Sorrel was still shaken. The day before had been one of the most exhausting she'd ever spent. Piper had cried so much, affected by forces none of them fully understood. On the way back to *Golden Petrel* her distress had been intensified by a downpour that had lasted an hour and left them utterly drenched. Back on board, Surgeon Barklee had ended up giving her a sleeping draught to calm her down and, thanks be, she had slept through the night and woken her usual happy self.

I wish I could say the same, Sorrel thought, but all they had learned ashore haunted her like a recurring dream. Every time she pushed the horror away, it returned: Piper was probably Prime Fox's child, a potential sorcerer, as was her brother, the Prince-regal, heir to the Basalt Throne. And Ardhi thought he had to die.

She glared at him. "You can't agree to be killed, just like that. It's – it's – unthinkable!"

"I knew the price of the kris then, and that I'd have to pay it one day."

"No," she said, pushing back that wretched impulse to weep, "Ardhi, please. Listen to me. On board *Spice Winds*, I learned what it was to have friends. You and Saker and Banstel, you made my life bearable! And now on *Golden Petrel*, I've learned what real friendship is. People who care about me, who care what happens to me and who have done their best to help me. Saker, Lord Juster, Surgeon Barklee, Banstel, Mate Finch, Mate Cranald . . . And you. How can you expect Saker and me to allow you to go meekly to your death? We won't do it!"

"My promise to the *empu* was made long before I met you." His troubled eyes were as dark and as deep as a forest pool. "I'm sorry."

She took a deep breath, steadied herself. *You have to find the right words, Sorrel. A man's life depends on what you say.* "Yesterday I learned that the child I love just as much as I loved my own is a sorcerer. Something so horrible, I – I find it hard to accept its truth. I am still battling to cope with even the idea of its possibility. A baby, born with no choice of the kind of person they will grow up to be? An evil man seduced a princess, in order to place his child on a throne. To place a sorcerer on a throne. That is true evil, as vile a scheme as can exist."

She paused, but when he opened his mouth to reply, she held up her hand to prevent his words. "No. You will listen to what I have to say. This Chenderawasi *sakti*: the Rani told Saker yesterday that the purpose of it is to protect your lands and thus yourselves. In both our worlds, if a person with a witchery acts in bad faith, their power is taken from them. Even without that, the power is always limited."

He nodded.

"You were eighteen years old when you made a mistake which had horrible consequences. You did your best to make amends. You couldn't bring the Raja back to life, but you did bring his regalia back, with the help of the kris."

He nodded again.

"The Rani told Saker *sakti* comes from the land, the sea, the sunlight. And that this *sakti* often accumulates in the blood and feathers and bones of special people, like Raja Wiramulia. Is your blood special in that way?"

This time he shook his head.

She was relentless. "The Raja's blood and bone and feathers were all used in the making of the kris. Because of the kris the plumes are here, in Chenderawasi. The kris did its job. It did its job *without your blood*. And yet you think your blood, your life, is still required? The Rani didn't tell you that. Nor did the kris."

"The *empu* said it was."

"You asked the blademaster to do something in a hurry, without the usual time for proper craftsmanship. What if he was afraid of failure and thought a sacrifice must be necessary to overcome the problems of crafting such a dagger in a limited time? So he sacrificed you, because he hated you for causing the death of his Raja. But what if it wasn't necessary? What if it was just something that gave him confidence when he needed it?"

"He would never have lied!"

"He didn't lie! He believed it. He was just wrong."

Ardhi was silent. He looked away from her, his gaze fixed on the decking.

He's uncertain. Good. She reached out a hand and closed it over his. "We don't want you to die. We especially don't want you to die for nothing." Underneath her hand she felt his fingers tense.

He has beautiful fingers. Climbing was his witchery; perhaps that had something to do with it. Most sailors had hands as rough as the hempen rope they hauled and as hard as the decks they scrubbed, and although he might not have been an ordinary seaman any more, he was still up aloft every day. Even so, his hands were elegant as well as strong.

"There's one way," she said, "that might tell you whether your death serves a purpose or not. Saker says the kris makes its own decisions."

"That's true," Saker agreed. "It jabbed me in the leg the day we first met. You say you didn't throw it at me: it left you and flew through the air to me. And what about when you broke into my room in Throssel Palace? You say it refused to return to you!"

"We think you should not allow the blademaster to make decisions about your life or death," Sorrel said. "You should ask the kris."

He raised his head to look from her to Saker and back again. "Princess? What princess? What evil man do you mean? And what throne?"

She shot a look at Saker. "Ah. That's something we have to tell you. It wasn't our secret to share," she said, "but the situation has changed and you should know everything now. You see, Saker and I are wondering if maybe your task is not finished yet. The Chenderawasi Islands are still in danger from Lowmeer."

"No, oh no." He was shaking his head, an appalled expression on his face. "I don't want to leave my home again. Don't ask that of me."

This time it was Saker who was relentless. "Will you ever be able to live here again?" he asked. "Isn't that why you are willing to die – because you have no life here any more?"

Sorrel had to turn away from Ardhi then. She couldn't bear to see his pain.

"We are going to tell you about who Piper is," Saker said. "Although that is perhaps not quite as important as who her brother is. Then you might understand why you cannot die, not yet." He leaned forward and tickled Piper's tummy; she giggled and squirmed. "You see, Ardhi, you have not done nearly enough yet to absolve yourself. You've barely started."

Sorrel winced. That was cruel. But then, if it saved his life . . .

39

The Outcast

Ardhi dropped his shirt on to the deck, and dived into the clear water of the lagoon. He swam underwater, clearly visible, with an economy of effort uncanny to those used to the cold oceans of the Va-cherished lands.

"He makes it look so easy," Juster said in Sorrel's ear.

She nodded. She'd been thinking the same thing. Ardhi was at home in the sea. He belonged here, in these islands with their beaches of dazzling white and waters so warm and translucent – and she and Saker were asking him to leave again.

"I haven't paid him yet for his services to the ship," Juster remarked. "Can I take it that he'll be returning? Because right at this moment, he looks as if he's trying to escape."

"He is," said Saker. "I don't think he can, though."

Ardhi surfaced and trod water for a moment. The twist of batik cloth he wore as a head band was still in place, as was the sarong he'd twisted up between his thighs. His kris he had thrust through the waist at his back.

He looks as if he is trying to go back to what he was, she thought. As if he can shed his sailor's clothes and turn back the clock. *But Saker is right; he can't return. They won't have him.*

They'd told him about Princess Mathilda, and the Prince-regal, about Prime Valerian Fox. He'd absorbed it all, but said nothing. Saker had attempted unsuccessfully to extract a promise that he wouldn't do anything until they'd talked to the Rani again, but all he agreed to was to think about it. A little later he'd divested himself of his sailor's clothes and dived over the side.

"I want to talk to you, Saker," Juster said. "I don't want to be caught napping by the arrival of a Lowmian ship. I need your help."

"What can I do?"

"Tell me when they appear on the horizon, of course. Or better still, *before* they appear on the horizon. So we can get clean away. I don't want to engage any ship until I'm sure it's laden to the gunwales with cargo."

"That's hardly likely to be the case if you are buying up all of the nutmeg harvest here!"

He grinned. "Exactly. *Spice Winds* is no longer my target. The other ships of the fleet will have a nicely varied cargo. Ideally, we sneak away before any Lowmian ship arrives here, lurk around the Spicerie until we can capture one or two of their fluyts, put our own sailors on board to sail them back to Throssel, and everybody goes home happy."

"Fundamentally flawed reasoning. The Lowmians will be extremely *un*happy."

"Which worries me not the twitch of a kitten's tail. My liege will be delighted."

"You are incorrigible. So you want me to take the longboat out and start patrolling the horizon?"

"You can be very obtuse, witan! If I wanted anyone to do that I'd choose someone who knows a cleat from a clewline. I want you to use your fobbing witchery, you ninny. What better lookout is there than a bird way up in the air, miles out to sea?"

"I can't exactly *talk* to them, you know. What do you expect me to do? 'Excuse me, Master Seagull, can you go look for *Spice Winds* and then come back and tell me the precise latitude . . .'"

"Tush! Of course you can. Talk to them, I mean. Ask nicely and they do all sorts of things for you! I've seen it, remember?"

He sighed. "You have no idea how difficult it is. I might get them to look, but how can they tell where the ship is afterwards? 'It was next to the most delicious shoal of minnow, and not far from some floating bladderwort.'"

"I have every faith that a witan of your intelligence will overcome any minor flaws in communication," Juster said blithely. "How long will it take before you have some birds on the lookout about twenty nautical miles from here?"

"I've no idea."

"Find out, will you?" With that, Juster disappeared to check the stowing of another load of nutmeg.

Exasperated, he slapped his palm down on the bulwark. "Beggar it, Sorrel. He's making a privateer of me."

Sighing, she said, "Nothing is clear-cut any more, is it? I discovered that when I killed my husband. The waters are always murky to me now."

"To me too."

"Look – Ardhi has met someone on the beach."

He shaded his eyes. "A woman. Let's hope it's a friend who'll be able to talk him out of this wish to sacrifice himself."

"I think I want to go ashore," she said.

"That's not a good idea. We don't know enough about these people, and your grasp of the language is still fairly rudimentary. I can't go with you, not if I have to help Juster."

She rolled her eyes. "Witchery . . ."

"And what if anyone here with a *sakti* witchery can see through your glamour? Ardhi can!"

"Yes, but I can spot folk with witcheries too, don't forget. And tailor my actions accordingly."

"Don't go alone, Sorrel. Wait until I can go with you." He pulled a face. "Right now I have to chat to some birds, although how I'm going to persuade them to tell me what they see, I've no idea."

"Tell them to come back and waggle their wings, or something."

"Wait for me and I'll go with you."

He didn't wait for her reply, though, and she pulled a face at his retreating back. *Vex you, Saker, I don't always have to do what you want and I don't believe you are any older or wiser than I am!*

Ardhi reached the shore and waded up onto the sands, squinting as the glare dazzled him. He felt behind his back to make sure he still had the kris, wrung out the cloth of his sarong as best he could and turned to look back at *Golden Petrel*. Juster was right. It was a beautiful vessel. However, its array of gunports, each one hiding a cannon, meant it could also be deadly. He must never forget that.

All this time I accepted that I was going to die . . . that it was neces-sary. What if Sorrel is right? Mentor Istanel had said something about superstition once. He'd called it the assassin of common sense. *If you can't see it, touch it, hear it, smell it, taste it or prove it exists, then begin to wonder about its reality.*

Standing on the beach, he watched the *prau* and canoes making their way from the port at the other end of the lagoon to where the ship was anchored while he considered all Saker and Sorrel had just told him. A sorcerer manipulating a princess so his son would one day sit on the Basalt Throne. A sorcerer who obviously hadn't bargained on the princess having twins. A sorcerer who probably had something to do with the Horned Plague. A sorcerer who had a financial interest in a fleet being built to trade in spices. Oh, Saker and Sorrel could talk of a Lowmian threat to Chenderawasi integrity, but what of an Ardronese one? It had never occurred to any of them that he would be just as worried about Ardronese incursions as Lowmian ones.

How could Chenderawasi fight ships with cannons and men with muskets? He shook his head in disbelief. Sometimes these Va-cherished folk could be so . . . so *imperceptive.*

He slipped the kris out of its sheath. The gold of Raja Wiramulia's plumes was as bright and as alive as ever – which meant that the *sakti* within was as powerful as ever. He touched the blade, seeking wisdom and thought he heard a whisper in reply; not words though. Never words.

"Ardhi?"

He whirled, the kris still in his hand.

And was stilled.

Lastri.

She smiled. "Are you going to stab me with that?"

Hastily, he tucked the dagger back into his waistband. "You? Never!" The words were husky, not at all the way he'd wanted to sound if he ever saw her again. And not the words he'd played in his mind all those years, either.

She was older, of course. A woman now, her face matured, calmer, but still as beautiful. His gaze dropped to her figure and his comprehension jolted him as he assimilated its implication.

She was pregnant.

"You – you're married."

She nodded. "This is our second child."

Oh, sands . . . There had been a time when they'd both thought her children would also be his. *We were seventeen. An age ago . . .*

She said calmly, gesturing at the protuberance of her abdomen, "I wanted you to hear it from me. I heard you were back."

He was speechless, wondering if she meant she wanted to save him the pain of hearing it from someone else – or revel in his pain when he heard it. In shock, he realised he had no idea which was true. She was no longer the person he'd known. He couldn't even guess whom she had married.

He forced a smile. "You didn't tell me you'd wait. I hope you're happy."

An odd expression that crossed her face told him that she was the one at a loss now: she didn't know whether he was being sarcastic or genuine.

He gave a low laugh. "I've had four years to know this moment would come, Lastri. I loved you deeply once, but we were very young, and the tides have changed many times since. I hope you walked softly with the wind in those years."

"I wasted time in bitterness," she said. "But the waves come and go, and children change everything. The wind is kind now, as I hope it will be to you."

"Who—?" he asked, even though he knew the question should be irrelevant.

"Eka. He was always after me, even when you were here."

He blinked. *Eka?* Who never bothered with schooling, who cared for nothing but fishing and playing *sepak takraw* on the beach with the other village lads?

He was about to reply when they both heard the call of a Chenderawasi echoing over the forest, and they looked up to listen.

As the sounds faded away, she said, "My grandfather demands your death now that you have returned. Don't listen to him, Ardhi. He's a bitter old man who resented having to craft a *sakti* kris for a foolish young man." She nodded towards the ship. "When they leave, sail with them. There's nothing for you here, and you don't deserve to die."

"This is my land." The lump in his throat was large enough to make breathing an effort.

"Not any more," she said.

She turned on her heel and walked away.

Sorrel, leaning against the bulwarks, watched. When the woman left, Ardhi did not move for a long time. He just stood there, looking after her as she headed towards a canoe pulled up on the edge of the lagoon a couple of hundred paces away. He continued to watch while she paddled away towards the town without looking back.

Sorrel turned her mind to hitching a ride on one of the *prau* returning to the shore, hoping her grasp of the language would be enough to arrange to be deposited on the beach.

One last walk down the forest trail between the village of the metalworkers and the lagoon, avoiding the port and the town and its bustle. . .

He dawdled, stretching his life for extra moments of memory. On the edge of the village, he paused for one last look at his childhood. Another village then, of course, in the south, but not so different. Men at their jobs, chopping wood, oiling their tools or cleaning their forges, the women pounding the red hot *lada* in the mortars, or grinding the rice flour – not in their kitchens but outside under the fruit trees where they could chat to their neighbours or watch the children play their games on the beaten earth.

He remembered a time when both his parents had been alive, and he'd been a child like that one playing there, wobbling along on the two half-shells of a coconut with the aid of cord he'd made himself from husk fibres.

Unseen, he watched the *empu* walk from forge to kiln and back again. He had aged more than four years warranted. Not only had the furrows in his face deepened and his hair thinned, but his back had bent almost double and his hands were so crippled Ardhi doubted he could still craft any kris, let alone a *sakti* one. The old man hobbled with the help of a cane, and stopped dead when he realised who it was watching him. Ardhi came closer, but the words of greeting dried up in his mouth.

Villagers began to gather around them, alerted by the bright-eyed children who'd seen his approach. Their silence was strange; even the youngsters were quiet. No one greeted him; no one even met his gaze. Except Damardi.

Fixing Ardhi with a glare from under the wild thicket of his eyebrows, the *empu* said, "So. You've come back. Wearing my kris still."

"The one you made me, certainly. But it is mine, *empu*, and it knows my hand. It has crossed many oceans and many lands since it left your forge. It has done all that was asked of it, and more." He'd kept his tone even, polite and – he hoped – unflinching.

"Give it to me."

He made no move to obey. "You told me that for the *sakti* in this kris to come to life, it needed my promise to die. I gave that promise. You said it was this kris which would drink my blood when I returned." He drew it from the twist of cloth at his waist, turned it over and over in his hands. "You crafted it, yet it was also my sweat that dropped into its molten metal. If it wants my life, so be it. But be careful, *empu*, for it has a mind of its own. Do not go against its wishes."

The old man snorted. "You mannerless boy! You would tell me what to do?"

"A warning in good faith can be neither bad-mannered nor an order, *empu*." He handed it to the bladesmith, hilt first, and knelt on the bare earth. He knew how executions were carried out: a blade driven behind the collarbone downwards into the arteries to the heart.

A quick death.

Damardi stepped forward and placed a hand on his right shoulder, as if to hold him in place.

A stir ran through the watching crowd. Not voices, but rather a shuffling of feet, an unsettling catch of breath that ran like a contagion from person to person. They knew his guilt, they knew of the promise given, yet still they dreaded an execution. Death was never to be taken lightly. Nonetheless, he knew no one would intervene. This was between him and the blademaster – and *Sri Kris*.

Or so he thought, until a voice rang out, clear and imperious, coming from the line of coconut palms behind him. He turned his head to look, but saw no one there. The blademaster glanced around as well, his expression more annoyed than worried.

The words had been clear, if strangely accented, and they were immediately repeated. "Do not kill him!"

He recognised the voice but for a moment he couldn't place it.

And then, a third time, "Do not kill him!"

Recognition came, and with it, horror. *Splinter it. That's Sorrel.* He finally located her standing next to a coconut palm, blending herself into the trunk. She was holding a fallen coconut, and while he watched, she lobbed it towards the blademaster. It fell with a thud and rolled to his feet. To the villagers, it must have appeared to fly upwards without cause, before falling out of the sky.

There was a stunned silence, then one of the children screamed, "*Pontianak! Ghosts!*" Youngsters squealed and fled in every direction, but most of the villagers just looked around in bewilderment, still seeking to know who had called out the prohibition.

Sorrel stepped out from under the palms. She was still using her glamour, this time creating a curtain around herself, supposedly of golden plumes, and within the centre, instead of her own form, she had approximated the outline of a giant kris. The whole creation wavered and undulated as if she found it difficult to manage. The result was mesmerising.

Ardhi groaned, wincing. She was as foolish as a cross-eyed crab! Damardi would never forgive her if he saw through her witchery.

A chorus of voices yelled warnings: "*Adua! Hantu! Lari!* Look out! Ghosts! Run!" Some of the watchers scattered, disappearing into their houses and closing the doors. Others, braver, remained to stare.

The *empu* looked back at Ardhi, suddenly uncertain. "Is this your doing?"

"Of course not. It might be *Sri Kris*, though." In a way. *Oh, Sorrel, have you any idea how much danger you are in?*

Of course she did. *And I'll wager she's relying on me knowing that I have to stay alive to make sure she escapes. The devious, sneaky, duplicitous . . .*

Damardi, refusing to look at the glamour, eyed the kris and opened his grip on the hilt so that it lay across his palm. The blade writhed there like a living serpent, the wisps of a plume catching the sunlight.

Ardhi smiled and held out his own hand, palm up. The kris flipped from Damardi to him, landing its hilt on his palm without any further action from either of them. He raised his gaze to look at the *empu*. "Do you want to try again?"

Damardi glanced around. A couple of the village elders and some of the young men were still out in the open, but all of them were standing well back. Sorrel had dropped her outrageous glamour and was once again blending into her background, as well concealed as an octopus on the reef.

"No," Damardi said. "The kris has spoken. I heard it speak." He turned and hobbled away, his head bent.

Ardhi took a deep breath. Pity for the old man shivered through him, but he did not linger. He slipped the kris back into its sheath and headed off the way he had entered the village.

As he walked past Sorrel, he did not look at her, but said, "That was such a lack-witted thing to do!"

"Wasn't it just?" she asked as she fell in next to him, still maintaining her glamour. "And it worked, too."

"It wasn't necessary."

"You don't know that."

"Do you mind if I speak Pashali to you? I want to be quite clear in what I say."

"If I don't understand, I'll tell you. But I'd rather use my own tongue to say things." She smiled at him. "I think it works better that way."

"So do I."

"What do you want to tell me?"

He looked back over his shoulder. There was no one about; no one had followed them. He said, "It was always the decision of the kris, Sorrel. Always. We have to follow the *sakti*, because that's what is best for our islands. And what is best for our islands is best for us. If the kris wanted me to die, I would have, gladly, knowing it was the right thing to happen."

"Oh, you are unbelievably irritating! I could *never* think that way. I have a will. Your *sakti* might have got me here, to your islands, but it can't tell me what to do. That's *my* decision. Just as it was yours, just then, to walk away." She dropped her glamour. "I couldn't have lived with myself if you'd died and I'd just looked the other way."

He stopped dead. "So you just left the ship and followed me? Just like that? I still don't understand why you would do something so – so foolhardy!"

"Because you are a friend! Why else? Friends look after one another."

"Yes, but knowing me has cost you so much. Chenderawasi *sakti* has taken you away from your world. I – I've always thought you must hate me and were just too polite to say so."

She started laughing. When she regained control of her amusement she said, "Believe me, I'm rarely too polite not to say what I mean. Too scared, yes, often, but never too polite. You are the polite one."

It was his turn to laugh. "No. I've always been the ill-mannered lad who didn't respect his elders the way he should. If I've held my tongue, it was because I – like you – was scared." He heaved a sigh. "I think I've been scared ever since Raja Wiramulia died. Out of my depth, trying to swim with the current, yet not understanding the tides."

"That – that's just the way I feel too. It wouldn't matter so much, except . . . except there's Piper." Her voice caught and wobbled.

"I'm not sure I know how to help her," he said sadly.

"I'm not sure we have a right to ask you to do so." They exchanged a look and she slipped a hand into his. "I think all this has cost you more than anyone should have to bear."

"It was all my fault to begin with, so I've no right to complain."

"The woman on the beach just then—"

"She married someone else. It was all a long time ago now. We were little more than children growing up together and making silly prom-ises to one another. That was before I sailed away to Pashalin. Afterwards, we met again, and perhaps something could – would – have come of it if – well, if I hadn't been responsible for the death of the Raja. Leaving her broke my heart, and possibly hers too, but hearts are easily mended at that age."

"Are they? Not yours, I think. Not so easily." She sighed. "All we can do is support each other. Right now, I think I had better go back to the ship before Saker finds out I sneaked off on one of the *prau*."

"Foolish. But . . . unbelievably brave." He smiled at her. "I will remember."

My heart, he thought, *has long since mended.*

40

Sliver of Hope

Sorrel, seated amidships in the pinnace, looked over her shoulder as the three of them sailed out of the lagoon and into the open ocean, on their way to Batuguli. Dawn was breaking over the sea to the east, and Ardhi had said it was a two-hour sail to reach their destination. Piper was in the capable arms of Surgeon Barklee once more, but she couldn't help feeling a twinge of guilt at leaving her behind.

Is there no shorter way, by road?" she asked Ardhi.

"We don't have roads."

"All right, by path, then."

"We sail everywhere. That's as it should be. We live on the coast. The interior is the home of the Raja's Chenderawasi. We do not trespass there without a reason."

"Why would the Rani ask us to meet her at this particular place?" Saker asked. He gave the sail an anxious glance as he spoke. Ardhi had earlier given him a quick lesson on managing the mainsheet, but from the look on his face, he wasn't sure he could.

"To remind me of my past, of my guilt," Ardhi said. "It's not far from the forest pool where the Raja was murdered. It's on the bay where the Lowmians anchored after listening to my drunken rambling." He shrugged. "I can hardly blame her."

It hurts you nonetheless, Sorrel thought. *But then, that's what the Rani wants, I suppose.* She wanted to say something to comfort him, but had no idea what words could possibly assuage such hurt. *When you know you are to blame, there is nothing anyone can say to make it better.*

As the boat scudded along the coast, she tried not to consider the past or worry over what was about to occur, but even the scenery conspired to unsettle her. The interior Ardhi referred to was rugged and forbidding, utterly unlike the hills of her childhood or anywhere she'd lived since. In appearance, these were not hills, but mountains. Crags and peaks and ridges towered high enough to be scraped by the frowning underside of passing clouds. The steep slopes were streaked with the tears of waterfalls, and every cranny, every hollow, every protuberance was draped in lavish verdure. It was magnificent – and terrifying. There was nothing subtle. Nothing gentle. Nothing tamed.

Sweet Va, we barely tickled the foothills on our walk to see the Rani. These people live on the fringe of something . . . She hunted for the right word. Primal, perhaps? Ancient, certainly.

The beaches and the fringing reefs were so beautiful they took her breath away, but that scenery was alien to someone from the Va-cherished Hemisphere. The sunlight was brighter here, the colours more brazen, the fish more gaudy. The white sands glared; the blue of the ocean dazzled.

"What are you thinking?" Ardhi asked.

"That this place makes me feel pale and colourless."

He shook his head. "You could never be colourless."

Saker gave him a surprised glance and Sorrel blushed. Ardhi changed the subject, ordering Saker to haul on the sheet. The sail flapped, then caught the wind as the boat changed direction and sped on its way.

"Have you had any luck with your bird lookouts?" she asked Saker.

He shook his head. "I've ten or so patrolling. I *think* they are doing what I ask, which is to look for ships as they hunt food, but it's like – like talking to Piper. You can't be sure how much she understands, or how long she will remember what you told her, or whether her crying means, 'I've hurt myself', or 'I'm scared', or 'I'm hungry'." He sighed. "I hate controlling them. They should be wild and free."

"And perhaps that is one reason why you have that particular witchery," Ardhi said. "You respect the birds."

"I don't remember thinking about birds one way or another before the witchery was granted."

"A Shenat witan would always respect living creatures, though," she said. "Why do you think you were granted the ability to climb, Ardhi?"

"It happened after Raja Wiramulia died." He frowned. "I'm not sure, but it could have been to be a good sailor on one of your tall ships. It's dangerous there in the rigging. *Sakti* needed me alive."

The witchery knows . . .

Or was it Va? Or the unseen guardians? The Avian Chenderawasi? All three? She was no longer certain of anything.

An hour later they sailed into a bay. Halfway along the beach, boulders were piled up into a tumbled heap, interrupting the curve of the sand.

"That's where we're going," Ardhi said.

"Now I understand why the Rani chose this place," Saker said. "It's so she can stand on top of the tallest rock over there and look down on us on the beach."

Ardhi ignored that, and his face was unreadable, but Sorrel noticed the slight tightening of his hand on the tiller. What was the matter with the two of them? It was as if they didn't like one another any more. Ardhi turned the boat towards the sandy shore, and when the wind had spilled from the sail, he ran the pinnace up on to the sand. As they left the boat, a bird gave a call from the trees. She spun around, but saw nothing. The sound carried, loud and mellow, filling the air.

"One of the guardians," Ardhi said, "telling the Rani we're here."

It was hot on the exposed sand, so she walked over to the shadow cast by the largest of the boulders. Ardhi and Saker stayed where they were, neither of them talking. She looked from one to the other, wondering what had gone wrong. *It's Saker*, she thought. He was not only devastated by the idea that Piper could grow up to be something evil, but also tormented that he couldn't do anything about it. He'd thought that bringing her to the islands would solve something, and it hadn't.

How tired I am, she thought with surprise. *Tired of going where the current takes us. When do I get to make the decisions?*

Even now, because she couldn't speak to the Rani herself, she was extraneous. She couldn't argue the case for Piper. She couldn't even understand what was happening until one of the men explained afterwards. Rage coursed through her.

I count, she thought. *And so does Piper.* It wasn't right that either of them were just so much flotsam on the surface of the ocean, unable to chart their own course.

A moment later, a shadow swept across the sands. Sorrel looked up in time to see the Rani glide overhead, the air whispering through her feathers. She had something gripped in her claws. She landed on the tallest boulder and Sorrel almost laughed. Saker had the Rani's measure.

Ardhi was tight-lipped as he knelt and made a gesture of abeyance. Saker removed his hat and bowed as well, but Sorrel – in a fit of pique and bravado – stood ramrod straight and looked the bird straight in the eye.

Your magic brought me here against my will, she thought. *And I think that I am just fed up with the arrogance of royalty!*

Saker was annoyed. What in all this forsaken land was Sorrel doing, standing there as if they weren't the ones who wanted something? Piper's future depended on what was about to be decided! He glared at her, but she wasn't looking his way.

I have discussed this matter with our elders and we have made decisions, the Rani said. She smoothed down some of her ruffled feathers with her beak and shook out her tail.

"We will abide by them," Ardhi said.

But the lascar didn't possess the right to decide that for Sorrel and him, Saker thought, his annoyance growing.

There is more than one problem here, the Rani continued. *We desire to halt your traders coming to our islands until such time as you have proved your worth and integrity. That first problem is ours, rather than yours.*

She turned her head to eye Saker beadily, as if she counted him as one of those lacking worth and integrity. *The second problem is one we share: the future possibility of a sorcerer on the throne of this land you call Lowmeer. If this occurs, no one is safe anywhere, including the Pulauan Chenderawasi. A sorcerer abides by no rules save his own.*

The third problem pertains to the child you guard. This is your problem, not ours, as is the fourth problem, the sorcerer who sired her. Do you agree with this assessment?

Ardhi looked across at him, and Saker nodded.

"Yes," said Ardhi. "Although that latter sorcerer might be a problem to you too. He has an interest in the spice trade."

She flared her neck ruff as if that statement had unsettled her. *The first problem Chenderawasi humans will solve themselves. They will sell their nutmeg in Serinaga, or sell to those Pashali who come here and are known to us already. If any more of your ships come, they will be sunk. Your task will be to extend that message to your Rajas, so that they are warned.*

"That will be done," Ardhi agreed.

Pickles 'n' pox, Saker thought. "I don't think you realise the power of the cannon that ships from Lowmeer and Ardrone—"

That is not your concern, she interrupted. *Next time we will be prepared. We have* sakti, *and it will be used, just as you must use your witcheries to save yourselves from the sorcerers.*

Ardhi dug him in the ribs with an elbow, and Saker subsided.

So we will solve the first problem, and you will solve the others. But we will aid you with those. She bent her head to pick up one of the items she'd been carrying in her claws. *One of these is for each of the twins.* She dropped what she was carrying down to Sorrel, who, startled, just managed to catch the falling items.

She turned them over and over in her hands. They were identical circlets woven from soft golden filaments. She guessed they had been made from the Raja Wiramulia's regalia plumes.

"What are they for?" Saker asked.

While a sorcerer wears this, the sorcerer's evil will remain subdued, their power weak. The children should begin wearing these as soon as possible. Your dilemma will be this: once the children are old enough, they can remove it, or someone else can. And once they've removed it, or someone else has, they'll never want to put it back on again. Be wary, for their sorcerer parent will sense its presence, the same way he smells that smudge on your hand, Saker.

"So," he said, "it's a temporary solution." He looked over at Sorrel. "I'll explain later."

The best solution for everybody would be to kill both children, the Rani added.

"That's the one thing we won't do."

She clapped her beak together several times, and he guessed it was a gesture of scorn, an Avian snort of disgust as if to say there was no understanding humans. *Allow them to live, then you must remember, their children will also be sorcerous.*

There is one other thing we have to help you, she continued. *Ardhi, you have your kris. If you choose to stay in Chenderawasi, you must surrender it to me. If you intend to leave, then you may take it with you, and use it in the service of ridding the world of these sorcerers. You other two humans will need something stronger than the witcheries you have. We have little knowledge of your world or your sorcerers, so what we have crafted is simple and may or may not help. Because we cannot trust you, it is also limited.*

She leaned over the edge again, this time dropping two pieces of bambu down to Saker. They were identical, about the length and width of his thumb. One end was solid, the other had been corked with a carved stopper, also made of bambu, all of it carved with intricate patterns. Wordlessly, Saker handed one over to Sorrel.

Each contains three small pieces from the Raja's glory plumes. Each piece can be used only once. Beware, for there is often a sting in the tail. Ardhi knows.

"Thank you," Saker said. "But—"

That's all. Ardhi knows the stories. She looked from him to Ardhi to Sorrel. *You have accomplished much together as a ternion. Yet two males and a breeding female rarely works when neither male is subordinate, so remember: those who fly alone, die alone. Think well on that.*

"Ardhi must make his own choices," he said. "I have no right to ask him to leave Chenderawasi again."

Perhaps not, she agreed. *But it is more complex than that, isn't it, Ardhi? Just remember, the cockbird may pose the question, but it's the hen that has the answer.*

With those words she lifted into the air and was gone in a burr of beating wings.

Saker stared at Ardhi, speechless.

There was a long silence, while Sorrel looked from one to the other, waiting for them to explain what had happened.

"Oh, blistering pox," Saker muttered finally.

"Right," Sorrel said. "I want to know every word that was said. Every. Single. Word."

The wind conspired against her. Saker gave a sketchy outline of the Rani's words as they pushed the boat back into the sea, but after that, a rough sea made talking difficult. Words were snatched away as soon as they were uttered, and steering the boat and managing the sail occupied the men's full attention. A proper discussion would have to wait, and so would an explanation of why the Rani's final words had silenced the two men so effectively.

Sorrel held on to the two pieces of bambu and the two circlets. She didn't dare unstopper the bambu in the wind, but she did examine the woven circles. They were gold-coloured, but it was obvious they weren't metal. They were far too light and if she had not kept a grip on them, the wind would have ripped them away. They were both the same: strands of golden filaments woven into one flexible chain without a catch, to be worn around the neck, she assumed. From what Saker had told her, it came from tail feathers. She had no idea how it could be so strong, but it obviously was.

She looked forward to hearing all the details, but just as they sailed into the lagoon, Saker received a garbled picture from one of his seabird lookouts.

"A tern has returned. It seems to have sighted a ship just over the horizon," he told Lord Juster as soon as they had clambered up the pilot's ladder on to the deck of *Golden Petrel*. "From the picture I'm getting in my head, it could be a Lowmian vessel."

"Can you ask it to take a look at the flag?"

Saker shot him a look of irritation. "By all the acorns on an oak, have you any idea of how clay-brained ordinary birds are? It's almost all I can do to stop them thinking with their stomachs!"

Juster ordered the ship's company to prepare for immediate sailing.

Sorrel, after retrieving Piper from Barklee, soon discovered that the word "immediate" was more the captain's optimism than fact. Although the activity on board changed from being merely busy to frenetic, it was obvious departure was still hours away. There was loose cargo and provisions to be properly stowed, Chenderawasi traders and labourers to be paid, sailors on shore leave to be found, sails to be readied.

When she saw several of the new sails had red emblems she did not recognise, and that painted canvas was being draped over the sides of the ship and hung in odd configurations along the deck, she turned to Saker in puzzlement. "What's going on?"

"He's changing the appearance of the ship. From a distance, especially as it gets dark, our shape won't look like *Golden Petrel*'s. The emblem is a Pashali one. If the Lowmians don't recognise us, they won't attack. Juster has decided to leave them to the Chenderawasi to deal with. The islanders don't want our arguments fought on their soil."

She was incredulous. "Lord Juster had all this prepared from the time he left Throssel?"

"This ship is a privateer, Sorrel. This is what they do. Pretend to be someone else, fly the wrong flag, deceive the unwary, and then at the last moment reveal their true colours and attack."

"That – that's *dishonest!*"

He quirked an eyebrow and she found herself laughing. "All right, I'm clay-brained, I know."

"At least this time, he's doing it so that they leave us alone and aren't suspicious of anything being awry when they anchor in the lagoon. They'll find out soon enough, I suppose, when none of their factors are there to greet them."

Her stomach twisted unpleasantly. "They have cannon. From an anchorage here, they could bombard the town. Innocent people could die!"

"No one has asked for our help," he said gently. "In fact, quite the opposite. They want us gone."

"Ardhi—"

"Ardhi is going into Bandar Ruanakula, with Juster's permission, to warn the mayor, *Tuan Sri*. Look, why don't you go below? I'll come down and see you later, to tell you everything. Juster has a couple of things he wants me to attend to, but really most of the time, we're just in the way."

She looked around at the bustle and realised he was right, so she nodded and retreated to her cabin. She played with Piper, fed her when she was hungry, then put her to sleep on her bunk in the mid-afternoon. When she was hungry herself, she picked up some fruit, bread and cheese from the galley and returned to the cabin.

A few minutes later Saker was knocking at her cabin door. She let him in and went to sit on the edge of the bunk. He seated himself on the cabin's only other item of furniture, a sea chest.

"I want to know everything the Rani told you," she said.

"That's why I came," he said, and launched into an account of all that had transpired between him, Ardhi and the Rani. When he'd finished, she picked up one of the circlets. "Shall I put it on her?" she asked.

He nodded.

She lifted the sleeping child and slipped it over her head. It was too large – large enough for the adult she could one day be. Piper stirred, then settled. "I suppose that offers us some hope – especially if we can keep the Prime away from both the children. At least he doesn't know that Piper even exists."

"He has to die, Sorrel. We have to stop him."

"Just like that? Where did either of us learn how to fight a sorcerer? Someone who already has a position of power – who is even supposed to be your superior!" She picked up one of the bambu pieces, pulled out the stopper and tipped the contents into her palm.

Three delicate barbs from a plume nestled there. They looked as fragile and insubstantial as bubbles. The skin of her palm tingled.

"And these are our weapons." She looked across at him. "I hope you've got more ideas than I have what we can do with these."

"Not a clue."

"You say the Rani said they came from the Raja's glory plumes?"

"I asked Ardhi about that before he left the ship. He said glory plumes are tail plumes, not regalia plumes from the breast. That means they aren't as potent."

"Wonderful."

He checked the second piece of bambu, confirming that the contents were identical. "Is it my imagination, or are they glowing?" he asked.

"When I first saw the regalia plumes, back in the Regal's castle in Lowmeer, they glowed. I looked through them, and saw this place. I smelled it. I didn't know where or what I saw, or what I smelled, but it was this island, and the perfume was nutmeg flowers. And then once, when you were wearing Ardhi's kris, I saw a golden glow. I smelled this world again then, too. And I heard the Raja's song. I was standing in the palace in Ustgrind, looking at the kris – and I heard a Chenderawasi Avian singing."

She put the barbs back into the bambu. "You say the Rani said Ardhi he could stay if he wanted. Has he told you he will?"

"Not yet."

She fixed him with a hard stare. "You haven't told me what the Rani said when you informed her you'd no right to ask Ardhi to leave the islands."

"Ah, yes." He rubbed a hand over his head in a gesture of embarrassment. "She said we were a successful ternion and we shouldn't split up. She implied that if we did, we might not be successful. She said it like a warning."

"What's a ternion?"

"A group of three."

She sent him a sidelong glance and raised an eyebrow. "And—?"

"And what?"

"Whatever it is she said that you're not telling me."

"Well, nothing really. She just intimated that a group of two men and one woman doesn't always work out well. What she said, ah, embarrassed both of us. That's all."

"Oh." She thought about that. "Oh, I see! Well, that doesn't apply to us, does it? I mean, neither of you are interested in me as more than a friend, and I'm not looking for a husband, so there's no reason we can't still be a – what was it? Ternion? How the pox does a bird even know a word like that?"

He laughed. "You may as well ask how a bird can talk to me inside my head." Then he added, more seriously, "They're not birds and we make a grave mistake if we think they are. Call them Avians instead. As for their language, I think the *sakti* plucks the words out of my mind and translates her thought using the words I already know. In fact, I doubt she uses words at all. Her language is not one of words, but of song and movement and flight and feathers! I guess we shouldn't ask how to understand the wonder of witcheries either, but just be thankful they exist."

She was about to reply when there was another knock at the door. Juster's voice called out, "Sorrel, are you in there?"

She pulled a face at Saker and rose to open the door.

"Have you seen Ardhi?" Juster asked. "He's supposed to have been back by now, but there's no sign of him!"

41

Farewell to Chenderawasi

After Saker told him there was a Lowmian ship heading towards Bandar Ruanakula and after Juster said they were leaving, all Ardhi wanted to do was warn his cousin.

Mate Grig Cranald was organising the last of the payments for the ship's revictualling, so when he arranged for the longboat to pay a visit to the town, Ardhi asked to go with them. He parted from the others on the town jetty. "I get *prau* to take me back to ship," he assured Cranald.

"Better be hurrying then," the third mate replied. "Cap'n will be a mite churlish if he has to leave the lagoon without you keeping an eye on the helmsman!"

Ardhi hurried along to the *balai kota*, the largest building in the town, where his cousin, *Tuan Sri* Imbak spent his days dealing with town affairs. The outside – with its massive soaring roof of palm thatch – had impressed the Ardronese sailors; inside it was not like any town hall of their experience and he'd heard their more disparaging remarks. "More like a village market day," he'd heard the bo'sun say.

Ardhi knew what he would find: his cousin sitting crossed-legged on the Pashali carpet at one end of the main hall, receiving petitioners, complainants and advisers. Discussions were held over cups of ginger tea flavoured with cloves, cinnamon and pandan leaves – served with sweet rice cakes if the visitor was considered an important man.

At the other end of the hall, the *kerani besar*, who was the man in charge of who would see the mayor and when they'd see him, tried to assemble waiting townsfolk and officials into some semblance of order.

Ardhi knew he'd be the last to be attended to, and he couldn't afford to wait. Immediately he entered the hall, conversation began to cease around him, only to be followed by a hiss of whispers and a buzz of disapproval. He didn't halt, not even when the *kerani besar* jumped up to detain him. Instead he marched across the hall to his cousin, addressed him by the required honorific and added starkly, "Lord Juster wishes to inform you there's a vessel approaching. It has not yet been identified, but it could possibly be the Lowmians returning for their nutmeg and their factors."

When the uproar from that announcement had died down, Imbak cleared the hall of everyone except himself, his three main advisers, his two personal guards – and his cousin.

"You have gall to come here with this news," Imbak snapped, his eyes blazing.

"I came to warn you. My ship is leaving; the other, if it is indeed the Lowmian ship, is your enemy. Lord Juster's is not."

"*Coward!*"

Ardhi turned to leave.

"Wait! You *dare* to turn your back on me?"

"Elder Cousin, I am leaving and I will never return. That is punishment enough. There is no greater pain than exile."

"It's what you deserve. But not until this new ship is a wreck and these murdering sailors are dead."

"Attack them at night when—"

"*You* will lead the attack. You brought them here. You kill them." He made a gesture to one of his guards. "Iwan. See that Ardhi does not leave the island until this Lowmian ship is sunk. If he tries, kill him."

Iwan gestured his obedience and fingered the hilt of his kris. Ardhi knew him; he was Eka's father, Lastri's father-in-law. Now he glared his contempt and loathing.

"There are guns and gunpowder left behind by the factors," one of the advisers added. "We do not know how to use such things, but doubtless this traitor has learned the workings of such horrors. Let him fight fire with fire."

Iwan smiled.

Ardhi's heart sank. He was trapped.

The sun was low in the sky as *Golden Petrel* edged out of the lagoon. Saker stood with Juster and Finch and Forrest the helmsman, watching their progress.

Ardhi was still missing, and Juster was furious. He'd had to prevail on several local fishermen with a *prau* to guide the ship through the opening in the reef. Once out in the open ocean again, he had Forrest steer away from the island group, rather than thread their way through the islands as Ardhi had done for them on their way in.

"I don't want to take risks in the dark," he said to Saker, the words more growled than spoken. "But that is going to bring me much closer to that Lowmian ship than I anticipated. I hope our disguise is good enough."

Saker stared at the ship now in full view, bearing down on them fast with a following wind, whereas *Golden Petrel* was making slow progress. "Is it indeed *Spice Winds*?"

"You don't recognise the fluyt you sailed on?"

"All fluyts look alike to me."

Juster stared at him in disbelief. "Pickle me sour! I do *not* understand you lubbers with your soil-clogged boots. Yes, that's *Spice Winds*."

"Do you think they'll be firing at us?" Cranald asked. He was jotting some calculations down on a slate. "If we hold course, we'll pass within range."

"We just have to hope they won't recognise us."

No one said anything.

"All right, get some birds out there, Saker. I want to know what's happening on board. For example, whether the gunports are open on the port side where we can't see them, the number of sailors on the topdeck, whatever you can give me."

"Birds can't count past two or three," Saker muttered, but called on all the nearby seabirds he could find anyway.

He felt as miserable as a soused herring in a firkin. Why had Ardhi not come back to the ship? He'd been so certain the lascar would join forces with them again, that the man wouldn't want to stay where he would be shunned and friendless.

What's the use in living in a paradise if you have to do it alone? Leak on you, you muckle-top, Ardhi! How will we win this battle without you?

But perhaps something had happened to him. Perhaps the *Tuan Sri* had ordered his death or imprisonment.

I should have gone after him. I should have looked for him. What kind of a friend am I? A beef-witted witan who was curdled crazy enough to be jealous! The Rani was right – if Sorrel wanted a man in her life, the choice was hers, not his, not Ardhi's.

"Those birdies of yours see anything, witan?" Juster asked.

"All looks normal as far as I can tell. But it's hardly a clear picture I'm getting inside my head, you know. Mostly they're focused on what they can see to eat in the wake."

You'd better be alive, you dagger-wearing addle-pate! Because, I swear, I'll come looking for you one day.

"Order a change of tack to port, Mister Finch. That'll take us further away, and make it clear we aren't intending to offer them a broadside. But I don't think they'll want to harm us. They're a merchantman, after all. They don't want a battle on their hands and holes in their hull."

"We'll be presenting our rump to them!" Finch protested to Juster. "Like a catamite waiting t—"

"Watch your language, Mister Finch! There's a cleric present."

Fiddle-me-witless, how do I tell Sorrel that Ardhi didn't come back on board and we sailed without him?

Captain Lustgrader lowered his spyglass.

"They've changed tack," he muttered. "They don't want an argument."

"I never seen a ship like that one," the helmsman said. "Got it rigged like a merchantman or a privateer, not a Pashali trader, for all they got that Javenka emblem on the mainsails!"

"No reason why they can't learn shipbuilding from their betters," Lustgrader said. "Va knows, they see plenty of fine sea-going vessels from our hemisphere when they come to Karradar. It's not Dornbeck's ship; he wouldn't be turning tail and running away like this one is. Ignore them. We want to enter the lagoon before the light goes."

It would be a close thing. In these southern climes, the light faded from the sky quickly after the sun had set. Va-forsaken place indeed! Still, a good place to make a tidy profit from the ignorant. He had every expectation that his factors had the last couple of nutmeg harvests ready for shipping.

He studied the wind, the angle of the sun, and ordered all the square-rigged sails furled. He'd brought a vessel into the lagoon before, when he'd captained the carrack *Spice Dragon*, but that time he'd surveyed the entrance in the ship's longboat first.

Well, I won't have to do that this time, he thought. He had the chart he'd drawn then pinned to the binnacle. *Damn, what is that smell? Stinks like a perfumed bawd! Must be the nutmeg flowers . . .* He'd heard they had a stench to them. Last time they had not been flowering.

About half a mile out from the breaking waves along the reef, a *prau* sailed out towards them with five young men aboard. They were dressed in their woefully inadequate garb, chests barely covered with loose waistcoats in a deplorable mix of ghastly colours, their heads uncovered except for a twist of cloth worn as a ring around the level of their brow. Then that stupid cloth they wore around their thighs. Like a woman! Well, except for the bare legs and bare feet. By Va, they were always so immodest and – and *sensual*. Lewdsters all, and he was hanged if he could tell them apart.

One of the natives called up to the deck, pointing to his chest. He had a huge goitre on one side of his face that distorted his features. "Greetings," he said. "Name me, Yandi. Me Factor Rudman's helper. He sends Yandi to show way into lagoon. Big storm came – change reef much. Not like before. Much different now. New way in now. Yandi show. Me come on ship?"

Lustgrader subdued his distaste. Let no one ever say he was a man who would hurt his chances to salve his pride; pride was the work of A'Va. "Lower the pilot steps, Tolbun," he said and smiled benignly down into the *prau*. "Greetings, Yandi. Come aboard."

The *prau* came alongside the moving ship with surprising ease, and Lustgrader had to agree that these heathen bastards knew how to sail. The *prau* disgorged the man who spoke at least a few words of a respectable language, and pushed away from *Spice Winds* without so much as bumping the woodwork. The man climbed up, grinning like a dog.

"Cap'n!" he said, his mouth slitting his brown face, "Factor Rudman sends many greetings." He pointed to the north. "Opening through reef that way. Yandi show!"

Without waiting for instructions or permission he leaped across the deck up to the fo'c'sle and out on to the bowsprit, where he stood with his arm pointing in the direction the ship should take. Lustgrader shrugged and nodded to the helmsman. "Do as he says." He turned to the man he had promoted to first mate after Tolbun's death. "Alert the lookout aloft to be especially vigilant. Put young Guldon up in the bows to keep an eye on this native."

He wasn't worried; a fluyt was built with a shallow draught to allow it to enter river mouths and poor anchorages. Ahead he thought he could see the place where the waves failed to break; in fact, another *prau* – with its sail raised – had just passed through, its prow cleaving through what must have been a gap in the coral.

The forward momentum of *Spice Winds* was now reliant on the spanker and jib sails, giving it more manoeuvrability. The breeze was from just the right quarter and not too strong.

Yes, he thought, proud of his ship, *she can do this*.

The native fellow appeared to know what he was doing, but even if he hadn't, Lustgrader's helmsman was probably the most skilled the fleet had. Aloft, the lookout was signalling all was well; the mate had their most experienced tars on the jib halyards and spanker sheets and Jemson was calling out the depths off the port quarter. Lustgrader gave a glance around. Everyone's attention was exactly where it should be, focused on their immediate job, alert for changes. He nodded to himself as the ship lined up with the gap perfectly. The waves would carry them in. He could see the flat water of the lagoon beyond, sparkling in the last rays of the setting sun. Some boats – canoes? – were setting out from the shore, too far away to be sure who was in them, but he suspected it would be the factors, coming to welcome him. Poor wretches, marooned in a hell-hole like this one for so long, surrounded by ignorant savages. Well, at least they had managed to teach this Yandi fellow how to speak a civilised tongue.

The fellow, balanced on the bowsprit and holding on to the foremast stay, turned to look back at him. He was grinning again – and the goitre on his face was gone. Lustgrader blinked, and was still trying to make sense of that, when the man shouted at him, his grasp of the language suddenly much improved. "Aie, captain, remember me? Ardhi the lascar? You did not believe me when I told you your sailors killed Raja of Chenderawasi! Believe it now as you lose your ship."

Every eye was riveted on the lascar. He moved before they were even sure what was happening. One moment he was on the bowsprit, then he had launched himself out and away in a curve through the air as elegant as a diving gannet.

Next, just as it seeped through to Lustgrader and the crew that all was not well, just as the captain opened his mouth to give he knew not what command—

A brilliance flashed to obscure his vision; a roar of an explosion rendered him deaf. *Spice Winds* juddered under the shock wave, and he staggered on the deck. He might have recovered his balance if the ship hadn't then ground to an abrupt, shuddering halt. A halt so sudden, everyone standing was flung forward to sprawl on the deck or slam against the structures. A moment later the ship lifted on a wave and moved forward again. This time the accompanying noise was the most ghastly of sounds: the never-to-be-forgotten slow cracking and grinding of a ship's hull ripping open in its death knell, its guts exposed as the ocean rampaged in.

Lustgrader, his sight and hearing returning, had time for only one last coherent thought as he struggled to rise. He was facing the stern of the ship and in disbelief he saw the aftcastle with its officers' cabins slowly subside below the level of the deck, only to be then obliterated by a cloud of dust and smoke.

Those savages on the boat, he thought, *they blew up the rudder while we were all looking ahead.*

With the rudder, the underpinnings of the stern cabins had gone as well. If he'd had longer to think, he might have appreciated the irony of what they'd done. They'd copied his attempt on *Golden Petrel*, but with far more success. With a little more time, he might even have realised the ship had been simultaneously guided onto the reef, just to make doubly sure it was doomed.

If he'd had a moment more, he might have seen the war canoes stroking across the lagoon, through water now shadowed by the island as the sun set. He might have heard the war drums.

However, he had none of those moments. He didn't even see the instrument of his death. One of *Spice Winds*' two small gun carriages on the weather deck broke loose from its moorings as the deck tilted and, still bearing its cannon, it ploughed into him and crushed his chest against the base of the mizzen mast.

* * *

After diving from the *Spice Winds*, Ardhi swam to the *prau*. It was Eka's boat, and it was one of Eka's regular fishing mates who hauled him over the gunwale.

Eka was at the sweep, and directed the *prau* away from the ship. "Everyone ready?" he asked. "No mercy. Not to anyone." He shipped the sweep and pulled out his kris. "They all die."

"What about him?" one of them asked, jerking his head at Ardhi and flipping his own kris from hand to hand.

"He and I have an agreement. I don't break my word. When we are done here, we sail after the other vessel and deliver Ardhi back to them, the scum that he is."

And you've made that sound so honourable.

The reality had been different. Eka had wanted him dead with a passion, and would have happily killed him once his part in the deception was over. Just before they left the shore for the *Spice Winds*, Ardhi, his kris in his hand, had drawn him aside.

Quietly, he'd explained that he needed to catch up with *Golden Petrel*.

Eka shrugged, indifferent. "Swim after it, then," he'd sneered.

"No. You will take me. Even if you have to sail all the way to the Spicerie. All the way to Kotabanta, if necessary."

"Your mind is way out of your skull! I'm not doing anything for you." He jabbed a forefinger into Ardhi's chest. "This is your chance for redemption, Ardhi the Moray." He nodded towards the lagoon and the approaching ship. "Give us the time to blow it into splinters, and you can seek a place in death for your tortured soul. That is all I'll offer. If one of those pale men doesn't do it for me, I'll kill you myself when we're done."

"Look down at what I have in my hand, Eka."

For a moment Eka continued to hold his gaze, then he lowered it to look at what Ardhi held: the kris. "Made with Raja Wiramulia's bone and blood and his regalia. Now repeat those words as if you mean them – and watch what happens."

Eka snorted. "I'll kill you myself when we're done with this Lowmian ship. Tonight."

The kris glowed, lit by the gold flecks within. It writhed across Ardhi's hand and the tip hooked itself into the front of the sleeveless jacket Eka wore. From there it squirmed its way upwards like a snake on the bark of a tree. At the neck of the jacket, the blade slid up until the point was jabbing into Eka's throat under his chin.

Eka, white-faced, laid his hand on the hilt, anchoring it against his chest in a tight hold.

"You see?" Ardhi asked softly. "I don't think it wants me dead. Not yet. Why don't you let justice take its course? The kris will kill me when the time is right. In the meantime, I will serve its will."

Eka remained motionless, scarcely breathing. Then he snatched his hand away from the kris handle as if it burned him. Ardhi caught the dagger as it fell. "We will catch up with *Golden Petrel*," he said, "when we are finished here."

When we are finished . . .

Such simple words. The reality made him sick.

Flames had a hold on *Spice Winds*. The ship was doomed, and those on board knew it. When the fire reached the magazine, not much would be left. The longboat was launched; the pinnace was just dropped over the bulwarks. Sailors were grabbing anything that floated and jumping into the water, all pretence of fighting the flames abandoned.

They splashed and kicked and rowed away from *Spice Winds*, desperate to save themselves. In the dusk light, they saw the waiting craft and headed that way. They thought they were going to be rescued. They thought there were Lowmian factors ready to aid them . . . until the clubs descended, smashing their skulls even as they reached out for a helping hand to those in a *prau*. Knives slipped between their ribs when they grabbed the side of the canoes.

The screams began.

He knew them all. Every single man. He knew the men who had despised him for his difference and ridiculed him. He knew those who had been kind and those who had been indifferent. And before the night ended every one of them would be dead. Pretending he heard nothing, he sat still, staring at the sky as the brightest stars were unveiled. When someone called him by name, begging for his help, he did not move. When Eka and his friends laid into the men in the water around them, when they pulled sailors out of the pinnace and the longboat and murdered them, he did nothing, not even when he was sprayed with blood and bone as Eka's men raised their bloodied clubs above their heads. Around the *prau*, gore swirled. Fish made the water boil with their frenzied feeding.

At his side in its sheath, the kris was still and dark, as if it too wanted no part in this ghastly massacre.

Every single death layered itself into his conscience, another piece of leaden guilt to weigh him down. Not one of these sailors would have been here to die this night if he had not first brought *Spice Dragon* to the isles of Chenderawasi.

They sailed all night, taking it in turns to sleep and steer. Even as he napped, Ardhi kept the kris in his hand, relying on the power of its *sakti* to keep him safe, but he need not have bothered. Eka and his friends were subdued, cautious in their dealings with him.

In the morning, they briefly called in at a beach, pulling the *prau* up on the sand, splashing the interior with water, then tipping it out to wash the blood away. They swam to cleanse themselves, their elation at their victory muted. One of them shinned up a coconut tree to collect some of the young fruit, so they could drink the cool milky water and scoop out the soft white flesh with their fingers.

And then they sailed on.

42

Changes

Sorrel stared at him, furious. "Lord Juster told me he was sending men to look for him. Why didn't you tell me they didn't find him?"

Saker, unable to sleep, had come up on deck just before dawn. He'd been tossing and turning, worrying about what they would find when they finally reached Ardronese shores again, and how they could fight Prime Valerian Fox. He'd thought they'd have Ardhi's dagger to help them; he'd thought Ardhi would be able to explain something about how to use the wisps of the tail feathers to help them, but they'd never had that conversation.

Ardhi had never returned to the ship. Now they were on their own, with no idea of what would confront them when they returned to Ardrone.

Confound you, you bilge-rat of a lascar! Why were you so intent on revenge against Lustgrader that you remained behind?

And now here was Sorrel, up early, with Piper wide awake in her arms, railing at him.

He tried to explain. "If I had told you, there was nothing you could have done. You looked tired last night. I thought you'd be better off for a good night's sleep."

Her glare was not encouraging. "Why didn't Lord Juster wait for him?" she asked.

"Sorrel, we couldn't wait. Not with *Spice Winds* sailing into port. There would have been a fire fight in the lagoon. It's not our land, and we have no right to bring our arguments into their parlour. Ardhi obviously didn't want to come with us. We have to let him go, if that's what he wants."

"We don't know that was what he wanted! That *Tuan Sri* man might have taken him prisoner. He might be dead!"

"He chose to go back. He never told me why, but if he was in danger, he must have known it, and for some reason thought it worth the risk. Maybe I shouldn't have made the decision to let you go to bed without knowing, but even so, we certainly didn't have the right to make decisions for Ardhi."

She stamped a foot at him, an action so uncharacteristic he could only stare.

"You don't understand!" she snapped. "There is no way Ardhi doesn't want to sail on this ship."

"How can you be so sure?"

"Because I *know* him. He has nothing to stay for! He's a proud man, and a deeply traumatised one. To stay would mean being ostracised for the rest of his life. He could never marry. His own family don't want to see him. The woman he once loved married someone else. His own grandfather won't see him."

She took a deep breath and laid a hand on his arm. "With us, he has a reason to live. For a start, he adores Piper. But there's two far more potent reasons. Prime Fox is a sorcerer, and he has a huge financial investment in the Ardronese spice fleet to the Va-forsaken Hemisphere. And the heir to Lowmeer is probably growing up to be a sorcerer. Ardhi has a reason to live: to protect Chenderawasi by dealing with the dangers to its existence brewing far from its shores. He may never see his home again if he comes with us, but he'd not turn down the chance to help keep the islands safe. Never!"

"But he's not here. And that was his choice. Sorrel, last night, just as the sun set, we saw a flash of light in the lagoon. Then we heard an explosion."

"You think the Lowmians were firing on the town?"

"No. I don't think they would have had time to realise the factors were all dead. We think someone blew up the ship. It had to be Ardhi, along with some folk from the town. They probably had explosives from the factors' stores and Ardhi has the knowledge to use them. Perhaps that was his way of earning back his place among his people. An execution of justice that would restore his reputation."

She thought about that, then shook her head. "His actions resulted in the death of their Raja. I know it's hard for us to understand, given that the Raja is not human, but Raja Wiramulia was both their wisdom and the . . . the *being* who granted them their witcheries, their *sakti*, through his regalia. Imagine if it was *our* unseen guardian, and we only had one of them. How would we feel if someone came from outside and killed that guardian?"

He considered that, and his imagination told him she was right.

"It's worse than you know," he said grimly. "Ardhi told me the young Raja is not old enough to grant witcheries. His plumes do not have the strength yet, and true, vibrant *sakti* has to come from mature moulted plumes of the rightful Raja."

"I see. So the death of Raja Wiramulia was particularly tragic because he didn't have an adult male heir."

He nodded. "People here can never look on Ardhi the same way again. He was heir to a Datu who ruled a huge chunk of these islands. Now he's the most despised man in Chenderawasi."

She gave a grunt of exasperation, shoved Piper into his arms and walked away. For a moment, he watched her go, then followed her. Piper chattered to him in her own language of coos and aahs, bopping him on the nose with her fist and grinning when he pulled a face. "Da-da-da," she said, and his heart melted.

Sorrel had gone straight to Forrest at the helm, demanding that he show her where they were on the chart Ardhi had drawn for him.

"Here," Forrest said, and pointed at the map now attached to the binnacle table. "See that peak marked there? That's that one." He turned to view the coastline they were following at a distance and indicated a conical pimple rising above the backbone of the range.

"And what route did we follow through the islands on our way into Bandar Ruanakula?" Sorrel asked.

He leaned over and traced a line on the map. "This way. But Ardhi knew every rock and reef and the cap'n doesn't want to risk that route without him. We'll go this way." He ran his finger around the outside of the island group. "It's much longer, but it will be safer."

"Then we have to wait here," she said, "for Ardhi."

Saker looked at where she'd placed her finger on the chart. She was indicating where the two routes intersected. Ardhi had scribbled names onto the map in Pashali script, naming many of the features, and Saker read the words next to her finger: *Pantai Emas, Pulau Dena*. "Golden beach, Dena Island," he translated. He looked at her in hope. "You think he'll follow us?"

"If he's alive and free, he is already following us," she said with certainty.

"It's possible that if they wanted his help, they forced him to stay behind. And then, once the Lowmian ship was sunk . . ."

"He'll come after us, I know he will." She looked at Forrest. "Who'd get there first?" she asked him.

"You can never be sure of anything when you rely on a wind!"

"Oh, yes, you can," she said, "when you have the right dagger."

Forrest blinked, looking at her as if she'd taken leave of her senses. "You'll have to talk to the captain about it."

"We will," she said.

Saker pulled her away to the stern, where he sat down on a hatch cover and dug a hand into his pocket. He'd collected a pile of coloured pebbles and shells, and he spilled them out on to the deck for Piper to play with. She gave a gurgle of delight and slid down from his lap on to the decking.

"Can you ask the birds to find him?" Sorrel asked. "You did tell me you sent a message to the Pontifect by bird!"

"I've no way of knowing if those messages ever arrived," he said. "I sent six different birds all with the same message. All I could do was to imprint a scene on their minds, and couple it with an intense desire to be there. The picture I tried to recreate was of one of the Pontifect's guards standing in front of her palace looking at the Ard River and the setting sun. That way a bird might have been able to orient itself by the sun until they found the right place. But it was such long odds, Sorrel. There's even a possibility that they'd mistake the sunset for a sunrise and head off in completely the wrong direction – and that's if they responded in the first place. Worse, they were all seabirds, and Vavala is on a river, not the sea. I lost contact with each bird about a day after they left me."

Piper offered him a shell and, after duly admiring it, he handed it back. She held it out to Sorrel instead. "That's lovely, darling," she said absently.

"I could try to send a bird to Ardhi," he said, "but what would I tell it to look for? Look around! There are *prau* out fishing all along the coast, probably more still within the shelter of the other islands. How can I tell a bird which one I'm interested in?"

She heaved a sigh. "Oh. I'll speak to Lord Juster. Perhaps he'll be prepared to wait for Ardhi. Keep an eye on Piper, will you?"

He let her go, ruefully aware that she had more chance of influencing Juster than he did.

Sorrel found the captain in his cabin with Grig Cranald. He'd never made a secret of his affection for his third mate, so she was unsurprised to find them sitting at ease in the luxury of the cabin, sipping brandy from ornate goblets. They both rose to their feet.

"I'm sorry to disturb you," she began.

"Not at all," Juster said. "Is this a social visit or business?"

"Regrettably, business, my lord."

"Then would you mind leaving us, Grig, please?"

The third mate nodded amiably and left them alone. Juster bade her sit and offered her a drink, which she declined. When she opened her mouth to apologise for disturbing him again, Juster silenced her with an upheld hand. "I never let my private affairs interfere with the running of my ship and everyone knows that, especially Grig." He sat down opposite her, picked up his brandy and asked, "What is the problem, Mistress Sorrel?"

"I regret I always seem to have problems when I come to you," she said. "And I appreciate what you've already done for me—"

He smiled at her. "But?"

"It's about Ardhi."

He listened while she explained, but when she ended by asking him if he would give the order to wait for Ardhi if necessary, his immediate reply was a shake of the head. "I'm glad to be rid of the lascar," he said. "Not that he wasn't a fine addition to the crew, but I mislike his magic, his plumes and his dagger. I don't want anything to do with this Chenderawasi sorcery and I'm delighted he's gone. What belongs in the Va-forsaken Hemisphere is best left there, mistress."

"We spoke to the Rani of Chenderawasi. She is the, ah, regent I suppose we'd call it, for her young son, the present Raja. She told us that Piper, and therefore probably the Prince-regal, is infected with sorcery. The only hope we may have for both the Regala's children is Ardhi's—"

He cut her off. "No. I can't believe that. If our hemisphere has a problem with sorcery, then we should look to our own witcheries. Or to Va." He stood, indicating it was time for her to leave.

She didn't move.

He frowned, saying, "Listen. Saker is a friend, and I was glad to help him back in Ardrone. But my ship and its crew comes first. After them, my liege lord. And all I've had since Ardhi came on board is trouble. And he has no right to come between you and Saker—"

She gaped at him. "Whatever do you mean?"

"I'm not blind. I've seen the way they look at you, both of them. Saker's a fine man and he deserves a fine woman. The lascar has no right to—"

She jumped to her feet, outraged. "No, *you* have no rights to say such a thing! Saker and I are no more than friends, and Ardhi has no interest in me. And I have no interest in either of them! How can I *think* of love when we are in such danger! All I care about is Piper and fighting the thing that has – has contaminated her. Lord Juster, there are such huge troubles facing us all, and I can't understand why you think such – such flibbertigibbet things can possibly be important to anyone at all right now."

They stood staring at each other, and she wondered for a moment which of them was the more surprised at her outburst. "I think," she said finally, "Saker might explain what's at stake better than I can. Excuse me."

She headed for the door, but he was there first, opening it and bowing her out.

Lord Juster never forgot his manners.

Outside in the companionway, she paused. Her heart was pounding, betraying her. For a moment she leant against the wall and allowed her desire – and, yes, love – to wash through her. Bottled up emotion she had refused to acknowledge was momentarily set free to scour her equilibrium, leaving her shaken. *This*, she thought, *this is why I must not love; it weakens me when I must be strong.*

* * *

When Sorrel returned to the deck, one glance at her face was enough to tell Saker that Juster had turned down her request.

"I do have another idea," he said. "Maybe – maybe we can do something else. Perhaps you'd better ask Barklee if he would mind taking care of Piper for a while. Then, on the way back, get one of those fish I saw Banstel catch this morning from the cook, and bring me a quill and ink and piece of parchment. Oh, and some twine."

She didn't waste time asking him why, or what he was thinking of doing; she just nodded, picked up Piper and left.

He liked that about her. Sweet Va, there was so much he liked about her . . .

He fumbled for the leather thong around his neck, on which he'd hung his piece of carved bambu. Easing the stopper open, he sheltered the contents from the wind, then teased out one of the barbs before restoppering the others safely inside the bambu. He looked up into the sky. There was only one bird nearby, a sea-eagle. It was ideal – a strong flier with sharp eyesight.

Closing his eyes, he tried to remember the words the unseen guardian of the Chervil Shrine had planted in his head, the day he'd been given a witchery. *All creation is one entity. You, the land and the sea – you know in your heart they are all one, and therein lies duty and power and salvation. You will surrender your will, again and again. It is a harder road than you ever dreamed.*

Sorrel returned without Piper and gave him the fish, then disappeared to find the other items. The sea-eagle spiralled down in lazy circles in answer to his call, to land on the bulwarks as he sent soothing thoughts its way. The swabbie on deck cleaning the scuppers shook his head in disbelief.

He approached the bird slowly and laid the fish down next to its foot. It accepted the offering, anchored it with its claws and began to tear at the carcass.

The bird showed no fear as it ate, and no interest in him. He glanced down at the wisp of feather he held, and tried to think how he could use it to enhance and awaken more of a connection to the eagle.

Sorrel returned with the remainder of items he'd wanted. Leaving the bird to eat its fill, he wrote a note to Ardhi. Then, needing both hands, he put the shaft of the barb into his mouth while he folded the note tight and wrapped it with twine. As the eagle finished the fish, he sent calming thoughts its way and reached out to tie the string to the bird's leg.

"Be careful," Sorrel said, eyeing the bird nervously.

As he bent his head down to see what he was doing, he knew the cruel curve of its upper mandible could rip his eye out in a blink. *Starve your imagination, you scaremonger.* He tugged the string to see if it would hold and ran a fingernail under it to make sure it wasn't uncomfortably tight. He was just straightening up when the bird made a sudden lunge at the feather barb.

Instinctively, he tightened his jaw.

The bird nipped the feather in two. He jerked back, gasping, choked on the small piece in his mouth and swallowed. Wings flapped, powerful, beating the air around him. He closed his eyes and swallowed again. Sorrel shrieked. He opened his eyes.

The sea was rushing past, several paces under him. He tilted sideways, and so did the horizon. Sunshine sparkled. Images flashed into his eye like lightning, as detailed as brush strokes on a painting. Disoriented, he wanted to vomit. Tried to call out, but no sound came. Smells overwhelmed. Water, salt, wetness, fish, nutmeg blossom, wet sand, damp forest, seaweed, feathers. Sounds: the rush of air in his ears, through his feathers . . .

He didn't have feathers.

Did he?

His feet weren't on the deck. He couldn't feel the deck. He was suspended in air.

He started to scream, but most of the sound was all in his head.

43

Saker and the Eagle

Sorrel, shocked, leant over Saker. He was lying on the deck, staring up at her in horror.

"Are you all right?" she asked.

He squeezed his eyes shut and shook his head.

"You swallowed part of the barb. Perhaps you should try to cough it up . . ."

He shook his head again, without opening his eyes.

She looked up to watch the eagle in the sky. She'd seen it beating its wings to avoid dropping into the water; now it had found rising air and was beginning to circle, higher with every circuit.

"Shall I fetch the cap'n?" Banstel asked. He wasn't the only one who'd come to her aid when Saker had screamed and collapsed. She was surrounded by concerned faces.

"Please. And bring Saker a drink of water."

She lifted his head onto her lap. His breathing was normal, but his face looked bloodless. She held his hand, touched his cheek, spoke to him. He didn't react.

When Lord Juster came, she told him what had happened and he ordered Saker carried into his stateroom. Once there, he sent everyone away except the three of them and shut the door.

"Let me get this straight. He swallowed a part of one of these magical plumes?"

"Yes, and so did the eagle. I think – we don't always have much say in . . . in what the magic does."

"What do you think happened?"

Oh, vex it, no matter how I explain this, he won't like it. She didn't answer his question. Instead she said, "I think we have to find Ardhi."

He groaned. "I thought we'd finally left all this *sakti* sorcery stuff behind. Are we never to be free of it?"

With a sinking heart, she realised he'd put his finger on the truth: they would never be free, at least not Saker, not Ardhi, not Mathilda's twins and not herself either. Hundreds of years in the past an evil man had sown the seeds of a canker, and no one had ever rooted it out.

"We're the unlucky ones," she whispered. "We have to destroy the blight. And we need the *sakti* to do it. We need Ardhi's dagger."

Juster didn't reply. He poured brandy into a glass, swallowed a draft as if it were water, then sat on his bunk. He raised Saker's head and pressed the glass to his lips. "Drink up, my lad. I think you need this."

With liquid poured into his throat, Saker spluttered and swallowed. More coughing followed, but at least it had the effect of opening his eyes. He looked at them both, then whispered, "I'm flying. Sorrel, I'm in the air and the sea is . . . is . . . way down there. What if I fall? Juster, I'm *flying*."

Juster threw up his hands. "Have you been smoking my supply of Pashali kif?"

"Find Ardhi," Sorrel said. "Fly on until you find him, Saker. Give him the note you wrote."

"Not you too," Juster said with a groan. "That's it. That kif goes into the ocean!"

Ardhi hated looking at Eka. The man wore an expression so stark, so forged with dislike and contempt, so unbending, it could have been a mask. Luckily, as Eka was at the tiller of the *prau*, Ardhi could avoid looking at him as the boat skimmed its way through the islands.

It was the morning after they'd left Bandar Ruanakula. He had no idea where this journey was going to end; he could only hope that the kris would use its *sakti* to find the other wisps of Raja Wiramulia's regalia, the ones Saker and Sorrel had. None of this had worked out the way he wanted, but he didn't see quite how he could have done anything differently.

It was about two hours after dawn, and they were still hours away from being able to intercept the route of *Golden Petrel*. One of the *helang laut*, the eagle fisher-kings of the air, appeared overhead. It spiralled down with the boat at its centre, casually moving no more than a feather or two to alter direction. Ardhi watched it and wondered. When the blade of the kris moved in his hand, he knew there was *sakti* involved. He held the kris up into the air in full view.

"Halt the boat," he ordered.

Wordlessly, Eka swung the tiller over to spill air from the sail, and the boat slowed.

"Just sit quietly," he said.

The bird made one pass over the *prau* just above the mast. He watched it, gazed into its unblinking eye. On its next pass, it extended its powerful legs, dipped lower than the boat so that its wingtips almost brushed the water, then rose slightly, reaching forward with its feet. Its momentum hauled its body upward until it gripped the gunwale and stood erect. It ruffled its wing feathers into a neat fold at its back and eyed Ardhi. Eka's friends, wide-eyed, scrambled out of the way.

The glare was uncanny. It sent a shiver through Ardhi, raised the hair on his arms.

"It's got something on its leg," Eka whispered. He had stayed at the tiller, refusing to show any fear, but his voice quavered anyway.

Ardhi wrenched his gaze away from that penetrating eye. Saker had sent him a note.

Slowly, taking every care not to startle the bird, he reached out. Using the kris, he cut the twine and retrieved the piece of folded parchment. He read what was written there, then turned to the others to say, "*Golden Petrel* will meet us at Pantai Emas on Pulau Dena."

He looked back at the eagle and shivered. *Saker?* Shells, he could see Saker in its eyes. "We'll be there," he murmured. "Before sunset, if the winds are kind." He lowered his voice even more. "Courage. The *sakti* will guide and guard you. I promise."

The bird stared, and he wondered if what he read there was not hate. Then, in a human gesture, the sea-eagle nodded and launched itself into the air.

Skies above, he thought. *Where are we going with this?* The only thing he knew for certain was that he was leaving Chenderawasi for ever. He would live the rest of his life in the Va-cherished Hemisphere and it would be there that his body would be laid to rest. The thought was devastating.

*   *   *

Saker had rarely felt so ill. His conscious mind had returned to his own body, but his whole being revolted at what had happened to him. His stomach heaved, but some small part of him was aware he was lying on the bed in Juster's cabin, so he strove to quell the nausea.

Certainty flooded his mind, unwelcome, horrifying. *It will happen again.*

He sat up on the edge of the bunk to face the two people staring at him. Sorrel, who had been kneeling beside the bunk and holding his hand, quickly let go and stood up. Juster didn't move. He was leaning against the closed cabin door, arms folded, looking thoroughly annoyed.

"What the blistering blazes are you up to, Saker?" he asked.

"Sorry, my lord," Saker said, deliberately formal. "I didn't ask for this. And I'm afraid you have a rendezvous to make, in order to pick up Ardhi."

"I can't think of a single reason why I should do that."

"Because if you don't, something worse may happen to your ship."

Juster raised an incredulous eyebrow. "Are you *threatening* me?"

"No, of course not! You know me better than that. It's a warning. Juster, I'm sorry, but this *sakti* – Chenderawasi witchery – has a nasty way of making things happen to achieve its ends. Believe me, I know that first-hand. I've just been flying around in the head of a bird. Have you any idea how – how *petrifyingly* scary that was?" He drew in a calming breath. "Please delay our journey long enough to find and bring Ardhi on board. If you do, I suspect you'll have a great deal of good luck thereafter, at least with anything to do with natural forces. Such as the wind."

There was a long silence, while Juster considered his words. In the end he said merely, "Are you prepared to swear that this *sakti* is not innately dangerous to the Va-cherished Hemisphere?"

"Yes, I am. We have to achieve a – a *union* of the magic of two hemispheres, because if we don't, we will lack the weapon we need to fight something evil."

"Surely we can manage to defend our own interests—" Juster began.

He interrupted, "Can we? Prime Valerian Fox is tapping into a rather nasty form of magic. He is already undermining the Shenat and their shrines."

"On top of that," Sorrel added, "there's so much happening in Lowmeer that is . . . sick. Regal Vilmar had first-hand experience of Chenderawasi plumes, and instead of acknowledging that anything that powerful is best left alone, he sent Lustgrader's fleet to bring back as many as they could. And that's just a start."

Juster tensed as he looked from her to Saker and back again. "Go on."

"The heir to the Basalt Throne is probably Fox's son, inheriting his sorcerous blood. Imagine a sorcerer having the power of a monarch."

A fleeting expression of horror crossed his face. "What makes you think that?"

"The *sakti* of the Rani identified Piper as inheriting the blood of a sorcerer. The Prince-regal is her twin."

Juster swore richly.

"There's also another point of view to be considered," Saker added. "If Lowmians prevail in this hemisphere, the Chenderawasi will have to fight to maintain their—" he hunted for the right words "—way of living, their right to live that life as they want. The plumes are an integral part of their life and their witchery. The Lowmians want to own that part, and they don't care how they attain it. Fortunately, I think we – the Chenderawasi and us – have thwarted that ambition for the time being. But we have more to do."

Juster winced and began to count on his fingers. "One, stop Fox. Two, stop the Lowmians in the Va-forsaken Hemisphere. Three, ensure that whoever sits on the Lowmian throne is not a sorcerer. Are you *sure* that's all?"

"That about sums it up," he agreed.

Juster sat down abruptly on the wooden trunk next to the bed and sank his head into his hands. "Well, that's simple then, isn't it? The three of us, and Ardhi. We can do that with our eyes closed."

They exchanged looks.

"There's Fritillary Reedling, too," Saker said.

"And Mathilda," Sorrel added.

"Prince Ryce?" Saker suggested.

Juster rolled his eyes. "A privateer with one ship, a disgraced witan and some birds, a woman with a glamour, a middle-aged female Pontifect, a lascar with a dagger, a spoiled brat of a princess with an interest in putting a sorcerer's child on the throne and an ineffective prince. Yes, we shouldn't have any trouble saving the world, should we?"

Neither of them could think of anything to say.

Juster groaned. "Sweet Va, *we have a sorcerer's child on board*! What the slumbering beggary did I ever do to deserve all this?"

Saker opened his mouth to reply.

"Don't you *dare* answer that, witan," Juster said.

"All right, I won't. Right now, all you need to decide is whether to pick up Ardhi, or not."

Juster snorted. "Leak on you, Saker." He stood up, frowning as if his head ached. "Where do we find this confounded lascar?"

44

The Smutch in the Sky

"Someone to see you." Barden, leaning on his walking stick, fixed Fritillary Reedling with an unrelenting stare telling her that whoever it was, this was someone she had better not refuse to see.

She leant back in her chair, stretching her aching back. On the desk in front of her were two piles of reports, one heap already perused, the other higher one as yet unexamined. All of it depressing. The Horned Death outbreaks continuing, the Primordials still throwing stones at clerics affiliated to chapels, Prime Valerian Fox's power now unassailable in Ardrone, King Edwyn ill and blind, Prince Ryce and his family holed up in a castle, the Lowmian court in turmoil as the Regala argued with her councillors – and worst of all, increasing numbers of fools joining the Grey Lancers, as they had become known.

She looked up at Barden. "I hope whoever it is has good news," she said.

"I doubt it. He says his name is Lord Herelt Deremer."

She sat without speaking, incapable of movement, her only thought being how little she wanted to see him.

Barden was staring at her, waiting for her reply, so she asked, "Did he say anything else?"

"No."

"Any opinion about him?"

"He has a fine tailor. Masterful bootmaker, too."

She rolled her eyes. "Make him comfortable in the small reception room downstairs. I'll come down when I am ready, in about an hour. Let's see how he takes the wait. Have some Staravale port on hand; he used to like it, I remember, although that was a long time ago."

"And your guards?"

"Ah, yes. I don't think he'll risk an assassination in the palace, but by all means ask the guards to search him for weapons, then place five of them outside the door. Oh, and send for Agent Brantheld and Peregrine Clary. Do you know where they are?"

"Proctor Gerelda did say she was going to check the city defences again over the next few days to make sure the new regimen has been implemented, and Peregrine has been in the Swordsmen's Guild for training all this month. I should be able to round them up."

Once Barden had gone and she could stop the pretence of composure, she stood and started to pace the room with long angry strides. The very thought of Herelt Deremer aroused her to throbbing rage; she could feel the ire pulsing through her body like too much bad wine. And to think she'd loved the rotten weasel once upon a time. Wholeheartedly too, giving herself over to a passion she'd never felt since. What a giddy-brain she'd been back then!

Breathe deeply; calm down, you fool.

Who would have thought he'd turn up here after she'd ignored his call for an alliance?

Sweet Va, she supposed it would be interesting to see how much Herelt had altered in, what, twenty-five years? He'd been a good-looking man back then.

But first she needed to calm herself. One thing was for sure: she did not want Lord Herelt Deremer to think the idea of meeting him again had in any way agitated her.

He was still a handsome man.

How annoying . . . They were the same age, but now she looked more like sixty, while – apart from appearing to be fatigued at the moment – he had worn well. Killing babies had not left its permanent mark on his face.

No, wait. When she looked more closely, it was there, in his eyes. The hardness of a man who had seen too many deaths. Killed too many innocents. A coldness.

He stood up when she entered, but did not smile.

She closed the door firmly behind her and crossed the floor towards him. "The years have treated you well, Herelt. Who would have thought I'd be the one to age so poorly! I shall have to take Va to task for injustice, I think."

Shut up. You're rambling.

"Your face may have changed, but your tongue hasn't," he said, still without the hint of a smile.

She was the one who smiled, not at his words, but at her discovery that she felt nothing. No regrets over her own behaviour, no lingering affection, not even a vestige of anger, at least not on her own account. For the others he had hurt, for them she could still feel the rage.

"Did you not get my message through Brantheld?" he asked.

"Yes, I did." She didn't ask him to sit.

"I did not receive a reply."

"No. Apparently, it escaped your notice that I represent Va-faith and, as such, I cannot countenance an alliance with an organisation whose main activity appears to have been to murder twin babies."

"That's an over-simplification, and you know it. What should be of more importance to you is that I have already brought that activity to an end."

"How *generous* of you. And how much did that have to do with Regala Mathilda, I wonder?"

He gave a slight shrug. "She did tell me to disband the Dire Sweepers or she'd see me strapped to a traitor's wheel. We negotiated, and there's no more twin murder. Actually I'd already stopped it anyway, but she didn't know that."

Well, fobbing pox, that's the truth! The information her witchery gave her was unequivocal.

"We are still seeking out victims of the Horned Death, however," he added.

"Still murdering, in fact."

"Mercy killing. No one recovers, you know that, and they do spread the disease. We save lives. Fritillary—"

"You don't have the right to use my name, not now. You lost that right, long ago. Had I known what you were when we first met, I would have killed you there and then."

He inclined his head, ever the polite nobleman. "Your reverence, you need me now. You need an army. You need the Dire Sweepers. Because there's one thing I do know: Valerian is not like his sorcerer forebears. He is more powerful, more greedy, more ruthless. His ambition exceeds all others. He's building an armed force, and there are contingents of them in every country of the Va-cherished Hemisphere, recruited by his many illegitimate sons – born sorcerers, every one."

He sounded so rational, so sincere, so genuine. And every fibre of her witchery was telling her that he utterly believed what he was saying.

Yet everything she knew about him told her a different story of his honour. He had deceived her with another woman. He had abandoned them both. Even when they'd first met, he'd already been a murderer; he'd admitted that much to Gerelda. He now headed the most conscienceless band of cutthroats ever in existence. He'd tried to kill Saker for no other reason than that the witan had seen too much one night during a killing spree of the Sweepers in a Lowmeer fishing village, and he recognised Saker as one of her agents.

"I can't see any reason to believe you," she said. It was a lie: her witchery gave her every reason. "You are seeking legitimacy because you've lost the protection of the Vollendorn line."

He was still standing, his hands by his side, his gaze steady. The bleak tragedy she read in his eyes brought a bitter taste into her mouth. *Don't be fooled. You've been fooled by him before.*

"You do need me, nonetheless," he said. "King Edwayn does whatever Fox wants. Prince Ryce is helpless. The Principalities are riddled with little pockets of Fox's lancers, all ready for his signal to act – and he is ready to give it, any time now. Lowmeer is rotten with the devil-kin we haven't been able to find, all sucked dry and spreading the Horned Plague before they die of it themselves."

He's pleading? She felt sick. "Sorcery makes even less sense to me than A'Va. If I were a sorcerer, why go to all this – this falderal of Bengorth's Law and devil-kin and twins? Unless you can explain that to me, you are not leaving this room a free man."

"Do you mind if I sit first? It's been a difficult day."

That at least had the appearance of truth. Not even the smart cut of his clothing could hide his weariness. She subdued a twinge of uncharitable gratification and waved her hand at the chair he had vacated. "One chance, Herelt Deremer. Explain the Fox family to me. Tell me what sorcery is. Give me all you know. Then, and only then, we might have something to discuss."

He sat and picked up the port Barden had given him earlier, turning the goblet in his hands without drinking. She remained standing, looking down at him.

"Let me start," he began, "by telling you how I came by this knowledge. I had a lot of time on my hands after I was wounded – a knife wound in my back." He glanced at her, smiling slightly. "I was fighting one of your agents at the time: Rampion. I suppose he told you. Anyway, while I was recuperating, I started doing some research to answer questions I had. Like your agent Gerelda Brantheld, I started with old documents. I looked at history. The Deremers had some old family diaries. There were collections of old tales and stories in our library. Then I started poking around in the Grundorp University Library, and speaking to my old professors. I put information together.

"The last thing I did was kidnap a son of Valerian Fox. In the end, he was extraordinarily obliging."

She flinched away from him in distaste; the truth was there, saturating his words until she could smell their stink.

He gave a hollow laugh at her cringe. "Oh, Fritillary, what I did to him was nothing compared to what he'd done to others! He was one of the fellows I call the Gaunt Recruiters, coercing people into Fox's Grey Lancers."

This time she didn't chide him with using her name. His pain was real. His disgust was real. *But how is what he did forgivable, no matter how sorry he is? The Sweepers killed babies!*

She folded her arms and looked away. "Stop blathering, and get to the point, Deremer."

"The Fox family keep to themselves, scattered over some twenty different estates in all the countries of the hemisphere. The patriarch of the family – now Valerian – is always in total control and is usually long-lived. Valerian's father was an exception and I have reason to believe it's because your Prime killed his pa, but that's not important. In the end, I concluded the Fox patriarchs had access to some kind of supernatural power that prolonged life, just as shrine keepers do. They also use their sorcery to bind their underlings and minor family members into a kind of obedient slavery, even though they live in opulence, surrounded by plenty.

"I don't know the source of the sorcery, but Bengorth's friend Ebent Voss was probably the first sorcerer of the Fox line. History tells us he was a very sickly fellow who helped Bengorth seize the throne, along with my ancestor. I think he was the first to discover a sorcerer could use small amounts of sorcery to seize other people's life-force and add it to his own. His victims were young, and after having part of their life sucked out of them, they'd eventually become diseased, grow horns and die young and insane. And so the Horned Plague was born. It can spread to those around the initial victim, mostly to family members or neighbours. Nasty.

"Unfortunately for Ebent Voss, he was touched by scandal. There were rumours about children disappearing and his involvement. Because of that scandal, I think Bengorth Vollendorn found out what he was really doing.

"According to my ancestor's diary, Ebent Voss and Bengorth had a massive falling out. I suspect Voss told Bengorth something like this: 'You're dead if you tell anyone what I can do. Keep quiet and I'll make sure your family stays on the throne and I'll use my sorcery to ensure Lowmeer prospers under your reign.' That is how Bengorth's Law started."

She sat down. "But that's not how it is now."

"No. When Bengorth Vollendorn died, Ebent Voss disappeared from court and changed his name to Fox. After that, it was A'Va's devil-kin – supposedly – who made the threats to the Vollendorn regals. Bengorth's descendants had no idea that it was a sorcerous thing, with Fox family members involved. My ancestors, the Deremers, didn't know either. The diary that recounted the original tale was deliberately concealed, presumably by Aben Deremer, the very first Deremer involved. So Aben's successors, my ancestors, pledged their lives to ridding Lowmeer of twins, believing twins became devil-kin who spread the Horned Plague, all caused by A'Va. And all the time it was a single sorcerer, sucking their life essence to extend his own."

She had trouble understanding the horror of it. "The *same* man through the centuries?"

"No, no. One at a time. First there was Ebent, who lived to be close to a hundred and fifty; after he died, his son. Then his grandson – who was Valerian's grandfather. I think there's rarely more than one adult sorcerer at a time. They don't like their own kind. At least, they didn't until the present.

"Valerian is the exception. He appears to have set out to have as many sorcerer sons as he could, each with a different mother selected from within different Fox estates. No daughters. Perhaps he killed the girls. Perhaps he uses his sorcery to determine all his children are male. As far as I know, he's never showed any of them how to replenish their life force when they expend it using sorcery. So the young men are all gradually dying, worn out."

"A caring father indeed! So who – or what – were the devil-kin who appeared to the regals?"

"Probably the sorcerer himself, disguised by his sorcery, using his powers. I suspect the one who appeared to Regala Mathilda recently was one of Valerian's sons. The Foxes muddied the water all along the line to confuse matters, and to make twins the target of Vollendorn wrath. At the same time, no one is going to be worried by the death of twins if they are to blame for a plague. That enabled the Foxes to target twins, or one in a set of twins, when they were still babies or toddlers. Twins were their prey. They were never more than innocent children the Fox family fed on to increase their longevity."

She said slowly, swallowing back the bitter taste in her mouth, "So the Horned Plague in twins is a result of a crime committed years earlier when the victims were young, a slow death that only really begins to kick in when they hit puberty. How better to disguise a voracious appetite for life, than to find a group of innocents to blame at the same time as you suck the life from them. How did they know where to find twin babies to satisfy their hunger?"

"I don't know. Possibly they coerced midwives to tell them. Or maybe they used sorcery to sense a double birth."

"And the Dire Sweepers went haring off, for generations, killing the innocent victims."

"Yes." The word was as stark as the expression on his face. "The matter became a muddle of lies and distortions. The Foxes distanced themselves from the Vollendorns. They even invented a mock Shenat branch of the family and shifted the base of their public face to Ardrone, while keeping their vile sorcery mostly on the Lowmeer side of the border."

Sweet Va, this is hard to hear. She wanted to block her ears, leave the room, forget all she'd heard. Instead, she sat straighter, raised her chin. "Go on."

"Valerian Fox was in Lowmeer a lot before he was the Ardronese Prime. On those trips he fed himself on the life force of many children at a time. He travelled from one Fox estate to another, selecting Fox family women to give birth to his children. Once he became a Va-faith Arbiter, and later still, the Prime of Ardrone, he actually had connections within the Lowmian network of clerics working to save twins – who were only too glad to tell him where they were being placed."

She closed her eyes, unable to look at him. "I don't think I've ever heard such a disgusting recital of iniquity. Your whole family has spent hundreds of years killing innocent children for nothing."

"Yes. We were all as blind as hedge-born moldwarps."

Her stomach roiled and she swallowed back the bitter taste of bile in her mouth. "Do you have any other horrors to tell?"

He glanced away from her stare, as if he couldn't say the next words while meeting the condemnation in her gaze. "Only this. The limitation on sorcery has been that each time you use it, it eats away at your own lifespan. So being a sorcerer was always a balancing act between using sorcery without growing too weak, then rejuvenating oneself by sucking the future life from a child, the younger the better. The ultimate aim was not just to maintain your power, but to add to your lifespan – all without killing yourself with too *much* youth. Apparently there's an art to it."

She grunted.

"Get it wrong and you can kill yourself," he added. "Fox is not passing on this art to his sons, at least not the ones I know about. These recruiters of lancers are all his sons, all young men, all sorcerers using their power and they grow weaker, day by day. I would imagine that mostly they don't understand what is happening to them. Either that, or they think their father will show them how to extend their health and their life as soon as they have proved themselves."

"I did wonder—"

The door was flung open without a knock. They both turned to look. Gerelda was in the doorway, wearing her travelling attire and her sword, her hair dishevelled, and an expression on her face that didn't bode well. Palace guards were clinging to her arms to prevent her from entering the room. She said, "Your reverence, it's started.

Vavala is under attack. I think you had better come and look at this. And tell these fools to leave me alone!"

Fritillary waved a hand at the guards, and asked as calmly as she could, "Look at what, Gerelda?"

"The sky! The fobbing sky! You need to come out on the terrace."

Birds? She wondered. *More of Saker's birds?*

But it wasn't birds. When she and Deremer followed Gerelda and stepped out on to the palace terrace, she raised her face to look. It was a lovely spring day, and the blue of the sky was dotted with clouds – the kind of fluffy white ones that children like to stare at until they see shapes of people and animals.

Across that balmy background was a splash of dark. A dirty mark, as if someone had thrown sludge from a giant pail, splashing the filth in a noxious stream. It commenced near the horizon in the east and trailed off towards the west, stretching over more than half the vault of the sky.

"The mark of the tar-pit," a voice said at her elbow. She looked down to see Peregrine standing there, his gaze fixed on the stain across the clouds. "The black smutch."

"It's just smoke," she said, and didn't believe her own words.

They weren't the only ones out there on the terrace. She was surrounded by palace guards, and most of the palace staff as well. Even Barden had hobbled out, leaning on his stick. She was in the midst of her friends and in no danger, but the dread she felt was eroding every sense of normality or safety.

"Barden," she said, the calm in her voice a complete contrast to the clamour in her chest, "I want a message sent to every cleric in the city, calling on them to remind people we are under the protection of Va and to have faith and courage. Tell them I will lead a service in the main chapel in an hour. Another message to the captains of the palace guard and the city guard, telling them to expect attack from any quarter, including, it seems, the sky. A third message, send to every shrine keeper in the land: 'Prepare the Oak.'"

Only then did she turn to Deremer. He was still gazing at the sky, facing away from her. She touched the back of his shoulder and a sharp tingle shot up her arm. She jerked her hand away and looked at her fingers.

He'd winced at her touch and now he turned to face her. "Sorcery," he said, nodding at the sky. His tone held no satisfaction. "This is a sign to his scattered supporters. Proctor Brantheld is right; he is launching his attack. I hope you are ready."

Her heart thudded uncomfortably. "Far from it."

"Do we have an alliance, your reverence?"

"We certainly have something to discuss."

As they filed back inside once more, she rubbed the tips of her fingers together, frowning. They prickled still and for a fleeting moment of disorientation she thought they glowed.

She dismissed the thought, and began to plan.

ACKNOWLEDGEMENTS

For all the folk who helped – I don't know how I would do any of this without you. For my husband, for his unflinching support; for Alena Sanusi, who keeps me strong; for Margaret and Perdy who offer suggestions; for Karen Miller who pushes me to do better; for Donna Hanson who knows how to be a good friend even from a distance; for all the beta readers like Jo Wake, who do it for free; for all the people at Orbit, especially Jenni and Joanna.

It is also for all my readers, without whom I would be truly lost; for those who review my books and recommend them, because you make it all feel worthwhile; for those who review my books and are critical, because you make me try harder.

For all of you: I hope you like the finished product.

This book is my poor tribute to my love affair with South East Asia and my husband's people. Although I have used a number of Indonesian/Malaysian words in this volume (often spelled in outdated ways in keeping with the times portrayed), and although the setting owes much to the places where I have lived and worked, or which I have explored, this story is set in fictional lands. The real spice islands, alas, possessed no *sakti* Chenderawasi in times past when sailors and traders came to plunder nutmeg, mace, cloves and cinnamon.

extras

orbit

www.orbitbooks.net

extras

about the author

Glenda Larke was born in Australia and trained as a teacher. She has taught English in Australia, Vienna, Tunisia and Malaysia. Glenda has two children and lives in Erskine, Western Australia with her husband.

Find out more about Glenda Larke and other Orbit authors by registering for the free monthly newsletter at www.orbitbooks.net.

if you enjoyed
THE DAGGER'S PATH

look out for

THIEF'S MAGIC

book one of the Millennium trilogy

by

Trudi Canavan

CHAPTER 1

The corpse's shrivelled, unbending fingers surrendered the bundle reluctantly. Wrestling the object out of the dead man's grip seemed disrespectful so Tyen worked slowly, gently lifting a hand when a blackened fingernail snagged on the covering. He'd touched the ancient dead so often they didn't sicken or frighten him now. Their desiccated flesh had long ago stopped being a source of transferable sickness, and he did not believe in ghosts.

When the mysterious bundle came free Tyen straightened and smiled in triumph. He wasn't as ruthless at collecting ancient artefacts as his fellow students and his teacher, but bringing home nothing from these research trips would see him fail to graduate as a sorcerer-archaeologist. He willed his tiny magic-fuelled flame closer.

The object's covering, like the tomb's occupant, was dry and stiff having, by his estimate, lain undisturbed for six hundred years. Thick leather darkened with age, it had no markings – no adornment, no precious stones or metals. As he tried to open it the wrapping snapped apart and something inside began to slide out. His pulse quickened as he caught the object . . .

. . . and his heart sank a little. No treasure lay in his hands. Just a book. Not even a jewel-encrusted, gold-embellished book.

Not that a book didn't have potential historical value, but compared to the glittering treasures Professor Kilraker's other two students had unearthed for the Academy it was a disappointing find. After all the months of travel, research, digging and watching he had little to show for his own work. He had finally unearthed a tomb that hadn't already been ransacked by grave robbers and what did it contain? A plain stone coffin, an unadorned corpse and an old book.

Still, the old fossils at the Academy wouldn't regret sponsoring his journey if the book turned out to be significant. He examined it closely. Unlike the wrapping, the leather cover felt supple. The binding was in good condition. If he hadn't just broken apart the covering to get it out, he'd have guessed the book's age at no more than a hundred or so years. It had no title or text on the spine. Perhaps it had worn off. He opened it. No word marked the first page, so he turned it. The next was also blank and as he fanned through the rest of the pages he saw that they were as well.

He stared at it in disbelief. Why would anyone bury a blank book in a tomb, carefully wrapped and placed in the hands of the occupant? He looked at the corpse, but it offered no answer. Then something drew his eye back to the book, still open to one of the last pages. He looked closer.

A mark had appeared.

Next to it a dark patch formed, then dozens more. They spread and joined up.

Hello, they said. *My name is Vella*.

Tyen uttered a word his mother would have been shocked to hear if she had still been alive. Relief and wonder replaced disappointment. The book was magical. Though most sorcerous books used magic in minor and frivolous ways, they were so rare that the Academy would always take them for its collection. His trip hadn't been a waste.

So what did this book do? Why did text only appear when it was opened? Why did it have a name? More words formed on the page.

I've always had a name. I used to be a person. A living, breathing woman.

Tyen stared at the words. A chill ran down his spine, yet at the same time he felt a familiar thrill. Magic could sometimes be disturbing. It was often inexplicable. He liked that not everything about it was understood. It left room for new discoveries. Which was why he had chosen to study sorcery alongside history. In both fields there was an opportunity to make a name for himself.

He'd never heard of a person turning into a book before. *How is that possible?* he wondered.

I was made by a powerful sorcerer, replied the text. *He took my knowledge and flesh and transformed me.*

His skin tingled. The book had responded to the question he'd shaped in his mind. *Do you mean these pages are made of your flesh?* he asked.

Yes. My cover and pages are my skin. My binding is my hair, twisted together and sewn with needles fashioned from my bones and glue from tendons.

He shuddered. *And you're conscious?*

Yes.

You can hear my thoughts?

Yes, but only when you touch me. When not in contact with a living human, I am blind and deaf, trapped in the darkness with no sense of time passing. Not even sleeping. Not quite dead. The years of my life slipping past — wasted.

Tyen stared down at the book. The words remained, nearly filling a page now, dark against the creamy vellum. Which was her skin . . .

It was grotesque and yet . . . all vellum was made of skin. While these pages were human skin, they felt no different to that made of animals. They were soft and pleasant to touch.

The book was not repulsive in the way an ancient, desiccated corpse was.

And it was so much more interesting. Conversing with it was akin to talking with the dead. If the book was as old as the tomb it knew about the time before it was laid there. Tyen smiled. He may not have found gold and jewels to help pay his way on this expedition, but the book could make up for that with historical information.

More text formed.

Contrary to appearances, I am not an "it".

Perhaps it was the effect of the light on the page, but the new words seemed a little larger and darker than the previous text. Tyen felt his face warm a little.

I'm sorry, Vella. It was bad mannered of me. I assure you, I meant no offence. It is not every day that a man addresses a talking book, and I am not entirely sure of the protocol.

She was a woman, he reminded himself. He ought to follow the etiquette he'd been raised to follow. Though talking to women could be fiendishly tricky, even when following all the rules about manners. It would be rude to begin their association by interrogating her about the past. Rules of conversation decreed he should ask after her well-being.

So . . . is it nice being a book?

When I am being held and read by someone nice, it is, she replied.

And when you are not, it is not? I can see that might be a disadvantage in your state, though one you must have anticipated before you became a book.

I would have, if I'd had foreknowledge of my fate.

So you did not choose to become a book. Why did your maker do that to you? Was it a punishment?

No, though perhaps it was natural justice for being too ambitious and vain. I sought his attention, and received more of it than I intended.

Why did you seek his attention?

He was famous. I wanted to impress him. I thought my friends would be envious.

And for that he turned you into a book. What manner of man could be so cruel?

He was the most powerful sorcerer of his time, Roporien the Clever.

Tyen caught his breath and a chill ran down his back. *Roporien! But he died over a thousand years ago!*

Indeed.

Then you are . . .

At least as old as that. Though in my time it wasn't polite to comment on a woman's age.

He smiled. *It still isn't – and I don't think it ever will be. I apologise again.*

You are a polite young man. I will enjoy being owned by you.

You want me to own you? Tyen suddenly felt uncomfortable. He realised he now thought of the book as a person, and owning a person was slavery – an immoral and uncivilised practice that had been illegal for over a hundred years.

Better that than spend my existence in oblivion. Books don't last for ever, not even magical ones. Keep me. Make use of me. I can give you a wealth of knowledge. All I ask is that you hold me as often as possible so that I can spend my lifespan awake and aware.

I don't know . . . The man who created you did many terrible things – as you experienced yourself. I don't want to follow in his shadow. Then something occurred to him that made his skin creep. *Forgive me for being blunt about it, but his book, or any of his tools, could be designed for evil purposes. Are you one such tool?*

I was not designed so, but that does not mean I could not be used so. A tool is only as evil as the hand that uses it.

The familiarity of the saying was startling and unexpectedly reassuring. It was one that Professor Weldan liked. The old historian had always been suspicious of magical things.

How do I know you're not lying about not being evil?

I cannot lie.

Really? But what if you're lying about not being able to lie?

You'll have to work that one out for yourself.

Tyen frowned as he considered how he might devise a test for her, then realised something was buzzing right beside his ear. He shied away from the sensation, then breathed a sigh of relief as he saw it was Beetle, his little mechanical creation. More than a toy, yet not quite what he'd describe as a pet, it had proven to be a useful companion on the expedition.

The palm-sized insectoid swooped down to land on his shoulder, folded its iridescent blue wings, then whistled three times. Which was a warning that . . .

"Tyen!"

. . . Miko, his friend and fellow archaeology student was approaching.

The voice echoed in the short passage leading from the outside world to the tomb. Tyen muttered a curse. He glanced down at the page. *Sorry, Vella. Have to go.* Footsteps neared the door of the tomb. With no time to slip her into his bag, he stuffed her down his shirt, where she settled against the waistband of his trousers. She was warm – which was a bit disturbing now that he knew she was a conscious thing created from human flesh – but he didn't have time to dwell on it. He turned to the door in time to see Miko stumble into view.

"Didn't think to bring a lamp?" he asked.

"No time," the other student gasped. "Kilraker sent me to get you. The others have gone back to the camp to pack up. We're leaving Mailand."

"Now?"

"Yes. *Now*," Miko replied.

Tyen looked back at the small tomb. Though Professor Kilraker liked to refer to these foreign trips as treasure hunts, his peers expected the students to bring back evidence that the journeys were also educational. Copying the faint decorations on the tomb walls would have given them something to mark. He thought wistfully of the new instant etchers that some of the richer professors and self-funded adventurers used to record their work. They were far beyond his meagre allowance. Even if they weren't, Kilraker wouldn't take them on expeditions because they were heavy and fragile.

Picking up his satchel, Tyen opened the flap. "Beetle. Inside." The insectoid scuttled down his arm into the bag. Tyen slung the strap over his head and shoulder and sent his flame into the passage.

"We have to hurry," Miko said, leading the way. "The locals heard about where you're digging. Must've been one of the boys Kilraker hired to deliver food who told them. A bunch are coming up the valley and they're sounding those battle horns they carry."

"They didn't want us digging here? Nobody told me that!"

"Kilraker said not to. He said you were bound to find something impressive, after all the research you did."

He reached the hole where Tyen had broken through into the passage and squeezed out. Tyen followed, letting the flame die as he climbed out into the bright afternoon sunlight. Dry heat enveloped him. Miko scrambled up the sides of the ditch. Following, Tyen looked back and surveyed his work. Nothing remained in the tomb that robbers would want, but he couldn't stand to leave it exposed to vermin and he felt guilty about unearthing a tomb the locals didn't wanted disturbed. Reaching out with his mind, he pulled magic to himself then moved the rocks and earth on either side back into the ditch.

"What are you *doing*?" Miko sounded exasperated.

"Filling it in."

"We don't have time!" Miko grabbed his arm and yanked him around so that they both looked down into the valley. He pointed. "See?"

The valley sides were near-vertical cliffs, and where the faces had crumbled over time piles of rubble had built up against the sides to form steep slopes. Tyen and Miko were standing atop of one of these.

At the bottom of the valley a long line of people was moving, faces tilted to search the scree above. One arm rose, pointing at Tyen and Miko. The rest stopped, then fists were raised.

A shiver went through Tyen, part fear, part guilt. Though the people inhabiting the remote valleys of Mailand were unrelated to the ancient race that had buried its dead in the tombs, they felt that such places of death should not be disturbed lest ghosts be awakened. They'd made this clear when Kilraker had arrived, and to previous archaeologists, but their protests had never been more than verbal and they'd indicated that some areas were less important than others. They must really be upset, if Kilraker had cut the expedition short.

Tyen opened his mouth to ask, when the ground beside him exploded. They both threw up their arms to shield their faces from the dust and stones.

"Can you protect us?" Miko asked.

"Yes. Give me a moment . . ." Tyen gathered more magic. This time he stilled the air around them. Most of what a sorcerer did was either moving or stilling. Heating and cooling was another form of moving or stilling, only more intense and focused. As the dust settled beyond his shield he saw the locals had gathered together behind a brightly dressed woman who served as priestess and sorcerer to the locals. He took a step towards them.

"Are you mad?" Miko asked.

"What else can we do? We're trapped up here. We should just go talk to them. Explain that I didn't—"

The ground exploded again, this time much closer.

"They don't seem in the mood for talking."

"They won't hurt two sons of the Leratian Empire," Tyen reasoned. "Mailand gains a lot of profit from being one of the safer colonies."

Miko snorted. "Do you think the villagers care? They don't get any of the profit."

"Well . . . the Governors will punish them."

"They don't look too worried about that right now." Miko turned to stare up at the face of the cliff behind them. "I'm not waiting to see if they're bluffing." He set off along the edge of the slope where it met the cliff.

Tyen followed, keeping as close as possible to Miko so that he didn't have to stretch his shield far to cover them both. Stealing glances at the people below, he saw that they were hurrying up the slope, but the loose scree was slowing them down. The sorceress walked along the bottom, following them. He hoped this meant that, after using magic, she needed to move from the area she had depleted to access more. That would mean her reach wasn't as good as his.

She stopped and the air rippled before her, a pulse that rushed towards him. Realising that Miko had drawn ahead,

Tyen drew more magic and spread the shield out to protect him.

The scree exploded a short distance below their feet. Tyen ignored the stones and dust bounding off his shield and hurried to catch up with Miko. His friend reached a crack in the cliff face. Setting his feet in the rough sides of the narrow opening and grasping the edges, he began to climb. Tyen tilted his head back. Though the crack continued a long way up the cliff face it didn't reach the top. Instead, at a point about three times his height, it widened to form a narrow cave.

"This looks like a bad idea," he muttered. Even if they didn't slip and break a limb, or worse, once in the cave they'd be trapped.

"It's our only option. They'll catch us if we head down-hill," Miko said in a tight voice, without taking his attention from climbing. "Don't look up. Don't look down either. Just climb."

Though the crack was almost vertical, the edges were pitted and uneven, providing plenty of hand- and footholds. Swallowing hard, Tyen swung his satchel around to his back so he wouldn't crush Beetle between himself and the wall. He set his fingers and toes in the rough surface and hoisted himself upward.

At first it was easier than he'd expected, but soon his fingers, arms and legs were tiring and hurting from the strain. *I should have exercised more before coming here. I should have joined a sports club.* Then he shook his head. *No, there's no exercise I could have done that would have boosted* these *muscles except climbing cliff walls, and I've not heard of any clubs that consider that a recreational activity.*

The shield behind him shuddered at a sudden impact. He fed more magic to it, trying not to picture himself squashed like a bug on the cliff wall. Was Miko right about the locals? Would they dare to kill him? Or was the priestess simply gambling that he was a good enough sorcerer to ward off her attacks?

"Nearly there," Miko called.

Ignoring the fire in his fingers and calves, Tyen glanced up and saw Miko disappear into the cave. *Not far now*, he told himself. He forced his aching limbs to push and pull, carrying him upward towards the dark shadow of safety. Glancing up again and again, he saw he was a body's length away, then close enough that an outstretched arm would reach it. A vibration went through the stone beneath his hand and chips flew off the wall nearby. He found another foothold, pushed up, grabbed a handhold, pulled, felt the cool shadow of the cave on his face . . .

. . . then hands grabbed his armpits and hauled him up.

Miko didn't stop pulling until Tyen's legs were inside the cave. It was so narrow that Tyen's shoulders scraped along the walls. Looking downward, he saw that there was no floor to the fissure. The walls on either side simply drew closer together to form a crack that continued beneath him. Miko was bracing his boots on the walls on either side.

That "floor" was not level either. It sloped downward as the cave deepened, so Tyen's head was now lower than his legs. He felt the book slide up the inside of his shirt and tried to grab it, but Miko's arms got in the way. The book dropped down into the crack. He cursed and quickly created a flame. The book had come to rest far beyond his reach even if his arms had been skinny enough to fit into the gap.

Miko let go and gingerly turned around to examine the cave. Ignoring him, Tyen pushed himself up into a crouch. He drew his bag around to the front and opened it. "Beetle," he hissed. The little machine stirred, then scurried out and up onto his arm. Tyen pointed at the crack. "Fetch book."

Beetle's wings buzzed an affirmative, then its body whirred as it scurried down Tyen's arm and into the crack. It had to spread its legs wide to fit in the narrow space where the book had lodged. Tyen breathed a sigh of relief as its tiny pincers seized the spine. As it emerged Tyen grabbed Vella and Beetle together and slipped them both inside his satchel.

"Hurry up! The professor's here!"

Tyen stood up. Miko looked upwards and pressed a finger to his lips. A faint, rhythmic sound echoed in the space.

"In the aircart?" Tyen shook his head. "I hope he knows the priestess is throwing rocks at us or it's going to be a very long journey home."

"I'm sure he's prepared for a fight." Miko turned away and continued along the crack. "I think we can climb up here. Come over and bring your light."

Standing up, Tyen made his way over. Past Miko the crack narrowed again, but rubble had filled the space, providing an uneven, steep, natural staircase. Above them was a slash of blue sky. Miko started to climb, but the rubble began to dislodge under his weight.

"So close," he said, looking up. "Can you lift me up there?"

"Maybe . . ." Tyen concentrated on the magical atmosphere. Nobody had used magic in the cave for a long time. It was as smoothly dispersed and still as a pool of water on a windless day. And it was plentiful. He'd still not grown used to how much stronger and *available* magic was outside towns and cities. Unlike in the metropolis, where magic was constantly surging towards a more important use, here power pooled and lapped around him like a gentle fog. He'd only encountered Soot, the residue of magic that lingered everywhere in the city, in small, quickly dissipating smudges. "Looks possible," Tyen said. "Ready?"

Miko nodded.

Tyen drew a deep breath. He gathered magic and used it to still the air before Miko in a small, flat square.

"Step forward," he instructed.

Miko obeyed. Strengthening the square to hold the young man's weight, Tyen moved it slowly upwards. Throwing his arms out to keep his balance, Miko laughed nervously.

"Let me check there's nobody waiting up there before you lift me out," he called down to Tyen. After peering out of the opening, he grinned. "All clear."

As Miko stepped off the square a shout came from the cave entrance. Tyen twisted around to see one of the locals climbing inside. He drew magic to push the man out again, then hesitated. The drop outside could kill him. Instead he created another shield inside the entrance.

Looking around, he sensed the scarring of the magical atmosphere where it had been depleted, but more magic was already beginning to flow in to replace it. He took a little more to form another square then, hoping the locals would do nothing to spoil his concentration, stepped onto it and moved it upwards.

He'd never liked lifting himself, or anyone else, like this. If he lost focus or ran out of magic he'd never have time to recreate the square. Though it was possible to move a person rather than still the air below them, a lack of concentration or moving parts of them at different rates could cause injury or even death.

Reaching the top of the crack, Tyen emerged into sunlight. Past the edge of the cliff a large, lozenge-shaped hot-air-filled capsule hovered – the aircart. He stepped off the square onto the ground and hurried over to join Miko at the cliff edge.

The aircart was descending into the valley, the bulk of the capsule blocking the chassis hanging below it and its occupants from Tyen's view. Villagers were gathered at the base of the crack, some clinging to the cliff wall. The priestess was part way up the scree slope but her attention was now on the aircart.

"Professor!" he shouted, though he knew he was unlikely to be heard over the noise of the propellers. "Over here!"

The craft floated further from the cliff. Below, the priestess made a dramatic gesture, entirely for show since magic didn't require fancy physical movements. Tyen held his breath as a ripple of air rushed upward, then let it go as the force abruptly dispelled below the aircart with a dull thud that echoed through the valley.

The aircart began to rise. Soon Tyen could see below the capsule. The long, narrow chassis came into view, shaped rather like a canoe, with propeller arms extending to either side and a fan-like rudder at the rear. Professor Kilraker was in the driver's seat up front; his middle-aged servant, Drem, and the other student, Neel, stood clutching the rope railing and the struts that attached chassis to capsule. The trio would see him and Miko, if only they would turn around and look his way. He shouted and waved his arms, but they continued peering downward.

"Make a light or something," Miko said.

"They won't see it," Tyen said, but he took yet more magic and formed a new flame anyway, making it larger and brighter than the earlier ones in the hope it would be more visible in the bright sunlight. To his surprise, the professor looked over and saw them.

"Yes! Over here!" Miko shouted.

Kilraker turned the aircart to face the cliff edge, its

propellers swivelling and buzzing. Bags and boxes had been strapped to either end of the chassis, suggesting there had not been time to pack their luggage in the hollow inside. At last the cart moved over the cliff top in a gust of familiar smells. Tyen breathed in the scent of resin-coated cloth, polished wood and pipe smoke and smiled. Miko grabbed the rope railing strung around the chassis, ducked under it and stepped on board.

"Sorry, boys," Kilraker said. "Expedition's over. No point sticking around when the locals get like this. Brace yourselves for some ear popping. We're going up."

As Tyen swung his satchel around to his back, ready to climb aboard, he thought of what lay inside. He didn't have any treasure to show off, but at least he had found something interesting. Ducking under the railing rope, he settled onto the narrow deck, legs dangling over the side. Miko sat down beside him. The aircart began to ascend rapidly, its nose slowly turning towards home.